INTO THE LYONS DEN

A Novel

by

Donni De-Ville

De-Ville Publishing
Nashville   -   Chicago   -   London

De-Ville Publishing is a division of De-Ville
Entertainment & Publishing Co., Chicago, IL.
While this book is a work of fiction, many of the
characters, places and incidents are based upon
actual events and acquaintances, some living, others
dead. Resemblances are intentional and not merely
coincidental. Some names have been changed.

Copyright © 2005, 2010 by De-Ville Entertainment &
Publishing Company

All rights reserved, including the right to reproduce this
book or portions thereof in any form whatsoever. For
further information, contact the author via her website,
http://www.donnideville.com or via email at sales@
donnideville.com.

ISBN-13
978-0-9771757-1-0
ISBN-10
0-9771757-1-5

Manufactured in the United States of America.

For information regarding special discounts for bulk
purchases, please contact the author at http://www.
donnideville.com or via email at sales@donnideville.
com.

FOREWORD

Sex, artistically written, a hint of lesbianism, heart-breaking romance, drugs, mayhem, gruesome murders with a serial killer running riot, make up this breath-taking, hard to put down, non-stop action story! Set in London, England, with a romantic start, the story soon turns into an exciting, mystery thriller.

Viv, the main character, a beautiful, sexy woman, is fraught with fantasies about her first lover. The short affair occurred sometime ago, and now her body cried out for the loving touch of a man. Not just any man. He had to be tall, muscled, strong, and handsome like her first love. In desperation, she puts her pride aside and signs up with a dating agency run by Dandy and Daniel Lyons.

Through them she meets potential partners, but all is not as it seems. At the same time she is sexually drawn to Daniel, but hides her infatuation, hoping he and his wife will not notice her awkwardness around him. Deciding to view more videos of prospective dating material, she sees one that looks similar to Daniel, and becomes enamoured of him immediately. The Lyons offer to take Viv to a party to meet the man socially brings fresh troubles. However, the man looking after the liquor, Alex, is spiking the drinks of some of the more attractive ladies. Viv ends up being mauled by Alex in the gardens only to be saved by a fantasy of a man, who takes her to a special place, (the den) in the house.

The next morning a party reveller is found murdered. The police suspect and arrest Daniel for the crime. Viv's, new friend's, including a helpful, transgender pal, set out to prove his innocence. At the same time, gays are being killed and mutilated by a serial killer. One of the friend's meets up with him, and is brutalized, by the madman. It seems the ladies' attempt to prove Daniel innocent, sets off a string of incidents that finally lead to the killer's apprehension, the identity of which brings this amazing, breath-taking story to an unexpected and utterly shocking conclusion! This is a story you will not forget.

--- Victor Farrell ---

Author of Occult & Supernatural books.

PREFACE

This story will affect men, women and gays alike. Touching inner feelings not openly admitted to, not even to you! Viv, 35 years old, searching for love, found the dating agency brought excitement, danger and heartbreak instead. The ending does not let the reader down and the story will never be forgotten. Fast moving, compassionate and racy! This is semi-soft erotic, mystery, thriller novel that is impossible to put down. A very absorbing story based on some true, slightly exaggerated, life events and characters.

A compelling story enacted around the Lyons Dating Agency, which is the backdrop for Viv, a lonely woman in search of her perfect partner and love. Instead, she encounters a baron, a lover, a transvestite, detectives, police, murders, a serial killer who travels throughout Europe. It was a huge change of pace from her mundane life, working in a London office. There is a very strong storyline all the way through the book.

Emotion, lust, romance, intrigue and death are part of the plot. The story is frightening in places and extremely sad in others. There are many twists which the reader does not expect and each chapter ends with a cliff-hangers. This story is unlike any you would ever have read anywhere and it will feel as if you are watching it on television or at a movie!

A must read for all fans of thrillers, and mysteries, with every chapter containing an unexpected turn of events, as does the ending, which could not be guessed at. This book is for anyone hungry for something new and exciting. The readers' appetites will be whetted from the very beginning of this adventure as they consume its contents as the main course for thrills, excitement and the unexpected.

Into The Lyons Den is a fast action-paced story covering everything from lust, mayhem, kidnapping and murder, to unexpected moments of humour and tenderness. The very first page draws one into the woven fabric of an attention grabbing masterpiece by the author Donni-Jay De-Ville. Such stories are written by those who have experienced much of what they write about.

An unforgettable write!

Victor Snow

INTO THE LYONS DEN

Chapter One
Remembering the Man Viv Would Never Forget

'*Life is boring and fast becoming unbearable*,' Viv realised as she walked to the bus stop. It had lacked fun and any promise of a serious relationship for much too long. Not since Lawrence, her first lover, or her later disastrous marriage and divorce from Gavin, had she felt so depressed and alone. '*At least I'm not going through **that** kind of hell*,' she thought, remembering how traumatic it had all been, the good and the bad. It was difficult to know what happiness felt like, as she went through the motions of life without any excitement in it. Waking up each day meant going to work and after that, the return home only to re-live the way things used to be. She felt as if her soul had gone into hiding.

Little did Viv know what fate had planned for her. Soon her world would be turned upside down and inside out. She was about to experience the most turbulent trials of her life. The soon-to-be events would prove both exciting and disastrous. She reached the bus-stop just as the bus arrived, on time for a change. After Viv had seated herself and paid the ticket, she lapsed into her favourite daydream of that initial, incredible meeting and affair with Lawrence all those years ago. He was her first love, someone she was unable to forget although she often tried to, and the whole memory remained as vivid as if it happened yesterday. She re-lived it often and felt certain she would remember it with clarity her whole life through....

* *

It had been a spring holiday fourteen years ago, when Viv took a week's holiday vacation, from her secretarial employment, to celebrate her twenty-first birthday. There were no close friends to share it with her, so she travelled alone to a resort, staying at The Seine Hotel, in Bournemouth. Many associates told her it was a good place to holiday. A change of scenery and a break from her life, or lack of it, was exactly what she needed. Bournemouth was a relatively busy seaside town just a few hours drive from London. It was an interesting, pretty place with shops clustered in between family-owned 'bed and breakfast' houses, which were so common in this area. They were the bread and butter of the majority of the townsfolk's existence.

The summer season ran from the end of March until early September. During this time, the bed and breakfasts provided a base of operations for thousands of tourists. They flood the town for its idyllic location. Each day the throngs of people ambled up and down the streets in quest of ways to break the summer boredom. The hotels that dotted the coastline were few and typically sold out months in advance. They provided some relief in the form of entertainment performed by many of the UK's good, but struggling comedians, musicians and singers.

The journey by train had been interesting, as Viv had talked with people and passed the time very pleasantly. After a taxi ride to her destination, she had signed into the hotel and carrying her own luggage, was shown to her room. She felt relieved to have this time to herself, away from her colleagues and all the hubbub of office work. She unpacked and after tidying everything away neatly, went down to the restaurant to have a meal. There were many dishes to choose from, but she sought a light lunch of chicken salad. Afterward, she wandered around the more interesting shops and enjoyed casual talk with shop assistants. Although not in the mood to make serious purchases, she always loved to window shop.

Buying things on impulse was not her usual way, but on this occasion Viv bought pretty ornaments of sculptured crystal dolphins, gracefully balancing on colourful imitation waves. Nothing much else had caught her eye, but she felt as good as if it were the Christmas season. Occasionally, she caught her reflection in a window and wondered how long it would be before the face looking back became an older, unrecognizable one. She shuddered with the terrible thought that time was racing by and she had accomplished hardly anything to be proud of.

On her return to the hotel, Viv entered the lounge to watch the comings and goings of the guests. There seemed to be quite a mixture and as usual, she found people-watching most enjoyable. Light conversation ensued with several of them and she was pleased to have chosen this standard of hotel to stay in. After the last friendly person had moved away from her table to join some other friends, she decided to go to her room. Viv wanted to make the most of the next few days, so intended on an early night's sleep, hoping to make a good start and find out everything there was to enjoy in this town.

After a relaxing bubble bath which soothed her taut muscles, Viv laid down on the comfortable large bed. Then after a few moments of studying the recently painted ceiling, she climbed into the bed. The sheets were crisp and smelled good. The pillows and mattress were just as she liked, but after half an hour, it was obvious her mind was not tired enough for sleep. Each time it appeared she would drift off, unwanted thoughts popped into her head. She was still partly back in the office, but her feelings now were mainly of anticipation. Viv had never taken a holiday on her own before and she wondered how many interesting people, particularly men, she might be about to meet. No matter how much she tried to clear her mind, it was hopeless. She felt far too restless and after a couple of hours slid out of bed. Viv decided to go for a walk around the building, so dressed again, touched up her make up, picked up her handbag with her purse in it and went down by the hotel bar.

Viv walked close to the bar entrance and noticed many lonely, male eyes turned her way. Suddenly feeling uncomfortable about walking in alone and not wanting to become a spectacle, she made an abrupt turn. Laughing guests had arrived in the foyer in front of her, and the night looked inviting through the hotel's slowly closing door. Viv walked between the guests, toward the door and went outside. A walk on the beach near the hotel in the warm, summer sea breezes would be sure to relax her. She stopped briefly, breathing in the aroma and enjoying the feel of the warm air carried on the breeze.

Viv looked both ways, choosing the direction with the least amount of people ambling along the path. Whilst walking she stared up at the beautiful, bright moon which overlooked the glistening bay. It was hard not to think of the many couples deeply in love with their arms around each other, who might be looking up in the sky at the same time. Suddenly, from out of nowhere a deep voice startled her.

"Nice night for a walk. Are you out here alone, or is someone going to join you?"

Viv turned and saw the large, partially lit silhouette of a man. She took a few seconds to regain her composure, but was pleasantly surprised at this confrontation.

"Oh, yes, just me, and it is a lovely night," she replied smiling, not wanting the stranger to sense her immediate interest in him. "I needed the sound and smell of the sea to help me relax. The atmosphere is so very beautiful at night."

Something about him attracted her, possibly his size as well as the timbre of his voice. When he stepped in closer, it became obvious. He appeared to be at least six foot three inches tall, with broad shoulders, striking blue eyes and an irresistible smile. His yellow vest showed off his biceps and tight middle. Viv attempted not to look anywhere else, but her eyes glimpsed his large thighs, noticeable, even in his cargo pants. Everything seemed to fit his body as though it were tailor-made for him. The man was now holding out a large hand and introducing himself as Lawrence.

"Hi," she said, hoping he never noticed her eyes roaming over him. She offered her hand, saying, "I'm Viv."

They chatted easily as they continued to stroll along. It turned out, Lawrence was a friend of the manager of the Seine Hotel, which was the very one she had a room in. Lawrence went on to say he lived in Grenada, near the Spanish coast, and sailed his boat to this town about three or four times a year. Sometimes it became necessary for him to get away from the hectic schedule of his job as owner of a large construction business. He explained that his long work hours made it difficult to unwind when he took these short holidays.

Lawrence also explained his habit of taking long walks, late into the evening to relax and enjoy the evening breeze. If first impressions meant anything at all, Viv was immediately impressed with his presence beyond just the physical. Lawrence was the type of man who commanded respect. He had panache, was confident, straightforward and assertive. Virtues possibly gained within his job, where he would sometimes have to deal with difficult customers. This was the rare kind of man Viv hoped might exist but had not seen anywhere except on the television.

She simply could not refuse when he invited her out on his boat, and she readily agreed to meet on the dock near the hotel the next morning. He escorted her back into the hotel, where he had a room also. They reluctantly parted and he leaned forward to give her a light kiss on the lips. It was a gentle kiss and she responded in kind, but his kiss was enough to let her know that he could mean business, given time.

* * * * * * * * * * * * * * * * * * * *

Chapter Two
Bitter and Sweet Memories

The next morning Viv awoke wondering if Lawrence was a reality. Her heart beat faster as she remembered his looks. She hurried across the room to the open window and looked out across the bay. The sun had risen a few hours earlier, burning off the morning dew, and the air coming in smelled crisp and fresh. It was a perfect day for a jaunt on Lawrence's boat, although she felt slightly apprehensive about meeting a stranger like this. Also, Viv was not so keen on the water these days. She thought back to the time she was a teenager when her friends had talked her into Jet-Skiing on a stormy day. They insisted it was the best weather to have Jet-Ski fun. Hesitant at first, but finding herself caught up in the excitement she had gone along, with the intention of talking her way out of it and watching them Jet-Ski instead. The weather was just as her crazy friends liked it; stormy, dark, with bad gales and a rough sea.

At first she seemed to be successful in getting out of this dangerous situation, but then they had called her '*chicken.*' It was well known she hated being called a chicken and soon found herself reluctantly climbing onto the offered pillion seat. There were three Jet-Ski bikes, and she was the only pillion passenger. At first it seemed fun, although scary. They had been gliding over the waves for five minutes or so, with her hanging on tightly, when they were suddenly thrown up high over the large waves. She looked down, and her stomach lurched as she saw the wave far beneath the Jet-Ski which seemed to be hovering in the air. It wobbled and just before turning upside down, Steve, her driver, yelled out, "Hold your breath!" She did, but was horrified that the bike might come down on her head. Fortunately, she had fallen more to the side of the bike which dropped into the water just after her.

Once under, she was unable to distinguish which way was up. Intuitively, she realised there was no option but to relax, and let herself float up to the surface. She reached daylight, but only for an instant before another wave engulfed her, pushing her back down at least five times. It was impossible to catch a single breath as each wave came too soon for her to breathe in any fresh air. Try as she might, it was also impossible to swim, and she could not even stay afloat. With little air left in her lungs, it felt like her time was up and she was about to die.

It was true about one's whole life passing by in an instant when death is inevitable. The speed of re-living each event was truly amazing and un-jumbled. Each memory came with emotions and made more sense than when she was actually living those incidents and events. Viv suddenly had the irrational thought of not wanting to be found dead on the beach, with her make-up all smudged or missing altogether. It seemed strange at the time of near death like this, that she should be thinking so calmly, but a warm and fuzzy feeling had taken her over.

Just at that moment, a hand grabbed her shoulder up and out of the water, into the sunlight and fresh air. Viv's saviour turned out to be Derek, one of the other Jet-Ski bikers who then called out to her driver, Steve, to hang on. He was still floundering in the water. Derek called out that he would be straight back for him. She did not have the strength to pull herself up onto the saddle of his Jet-Ski, so using one hand, he helped her hang on the side as he motored back to shore. Viv struggled to catch her breath in between swallowing sea water as the waves washed over her, but she reached the safety of dry land. Luckily, one of their other friends had seen and rescued Steve the same way. The capsized Jet-Ski was nowhere to be seen.

Viv gladly returned to the reality of her hotel room. Her arms were tight around herself and she was shaking, but not with cold. It was hard to accept she could have died that day just a few years ago. '*Good grief*,' she almost said aloud. '*I hope nothing like that happens again!*' Nonetheless, it was an experience that kept her out of the water ever since. At least the weather today was nothing like on that day and she was not going to be in the sea, just on it, protected in the middle of a boat.

She drew herself a bubble bath and manicured her already well groomed nails whilst the water filled. Best to look as good as possible, she mused. '*This guy might turn out to be a real dud, but if he was as good as he looked, who knows where it could lead? Could this man be the right one for me?*' It might be too early to tell within this short holiday, but she certainly hoped Lawrence could be that elusive one and only, her first and last. She finished her grooming and selected clothes for the day.

Viv was unsure of just how to dress for a day on a boat and hoped the outfit she chose would impress Lawrence. She picked out a lilac gypsy-style skirt and cerise off-the-shoulder blouse. The top seemed a bit revealing, but it felt comfortable and cool. *'Something to easily slip out of, if the situation warranted,'* she thought, wickedly. *'Gosh, I don't even know Lawrence, and I'm already screwing him,'* she laughed. With that naughty thought, she stepped into her high-heeled sandals and left for the dock.

Lawrence had found it difficult to sleep the previous night. Something about Viv not only got his attention, but seemed to bewitch him. It was something beyond her obvious physical attraction. After all, anyone could see she was gorgeous. Athletically built like him, but busty, something he appreciated in a woman. She also possessed a very confident and mysterious air, and he hoped to learn more about her.

He had already showered, breakfasted and was about to dress. It surprised him to see the beginning's of arousal. He unsuccessfully tried not to visualize the two of them entwined in love's embrace on the deck of his boat. Dressing had become difficult as he fumbled with his zipper, trying to get his pale blue trousers done up over the bulge that had appeared there. He suddenly realised women did have it easier in some respects; at least there were no obvious signs of their arousal. Finally, he finished dressing. He wore a light blue shirt opened at the neck. The sleeves were rolled halfway up his muscled forearms. He chose his favourite sunglasses, slipped them on and smiled happily into the mirror, hoping Viv would like what she saw. He then pulled on his open-strapped, leather sandals and headed off to meet the enigmatic woman.

* * * * * * * * * * * * * * * * * * * *

Chapter Three
The Fantasy

Viv arrived at the dock just as Lawrence appeared. They smiled at each other and hugged like old friends. Impulsively, he pulled her towards him again and kissed her gently, but with more meaning than the kiss of the previous night. As they pulled apart, both looked flushed. Holding her arm, he moved her forward, motioning out toward the end of the pier.

"That's my boat over there," he gestured happily.

He pointed to a thirty-foot sailboat that gently swayed at the end of its tether on the dock. It was a great looking boat, but she felt butterflies inside at the thought of going out on the sea again. Lawrence led her along and after helping her on board, she watched as he undid both of the tethers. Soon he was aboard and two glasses of chardonnay appeared like magic. It did not take long before both were enjoying the journey along the gently rolling sea.

Viv knew how drink affected her, but thought that refusing the next offered drink would be impolite. She sipped slowly, whilst feeling the effect of something akin to abandonment. Viv no longer worried about the sea taking her again and felt safe with Lawrence. As the time and journey passed along, she sat closer to him. An hour into the journey, after much small talk and several more glasses of wine, they became quiet and thoughtful.

Viv enjoyed looking into the bright, blue eyes of Lawrence and noticed how dark his hair was. Almost black, and it made a great contrast to his eyes. He hungrily returned her gaze. They both sensed this was the place and time to stop the engine, and Lawrence did just that. The drink had relaxed Viv enough to lower her inhibitions, and although she felt nervous with this about to be her first time, she knew it was going to happen. If not now, then very soon. She could not resist placing her hand on his thigh as he slipped his left arm around her waist. They sat back for a quiet moment's reflection. The only sounds were the occasional seagull call and the placid water lapping under the boat which rolled idly on the gentle swell. Everything seemed so perfect for both of them.

"We're quite alone here, Lawrence, not a boat anywhere in sight," Viv said half questioning. "Where exactly are we?" she added, not really concerned about that at all.

The only certainty being that she was here alone, in the middle of the sea with a man she had only met the night before. Normally, her alarm bells might have told her to panic. But, there was something about those deep blue eyes that hypnotized Viv into feeling she could easily bend to his will, no matter what that might be. She had finally found the chemistry she needed with a man and she was ready to be taken for that very first time. If it was his intention, it was hers too.

Lawrence grinned back at Viv, reading between the lines. She seized the opportunity to slide her hand along the inside of his left thigh. Her fingers brushed something solid and she quickly moved her hand back, slightly embarrassed. She lifted her face to his with an unasked question in her eyes. Instantly he kissed her on the lips. It turned into a long, lingering, gentle kiss. Tingles went through her whole body. Breathless, she pulled away from his embrace.

"Oh, Lawrence, I don't know you well enough for that kind of kissing!" she exclaimed half-amused, but fully aroused. She had briefly kissed other men before, but none had affected her in quite this amazing way.

Lawrence seized Viv tightly in his arms and covered her with long, deep kisses along her neck, shoulders and tops of her breasts. Then he pressed his entire body against hers. His strong, sailor's hands cupped her breasts and caressed them. He had a clean, compelling man soap smell about him and just a touch of expensive aftershave. As he fondled her breasts, there was a *need for sex* expression on his face, which added greatly to her arousal. He placed her hand on his erection which felt thick. *'A bit too thick?'* she wondered, trying to subdue her sudden, rising panic.

Lawrence sensed it and began to kiss her again, until she became relaxed. He then moved his hand onto her smooth thigh, slowly moving further along and up her silky skin. His fingers slid inwards and came closer to the part she longed for him to touch, but she instinctively moved away, holding her face up to him so that he would kiss her again. She had read sexy romance novels and hoped she did not appear to be a novice, but this was going much too fast for her. She had to tell him somehow.

"I want to wait until I've known you a bit longer," she managed, in between the kissing.

"Wait for what?" he asked, trying to look innocent.

"You know what I mean. I got carried away; it must have been the drink! I haven't done it before Lawrence, so I want it to be special and not rushed," she blurted out.

Viv had said it now and felt his body tighten, as he loosened his grip on her. Had she ruined it? How she yearned to have had some experience before, so the magic of this moment would not disappear.

"You really haven't done it before?" he asked, incredulously.

"No, I'm so sorry. Have I spoiled it for you?"

Lawrence leaned back, reached for the bottle and poured them more drink. He smiled broadly as he handed her the glass. Viv felt some hope that all would be well, but she could not be sure.

"Well, now, that being the case, why did you trust me to bring you out here on the sea where we'd be all alone and I might take advantage of you?"

"Hmmmm, she said thoughtfully. I suppose I ought to have suggested we had dinner, instead of going out for this trip." Viv wondered what would happen now and thought he would want to take her straight back or throw her in the sea, heaven forbid!

"You could have suggested dinner," he agreed. "But, so could I have suggested it."

Viv wondered why she had not thought about what she was doing, but looking at him, it was easy to know why. "I wanted to be alone with you," she said sheepishly, "and I trusted…. trust you."

"Fair enough and I am honoured you could trust me so readily."

Viv relaxed that he was taking her news so well and moved closer to him. He put his arms around her and kissed her gently. "I hope you want to see me again, so we can take it slowly," he said in between the kisses.

She felt happy and knew he was not offended. She was impressed with his control and knew he would wait until the time was right for her. Viv replaced her hand on his thigh. But, Lawrence gently removed it.

"Better not to do that just now, far too dangerous," he grinned, slowly moving his head from side to side.

Viv moved back slightly and apologised. She felt as if she were a little girl, not a woman of nearly twenty-one. She had forgotten about her birthday and told him it was the day before she had to return home. Lawrence said it was a special birthday and he would think of a lovely treat for her. Viv's eyes opened wide as she imagined what that could be. *Surely not 'that?'* It might still be too soon for her, but her time with him would be running out by then.

"I know what you are thinking," he grinned, "but I didn't mean that, unless you think it a lovely surprise? We shall have to see nearer the time, what it will be."

Viv felt better, although so much of her wanted that, '*that.*'

A wind had picked up and Lawrence said they should go back now and get ready for dinner at the hotel, or another restaurant of her choice.

She smiled at him. His voice possessed an assertive but gentle, deep tone, verging on the edge of a growl. There was something beyond simple lust that touched her regarding this man. She was pleased that he would be the one who would take her virginity, but she also hoped they would stay together. Intuitively she knew no other man could measure up to Lawrence. She also appreciated the innate tenderness he showed towards '*his woman.*' It was the kind she had read about when romances happened on board. The type sailors were supposedly prone to.

Lawrence stood up and stretched himself, his arms reaching far above his head. Popping sounds could be heard as he untangled his joints and rigid muscles. The engine was started and the boat moved along too fast, but she looked forward to having dinner with him that evening.

* *

Both Viv and Lawrence had gone back to their rooms to freshen up, and she welcomed the chance to assess everything before meeting up with him again. She had taken a shower and picked out her evening clothes. Tight low-rise trousers, dressy crop top and high-strap, wedge sandals. She put on her usual scent, Opium, as that would be the smell Lawrence would associate with her. There was an hour to wait, and she happily lay on top of the bed gazing at the ceiling, wondering what he would think of for a birthday surprise. She also imagined their bodies clasped together....

It soon became time for Viv to leave her room and she felt good. They had arranged to meet in the bar before going to dinner in the hotel. Viv confidently walked in this time and saw Lawrence immediately, even though his back was towards the door. He was the tallest and broadest man in there. All eyes were on her, and she felt so proud as she walked up and touched his shoulder. Viv was given a wonderful smile and quick kiss on the lips. They stood close together at the bar and had a drink while they chatted casually. She was pleased the chemistry was as strong as ever and Viv tingled all over as she looked at him. A handsome man, dressed in a white open-necked shirt and tight-fitting black trousers. His expensive looking black shoes were highly polished.

They were taken to their table amongst the many other customers. There was a three-piece band playing; a jazz quartet, piano, bass and drums. The musicians were of high standard and they took requests for the classic songs. Lawrence asked them to play Ray Charles's, *I Can't Stop Loving You,* with a dedication for Viv. As the music started, he surprised her by taking the stage and singing the song to her, whilst the piano player sang the harmonies.

'How on earth could a man who looked like him, also be able to sing like this,' she wondered. Viv did not take her eyes off Lawrence. Out of the corner of her eye, she noticed the women almost drooling over him, but he never took his eyes off her.

Although the meal was good, it was hardly noticed, but the night was magical. The couple danced, smooched and were able to talk during the slow songs as the music played at a decent level. They learned a great deal about each other, and although she had suspected there would have been other women, she still felt saddened not to have been the first for Lawrence. But she was pleased to have him now as there was, thankfully, no-one on the scene here or back in Grenada for him. Viv liked the sound of that and wondered if she would be living there soon. No harm in dreaming and hoping.

The days went by with them enjoying each other's company to the full, only separating to go back to their individual rooms at night. They had discussed the 'surprise' to happen on her birthday, and the main surprise was that they were going to spend the night with each other. With this thought in mind, they enjoyed the days and every moment socially, visiting anywhere worth seeing. All the time looking forward to the birthday date, but regretting they would be separating not long after, at least, temporarily. The day was planned for an exceptionally exciting time of visits to all the nearby places not visited previously.

Lawrence had many beautifully wrapped gifts for her and the most romantic birthday card, which she would always treasure. The whole day was filled with a magical joy. They hugged, kissed and laughed more than before, hinting at the night to come.

Then the night was upon them both, starting with slow undressing, more self-restraint and anticipa-

tion, champagne whilst cuddling in a bubble bath….
Viv had the best teacher and the best night ever……

* * * * * * * * * * * * * * * * * * * *

Chapter Four
The Painful Reality

The bus came to a sharp halt and jerked Viv back to reality. It was her stop, and she rose from her seat still disorientated from her vivid memories as she stepped off the bus. It surprised her that this memory had been so strong this time. Although the incident had occurred years ago, her body still tingled with the memories. This past happiness and depth of emotion reawakened itself occasionally, but never before in public. It happened usually in her night dreams but not always so intensely. The reality of today's memory shocked her, and it took the ten-minute walk home to shake off the haze of the sensual memory. Viv's mind was in turmoil and she found it impossible not to continue thinking about that tremendous time with Lawrence. Even the lyrics of that song he performed for her, 'I Can't Stop Loving You,' was so relevant now.

As usual, depression hit her as she thought of how good their continuing relationship had been. Viv often wondered if the heartbreaking decision she made to run away from Lawrence was the dreadful mistake she now believed it to be. No matter how much she had tried to think differently, her greatest fear was that when she was not with him, even whilst he was at work, another woman might be successful in taking him away. Lawrence was far too perfect a man, and it was difficult to believe that she would always be good enough for him.

It broke her heart to leave him and also to see the hurt she caused, but the fear of losing him was something she could not risk. Viv could not let herself think anymore on exactly how it ended, for her feelings were still too deep and the wounds were easily opened. She often found herself holding the gold filigree heart pendant on her necklace chain that had been one of the gifts from Lawrence on that memorable birthday. Viv was holding the pendant now and it helped her feel close to him. She ached for Lawrence and hoped somehow to see him again when she could cope properly with it.

By the time Viv reached her house the memory had begun to fade. But, she was now determined to do something to get her life back on track. She had been celibate far too long, even partly through her marriage to Gavin, who she picked on the rebound. She was determined to think of a way to find the right man. One who was not perfect, not too good-looking, but, he had to be similar to Lawrence. Somehow, she had to find another man who would understand her self-doubts and not inadvertently cause her to feel inadequate for not being the perfect woman. It irritated her that she did not have enough self esteem.

Viv, like many other women considered very attractive, needed constant assurance. She felt annoyed that a man could have such a hold over her due to the amount of love she felt for him. Viv needed the company of one special man, who she felt she could measure up to. Not up to Lawrence's calibre, but someone so similar, that she could relax and feel safe. She needed to find someone soon, before she could no longer resist the temptation and attempt to reconcile with Lawrence yet again, only to hurt them both when she would inevitably flee.

Her next move would be the start of many thrilling, sad and unusual encounters. Life would never be the same again.

* *

Viv opened the front door feeling great relief to be home again, amongst her familiar comforts and odds and ends collected over the years. She was very proud of her little three-bedroom house, nestled off and away by itself in a secluded cul-de-sac. She had managed to purchase the house with the help of a friendly bank manager, who had fallen for her good looks and charm. He had been the rare decent sort, who was satisfied with her company on the occasions she had agreed to dinner or an outing.

Viv loved this house, with its pastel-coloured walls, lilacs, purples, reds, pinks and blues. Even the clocks and banisters were painted just to provide bursts of colour wherever she went. She liked white clothing, but not the colour white as part of the furnishings or decorations. White felt and looked too cold and clinical a colour, reminding her of hospitals. However, Viv adored snow, the way it transformed the wonders of nature to make a magical scene. Viv put it down to how contradictory she could become at times. Predictably unpredictable, she had been called many times by those close to her.

Viv's shoes were off, and she was about to dress in something loose and comfortable, when she realized she had forgotten to do her small bit of shopping. She only needed to stock up on as few items and decided to retrace her footsteps back to the newsagent and grocery store. It was a local family owned business that did very well as it stayed open twenty-four hours a day. It was located in a small precinct of shops she had walked past only a few moments ago.

Viv knew all of the shopkeepers by name. It was good to go in and shoot the breeze with them, and she was always interested in hearing the latest news and gossip in their lives. Soon she was strolling from shop to shop but could not help noticing the beautiful blue colour of the sky. It immediately took her mind back to the romantic encounters with Lawrence. '*Stop it!*' she scolded herself and instead, tried counting the paving slabs and curb stones to keep her mind preoccupied elsewhere. Anything, to keep her from longing for the man she still desperately missed, needed and wanted, if only she was brave enough to trust herself to trust him, she would be with him now.

Viv arrived at the newsagent and quickly gathered together the things she required. Coffee, milk, toilet paper, the usual mundane items one needed to get by. Whilst standing at the checkout, she noticed the store manager glance at her and smile. Apart from the usual greeting, today he seemed too busy for a chat.

On many previous occasions, Viv had also spoken with his wife. She was a nice enough woman, although frumpy and unfashionable. She looked like so many other women who stopped taking care of their looks after many years of marriage to the same man. Viv thought it might be nice to be married and living a nice, average, simple life. Similar to the style this man and his wife enjoyed. Routine, with no chaos she supposed. The couple seemed happy enough.

As was the case with many men, he was not her type so she felt surprised when her mind began to imagine herself alone with this man. He was no fantasy, just a pleasant, sociable, but business-like newsagent and local store owner. She imagined their bodies thrashing about together on some faraway beach, whilst waves licked at their naked bodies. This image did not give her any physical feelings, so it made no sense visualising in this way.

Once again, Viv forced her mind back to the here and now. She paid for her groceries, smiled courteously and left for the short walk back. On arrival at her house for the second time, she felt like weeping. She had a decent job and lovely, cosy home with its beautiful rattan and cane furniture. But, deep down she felt extremely lonely, physically aching to find that elusive 'Mr. Right.' Or rather, 'Mr Nearly Right,' who probably did not exist, leastways not for her, and it hurt to realise she would always pine for Lawrence.

Viv had believed Lawrence was her *special* person and felt he would always be. With those exact looks that excited her, he also possessed absolutely everything a woman could desire, including money. It was other women she could not trust, and to lose him, have him walk away, would have been the complete end of her. It would have felt even worse than the heartache she suffered by walking out on him and worse than the grief she continued to feel all this time.

Viv could not make a life with Lawrence for another reason. He had to be absent a good deal of the time with his work and missing him, wondering if he were safe from harm, as well as from women, would have been unbearable too. Viv yearned for his touch, his kisses, just all of it! Women everywhere threw themselves at Lawrence, and she was afraid that one day he might be tempted, which would have torn her heart out completely. In the end she broke off all physical contact, but stayed in casual contact, retaining the fantasy of him as her perfect lover, although it left her miserable and empty. It was during an attempt to end this feeling that she became involved with Gavin. Then promptly found herself in worse depths of despair and entrapment with the marriage, followed by the horrific consequences of the divorce. He had even tried to take her beloved little Chihuahua, Mia. Viv still missed Mia who had died of old age just a few years ago.

Viv kept in touch with Lawrence, as neither could let go completely. Lawrence hoped to change her mind, but the fear of losing him made it impossible to accept him. Over the last few years they had exchanged the occasional letters, emails, cards, and she often, without knowing if it would truly transpire, promised to visit him. She always became too afraid of having all her feelings aroused only perhaps to leave him again and bring all their pain back to the surface. Lawrence was living permanently in his villa near Grenada, on the Southern coast of Spain. As far as she knew, he never found another woman. A massive sigh escaped her.

Viv brought her thoughts back to the immediate problem. She appraised herself knowing that men found her attractive, often making nuisances of themselves. Initially, she might enjoy their company but would soon tire of them, finding them boring. Inevitably, conversations turned into discussions about their material wealth. They were always trying to impress her with their acquisitions and powerful business positions. In effect, they hoped she would want to marry them and, unwittingly, become another possession. A new decorative acquisition to make them feel more 'macho,' and have something new to brag about to other men. Viv was a woman never to be a 'notch' on anyone's belt.

What most men did not realize though, was this type of discussion only made them come over as self-centred. Also, perhaps men appeared unattractive to her, because they were. Especially, compared to a man like Lawrence. Viv needed that same complete 'chemistry.' The charm she had seen in Gavin, the man she had married on the rebound from Lawrence, had a small amount of what she needed. But his love of alcohol ruined even that.

Viv had been celibate for so long now and something had to be done about it. The question was, where and how to find *him*? Viv panicked for a moment. Could it be he was not out there at all, and if he were, would she ever meet him? If she found the near perfect man, almost like Lawrence, would he care enough for her? And the big question…. Would she run away as she had done from Lawrence? She hated these thoughts because they always left her mind in a mess. It did not surprise her to notice she was holding the pendant again.

Viv decided on a strong coffee and refreshing shower. Afterwards, draped in towels from head to foot, she sat quietly at her dressing table. Her eyes wandered around the bedroom and thoughts of changing the décor of her home re-surfaced. It needed *something.* More decorative lamps would be good, and larger mirrors could be added through-out the house to make the place look more spacious. A Mediterranean mural to cover one of her walls in the lounge would make it feel as if she were at the beach. Her mood lifted as she reminded herself of how lucky she really was.

Viv had purchased and moved into the house just a few years after her horrible and prolonged divorce from Gavin, the abusive, alcoholic. She had mar-ried him at a relatively young, twenty-three years of age. He frequented the club where she worked as a dancer. This job had come her way unexpectedly one evening whilst out with friends at the club. The owner had invited her to dance there professionally, so she did, for fun and to supplement her secretarial salary.

It was at the club where she first met Gavin, who appeared to be a charming man. Tall, very attractive with his blow-dried, blondish hair and muscular body. He was also a skilled fighter with a reputation and everyone feared him. She felt safe in his company and proud that he wanted her. After all, no one messed around with her whilst she was with him and that was a terrific feeling.

Viv believed she loved him at first, although it felt more like admiration than love, and not particularly lust. They soon married and moved into a large flat with a colourful, large garden, preferring to stay in their home town of Cornwall to begin their life together. Their friends were nearby and all, including her, hoped to move to Spain when they retired. It was the *in* thing to do. It was also Viv's secret, knowing that Lawrence was living in that country.

Gavin seemed compatible with her, but after their marriage his many dark, secretive sides were revealed to her. The first thing he made her do was give up dancing, so she went back to work full-time in an office. The second was not being allowed to go out with her girl friends. She had no physical or emotional freedom and soon felt like a prisoner.

Even though Gavin was a highly intelligent man, the effects of alcohol changed him dramatically. Whilst some men became merry and silly with drink, it turned Gavin irrational, jealous and his motives or actions difficult to comprehend. He also lived his life under the assumption that every man wanted his woman. Gavin instigated constant fights, attacking any man, anywhere and at anytime. It almost turned her into a nervous wreck as she was unable to even greet a male friend in passing.

By the time she reached twenty-seven years of age, the marriage was over. The divorce had turned into a bitter experience. Gavin would not face the inevitable and at first, stalked her. Viv had heard that he was drinking more heavily than ever. She feared this dark, evil side to his nature and had come to know it well. Her nerves were a mess if she went out shopping or to some of their favourite bistros, bars or restaurants in case she bumped into him.

Viv wished she had seen his true nature before they married. Instead, the marriage had caused her hell and then the exhausting, time-consuming divorce. Viv feared for her life the entire time, but never mentioned it to Lawrence on the occasions they were in contact. It would have been too humiliating for her. Viv had stayed alone for the past ten years, enjoying a certain kind of peace. It seemed impossible for her to trust another man, even if he seemed trustworthy. But Viv also knew that time healed, erased memory and that love had no rules so she still hoped to have a partner one day.

Viv often remembered back to when she was *one of the crowd.*' There were so many fun dances and parties, with friends dropping by all the time. Well, sometimes it was inconvenient, but it was good to be popular. She frowned slightly, remembering friends who came along with their seemingly endless troubles and depressions, mostly over men or money.

When Viv moved away from Cornwall, she lost touch with her friends. They all thought her crazy to move as far away as London, just to keep out of the way of her ex-husband who continued to live in Cornwall. The truth was she needed to start a new life where he could not find her. Unfortunately, Gavin had become too friendly with some of her closest friends and could track her down, if she continued to keep in touch with them.

Then on moving to London, Viv had found employment in a solicitor's office. She was not enamoured with the work and longed to do something more interesting, but it kept her going. In the ensuing years, Viv only dinner-dated and felt very proud of her independence, or so she thought. But sometimes, she really missed the closeness and clean soap smell of a man. The smell of Lawrence.

Viv loved the thought of cuddling up at night, like spoons. What great comfort it would give her and how much better she would sleep with someone close by to offer his love and protection. It was only at these lonely times she became aware of the empty atmosphere of the house and wondered if she should go to Lawrence, before it became impossible to reconcile. They still had chemistry with each other, but for how much longer?

It was all too much to think about at the moment. Besides, she was hungry having not eaten all day, so perhaps it was her empty stomach that made her feel so down right now. At the same time, the prospect of eating alone tonight took the edge off her hunger. As usual, she was a mix of emotions, all conflicting.

Viv sat down at the glass-topped, rattan table, which was one of her favourite pieces of furniture she had managed to hang onto. She held a cup of coffee and the local newspaper which she had bought particularly for the personal classifieds. Instead of seeing the print, on gazing down at the front page she saw images of her life. It had taken a very long time for her to want to share her privacy, years in fact, but now the yearning had to be faced. She would look for her Mr 'Nearly' Right. Lawrence was in her heart, her mind and flowed through her veins, he would always be there. But, there was a small untouched portion of heart which she could allow for a new man and that was all she could give.

* *

Chapter Five
The Dandy Lyons Marriage Agency

There were no chances to meet a potential partner at work as they were all so average. The women who worked there were all far too conventional, for her tastes and had nothing in common with her either. As a result, she never socialized with them.

Viv's attention returned to the newspaper as she remembered a *'Personal Ads' column* somewhere and glanced through until she found the relevant page. There were more lonely people advertising than she imagined and unfortunately, she could identify with most of them. Everyone wanted to find love, happiness and, *'sex.'* After all, it was common in the morality of today and a woman could admit to enjoying it at last. It was difficult not to think of the murderers who may find advertising or responding a handy way to find victims.

People seemed to drift from one relationship to another far too casually. How was it even possible to really get to know each other any more, to develop a partnership with common goals or interests? As a result, those her age and older, unable to find a partner through conventional means, seemed to be turning to other methods such as these.

She read aloud; *'PRETTY, GREEN-EYED MOTHER OF YOUNG GIRL, seeking a professional gentleman to share life with...'*

'RESPECTABLE, GOOD-LOOKING, solvent gentleman with GSOH, hoping to find soul-mate. Possible love and marriage?'

Most of the abbreviations were easy to decipher and she ignored the more complicated ones. Viv tried to imagine meeting a stranger on a blind date. *'What if it became so unbearable or boring that she wanted to leave before the evening was over? Besides, where would they go?'* She smiled. Was she really considering this option seriously? *'Why not?'* It seemed unlikely to meet that someone special in her everyday life. That was most unlikely and probably impossible, as she did not 'hang' out anywhere.

Viv knew she was still a desirable, good-looking woman. Although nearly thirty-six, she certainly did not look her age, maintaining herself through rigorous, home yoga exercise and good diet. She lived alone, so there were no hassles from a man to put up with, who wanted fried food or who could have stressed her out enough to cause wrinkles. As she read on, the number of advertisements continued to surprise her. There were so many columns all of similar wording. Unfortunately, not a single person sounded interesting enough for her to reply to, but the idea of writing her own advertisement intrigued her....

'How would it go?' she wondered. A little voice inside her head replied; *'SEX-STARVED, CURVY, DARK-HAIRED BEAUTY, NEEDS A MAN,*

IMMEDIATELY, IF NOT SOONER!' She laughed aloud…. That would certainly attract some replies!

Viv was about to discard the newspaper and make herself another coffee, when she noticed advertisements for marriage dating agencies. One in particular caught her eye. *'THE DANDY LYONS MARRIAGE AGENCY.'* Such a corny name, but it stood out from the others. She noted the address and telephone number just in case she might prefer to give them a try, or rather, muster the courage to do so.

Later on that evening, Viv attempted to write a serious advertisement to no avail. She had already tried to answer some, but the end result was laughable. If she were serious about finding her 'man,' then it had to be achieved through the proper channels, which should be the safest method of meeting men. She wondered about the various alternatives, finally settling on the idea of one of the dating agencies, the one with the corny name. The agency surely had a system to weed out the *'weirdo's* and *'undesirables.'* A reputable agency would have security systems in place. But, she could not help feeling sceptical and not sure the bother would be worth it.

The following day after finishing work at lunchtime, Viv made her way to the dating agency. This particular agency, *'The Dandy Lyons Marriage Agency,'* impressed her, not only due to the memorable name, but since it advertised dating for the *'discriminating'* single with the intention of marriage. It was not just for meeting sexual partners….

'I'm certainly discriminating enough,' she thought.

'*After all, I don't trust any men!*'   She decided this agency was also better, since it offered personalized consultations and video viewing of its members.

Viv smiled, remembering her useless attempt to phone the agency earlier that morning. The person on the other end of the line seemed helpful enough. However, Viv soon found it difficult to say anything sensible and confused everyone, herself included. In the end, she hung up the phone in fits of laughter. It might be easier to see them in person and she hoped her voice would not be recognized on her arrival.

She arrived at the address, without having broken the ice, although her courage arrived slightly later than she did. The agency was located in a relatively new, almost all-glass building. It stood out prominently with its shiny glass windows reflecting the bright sunshine on this particular beautiful day. No way would she admit her earlier phone call. She hovered outside the building for several minutes, trying to look as if she had lost her way, glancing inside occasionally.

Viv's courage almost disappeared, until she envisioned yet another lonely Christmas, decorating the rooms on her own, sipping a liqueur, eating the odd snack, usually Twiglets which she loved with only herself for company. There was no point in cooking for one. She imagined looking at her predictably few Christmas cards, placed on the mantelpiece above the burning fireplace in the front room. This image was all she needed for the extra push to enter the building. With a false air of confidence, she walked to the security desk, signed in and was then directed over to the shining bank of elevators which led to the agency and her true destiny, or so she hoped.

Viv entered and pushed the button for the 5th floor where the agency was located. She listened to the gentle *'ding ding'* as it lumbered up the levels. On arrival at her floor, she took a deep breath and walked straight into the agency. The receptionist was an attractive lady seated behind a computer at a work station. Viv imagined the lonely men who confronted her each day. They must fancy her like mad and hoped, through the agency to find someone just like her. The woman looked up and gave Viv a warm smile, which she easily returned.

"Hello, I could do with some help," Viv said nervously. "I'm interested in using your services."

"Well, I hope we manage to help you!" the receptionist pleasantly responded whilst handing her a clipboard and pen, along with some forms to fill. A chair was pointed out where Viv could sit down in privacy to answer the questions. She made herself comfortable and examined the forms. They requested the usual information, such as name, address, telephone number, date of birth and place of employment.

Viv aimlessly filled out each line, beginning to think she had made a big mistake in coming to the agency. Her attention wandered and on looking up, noticed a dark-haired man with striking blue eyes, who observed her from an adjoining office. He smiled for an instant and then returned to his writing. Her heart lifted slightly, and she felt a tingling sensation in her lower belly.

'What a gorgeous man,' she thought. *'I can't believe it, he looks so much like Lawrence!'*

Viv forced her attention back to filling in the forms, returning them to the receptionist behind the desk, who accepted them with another happy smile. She arose from her workstation saying, "Just a minute please," and disappeared. Several minutes later, an even more attractive woman came to greet her. She was dressed in a white blouse with the top two buttons undone showing a dignified amount of cleavage. The woman wore a black, form-fitting skirt, with 4-inch stiletto, high-heeled shoes. The black leather shone as she stepped into the reception area to meet Viv.

"Hello there, nice to meet you. It's my pleasure to be able to help. My name is Dandy Lyons, but please call me Dandy," the woman smiled. "Come with me into my office," she continued, motioning Viv to follow her into the confines of the agency's private rooms.

Dandy escorted Viv to a rather large space which had a glass wall that allowed a good view of the workstations which dotted the agency's general work space.

"Please have a seat, Viv," said Dandy. She gestured toward the big, comfortable settee, whilst she positioned herself behind her desk.

"How can we help you?" she asked, her smiling face beamed.

Viv took a few seconds to find the right words. Her voice did not sound anywhere near as confident as she hoped.

"I need a man," she managed, horrified at how desperate that must have sounded. Regaining her composure she said, "I mean, I'm looking for a man, er… special man… a true companion and partner." Viv still felt her face burning with embarrassment, even after all the words were out. She had not meant to be so obvious.

"For yourself?" Dandy inquired.

"Er, yes," Viv replied nervously, confused with this strange question.

Dandy replied with a knowing smile, "I only asked because some people come in here on behalf of friends or relatives, or, at least they prefer to say so." She continued, "We have a personal profile questionnaire that we'd like you to fill out, so we can more specifically determine the exact type of man best suited for you. Would you like me to ask you questions, or would you rather have some time to read them and then think about the answers? We can talk afterwards. There's plenty of time and absolutely no rush," Dandy offered, hoping to ease Viv's nervousness.

Viv glanced at the attractive man seated behind the desk in the next office, separated only by the glass partition. He must have sensed her eyes on him as he had looked up almost immediately and smiled at her. She blushed and smiled back. *'Could he possibly be filling in a questionnaire as well? Why would anyone with his looks need to waste time filling out questionnaires to find a woman? Perhaps there was something wrong with this guy?'* Then she remembered her situation and what had brought her into the agency.

"Oh, yes thanks," she answered reaching to take the offered form, "I'll fill it in."

The questions were no problem at all, until she got to the ones regarding qualities in a man that she found most desirable. Viv looked up in a way that Dandy knew was asking for help.

"Are you stuck?" she asked.

Viv cleared her throat. "Well I'm not really sure I have a clear picture of the man I'd like to meet," she answered.

At the same time, she visualized herself and the man in the adjacent office entangled in a passionate embrace. Their half-dressed bodies were on the desk, in the heat of lovemaking, with papers and files flying all over the office. '*What on earth is wrong with me?*' She admonished herself.

Dandy smiled, "Think of the qualities you admire most, ones you prefer and you can write combinations down in the order of preference. Take your time. Oh, and don't forget to also put down the qualities you have to offer. Be honest now, this is no time for modesty."

Viv glanced once again at the man behind the glass partition. This time Dandy's eyes followed hers.

Dandy caught the attention of the man with the sexy blue eyes and gestured for him to come and join them.

"I met my husband through a marriage agency," Dandy said, pointing to the man who was now rising from his chair in the adjacent office. "That's one of the main reasons we decided to start up an agency of our own. Now you can see it's very possible to find the right man. Hopefully, you'll find your ideal partner just as we did!"

When Viv realized the man whom she had already started to fantasize about was married and, to the woman seated in front of her, she felt ill. The thought of her type of man not being available, caused something inside her to collapse. She tried not to show her disappointment as she handed back the questionnaire. Viv hoped Dandy was not a mind reader and refrained from returning the gaze.

"Are you interested in membership for three months, six months or the full year?" Dandy asked.

Viv felt very confused, in more ways than one. *'Perhaps this couple might not really be happily married and he wants to escape a bad marriage?' He might be hoping to find someone through his own agency to fall in love with,'* she found herself wishing. A pang of guilt hit her, of course that was rubbish. The man now took papers over to someone on his way out and it looked as if he would soon enter the office they were in.

The fees were disclosed and Dandy waited whilst Viv decided on which membership package she preferred.

"I'd prefer to start with a three-month membership and see how things pan out," Viv answered.

Dandy asked, "How would you like to pay, credit card, cash or cheque?"

Viv wondered if it were too late to back out. Deciding it was too late, she paid in cash and was handed a receipt.

Dandy passed Viv a file and said, "One of the men in here could be suitable. If not, don't worry, we've plenty more for you to look at. New potentials come in regularly and are added to the list."

As Dandy spoke, Viv studied the woman who had won Mr. Lyons' heart. She was a good match for him Viv had to admit, with her clear blue eyes, large, firm breasts and long wavy auburn hair. At a guess, her age could be mid thirties, although she appeared more mature.

Viv heard a chair being moved in front of her and looked up to see Mr. Lyons standing there. Her heart lurched almost out of her mouth. He was even better-looking close up, and his body seemed *just* as good. So similar to Lawrence, far too similar!

'Oh, no! He's definitely the one I want and he's not available!' She could hardly catch her breath.

He held out his hand and introduced himself as Daniel. Viv nervously took his hand and knew her heartaches were about to start all over again.

* *

Chapter Six

The Lyons' Set Up a Potential Partner

Due to the electrifying affect of Daniel's hand-shake, Viv was relieved when he left her to get back to his work. Dandy had asked if he could now make an important telephone call to the name and number she handed him on an invoice. Viv had the feeling Dandy was just laying claim to her man, a way of saying, *'this is my man, so back off!'*

Dandy's 'actual' voice brought her back from meandering. She was being asked to look through the files to see if anyone appealed to her. Viv turned page after page, convinced there would be no one interesting enough, until she noticed a particular photograph. It was of a mature man, with kind, blue-green eyes and rugged handsome features.

The words accompanying his photograph were not out of the ordinary, but he seemed a good choice. His interests included wildlife, the Arts, music and an occasional drink with a cigar.

"I see you've taken a fancy to Mr. Burgess, Viv," Dandy said. "He's a charming man who shares your interest in dancing. I can show you his video if you care to come into the next room?"

Viv nodded, but felt nervous as she followed

Dandy into a curtained room containing a large wall screen. Whilst the video was prepared, Daniel entered the room with a tray of wine and three glasses. Viv pretended not to notice him.

"Would you like a drink, Ms., er?" he asked with a smile.

"Desmond, Viv Desmond," she said quietly, glancing his way. Her stomach turned over making her feel almost sick. His were the sexiest eyes she had seen, in a long, long time.

Daniel spoke in a jovial tone, smiling at his wife. "We're celebrating our first year of running the agency."

Viv could not stop looking into his eyes and thought her heart would stop beating altogether. They were not her Lawrence's, but they were pretty damn close!

Truthfully, she replied, "Yes, I could do with a drink please, Mr. Lyons." She knew what alcohol normally did for her and hoped it would not have that same effect now, but she needed to relax. Her hand shook as she accepted the glass he offered. Thankfully, Daniel did not seem to notice, although he mentioned casually there was no need for her to be nervous as this venture could be the start of something wonderful.

Daniel also advised her, "If the gentlemen or ladies don't make the grade, they won't make it into the file. We can't take just anyone who comes in here. We want to keep the agency's good name and high standards. That's one of the reasons our monthly dues are a bit higher than the typical agency. We can eliminate all but the most serious candidates."

He continued, "Most of the bureaus call themselves agencies, but they really don't offer our level of service, screening or confidentiality." He smiled at her, "You can call me Daniel," he said, sitting down beside his wife. He aimed the remote at the large screen and pressed the play button. The video began.

"Hello," said the voice on the video. "My name is Henry Burgess. I'm thirty-eight years of age and own a small, but flourishing, sign printing business."

Viv only pretended to listen. The man on the screen was nice enough, but her attention was not completely there. *'He even has lovely shaped lips!'* She thought, imagining how they would feel on hers and then she saw his large hands. *'How come I never noticed that when we shook hands? He must be well endowed too, like Lawrence,'* she could not help remembering. It was impossible to stop getting carried away with these thoughts. The few sips of wine had taken serious effect.

The video voice began to filter through again. "….. and she doesn't have to be attractive, just well-groomed with a charming personality and a good sense of fun." Viv caught the last sentence of Henry's speech.

"Well, what did you think of Henry Burgess then?" asked Dandy.

"Very nice…. I think," Viv replied, somewhat uncertainly, surprised the video had finished. He seemed okay, but not all she hoped for in a man.

"Would you like us to set up a meeting with Henry?" asked Daniel.

Viv could not believe what that voice was doing to her, although it did not have quite that rumbling deep *'timbre'* Lawrence had. Her mind wandered off again into sexual fantasy land. Finally she managed to squeak out a response.

"Yes, please."

"Good, we can arrange that for you!" Dandy said, walking towards the door.

Viv was not sure what she had agreed to. The question had slipped her mind already.

"As soon as we can get hold of Henry, we'll call you. I feel sure we'll find you the right partner, sooner or later. Perhaps he might fit the bill, you just need to give him a chance."

Viv had taken the cue and was now standing by Dandy who gave her a quick warm hug, saying, "Bye for now then, Viv. See you very soon."

'Easy for you to say,' Viv thought, as she stepped out of the door. *'You've got my man! My looks won't last forever and I need him now,'* she reflected quietly, but felt tempted to scream her thoughts out loud.

When the door closed behind her, Viv felt lonelier than ever. The rain came down suddenly and began to soak through to her scalp and clothes. Visions of Daniel Lyons and herself, sheltering under some bushes from a violent storm, came into her mind. She could feel his lips on hers as they passionately kissed. The feeling sent goose pimples all over her body. Their naked, wet bodies pressed tightly together. She gasped, as she once again felt the hardness of a muscular man's body. Viv could feel and see it all vividly. The feelings were too much for her to bear. Her legs felt weak and wobbly as she continued on her walk back home.

Luckily, there was a bistro nearby. Entering the door, she collapsed into the nearest seat at an empty table. She still tingled inside and waited for the feelings to subside. *'Oh no,'* she thought, *'If I'm like this with imagination, how can I ever cope with being near to him again?'* It was obviously lust and not love she felt, but it had opened something dormant in her.

After all these years, she began to feel these sensual feelings resurfacing. As much as she wanted to save herself for a potentially permanent partner, Viv realized that she desperately needed sex, although still only with a real *'turn on'* of a man, whose needs would make her feelings far more intense.

"Cup of coffee, and something to eat Miss?" asked a voice suddenly.

She looked up to see the waitress. Viv was asked again if she wanted coffee, but it took a moment to collect her thoughts and respond.

"Yes, please, black will do fine," she replied. After this coffee she would walk home, determined to think of anything other than the emotions recently experienced.

Eventually, Viv arrived home completely soaked through. As usual, her umbrella had been left in the house. She was barely inside when the telephone rang. She rushed over to answer it dripping water everywhere as she picked it up.

"Hello?"

It was *'his'* voice, Daniel Lyons. Viv's heart fluttered madly and she found it difficult to speak, or even to hear the exact words Daniel said to her. She did catch him say that Mr. Burgess, Henry, was on the other line and would she like to be connected? She would love to be *'connected,'* but not particularly to this other potential date. She was put through regardless and the other unfamiliar voice began to speak.

"Hello, Viv, this is a bit embarrassing, but here goes… I'm Henry Burgess. You've seen my video?" He stated, rather than asked.

'What a dork!' Viv thought. *'He sounds too keen or too nervous.'* She made up her mind in an instant. *'Certainly no match here.'* No way could she ever be compatible with such a person as the man on the other end of the telephone seemed to be.

Henry did not wait for a reply but continued. "Luckily there was something in my details, or photo, that you liked enough to want to take this further." There was continued silence from her. "Are you still there? I've been given a very favourable description of you!"

Viv's heart lurched. *'What did he mean? Who had described her? Was it Dandy or Daniel?'* "I only went to the agency this afternoon," she replied. "It's way too early to take everything in, and I'm not sure if I should change my mind, about going through with any of this. In fact, I've only just got in the door and I'm still dripping rainwater all over the floor, Henry."

"Shall I call back later then?" Henry cheerfully asked, adding, "Although I'd prefer for us to arrange a time for tomorrow evening?"

Viv was taken completely by surprise at his direct-ness and slightly annoyed by it as well.

"Oh! So soon, Henry? I've hardly spoken to you, don't know you yet. Wouldn't it be better if we spoke a few times on the phone first?" She had actually hoped to dissuade him through the somewhat apa-thetic tone of her voice.

"Oh, I know enough about you and there is no bet-ter way to find out about me than to meet up and talk. How about it then? Tomorrow evening?"

Viv gave up all attempts to put him off. Although thinking he was a bit too pushy, she agreed to a time and gave him her address. She put the phone down wondering if she had made a terrible mistake.

'Imagine me giving my address to someone un-known?' She felt sick. *'Is this going to be something I'll regret?'*

For all she knew, he could be a serial killer who chose his victims through dating agencies. He sounded a bit forward, what if he turned out to be a killer? *'Oh, my God! I better phone Daniel right away and have him cancel the whole thing,'* she thought in a panic.

She walked around in circles and then thought, *'I must calm down, the agency has to be a safe bet. After all, they knew Henry, didn't they?'*

They must have passed him through the same screening she had to endure. Viv imagined Daniel's face as he grilled Henry with questions. *'After all, it would need to be a special man to go out on a date with 'his' girl, right?'*

She collapsed into her armchair. *'Have I really fallen for him? Or, is it lust I feel?'* She was hot and bothered by images of Daniel. Maybe this couple could be faking their closeness for the sake of their clients? Perhaps they were not really married? Maybe they told clients they were, in order to promote good public relations for the agency. Viv was confused. The last thing she needed were *'strange'* men in her life.

Viv was still extremely apprehensive about it all. She usually trusted her intuition, learned from bad experiences. Perhaps, there was a way to tell the Lyons that she had a change of heart? But then she would never find out if Daniel was happily married or not. What if the Lyons suspected the awful truth, that she really wanted Daniel? Well, she was in it now and might as well see it through. Arrangements had been made to see Henry tomorrow, and there was no decent way out. Viv was committed and now had to see where this would lead.

Her night sleep was very fitful and disturbing with dreams full of strangers who came up to her asking unusual questions. In one dream, an angry woman with auburn hair and green eyes relentlessly pursued her. Although obviously meant to represent Dandy Lyons from the agency, this woman was a hideous creature.

The creature had six arms and four legs. Each hand held a clipboard with a form attached. It chased her, demanding in a screeching voice for the forms to be filled in. Viv only just managed to force herself awake before the creature engulfed her with its many outstretched arms.

In yet another dream, she experienced a mixture of fear and eroticism. The dream started with a party in the woods. It soon became apparent she was the only female present and was being plied with drinks. Then, she was slowly stripped by numerous large men with the letter 'D' tattooed on their ample bellies. The significance of this letter escaped her, unless it stood for 'Daniel?'

The men queued up to have sex with her, one after the other. Erections bounced up and down as men danced around and chanted. Some even came back for another go at her. For some reason, Viv did not attempt to awaken from this dream. On reflection, she wondered if she had turned into a nymphomaniac or some kind of insatiable sexual demon. But why the large, overweight men? Actually, it all quite disgusted her. Perhaps her mind tried not to think of the muscular men who she really fancied?

At work, Viv found it difficult to concentrate on her work routine. She drifted back to her dreams from last night. What might they signify? Feelings about the dreams were very contradictory as part of her thoroughly enjoyed the sex, but another part felt so dirty and abused. It seemed ridiculous, but yesterday, she only had Lawrence on her mind. Now he had been joined by Daniel and Henry, albeit, in entirely different ways.

* * * * * * * * * * * * * * * * * * * *

Chapter Seven

Meeting One Man with Another on Her Mind

The afternoon slowly ticked by, and Viv's trepidation about the imminent meeting with Henry grew heavy in her mind. *'What would he be like? Would it turn out she liked him after all? Would he be able to replace her feelings for Daniel, not to mention Lawrence?'* She really hoped so. Her mind was in turmoil yet again.

She looked at all the letters on her desk. Some were finished, but a pile needing attention sat in the *'In'* tray. There was a never-ending amount of work, and it all seemed to be headed nowhere. Well, at least not in her direction. There simply must be a better life for her outside this dreary drudgery of paperwork and answering telephones.

Perhaps, Henry would surprise her by becoming the man of her dreams? It was too late to turn back now; she had to meet him. It would be impossible to tell the Lyons she no longer had an interest in their services and wanted her money back. Everyone, including her, had spent too much time on the whole process to stop now. By the same token, what would the future hold now that she had taken this fateful step?

Did she really agree to meet someone this evening? Viv managed to get through the day, in spite of how the past came back so vividly. One day she vowed to let go of her memories which caused her more pain than pleasure. It seemed obvious that her present inability to do so, could well threaten any hopes for her future happiness.

Once home, Viv tidied up quickly, then relaxed in a hot bubble bath, taking occasional sips of her favourite cream soda. Her makeup was reapplied using a precariously positioned mirror on the edge of the bathtub.

It suited her to use heavy eyeliner and even heavier mascara on her long eye lashes. This lent a somewhat Egyptian look to her appearance. Especially, as it complimented her coffee-coloured skin so well. Viv's parents had been Spanish-Bohemian and she inherited her dark complexion from them.

No one was quite able to guess her origin. She could be taken for an Italian or Greek, as well as Latin American. A fine bone structure and high cheekbones added to her mysterious appearance. Viv's full lips never needed lipstick as there was a natural reddish hue to them. She did, however, like to add some clear lip gloss.

Viv continued to prepare herself for Henry's arrival, then again realized she was about to meet a total stranger. The thought caused butterflies in her stomach and not in a good way. She imagined him wanting to have sex, and a hot flush swept through her. She certainly would not jump into bed with just anyone. It had been a long time and she would keep her reputation unspoiled. Especially now as she hoped to begin a whole new way of life which included stability.

Viv chose to dress casually and comfortably, in black Lycra trousers, black ankle boots and a longish emerald jumper. It looked so well with her long, dark hair. She picked up her black leather coat, walked into the lounge and waited for Henry. There were still many apprehensions, but she decided to make the best of the situation.

Henry rang the doorbell exactly on time. Nervousness flooded through Viv as she walked toward the door and opened it. When their eyes met she was aware he had made an instant judgment, just the same as she had. It all had much to do with visual compatibility, a kind of physical chemistry. The instant decision as to whether they would look good together or not. Henry was tall, had nice looks, big shoulders, but did not exude sensuality, which Viv needed to excite her. She was slightly disappointed, although she smiled to hide it as best she could. At least she would be escorted by a respectable looking man.

Viv had her character faults and one was her reaction to a man's appearance if considering him as a partner. Unfortunately, she was very driven by a certain type of look and could not fancy a man who did not meet that criteria, or come near enough. Broad-shouldered, tall, muscular, dark haired, yes, Henry was similar, but his hair was cut too short for one thing and he lacked the degree of sensuality which could attract her. Viv felt shallow as she knew that her judgment had been made on this chemistry alone.

"I'm Henry," he beamed, in his soft, low voice, introducing himself unnecessarily. He took her hand, completely encasing it with his own.

'Another man with large hands', she thought. "Pleased to meet you," she managed, in a slightly unnatural voice. "Would you like a drink Henry, or shall we go straight out?" It sounded too much to the point, but no other words came to her.

Henry noticed Viv's lovely face first, then her shape. He liked the complete package. He noticed her small waist, or, was it the large breasts that made it look so small. She was dressed in a casual but sexy way, and it suited his taste. "Mrs. Lyons said you were a good looking lady, but I never expected this!" He said. "Good looking is something of an understatement!" Henry hoped her personality was as likeable. If that was the case, he might turn out to be a very lucky man. That was, if she liked him too! Henry thought it would be wonderful to walk down the street with this beautiful woman on his arm. It would make him hated by every man they passed. He liked the thought of that as well. "I would love a coffee before going out, if it's not too much trouble," he said, then added straightforwardly, "Mrs. Lyons also said you had good taste in men."

Viv's cheeks began to burn. Henry obviously did not know the significance of that remark, and she was glad to escape into the kitchen. Whilst waiting for the kettle to boil, she refilled the sugar bowl. Some of it spilled, but that could be cleared up later.

'*How could Dandy make that remark,*' she thought. '*Surely she hadn't seen me appraising her husband?*' It was all far too embarrassing.

Viv was sure she would not enjoy this evening and was frantically trying to think of excuses to get away as early as possible. How could she convince Henry that she did not fancy him and at the same time, stop things before they moved ahead too seriously? Not for her, of course, but for him. Viv still remembered the agony of her failed marriage and the numerous men who had chased her during her time in Cornwall. She glanced at Henry, who was seated on the sofa as she placed the tray with the coffee and cups on the table in front of him. He picked up the coffee pot and began to pour, motioning for her to sit down by his side. She hesitated. It was a bit too close, but she did not wish to offend him, so complied.

"Oh, I didn't mean for you to pour," she said quickly.

"No, I don't mind, nothing wrong with a man helping or doing chores around the house!"

Viv smiled, "You are obviously not a male chauvinist pig!"

"I'm definitely proud to say I am not! I respect women. I am close to my mother who has an apartment in my house."

Alarm bells started to ring. '*A Mummy's boy was bad enough, but at his age?*'

"....and I enjoy a certain amount of housework. Even cooking can be a pleasure, rather than a chore! Can you cook?" he asked suddenly. It seemed incredulous to him that someone like Viv might also enjoy cooking.

She shrugged.

"Oh, come on, just a little bit?" he urged, trying to prompt her, noticing her eyebrows come together in the tiniest of frowns.

"I can, if I have to, but I prefer to help someone prepare a meal," Viv replied. "I don't mind washing up afterward, though."

Henry was right about her at least on this one count, but helping was better than not wanting any part of sharing the cooking. "I agree. It's much nicer doing things together."

Viv felt uncomfortable. Henry talked as though he were testing her, interviewing, with marks being scored. Did it occur to him that she might not be attracted to him whatsoever and that it did not matter if she liked cooking or not? Regardless, Henry rambled on. He was the one who continued to lose points. Viv wanted to fantasize about Daniel, not indulge in this shallow conversation. She would have to wait until Henry was gone.

"Have you seen many other women?" she asked, surprised at her forwardness.

"A few, five I think. I've been registered for eight weeks now." Henry asked if Viv intended to make a video and was visibly relieved to hear her say no. He knew she would be much sought after and did not want the competition.

Viv wondered how long it took Dandy to meet Daniel. *'Why did they have similar names?'* She heard Henry say he had no more interest in the agency. It sounded as if he had won a contest. *'How can some people be so presumptuous?'* She wondered how to let him down gently. After all, Henry did seem to be a polite, well-mannered person and he may be talking this much to make up for her quietness. Trying far too hard to put her at ease.

"Daniel, that is, Mr. Lyons, seemed quite pleased that you chose to meet me. I hope you'll give me the chance to be myself, instead of this person who's just prattling on!" Henry said, laughing.

He sensed that Viv was very apprehensive, or was her mind far away on thoughts elsewhere? He wished she would respond a bit more. It made him uncomfortable having to ask most of the questions and carry on this strained conversation, even though Viv was still a delight for him to look at. Henry knew he could not stimulate the conversation, whatever he said. Viv seemed too distracted. He began to think she might dislike him.

"I'm sorry, Henry, this has all gone too fast for me. It's not normally like this when I meet someone for the first time. At least, not usually, but I don't date much. Mostly, I'm quite relaxed, I think…. But right now, well, this feels like an interrogation!"

"It's all my fault, Viv. I'm so sorry," Henry apologized. "I'm asking so many questions and talking too much. Come on, get your coat, and let's get something to eat!"

He smiled broadly and Viv noticed his green eyes twinkle. She relaxed slightly, noticing he did have lovely kind eyes and a very pleasant smile. Maybe she could grow to like him? At least, enough to enjoy the evening.

She went over to pick up the remote to turn the television off, when a newsflash came on. They both listened and watched as a reporter talked about the latest serial killing. After it ended, Viv turned off the television. She asked Henry if the latest murder was anywhere near to where she lived.

"I can't say, Viv. From what I've read and heard in the news, the killer has moved over many areas. It's almost impossible for the police to know where he is." He added, "Did you realize that to date, this man has only killed gay men?"

"Good grief! Well, though I feel a bit better for myself, that's awful news! I hadn't even heard much, apart from some news reports a few weeks ago. I don't like to listen to such horrible news."

"Viv," Henry said as he walked closer to her, "I intended to take you to a restaurant, but if you'd prefer, we could get some takeaway food and drinks?"

"Oh, no!" She replied a little too quickly. "I'd prefer to go out." She was concerned that he might have amorous goings on in his head.

"You don't have to worry about me, lady," Henry said with a mischievous look in his eyes. "I'm always on my best behaviour! Come on, get your coat."

* * * * * * * * * * * * * * * * * * * *

Chapter Eight
Pleasant Reminiscing

Through half-closed curtains, Viv could hear the rain spatter against her window pane. She snuggled down lower, pulling the covers over her shoulders. What a wonderful evening it had turned out to be. They had a meal and visited several clubs. Henry turned out to be great company making her laugh most of the time. Given the opportunity to chill out, he talked in different accents and mimicked people, shamelessly.

Dinner was exquisite and the dancing was such fun. He greatly surprised her by being such a good dancer! She would have preferred more of the 70's and 80's music to the loud modern sounds. Some of the songs actually turned out to be her all-time favourites, like 'Roxy music' and 'Bad Company.' They even visited one club where 'Rolling Stones' music was played!

In between the various sets, the music sounded so similar that it became difficult to tell if the song had been changed. It was a shame that the music was so loud the conversation had to be 'shouting.' How were the young people supposed to find romance when they had to shout at each other whenever they went out for the evening? How could girls respond with dignity if they too had to shout back like 'drill sergeants' to be heard? Maybe romance was no longer considered a necessity in today's society. It certainly had begun to die out!

Apart from the loudness of the music, everything else had been just great. Viv only thought of Daniel twice or perhaps several more times, but she certainly enjoyed dancing with Henry, nonetheless. They moved well together and their rhythms synchronized well to the beats of the music. As it turned out, Henry was an avid musician who had once been part of a band. He played the drums and saxophone, two of Viv's favourite instruments. She loved the way the sax added true character to any musical number.

Henry studied music as a child and then joined a band when he got out of school. They played for a few years, enjoying moderate success as a melodic rock band. The group disbanded and each of them headed separate ways. Henry reminisced about those days and often wanted to join up with a band once again, if only in his spare time.

However, a band was a full-time commitment and Henry did not have the time with all of the hours he devoted to his work. Yes, Henry certainly had scored some points with Viv due to his musical background, but still, she approached the potential relationship very cautiously.

Viv snuggled further down into her bed and smiled. She remembered how well Henry took it when she did not invite him in for a 'coffee.' For the time being she would keep him on a leash, willing and eager, if the need in her arose. It had been left that she would call him soon to arrange another date. Henry's face had taken on a sad, *'little boy lost'* look. He would have preferred to arrange something more definite.

He managed to put on a brave smile, gave her a hug and a friendly kiss on the forehead.

"Good night, Viv," he called out getting into his BMW gold coloured Sports Coupe. He honked the horn and blew her a kiss before speeding off into the night. It was nearly 3 a.m. Viv knew Henry should not have 'honked' at that time of night, but it was just a little 'honk.'

Viv stretched out to her full 5' 7" frame, closed her eyes and relaxed in the warm feeling of anticipation. The handsome face of Daniel Lyons floated through her mind. She simply had to go to the agency tomorrow. *'After all, it would not hurt to browse through another file or two, would it?'*

Men on tap, what a thought, and if Daniel happened to be there she would deliberately make sure he had no effect on her. After all, he was taken, or was he unhappily taken? No, she must not think like that.

Also, there was a chance she might find a combination of Henry and Daniel. After all, with all the men in the world, there should at least be one! He must exist somewhere! Viv felt a twinge of guilt, wishing she could get to know Daniel better. *'Daniel,'* what a strong name. She went to sleep thinking what a dumb name 'Dandy' was and perhaps Daniel thought so too.

Viv slept in late the next morning. It was 11.30 a.m., by the time she managed to force her eyes open enough to see the telephone. She called the agency and was informed that since it was Saturday, the agency closed at 1 p.m. She had to fly! No time for the pleasuring session she had promised herself. That would have to wait until later.

When she arrived at the agency, Dandy welcomed her with a big smile, but Viv wondered if it was false.

"Hello again," she said and ushered Viv into a waiting chair.

Viv smiled back, annoyed at herself for not returning the same kind of warmth. She glanced sideways and noticed that Daniel was once again seated behind the glass partition in front of his computer. He continued working and did not glance up. Was he ignoring her? Why should he be? She suddenly realized he had no reason to know she was here at all. After all, it was Dandy she had spoken to earlier.

"Well, how did you get on with Henry?" Dandy asked.

"Oh, quite well," Viv replied quickly. "As I told you on the phone earlier, he's very good company…" She trailed off.

"But?" Dandy asked, with her head leaning to the side quizzically.

"Well, if you don't mind, I'd like to see if there are any more men on your files that might be suitable. You know, before I make a decision to see anyone regularly?"

"Yes, of course," Dandy said. "I guessed as much when you spoke to me earlier. Oh, by the way, Henry phoned us this morning. He's removed his profile from our records."

Viv was surprised and hoped he had not done that because of her. It seemed as if he had put all his eggs in one basket. '*A very frail basket at that too,*' she thought. Viv remembered Henry's comment about the video. She asked Dandy how much it would cost.

"I hope you don't mind me saying this, but I think it would be a bad idea for you." Dandy looked serious. "You might attract the wrong type of man." She came around the desk to face a confused Viv.

"You have obvious physical appeal. I feel sure that you'd prefer that asset to be secondary in a man's mind. Women like us have a need to be appreciated for who we are, not to be mainly a decoration on some man's arm just so he can boost his ego!"

"I see what you mean," answered Viv, with a laugh.

Dandy took off her jacket which covered a tight red shirt-waister. She wore a matching pair of red fitted trousers, with a shiny black belt around her slim waist. Strangely, their figures were quite similar. Dandy sat down beside Viv.

"I'll tell you why I'd like to help you. It's mainly because I made so many mistakes when I first started this method of trying to find my 'Mr. Right.' I hurt so many men unwittingly. I was tempted into having many sexual encounters. Too many! Although I didn't actually hop in and out of bed, it seemed like that, due to my becoming close to a few of the men. I made the mistake of thinking they were keen on the '*complete*' me." Dandy shifted in her seat, then continued.

"I realized the '*lust*' thing got in the way, preventing them having the time, or even wanting to get to know the real me. They thought I was what they were look-ing for from the start on appearance; I began to feel cheap, dirty and used. It felt as if I were losing my soul, it was such a difficult time. I almost gave up the hope of finding anyone that I was interested in, who could take his time to get to know me properly!"

Viv was amazed at this forthrightness and also that Daniel's beautiful wife should feel concerned enough to share her own experiences! *'Why would she be so kind?'* Viv wondered. Especially, as Viv had more than a sneaky feeling her interest in Daniel, was very obvious to Dandy.

Dandy continued, "I made a video. Stupidly, I dressed far too sexily and many men took an interest in me due to the physical impact. Of course, I made sure I either saw their photograph or a video of them before agreeing to meet them. It's the only way to see if there's any chance or potential for physical chem-istry. Many were handsome and some not so attrac-tive. It seemed the more ordinary the men were, the nicer they turned out to be. But those types were not so appealing to me."

Dandy was pleased to see Viv take it all in and con-tinued. "It was all so time consuming, but I would not compromise. It took fourteen months before I seriously dated. That was how I met Daniel. By then, I had a very toned down video. There were many shots from a distance, and had my coat on in some. That type of thing. It worked. Different men were choosing me. You see, the more modest man was probably worried about having an *'obvious'* woman as a partner and potential wife."

"Quite understandable really," Viv said. She could certainly see the sense in this. "So, Daniel picked this more *'laid back'* image then?"

"Yes, exactly that! Then of course when I saw his video, I knew he was the one for me. He was as great as he looked. I fell in love immediately!"

Dandy's happiness was infectious.

She continued. "If you don't feel that chemistry from the start, a relationship will never grow as well as it should."

"How long had Daniel been looking?" Viv asked.

"Only about 6 months," was the reply.

Viv wanted to ask more questions, but now was not the time or the place. She thought seriously about this agency dating, realizing it was not only meant for people who found it difficult to maintain a relationship. It was also a good way to meet a much wider spectrum and variety of people. If anything, it could prove a time saver over ordinary dating.

Dandy waited for Viv to focus her attention again.

Viv looked up. "I don't want to keep looking for as long as you did, though. It would drive me crazy!"

"You may get luckier than I did and have quicker results, too. Anyway, I've been working something out for you."

Viv interrupted her. "Do you think I should make a laid back video like you did then?"

"Not yet. It depends on whether my idea works or not. First, I must say Henry was one of the nicest on the books for a long time. But I know your problem.

You've set your mind on a particular look. What you need is that chemical reaction."

Viv nodded, and thought, *'Yes, just like the one I had on seeing your husband!'*

Dandy had sorted out some potentials from a different file, which she said were worthy of consideration.

"Henry's lovely, but he's not exciting. Maybe I need someone younger? Do you feel that Henry could be right for me?" Viv asked.

Dandy looked thoughtful. "Henry's very attractive in a rugged way. He'll certainly age well. He also has qualities which reveal themselves the more you get to know him."

Viv wondered if she might have felt some chemistry, had she been able to concentrate on Henry without Daniel on her mind. It was something she had not considered before.

"I may be wrong for telling you this, Viv, but Henry's besotted with you and thinks you're the right one for him. So much so, that he's lost money by taking his name off the register. If it turned out you weren't interested in him or unable to feel the same way, he said he'd put his energies back into his work. He doesn't want to waste any more time and is not interested in meeting anyone else."

Viv felt all kind of emotions, but was secretly pleased that Henry had taken to her to this degree.

With a slight twist to her mouth, she said, "I certainly felt very comfortable with him after just a little while in his company, but…"

"Don't worry, I understand," Dandy said smiling.

Viv sincerely hoped she did not understand at all. Dandy went over to the desk and picked up the new file she had prepared. She placed it on Viv's lap and then to her surprise, put on her jacket and coat.

"I'm afraid I must leave you now, as I have a dental appointment," she said.

"But you told me you had an idea?"

"It will all make sense to you soon. You just have to look at the file first. Daniel will help you. If you want to ask me anything later, you can always contact me here. Now don't rush, just relax and enjoy yourself."

Dandy slipped into the next office to talk to her husband. Viv sneaked the occasional glance through the glass partition. *'How could she do this? Leaving me alone with HIM?'* She felt incredibly nervous. *'Had Daniel already sorted out some videos for her? How embarrassing this was going to be! How horrible! How exciting! So confusing!'* Viv could not determine how she really felt. One thing was certain, her heart was beating madly.

Dandy returned. "Daniel will be out in a moment to help you. I must go now, otherwise, I'll be late for my appointment. See you later, Viv. Bye for now."

She had gone! Dandy had actually left her, and *'he'* was in there! About to come out, walk over to her and say, *'From the moment my eyes met yours I knew you had to be mine. Thought I already knew what love was, but this is much stronger.'* He would then take her hand, as his lips got closer and closer, *'..and I know you feel the same way too. I must hold you close to me.'* Viv visualized them kissing and his right hand cupping her breast. She felt faint.

* * * * * * * * * * * * * * * * * * * *

Chapter Nine

Viv Receives an Offer She Cannot Refuse!

"Hello."

Daniel never meant to startle her, but Viv visibly jumped.

"I'm sorry to have kept you, but I was just finishing off some work." His smile was the most wonderful thing she had ever seen. It gave her goose-bumps all over.

She managed a weak, "Hello." A loud silence followed.

His eyes seemed to penetrate her soul, searching inside, discovering things even she never knew about herself. He sat opposite and motioned to his laptop. He asked Viv if she minded him continuing with some important work. It would only take a few moments he said, whilst she studied the file. Viv nodded. She did not mind at all.

It would give her time to compose herself, if that were at all possible. She shuddered as Daniel's hand touched hers for a second when he opened the file in her lap. *'Such well-groomed hands. I must find something to dislike about him. Please, I simply must!'* She thought desperately.

Vanity made her wonder if he deliberately acted as if his wife were around to keep an eye on him. Or, perhaps he really was 'trustworthy.' Maybe he was so totally satisfied with Dandy that he never reacted to other attractive women. This was exactly the kind of man she wanted. Viv could not remember a time when left alone with a man or even the husband of a friend, that some kind of pass was not made.

Her hands were steadier now whilst she turned the pages. In between her thoughts, she forced herself to concentrate on the information and photographs.

"Here's a pen and paper, so you can take notes, if anything or anyone takes your fancy," Daniel said, as he leaned over and handed them to her.

'Yes, something has taken my fancy alright, but I can't do anything about it,' she thought unhappily.

A whiff of aftershave, or was it just his smell, permeated the air and sent the most exquisite tingle down her spine. His face was so close she imagined that he might kiss her. *'That's how it happens in the films,'* she remembered. Viv resisted the most incredible urge to meet his lips. Instead, she accepted the offered items. To her surprise, there seemed to be quite a few potentials in this file. Not in the same mould as Daniel, of course, but some looked promising.

Viv grew more confident as acceptance of the situation imposed itself on her. She became genuinely interested and read on, although she still turned the pages a little too fast. Occasionally, she jotted down a member's number.

"Anyone taken your fancy then?" Daniel suddenly asked.

'*Much more than you should ever know,*' she thought, imagining his lips softly closing over hers, yet again.

His sexy blue eyes looked straight into hers. "You're at the end of the file now, Viv," he laughed.

His laugh was so infectious, just like him. If he was a virus, she would be happy to catch it. Automatically, she pointed to a profile on the last page.

"This one!" She had to say something.

"Ah, yes, that's Baron Von Eider," he replied.

Upon closer inspection of the accompanying photo, Viv was amazed to see the resemblance to Daniel! At least through the haziness of the photo, as this was the most unclear of all of them. She did not have time to look at the profile details, as Daniel had already asked for her 'list.' Five numbers had been written on it. Daniel then asked her to follow him into the screening room. He motioned for her to sit down, although this time, much closer to him. The situation seemed dream-like. Viv must have been in a real daze, for she had not even noticed that Daniel had made coffee and was handing her a cup.

"Thanks, Mr. Lyons," she said, finding it difficult to be more personal and use his first name.

"Call me Daniel, rather than 'Mr. Lyons', it sounds too formal," he said, smiling.

She would have felt more comfortable calling him 'Mr. Lyons.' It reminded her that he was married. "Daniel and Dandy." She could not help but say their names aloud.

"Are they your real names?" She did not mean to

sound so impolite, and felt embarrassed. Previously, Viv had thought that *'Dandy,'* plus her surname, *'Lyons,'* was unlikely to be real.

Daniel did not seem to mind the question. "Our first names are genuine, but *'Lyons'* was acquired," he explained. "Dandy thought it was a good idea to change our surname, for the sake of the agency. It's corny, but people will remember the name. That's business and good marketing."

Daniel organized the five video tapes that Viv had marked down from a list of numbers. Each number referred to a different male client.

The lights went off and the screen lit up. The name of David Markham was announced. He was pictured seated on his sofa, talking casually and surprisingly relaxed. Viv understood why, when she heard that he had been an actor. She immediately dismissed him from her mind. From past experience, she had learned that actors, well most of them, could constantly play games and lie without being detected. They could make you believe anything they wanted you to. After all, that was their job! Their talent!

Daniel saw her disinterest. "Not keen then?"

Viv shook her head. He did not bother to question her further, but put on another video. It was extremely difficult for her not to stare at Daniel, but the few times she did, he had not noticed. By the time he played the fourth video, Viv needed to get out of the room as she could not control her thoughts. But, she hoped this last one might be the best. Baron Von Eider's video was about to be shown. How on earth had she forgotten about him? Even though she had not seen a close up picture, the man who seemed to resemble Daniel was about to appear on screen. Her concentration and optimism were now very real indeed.

As his video started, the first thing she saw was a beautiful mansion surrounded by rambling gardens. The lawns were bordered by rose trees and exotic looking bushes, shrubs and small trees. Orchards came into view and then the stables with some magnificent horses being led along a trail.

Daniel took a sidelong glance at Viv, who seemed to be enjoying herself now. He was pleased. Dandy had a previous long conversation with him about Viv and had taken a distinct liking to her. There were some similarities from when Dandy was younger, or so she told him. Daniel could not see this, but if she liked Viv, well it was all right. That was the reason he agreed to go along with this not as yet, totally thought out, *'plan.'*

The video rolled on. Everything looked marvellous and Viv longed to live in this wonderful place. Only one thing left to see, the man himself, but now the video had come to an end and the projector turned off. Viv looked up expectantly, only to see Daniel grinning back at her.

Viv wished he did not smile like that. It made her heart beat faster. She knew it was lust, but that was bad enough.

"There's more to this than meets the eye," Daniel said, implying that he knew much more than he was prepared to indulge. "But first, I must ask how you feel about that last video of the baron's details?"

Viv was not sure what he meant.

"Now that you've seen his home and photograph, along with the other information in the file, is he the kind of man you would like to have a relationship with?"

"Well, the profile photo was hazy and there's no sign of the baron on the video. But, the lifestyle is wonderful, yes, of course he would be worth meeting," Viv replied quickly. "He'd be everything a woman could possibly want, provided his character and personality matched his looks!"

She felt her face grow hot. Surely, Daniel knew how similar his looks were to the baron's, even with the photo not being clear.

"Why wasn't the baron, on the video, Daniel?" Viv asked, feeling strange using his name. "Why only an unclear photo in the file of this, baron?"

"You can see for yourself," he beamed, with another heart stopper. "In a much better way than a video could possibly show." Daniel fell silent whilst he searched for the right words. "How about accepting an invitation to a barbeque, at that very house?" He indicated towards the empty screen and continued quickly. "Dandy and I have been invited and you could come as our guest."

Viv found it hard to believe what had been offered. It made her feel excited and alarmed, all at the same time. "I'm not sure. That is, I'm not sure if I'm ready," she said quietly.

"Just think about it. You can watch the baron from a distance and if you want to know him better, that will be up to you. Anyway, Dandy and I are convinced that you will enjoy yourself. He always throws the best parties, and this is going to be a fancy dress barbeque. In fact, it's a dress *any way you want,* type of party."

Viv thought very hard. She had met enough wealthy men to know that they could be extremely cold. They usually expected far more in return than they were prepared to give. However, it was a chance to be near Daniel, even if his wife was present.

"The baron would not know you were there just to see him and if all goes well, the relationship would have a far more natural start," he persuaded.

After a short while, Viv felt intrigued and agreed it would be better than meeting as prospective marriage partners.

Daniel smiled broadly again. "Just trust me," he said. "I'll explain everything at the right time."

The words sounded to her, like *just love me.'* How would it be possible to have feelings for anyone else when she felt like this, and over a married man? But, she was determined to give it a try.

"Well, Viv? Do you accept?"

She drew a deep breath and nodded her head in agreement.

"Good, good. That's it then. Dandy will phone you nearer the time to discuss the details. The barbeque is on next Saturday evening which gives you a week to get geared up for it."

"Only a week away!" she gasped, feeling the weakness spread throughout her body, not just in her knees.

"You did say you wanted to see other men before knowing if you could commit yourself to one of them. Also, that you didn't want to wait as long as Dandy did, before she found her suitable partner!"

Viv was surprised that Dandy told him so much, but then it all had to do with business. It was not as if anything *personal' had* passed between them. Viv only thought about it for a few seconds before she agreed, stating it would be better than an interview type of meeting. *'A week is better than if the meeting was in a few days,'* she thought, feeling more comforted. She expressed her gratitude to Daniel for all the time that had been spent on her.

"You're so lucky to find someone like Dandy and her you!" She suddenly said aloud.

Daniel's face lit up with pride as he replied, "Dandy's so very different from anyone I've ever met before. She told you how we met I suppose?"

Viv nodded.

Daniel continued, "I had a few girlfriends before, of course, but none affected me as much as Dandy. We're very well suited to each other."

These words caused Viv some pain. Had he, in an underhanded way, just told her that she had no chance? Or, was he totally oblivious to the way she felt about him? She wanted to tell him he was the only man, or, the second, if Lawrence was counted, to affect her in such an immediate way. But she knew this could never happen. Instead, she managed to reply that she hoped she would find happiness just as they had done.

"We'll certainly do our best to help," Daniel said, as he motioned Viv toward the door. He side-stepped, allowing her to pass. At the door, he gently touched her shoulder for a second or two and said, "Don't look so worried. It'll work out all right."

"Thanks," Viv muttered, as she returned Daniel's smile.

She was glad to get away. He could not possibly have known how his hand on her shoulder, had affected her. An electric shock had coursed through her body and awakened deep sexual needs. *'How could he have remained so calm and unaffected?'* she wondered.

On the journey home, Viv reflected on the events of the past couple of hours. A feeling of apprehension and anticipation grew inside her. For the first time, she had hope, real hope. Her future no longer seemed so bleak or empty.

When Viv arrived home, she busied herself with housework and hoped the week would go by quickly. It felt as if she were about to go on her first date. But first she had to get through seven days, before the barbeque date finally arrived.

This time she recognized lust for what it really was. Luckily, she had not become acquainted with Daniel well enough to really fall for him. But what would happen on the night of the barbeque? What if Dandy left them alone in such a social situation?

'Oh jeez! Am I going to even want to try and get to know the baron?' It did not matter to Viv about living the life of luxury, if she could not feel that *'chemistry'* with the man. It could happen, if it turned out

Daniel was not really married and he showed his feelings for her. That was a long shot, but one could never know for sure.

* * * * * * * * * * * * * * * * * * *

Chapter Ten
Getting to Know about Henry

That evening when the doorbell chimed, Viv was far more composed than the first time Henry visited. When she opened the door to greet him, the pleasure on his face was genuine. Apparently, she had again chosen the right outfit to wear. A loose jumper and lacy sarong style skirt. These were her comfortable smart clothes which she liked to wear when relaxing at home, or for a casual outing. Henry seemed very pleased with the effect.

He had entered her home briskly, carrying several cartons of food. The waft of a very expensive aftershave accompanied him. He kissed Viv on the cheek, then made his way to the kitchen placing the food on the worktop. As if by magic, he produced a very unusual potted plant from another bag and placed that in the centre of the table. He asked Viv for two plates in order to prepare their meal.

"We have everything and more," Henry announced triumphantly. "I hope you're *really* hungry." He finished arranging the food on the plates before he remembered the drinks were still in his car. He went to retrieve them and returned with a bottle of wine and two bottles of cream soda. There was also a bottle of sherry which Viv said she liked to drink late sometimes, to get her brain ready for sleep.

He remembered that she mentioned liking cream soda, which was also a favourite of his. They tore into the barbequed ribs and talked easily. Viv laughed at Henry's humorous quips, although she worried about how to tell him about the baron's barbeque.

It annoyed her that she felt so guilty about it. After all, she had not made any commitments to Henry. Still, it would have been easier had she not known how infatuated he was with her. When Henry spoke, he always looked deep into her eyes and smiled in a certain way. She knew that look and had seen it before in the eyes of a few men who had fallen for her. Now, Henry already wore that look.

As it turned out, he had more in common with Viv, than she could have at first realized. For example, he was a budding author and written several poems and short stories. He routinely posted them to a writing website where authors reviewed each other's work. Henry continued to speak about his stories whilst they ate the delicious food.

Some of his stories were published in various magazines, but Henry had not so far received any real recognition. The printing business he owned and managed consumed most of his time, even though he had four employees. To Henry, writing was basically an enjoyable hobby, along with the camaraderie from the other writers on the site he befriended.

Viv also loved to write and had written several short stores, and articles. She had started a book, but it remained unfinished after several years. It was not that she lacked the patience to write. She actually loved it, but the book was autobiographical.

Whenever, she worked on her story, it conjured up too many painful memories.

She then needed to step away from it for several days, if not weeks and months. She would have loved to put her vivid memories down in the written word, but it was still too difficult. On the other hand, she knew that writing out all her hurts would be therapeutic and a way to release them from her mind.

"Perhaps you should write for television," Viv suddenly said to Henry. "There's so much rubbish on nowadays, they could use some good writers, I'm sure."

Henry considered this idea saying he might give it a try some time. They finished all of the food, and then Henry insisted on helping with the washing up. As they headed for the kitchen, he must have thought of his mother. He spoke of her as they carried the plates to the sink.

As it turned out, Henry's mother had dropped out of school at an early age to marry a military man, who was about eight years older than her. She was only seventeen at the time, and when she was twenty-two, produced their only child. Henry had been a blessing and his mother doted on him. He described his childhood as basically uneventful, but pleasant, with the extravagances expected with being an only child.

Henry went on to describe the house he now lived in. It was a white, two-storied, frame dwelling that consisted of two large flats he converted by himself, after his father's death. His father had worked diligently all his life at the same shoe factory. He did not leave much money, but as part of his legacy, ensured that his wife and son at least had the house. Henry's father was a very caring, decent man and Henry cherished the memories of their relationship.

Henry had attended a private school in Bedford. He earned a degree as an engineer and travelled the world with various jobs and companies. Although there had been a few casual relationships, he had never found his true love. His mother often reminded him about her greatest wish and it became painstakingly evident that she was not, as yet, a grandmother.

Henry said she would often chide him with; *'When are you going to find a nice girl and give me some grandchildren?'* His nose wrinkled as he said, "I didn't feel the need for children or to settle down. At least not then," he added.

Viv flinched at these words. She loved children, but felt no need for any just yet. Although thirty-five, she still had a life to live and plenty of time to have children, or not.

"I think it best to get one's affairs in order first, also experiencing life the only way possible with the freedom of being childless. Sacrifices always needed to be made, especially when everything began to re-volve around raising the children correctly."

Perhaps part of her reasoning was due to her own unhappy upbringing and the vivid memories she still carried of her own parents. They were totally unprepared for the responsibility. Perhaps that was why they were no good at it. In any event, she did not want to ruin Henry's mood, but she wished he was not taking it so fast. Henry sensed the discomfort and changed the subject by continuing to talk about his father.

"After his death, I gave up my job as an engineer and stopped travelling. I inherited the house with instructions to also have mother live there. With the money left after the conversion into separate flats, I started my successful printing business. We cater to a small clientele involved in publishing, magazines, calendars and mostly small print jobs. It's proven to be very lucrative, thankfully."

Henry was happy with his business, which was why the long hours did not bother him. He loved being his own boss, although it did have its headaches, especially when dealing with incompetent employees and their idiosyncrasies.

Henry and Viv returned to the lounge making themselves comfortable. Viv attempted to break the news of the upcoming date with the baron, but lost her nerve. Instead, she asked how many ladies Henry had already seen through the agency. He grinned, and then stretched himself out, resting his head at an angle against the back of the settee.

"I've seen a few," he said quietly. "They're not worth talking about though."

"Tell me anyway, Henry, I'm interested," Viv pressed. He began to look mildly embarrassed.

"Oh, well, the first lady that took my interest was Veronica. She was well-groomed, about mid-thirties. We met at a hotel downtown for lunch. I'm sure she said she didn't smoke or drink, but she did plenty of both. The whole thing seemed very tense with her and the conversation went more like an interview."

"What did you talk about?" Viv grinned.

"It seemed to be mostly questions, the majority on her part. She asked all about my business, like how long I'd been running the company. There were questions about my staff and if I'd had any affairs with any of them. She also asked if it was a lucrative business, about shares in other companies and how much property I owned."

Viv laughed, and Henry joined.

Henry continued, "I'm exaggerating a bit, but that's how it sounded to me. I knew what she was after."

Viv agreed that is was strange the woman had been so obvious.

"Veronica kept ordering Pina Colladas and downing them like she was in a race to drink all the alcohol in the world by a certain deadline. I'm not against drinking, but serial drinking, one after the other is quite another thing. Not only in between drinks, but even during the meal, she kept puffing away at her Cafe Creme cigars. It made me very uncomfortable and sometimes breathing the smoke made me feel nauseous, as I don't smoke, except for the occasional cigar."

Henry stood up to retrieve the bottle of wine. He offered Viv a glass and she nodded her head. She had some wine earlier to be sociable, but committed the crime of adding cream soda to her drink. It tasted good. She began to feel a mild, but pleasant buzz. The drink had the desired effect as it relaxed her, making it more comfortable to be with Henry. She hoped after another glass, she would finally get the nerve to tell him about the upcoming weekend at the baron's.

Viv knew she would have to say something soon and tried hard to find the words before Henry got back with their refills.

He reclined back on the settee, and Viv sat on the bean bag next to him. As she helped to arrange the cushions neatly behind him, her hand brushed against his jumper. The wool felt so very soft. She wondered if his mother had washed it.

"Who else are you going to tell me about?" Viv asked. "Tell me of the ones you got on with."

Henry did not want to continue this line of talk, but Viv was insistent. She needed more time to get her courage together. He looked as if he were having difficulty in remembering the others, but managed to dig out memories about two of the other women he met through the agency. There was Alice and their meeting in a coffee bar. Evidently, they spoke politely for an hour or so, before he managed to *escape.* He then told her of Deirdre. She had a nice personality and they met a couple of times for lunch, but it never went any further. There was no chemistry and not many shared interests either.

"Who else was there?" Viv prompted. "Surely you were a bit more successful than that!"

Viv knew the time had nearly come for her to explain things to Henry, and her mind wandered to the forthcoming event. How lucky to have an employer that allowed her at such short notice, to take time off. It would have been impossible to concentrate at work with the excitement of the barbeque coming up. Henry's voice drifted back through to her.

"There was only one embarrassing situation, but

you don't want to know about that one, I hope?" By the look on Viv's face, she did, so he continued.

"This one was some kind of a model who was beautifully turned out and good-looking, though in a plastic kind of way. I could tell she was pretty without the make-up, but she had changed her natural look and created a totally new image."

"We all do, when we wear make-up," Viv interrupted.

"Yeah, but it shouldn't be that obvious, I don't like 'over the top'. The lip liner was drawn right over the lip line, and her eyebrows were a completely different shape from anything normal!"

Viv laughed uncontrollably. There was such an incredulous look on his face.

Henry continued, "Her clothes were obviously expensive and so was her perfume. We arranged to meet in a restaurant, which wasn't such a good idea as it turned out. First, she was late. Then there was nothing on the menu that appealed to her and she made such a fuss about it!" He was re-living the humiliation as he continued.

"The waiter managed to talk her into one of their 'specials' and her mood improved. Her name was Olivia, by the way. Whilst we ate, she did most of the talking. I knew we were not compatible, but she was the most interesting out of all of them." Henry stopped speaking and Viv thought he looked embarrassed.

"Go on," she said, intrigued. "What happened then?"

His face had indeed gone a shade of pink. "Olivia said that although she had a great lifestyle, it would obviously change as she got older. It would not be possible to '*pull*' the same kind of man and she wanted to choose the right man to marry, now. Those were the exact words!" Henry tried to look offended, as he laughed. "She then started to ask personal financial questions. I was modest to the degree of total under-exaggeration!"

His face reddened even more as he went on to say, "She asked if I was virile and prepared to marry, as she wanted at least four children! Meanwhile, if I proved myself to be a good lover, she would plough money into my business! And then, she '*forgave*' me for using this personal contact '*scheme,*' to try and find the woman I wanted."

Viv found this story hilarious, even needing to wipe some tears from her eyes. Henry was not so amused. She had to ask another question. "This Olivia, was implying you were a gigolo, but worthy of being a husband then. Did you turn her down?"

"Of course, I turned her offer down! I couldn't trade myself that easily. Besides, the business was doing fine on its own," he added quietly. "Anyway, I'm not ready for children and especially, not in need of a wife like her!"

Although Viv was in fits of laughter, she noted that he did not seem ready for children either, even if his mother insisted.

"How did it all end? Did you tell her you'd think about it?" Viv found the indignation on his face highly amusing.

"Well, I merely thanked her for her offer. Said I preferred my uncomplicated life and that I was not fit enough for what she had in mind!" He laughed loudly at his comment and then added, "She took it very well. In fact, she took it too well really. It didn't do much for my ego!"

The atmosphere felt light-hearted and they both sat quietly for a few minutes. To change the mood would be sad, but it was now or never.

* *

Chapter Eleven

Time Together Helps Henry and Viv to Bond

"You do realize," Viv ventured, "that I may still be seeing others? Nothing wrong with that, is there? After all, we're both still available and playing the field, right?" She felt nervous about his reaction.

Henry's face tightened, and she could almost hear his indrawn breath. "I'm not seeing anyone else right now. Are you? I'd hoped that you'd give us a try first. I really thought that…" he stuttered, looking both dejected and defeated.

"I guess I'd built up too many expectations for this relationship. I should have discussed your feelings with you first. It was wrong not to have done so," Henry realised.

Viv imagined the crush of emotions and bitter, painful feelings of rejection that must be rolling deep down in his gut right now. She had not intended to bring him down so abruptly and felt sorry for it.

"It's a bit more complicated than that, Henry. There's something that I must find out."

The next problem was to tell him the rest. But, how much of her feelings should she expose, about her infatuation with Daniel and whether or not it was love or just lust? She liked Henry too much to keep the truth from him, but also did not want to hurt him further, or unnecessarily.

Henry waited, expectantly. All the while he stared at the drink in his hand before asking who his *'rival'* was. Viv explained about the upcoming September barbeque, but said it was more of a night out. To try and break the tension, she also added that there might not be another meeting with the baron anyway.

Henry smiled slowly and tried to joke. "It had to be a baron! Well, I hope he's spotty, with a huge aristocratic nose, awful breath, a large belly and is as boring as hell!"

Viv felt quite relieved that he tried to take it so well and also felt relieved that her news was out in the open. But Henry still looked tense as he pushed himself up into a sitting position.

"He *'is'* ugly I hope? *'Plain'* at least?" he asked hopefully. Although he knew that a woman of Viv's calibre would never fall for a plain old man, even if he was very wealthy.

"I'm afraid not," she replied honestly. Her brain attempted to find the kindest way to say more. *'I've got to tell him, I have to say it....'* Then she blurted it out, "He looks similar to Daniel!"

Henry groaned, totally deflated now. His nose crinkled. "But, Daniel's a very good-looking man! Correct? That's just not fair!" He moaned falling back on the settee in apparent disgust and misery.

Viv desperately attempted to play it down when

she told him looks were not everything. She even complimented Henry's looks which were handsome anyway. However, in spite of it all, she knew her preference was still for someone with great looks, panache and that elusive chemistry. She could not help being shallow in this respect and hated herself for it. By the same token, why should she not set high standards for herself?

Henry had not felt so terrible in a long time. A baron was bad enough, but with the looks of Daniel too! He groaned.

"I can't believe the Lyons' did this to me," he said. "I thought they liked me and knew how strong my feelings were for you. I really need to talk to them about this."

"Oh, Henry, the baron might prove to be boring. He might think too much of himself and be extremely arrogant." She still attempted to change the mood although it seemed irreversible at this point.

She wanted to console Henry and tried to, by taking his hand, but she sensed a slight withdrawal as she touched him. She removed her hand. It made her sad and felt almost as if he had accepted an early defeat. In a way, this also irritated her. After all, she did not have to choose a relationship with anyone and had only just started in her quest for a partner, anyway. Did Henry not have it in him to fight for her? At least, enough feelings to wait for her?

"I'm sure we'll still want to be friends, no matter what does or doesn't happen, Henry. Right?" She meant every word.

Henry smiled at her. Not a sexy smile, or a happy

one, but an extremely caring, genuine smile. He leaned over and put his arms around her. She leaned in closer to him and they both enjoyed the moment.

"I'm sure I won't like the baron as much as I already like you," she said. "Not when I get to know him better."

Henry was not reassured. "He's certainly got a good chance with you. After all, your life could be so luxurious. How could I begrudge you that?"

"Am I not even worth fighting for, metaphorically speaking, of course?" Viv asked.

Henry attempted a smile. "If you had liked us both equally, I still wouldn't have stood a chance. He's got too much going for him!" he said dejectedly. "Money, a title, houses, cars, servants…"

Viv tried to stop him, but he rambled on for a while before sitting still, in a crumpled silence. He was right of course, but she still had something more to admit. She told him seriously that he, Henry, had kindled a flame. Not much more than a flicker, but enough to know she did not want to lose him.

Henry listened intently, and then put his hands on her shoulders, turning her to face him. He looked straight into her eyes and told her that although they hardly knew each other, something had definitely passed between them.

"It's not lust," he said. "It feels as if we've known each other all our lives. As if you should have always been there in my life. Well, it feels like that to me anyway."

Viv did not feel quite the same, so she just acknowledged what he meant. She asked him once again, if it meant that they could only be the closest of friends, would that be enough for him?

He replied, "Well, in that case, it would have to be enough. I couldn't bear for you not to be in my life, so the hurt would cause me problems to begin with. I only hope that would be temporary. However, I wish the temptation of this other man was not being put in your way."

Viv tried to explain that she needed to try and change something that should not have been there in the first place. Henry sensed there was more she wanted to tell him.

"What's wrong? You can tell me." He spoke so kindly that she almost burst into tears.

Viv simply had to tell someone, she had to tell Henry. So many things had happened in the past few days, and too much of it hurt. She could not even work because her mind was in such a whirl and had taken time off indefinitely. Luckily, she had savings and sick days due her. Finally, she just blurted it all out to Henry.

"I also have strange deep feelings for Daniel! I know I shouldn't, I just can't help it Henry!"

Henry tried to assimilate this new disturbing information. The competition was with two men now. If it did not work out with the baron, what about Viv's feelings for Daniel? How would she cope with those? In a way Henry was pleased that it was a married man she had fallen for, as it might make it harder for her to fall for the baron. Either way, he realised he could be the loser.

Henry stood there wide eyed, as though searching the air for something else to say. Suddenly, his demeanour changed. "I've got a brilliant idea, Viv. I'm determined for you to get to know me better before you leave for this barbeque. At least allow me this opportunity."

Viv was truly surprised with his idea, but also thought it would be good for both of them. She agreed to his plan.

* * * * * * * * * * * * * * * * * * * *

Chapter Twelve
Marvellous Holiday Break

It was four o'clock, on a wonderful, sunny summer afternoon. Viv could hardly believe it. Yesterday, she was in London, today it was Spain. A place called Rosas to be exact, which proved to be a lovely, exquisite, unspoiled village with no British tourists. Many other nationalities clustered there, like French and Germans, but there was no English spoken. Viv expected Rosas to be slightly touristy, but it was not like that at all and she loved the many markets with the varied and unique merchandise. Bartering with the merchants felt exciting too, and she became reasonably good at it.

The only English she heard spoken was by Henry, who also spoke Spanish when it was necessary, calling it Catalan, which was understood in most parts of the country. She was impressed, since she only had a smidgeon of 'school French' to call upon.

Viv was extremely pleased she had let Henry talk her into being so impulsive, in coming away that very morning for a few days break. She now lounged on the patio seat in a white cotton flowing robe, bought at the hotel shop earlier. Sighing deeply, she looked around the white-walled patio and at the incredible views. There were a few fluffy, friendly looking clouds in the pale blue sky. It felt hot, but the cool breeze was sufficient to keep it all comfortable. There were also many new aromas to breathe in. When Viv looked over the low balcony with the safety fence, it was possible to take in the beautiful scenery of the 'Playa,' as they called the beach there and watch the gentle waves rolling in. Many people with children were on the sand or sitting on their sun loungers, with picnic hampers and sand mats laid out. Everyone seemed happy and making the most of the great day.

Viv loved the way Henry had controlled the complete travel situation. He even proved to be such a gentleman, hiring a two bedroom apartment in the rented villa. He spoke about going to unpack in *'his'* bedroom, which let her know there would be no problem with him expecting to share a bedroom with her. Viv had loved her bedroom on sight with its pretty pink walls and coverlets on the bed to match the wall. It was easy for her to relax and do as Henry asked her and to enjoy his company, recharging her batteries with little thought for the barbeque coming up. He told her the holiday break would make it easier for her to get things in perspective.

She knew that his underlying plan was to give her a chance to get more used to him, possibly to become too involved to want to attend the *'event,'* and she expected he might even try to talk her out of attending. But, this spontaneous break was a good idea for two reasons. It would help her get through the week without becoming a nervous wreck and she would learn more about Henry. This was something she wanted to do and knew he was well worth it. He was proving to be delightfully unique and a wonderful, considerate person.

Henry, dressed in a white open-necked shirt with rolled up sleeves, appeared on their patio with a tall jug of iced orange juice.

"Fancy a quick drink to stave off dehydration before we go for our walk? I must say Viv, you look very cool, meaning both *'hot'* and cool," he laughed.

She laughed easily, thanking him for the *'cool'* compliment.

They drank a glass each and then stepped out toward the beach. Viv took his arm as they strolled along through the gate and out onto the white concrete path. She watched his face as the very welcome breeze gently blew through his dark brown hair back, revealing some grey at the sides. His jaw line was strong with the hint of a dimple in the chin, lips well-shaped and his eyes a lovely grey-green shade. There was still an appearance of youth about the cheeks, which were slightly creased with laughter lines. His eyebrows were thick and a little unruly, like his hair. She smiled inwardly remembering her comment on not liking short hair. His reply had been that the hairdresser had cut it shorter than usual, but he could grow it longer, even than was normal for him.

Viv sighed. Hard to believe men like Henry still existed, so how on earth could she not see the potential to fall in love with him? He was easy to talk to, trustworthy and she respected him. He made her laugh and really cared about her feelings. He certainly was attractive. *'So, what's wrong with me?'* She sighed again. It was Daniel's fault! There did not seem to be any other apparent reason.

Viv wondered if, whilst her whole system now

yearned to be made love to by Daniel, how she could be affected by anyone else? The barbeque was the chance to short-circuit her emotions. Being in the company of two exquisite mortals, Daniel and the baron should help sort her feelings out once and for all.

If Viv never again had strong emotions in her life, she would always have the memory of all the anticipation experienced at this moment. Being on the edge, with all nerve endings buzzing in anticipation! Wonderful feelings and the memories would last a lifetime! If only she could bottle them, to preserve their longevity and the depth of the emotions.

Obviously, she would start with the pure physical cravings and surges of electricity toward Daniel. Then there was the excitement of spending the evening in close proximity to him, wondering if she would see any signs of his feelings towards her, innocent or not. Viv relished the possibility of a wealthy, equally handsome, titled, unmarried man, who might make her feel the same as Daniel did. She would much rather prefer that scenario, but would he have the same kind of bulging muscles showing through his shirt? Yes, that was shallow thinking, but the thought of potential raw passion was too great.

Viv had been celibate for so long, she felt like a volcano about to erupt and now she was experiencing the immense romantic feelings of this quaint little place called Rosas, hitting her squarely in the tingle buds. Instead of keeping it all in her head, there was the chance she would soon be living her erotic dreams and they were good, very good. It felt as if she were time travelling back eons to places where everyone was unhurried, relaxed and allowed to feel alive. She could really appreciate what life had to offer.

Then of course, there was dear, sweet Henry. It was not possible to label those feelings, except to say that he gave her a sense of having a safety net. They also had that rare thing called communication and there were even feelings of belonging. Henry was indeed very important to her, even if thoughts of the other men gave her more excitement.

The days were full, enjoyable, but went by too quickly. They made sure to get many adventures in and not to just lie on the beach, baking in the heat as too many tourists seemed to do. They both loved the same scenery, trips to other islands and the curio shops. Night-time dancing was enjoyed immensely and they even made some casual friends who joined up with them at various eating places. Sometimes she felt sad to think she may never talk to these new people again, as friendships made abroad can disappear as fast as they were formed.

Both, Viv and Henry, felt pity for the hungry, homeless dogs who begged for food, mostly beseeching with their sad eyes and not by becoming real nuisances. It was impossible not to feel great sympathy for them, and she knew remaining memories would continue to hurt her, long after arriving back home. The guilt would stay also, for not doing enough for them. But, that would have meant taking it on as a full-time job, not to mention recruiting hundreds of volunteers.

They had regularly fed some of the mongrels who appeared whenever they came outdoors. One friendly dog, a black and tan Dalmation/German Shepherd cross, with the most appealing large eyes, followed them whenever possible and they would share whatever food and adventure they could with her.

The dog had merely been called; 'Gross Chien,' (meaning; Big Dog) and they had heard others calling her that. She was neglected more than the other dogs when tourists threw food to them, as she was larger than most and probably would have eaten too much of the meagre rations. Or, perhaps due to her large size she already looked better fed. Her rib bones were not showing like the rest of the skinny dogs. Henry and Viv felt bad to be going back home only to *abandon* their new canine friends, especially, Gross Chien. When the time came for Viv to say good bye to them, she would shed many tears, but that would not be the case for the human friends for they could stay in contact.

The week had almost passed and she thoroughly enjoyed every moment. Henry had proved to be the ultimate gentleman and had not pressured her into sharing a room, but he had managed to creep into her heart, just a little bit, enough for her to care. They had cuddled and even kissed each other goodnight on retiring to their own bedrooms, but not once had she been tempted to want any more than that. Today would be the last day with Henry in Rosas, and that saddened her. This afternoon, Henry had arranged to meet her at the market and she made one last check in the mirror. The string-tie-up on the fitted bodice needed to be tightened, which she eventually managed. The emerald green material gently flared out from the hips and ended just above her knees. The colour of the dress flattered her the most, even more than red.

Normal standard sandals were so unflattering for legs, and luckily, she managed to find these higher-wedged, ankle-strapped sandals at Russell & Bromley's in Kensington when she was back home in London. The colour, green with a stripe of black was a good match for the green dress she wore now, bought in Madrid yesterday.

She thought about that Madrid outing. It had been a lovely day out, apart from the bull fighting posters everywhere which gave her a nasty reminder of the worst part about Spain. Henry loved the miniature bull she bought for him, although like her, he hated bullfights and loved the magnificent bull, so strong and gentle, if treated correctly. They both wished the matadors would fight each other instead.

Viv combed her long straight hair, wondering as usual if she ought to cut a fringe. She always decided against it when remembering how impatiently she waited for it to grow out the last time she made that mistake. She thought of Dandy, whose hair was wavy and shoulder length. If straightened out, it would probably be as long as hers. It was strange how similar their figures were. Viv tried to envision what she might wear on Saturday. What would Dandy wear? No, she would not think about that just yet. This was her time to be with Henry and to recharge her batteries, not to drain them.

Henry was easy to notice as he walked toward her, although he was behind a crowd of men. Some of them were arguing with each other, but Viv had become accustomed to this type of behaviour. Everywhere they visited there was always someone about to, or who had already, lost his temper, but it never came to blows. The people talked loudly and never cared who heard their conversations or arguments, but it was mostly the men with the aggressive attitude, not the women. These Spaniards reminded her of Greek people, who were just as loud but also basically decent people too.

Sometimes, immediately after an altercation on the verge of physical violence, the disagreeing pair would go off with their arms around each other's shoulders! Viv even witnessed an irate group of men break off temporarily from an argument to whistle, often in time with each other, at an attractive woman who walked past them, only to continue the shouting when she disappeared out of sight!

As Henry approached, Viv wondered why she had not noticed how tall he was. It became really noticeable when he walked amongst the Spanish men. He saw her now and was soon at her side. They kissed and he took her arm as they walked over to a hotel frontage where they sat down. The fragrance of the flowers, the aroma of food cooking with the recognizable smell of the ocean, delighted Viv. It felt all the better sharing it with good company, and Henry was very good company, but it had been difficult to keep her mind off memories of Lawrence. Too much reminded her of him. It continued to surprise Viv just how deeply she could still be hurt, even after all this time.

"Did you sleep well?" Henry asked.

"I certainly did thanks. It's been the same ever since we got here. It must be the sun and the wonderful fresh air!"

He was pleased. "It's our last day Viv, what shall we do this evening? Anything special you'd like?"

"I'll just go along with anything you want to do, Henry." She could think of nothing in particular that she wanted to do.

They had spent their days well and for the most part, had generally roamed around. Viv had not even found time to turn on the television in all that time and so had not heard any more of the serial killings. The evenings found them seated in the piano bars and of course most of the noisy customers joined in with the singing. Luckily, the enjoyment was not ruined by 'Karoake' and contrived entertainment. Nothing is as much fun as music played 'live' on the spot.

It was so easy to make friends with the holiday atmosphere. They had befriended a German couple of retirement age and a middle-aged French couple. When they all bumped into each other, sometimes planned, French was spoken by them all. Their efforts at English were far too difficult to understand. Viv managed reasonably well with the French language and helped Henry out with the odd word or too.

Viv had still not heard English spoken and began to miss the easy communication. Although some Spanish words made sense to her now with the repetition, it was easier to hear it than for her to verbalise. She only managed to speak the odd sentence or two and was not always understood, but Henry was ready to interpret for her.

Suddenly, Viv remembered a place that had been fun. "It might be nice to go to the 'El Cid,' nightclub again. We had a terrific time when we last went there. Would you fancy that?"

"Okay. We'll do that then," he said.

"Henry, you don't sound that keen. What did you have in mind then?" She asked.

"Well, although it was great there, I hoped we could spend part of the evening alone. Have a few drinks in the villa?" he asked hopefully. Time was running out for him and they would soon be flying back to England.

Viv agreed it would be best to spend some time alone with each other. A delightful breeze played through her hair and today seemed hotter than usual. Tonight would be their last night in Spain, and they had not spent that much time completely alone. Henry had been such a gentleman he had not even tried to make any real attempt to seduce her. She appreciated that. Viv suggested they have dinner at the piano bar, where a musician called Sancho, sang Ray Charles songs. The restaurant made incredibly delicious paellas there. They could dine there and then head back to the villa.

They had dined at the piano bar several times before, but usually sat at the back. This time, they had a front table which made it more convenient for getting up to dance and they both even stood by Sancho to sing some songs. They had a very fun time to remember and keep in their memories. Viv hoped it would not be the last time she felt so close to Henry. She suggested walking to a particular sentimental place, the one they first visited before they knew each other as well as they did now.

There was a strong atmosphere of sadness when they set off for their last walk. They followed the well-trodden footpath toward a cave which had steps set in the side and wound up to the top of the cliff. Viv tried to take in as much of the scenery as possible, wanting to make the images last. She loved the white-washed villas and their colourful courtyards. This would be missed once she was back amongst the cold grey of the concrete jungle of home.

The foliage seemed much greener and the skies much bluer in Spain. As for the sea, that colour was heavenly. *'Turquoise,'* she thought, watching the way it deepened where the reef formed a ring. Further out, the sea became an even darker colour. The reflections danced and twinkled upon the surface. A truly beautiful sight, set against the occasional fluffy cloud.

Viv would always remember the colourful people seated outside the restaurants. Mainly the locals as they argued and laughed, contradicting their emotions. It was all so natural. A dog barked, rudely breaking into her thoughts. She was so sorry about the dogs, there were far too many of them. Strays were everywhere, with their huge sad eyes yearning for attention and for people to take pity on them. Soon they would have to say goodbye to Gross Chien, and she was not looking forward to that.

The dogs need for food and affection was very apparent, and they really appreciated a pat on the head and a kind word, or two. *'Poor unloved, delightful creatures! Did they feel loneliness in the same way as humans?'* She hoped not! A vision of a dog marriage agency appeared in her mind. Inevitably, it reminded her of Daniel. Her stomach turned over and she felt a tingling sensation. It was hard to determine if it was a pleasant feeling or not.

Henry held her arm in support when they reached the cave and walked up the steps. Viv needed his help as it was further than she realized. At the top, they found a spot to sit, which was partly sheltered from the wind by a sparsely branched tree. The little bit of shade was appreciated as they both felt hot. Viv leaned against him and could not remember a time when she felt so happy, content, pampered and cared for.

A swift pang of regret shot through her like an icy wind. *'Will it be very different after tomorrow? Am I about to throw away something too good to lose?'* She wondered, almost feeling panic coming on. She looked at Henry and caught her breath. Her feelings for him were more than she cared to admit. What if his feelings became so hurt that he had to stay away from her, regardless of the outcome? Or, even worse, having to tell him she had chosen someone else?

Henry thought along the same lines, as he took Viv's hand which felt so tiny in his. He wanted to speak, but the words would not come. Sensing the sadness in her, he felt it better not to say anything in case he made her feel worse. This was the moment he had been dreading all along. He turned his head away from her, but not before she noticed the tears in his eyes. Tears immediately sprang to hers, and she felt like hugging him. Viv knew that would not be a good idea as it might cause him more hurt. She had no idea what to say either, so held his hand tighter and rested her head further against his shoulder. *'All I have to do is cancel the whole thing,'* she thought. *'I need never see Daniel or meet this baron! How can I hurt Henry like this, especially when it's hurting us both?'* The situation meant she had to see it through and hoped it would all work out well with nobody getting hurt, too much.

They sat with their private thoughts until the wind became too chilly and the light began to fade. They began to retrace their steps, but this time Henry's arm was tightly around her shoulder as they walked. It felt as if he were letting her know that she was his woman and in a way, it felt as if he were her man.

They decided not to freshen up at the villa first, but to go ahead and have dinner. A cab was hailed which took them to their favourite bistro. It was a quiet affair and although they both attempted to lighten the atmosphere with small talk, there was none of the usual laughter or banter. They enjoyed garlic sauced chicken, asparagus spears and sautéed potatoes. Neither of them felt hungry enough for dessert.

Part way through their meal, they noticed a group of waiters in the corner of the restaurant, surrounding a television. They spoke excitedly and flapped their arms around in animated gestures. When their waiter approached them with the bill, Henry asked if anything was wrong.

"Si senor! It is the serial killer! Sorry senorita, do not want to ruin your meal, but he is in Spain. The killer who kills the gay men, he is in Spain! El Diablo!" He tossed the bill on their table, mumbled in Spanish and then flounced off. They understood why he was so alarmed.

Neither wanted to spoil their last night, so they kept their thoughts on 'El Diablo' to themselves. The music eventually sifted through the tendrils of their thoughts until the shock of the news had dimmed. After a while, Henry signalled he wanted to pay their bill and an ashen faced waiter came to deal with it. They left the restaurant and flagged a taxicab. Viv strung some Spanish phrases together and was pleased when the driver understood her instructions.

Back at the villa, they showered, separately as usual. Henry poured them wine, adding a shot of cream soda for Viv. He then sat close beside her with their legs touching to get as much intimacy as possible. Whilst they had not spoken of their intentions, both were determined to be as physically close as they could be tonight, under the circumstances. It was fun to reminisce and enjoy the occasions all over again. They talked of the fun they had and recalled their only swim.

They had gone out in a dinghy, nearly as far as the reefs and Henry managed to convince Viv to jump in the water with him. She had already related her near drowning experience, but Henry said this would be much safer and he would take care of her. The water looked far too inviting and she risked jumping in with him. Henry kept hold of the rope, tying it around his waist so the dinghy would not float off. They swam around the dinghy and back the same way with Viv making sure not to swim far from him. Sometimes, she just held on to him and they looked down into the water.

Strange, coloured fish casually swam by them, not the slightest bit concerned by their presence and it was delightful. For a short while, Viv had been worried sharks might appear too, until Henry told her that as long as the fish swam slowly there was no reason to worry. They found it hilarious to point out the fishes that suddenly swam faster. Luckily, this did not happen often and they enjoyed their time in the water.

When Henry lifted her up into the dinghy, her bare flesh pressed against his. It had made him catch his breath and was a memory Henry would always cherish. He wished it could have lasted longer, but did not mention it. The last thing he wanted was to cause her more problems. He was determined to believe everything would work out well for them in the end.

Henry took a sip of wine as they came back to the present. He spoke quietly. "I felt sad that night, after the closeness of the swim, as you still only kissed me lightly on the cheek and went to your own room as usual. I had hoped for a lingering hug that night!" But, I'm glad we became closer quickly."

They both laughed at this comment, and Viv reminded him that the *'light kiss,'* occurred back in the early days, as since then, they had progressed to goodnight hugs and their 'kisses' were not just *'friendly pecks'* any more. They looked tenderly at each other, both yearning for even more closeness, but accepting the reality.

After all this reminiscing of their week together, they fell silent. Henry looked at Viv, sitting so close to him on the sofa. This, he thought sadly, could be their last evening together, ever. He had fallen completely in love with her. Now, it might be the last time he ever shared such closeness with her and it hurt him badly. It was also getting late and they had to be up early for the plane trip back.

As they were about to go to their own rooms, they hugged tighter than they ever had before. They held on longer, and neither of them wanted to part this time. There was only one thing for it. Viv suggested they lay together, but only cuddle for this last night. Henry eagerly agreed, wondering if he would be able to control his sexual feelings for her. He could not give up the opportunity to lie next to the woman he loved and to be with her all night long, especially, as he may be about to lose her. It seemed she really cared about him too, but Henry hoped he would not do anything stupid to make her think less of him.

* *

Chapter Thirteen
The Long Awaited Barbeque

Viv had arranged the last-minute details with Dandy over the telephone whilst still in Spain. Although feeling apprehensive, she looked forward to the barbeque and felt more at ease about attending. Surprisingly, she managed a decent night's sleep alone after returning to London on Friday night with Henry. She had cried over the good-byes with Gross Chien, and Henry was on the verge too. It had been a dreadfully sad flight over and an even sadder departure. They both believed and hoped it was only a temporary parting, but it proved very painful for both of them to separate, nonetheless.

They had not only *'cuddled'* that last night in Spain together. They had made satisfying love. Their bodies automatically responded to each other, and it had been an extension of their growing friendship. It had been a gentle type of emotional caring sex, rather than being passionate.

It was comforting and a way for Viv to say thank you to Henry, leaving a good memory for both of them. But, the worried look on Henry's face as they parted haunted her thoughts. Would she see him again? Would he want to? Would *she* want to? She would have to be disciplined and keep her mind on what was about to happen, or not happen, as the case may be. From time to time she visualized Henry, but forced her thoughts elsewhere.

"Why is everything happening so fast?" Viv said aloud. "I don't trust myself! I'm not in control any more!" The tears trickled down her cheeks again. She rushed over to a mirror and held a tissue against the corner of her eye.

"Waterproof, my foot!" she said aloud, wiping away a smudge. There was no time to refresh her make-up, she had already spent most of the day re-doing it, thanks to her sadness at the situation. She had also changed her outfits several times and had eventually settled on a red Lycra mini dress.

Viv put the finishing touches to her outfit by choosing a red and black, three-quarter sleeved, see-thru lacy patterned wrap top. The belt she chose was one of her favourites, a black stretchy one with a large, gold chrome buckle. Her black leather ankle boots, with tiny red motif design, were just right, too. They were also comfortable enough to stand around in.

She had now dressed, and began walking up and down her lounge in anticipation. Her thoughts had become a total mess. It perplexed her that she could look forward to seeing the baron as well as being in the company of Daniel again. She even wished Henry was coming with her. She missed him and wondered what he would be doing tonight. *I bet he's thinking of me and worrying his head off.* Viv thought, feeling a deep sadness. Tonight would prove many things to her.

The Lyons' arrived at Viv's home on time and Dandy looked radiant in her emerald green, Lycra shirt style top and matching pants. A fluffy, black lace-patterned cardigan wrapped around her shoulders. They complimented each other with Viv wishing she had worn green too, her favourite colour. Dandy loved Viv's red outfit and commented that it made her look devilish! Viv did not mind at all. Tonight she felt quite devilish as she followed Dandy to the car where Daniel waited for them. It was a restored, red MGB Roadster.

The passenger seat had been tipped forward, enabling her to climb into the backseat. Her face was just inches from Daniel's, as he said hello. She was overcome with an immense urge to kiss him. The smell of soap was still detectable under his aftershave and was something she particularly liked in a man.

Once she and Dandy were comfortably seated, Daniel asked if Viv had a good time with Henry. He had told them he was taking Viv away for a break. She answered that it was great, but did not want to say any more than that for now. Dandy asked if she was ready for the big evening.

"More than ready," Viv announced confidently, although feeling the opposite. Daniel pulled out into a gap in the line of traffic, and they were on their way. Silence prevailed as Viv studied the back of Daniel's head. His hair curled onto the collar and his ears poked out a little. She wanted to nibble on them.

Dandy started the conversation again by talking about Baron von Eider. "If he wants to know how you met us, just say it was at some party recently. He's got a lot of pride. He'll think you're only a guest, so you can relax and enjoy yourself!"

"How's Henry?" Daniel suddenly asked.

Viv tensed when she heard his name. For a second, she longed to be in his loving, safe arms. What was wrong with her, always wanting to be with the man she was not with?

"Oh, he's feeling a bit put out about tonight, but we had a terrific time in Spain," she replied.

"You're not regretting this, are you?" The Lyons' practically asked in unison.

"No. Not now anyway. I'm bound to be missing Henry after spending the week with him. I just have to concentrate on tonight! Anyway, I'm really looking forward to meeting the baron."

"That's the spirit," Dandy said. "Enjoy tonight and don't think any further!" Daniel nodded his approval.

* * * * * * * * * * * * * * * * *

Eventually, they pulled into a huge drive bordered by cedar and pine trees. The journey took nearly an hour and ended on the outskirts of London. It was dusk and the falling shadows gave an eerie, but beautiful atmosphere to the place.

Large signs placed by the roadside directed them to the designated parking area. Music, laughter and talk wafted over them long before they had a glimpse of anything, other than the rambling, ivy-covered house.

After finding a good parking space they walked behind the house to join the party people. Lights were placed in various strategic points and the place looked impressive, even in the half dark. Landscaping comprised of stone steps winding around various trees and bushes with a well kept lawn scattered with benches and some tables. The house lay back in the distance looking large and pretty, with lights on in most windows. Viv felt self-conscious walking amongst the oddly dressed people, many in fancy dress costumes she had never seen before, or would want to see again. Too many people were half-naked with feathers or bright shiny things dangling from various parts of their bodies, and several celebrity impersonators wandered around. Viv wanted to take it all in and her head constantly turned from left to right, in awe of the scene before her.

There were costumes from the Tudor and Medieval times, with plenty of masque wearers. Fairies flitted around prettily dressed and made up in a way she could not be sure whether some of them were male or female. Pirates wore swords in their belts, trying to look fierce. A few folk were casually dressed, as the Lyons' and she were. Dandy had said it was not imperative to dress up, and Viv was pleased not to. The creativity was quite astounding. Most were impressive looking and very imaginative. Viv wondered what she would have worn having witnessed this spectacle, but felt content with not being too much a part of it all.

They soon found a suitable place to stand, reasonably close to the delicious-smelling, barbequed meats table. Daniel went to find drinks and quickly returned carrying a tray with three glasses of punch. Viv took one of the glasses and after a large gulp, sensed it was heavily laden with alcohol.

"Is 'he' anywhere near us?" She asked.

"Take it easy!" Dandy said grinning. "I can't see him yet, but he's not that frightening!"

"Maybe he's not to you!" Viv replied with a giggle.

She liked Dandy very much, and this made her dislike herself for the illicit feelings she could not suppress toward Dandy's husband. She could not imagine preferring the baron, no matter how big a charmer he might be. Daniel had the same looks as her ideal fantasy *real* man, Lawrence. Even if the baron were that similar, she had met Daniel first. He was the original. As far as she was concerned, no one preferred a copy.

"Don't be so nervous," Dandy said. "As soon as he comes into view, we'll let you know so you can watch him."

The real reason for Viv's nervousness stood right in front of her! Daniel looked so good. His white satin shirt was slashed to mid-chest. Underneath, he wore a black vest. An abundance of dark hair protruded over the low neckline. His white trousers were cut tight and revealed too much muscular activity. His small waist was set off by his well-muscled thighs. The sides of his dark, thick hair was longish and swept back. Eyes so blue, they looked icy! A truly tantalizing and rare sight! *'Men like this could steal anyone's heart,'* she thought. *'It isn't my fault at all, I'm only human. I'm only a woman for heaven's sake!'*

Viv's attention was being called for, so she turned to investigate the source. She tore her eyes away from Daniel for a moment and found herself staring straight into almost identical eyes, except they had a positive twinkle in them! A definite twinkle of interest! Dandy had just introduced her to the baron. Viv was so astonished that she could only stare. She heard Dandy say something, but her voice did not come through properly. The only voice she could hear, resonated deeply, reminding her of all that was wonderful with the world.

"So, you are Viv! Good to meet you!" The new sensual voice said.

His eyes searched her soul. It gave her the physical sensation of ripples and vibrations shooting through every part of her body. Before she was able to respond and perhaps luckily, a rude, long-haired blonde woman intervened and whirled the baron away impatiently. It seemed she had to dance with him at that very minute, as her favourite song was being performed by a band that suddenly wailed in the distance on a makeshift stage.

"Have a good time," the baron called back to her, "I'll be sure to see you later!" He then disappeared into the crowd.

Viv's heart started beating normally again. His body shape, back and front, looked very similar to Daniel's including the face and voice; only the muscles were more exaggerated and the voice a little deeper. *'He certainly works out with weights seriously,'* she thought. But, if Daniel and the baron were dressed the same, the main difference would be that the baron had a moustache and his hair was longer! *'How could this be? There must be only one answer,'* she thought suspiciously.

No one spoke as Viv turned back to them. Daniel seemed distinctly uncomfortable, and Dandy appeared apprehensive as she looked at Viv, who stated the obvious.

"He's your identical twin brother, isn't he, Daniel?"

Dandy intervened. "We didn't want to deceive you Viv, but you may have been too embarrassed to go along with our idea otherwise."

* * * * * * * * * * * * * * * * * * * *

Chapter Fourteen
The Explanation

Viv was not sure how to respond, her thoughts had become very muddled. Daniel said he would give them some time alone so Dandy could explain the situation. He kissed his wife on the lips and left them to it.

'That kiss should have hurt me far more than it did,' she realized. *'Perhaps I can feel for someone else now.'* The vision of the handsome baron and the sound of his voice still resonated in her brain. *'What happens when there are two originals?'* To Viv, this meant a far worse problem.

Dandy ushered her over to a bench underneath a horse chestnut tree. When they were both seated, she explained. "You see, right from the start I knew the kind of man that affected you, by your reaction to Daniel."

Viv flinched. Her cheeks burned and she felt like running away. *'Surely a nun would have been affected by Daniel, not to mention having the same reaction to the baron? They were EVERY woman's type of man!'* She refused to feel guilty, but it did not work and she wondered how on earth Dandy could still like her. It seemed strange that Dandy did not consider her as real competition. *'How could love be that strong?'* she wondered.

Dandy continued. "Don't feel bad. We just wanted to help you. When you came back in to look at more files so soon after you met Henry, we understood."

Viv's cheeks burned even more. *What does she mean? 'We understood?' That means Daniel knows how I feel about him too! Oh, for heaven's sake!'* Suddenly, she longed for Henry's arms and safety, away from all these emotions. These new emotions were leaving her an emotional mess, which also hurt physically. Her stomach churned.

Dandy continued unperturbed. "Once a woman gets affected by a strong visual image, she keeps hoping to find it again. She has to keep looking, or she'll constantly feel let down, even by the best of men."

"How do you know so much about these things?" Viv asked, suddenly thinking about Lawrence. *'Yes, these men are so similar to Lawrence,'* she thought miserably.

"Through experience and not all mine, I'm glad to say," Dandy replied. "As Daniel's brother is not married, it seemed the ideal solution, if it worked out." She added, "We hoped to see him before he came over to us, and we would have kept you both apart until you spent a while watching him from a distance. It wasn't meant to happen this way. "

Viv wondered why Dandy had not fallen for the baron at the time she fell for Daniel and asked her about it. Dandy replied she did not meet his brother until they were secure in their own relationship. After a minute's silence, Viv asked how much Daniel knew about her feelings.

Dandy's voice came through her uncomfortable

thoughts as she replied, "He knew almost as soon as I did."

Viv thought about the time she was left alone with him in the office. *'How embarrassing, he knew how I felt! How will I ever be able to face him again?'*

"Dandy, how could you go off to another appointment and embarrass me like that?"

"That wasn't deliberate. I'd forgotten about that damned appointment. I can't say I was totally relaxed when I left you with my husband." She grinned. "But, I totally trust him and our relationship is very good. I knew, as well as hoped, that no harm would come from it."

"But, what if I'd tried it on with him? You don't know me at all yet!" Viv replied in a slightly raised, agitated voice. She was deeply relieved that nothing had been said or done, to regret now.

Dandy looked apologetic. "If that was the case and you had tried anything, Daniel would have told me. If you were too dangerous to have around, we would not have gone ahead with our plan."

"So I passed a test then?" asked Viv. "Thank heavens for that!" She was inwardly pleased now, knowing that she had been possible competition for Dandy. "What exactly *IS* your plan?" she asked, more curious than ever.

Dandy looked so sincere, that Viv reluctantly felt her trust returning.

"It was quite basic really," Dandy said. "We videotaped this place whilst BV, that's what we call the baron, was away on business. He's a few years older than us and never been lucky in love. He had begun to lose faith in the female sex."

Viv grew alarmed. "Do you mean he's going gay?" If that were the case, she did not want to be part of the conversion, no matter how delectable the prize!

"No that's not what I meant," Dandy said and laughed. "He's fed up because women keep throwing themselves at him, and he doesn't want a woman he can have easily. They're no challenge for him."

"Who was the woman who took him away to dance?" Viv had wanted to ask this question earlier.

"Oh, she's just one of many. He's not seriously seeing anyone."

Viv wondered how she could get near enough for 'BV' to get to know her, but, without it looking as if she were chasing him.

Dandy answered the unasked question by saying, "I can tell he was interested enough to make time for you during the evening. And, this evening," she reminded Viv, "had only just begun."

"I hope something good happens between you and BV." Dandy said. "I would love to see more of you, you're so, refreshing!"

"You make me sound like a fizzy drink!" Viv laughed in reply.

"Oh, I do hope we stay friends," Dandy said earnestly, as she touched Viv's hand.

Viv hoped so too, but that could only happen if she was able to think of Daniel as being, 'only' a friend. Suddenly, a loud unfamiliar voice cut into their thoughts. The voice called out for them to come over and get some hot food. The voice belonged to a man standing by a table laden with a huge array of freshly barbequed meats.

"I should eat something," Viv said. "The punch is strong, and I haven't eaten all day. What's in this stuff anyway?"

"No idea! But, I should eat too, only some friends are calling to me from over there," Dandy waved in their direction. "Do you want me to introduce you to them?"

"No thanks, Dandy, I need to eat something to sop up this alcohol first."

"Okay, you eat and I'll join you as soon as I can. I'll eat something then!"

After the food server was introduced as Alex, Dandy took another glass of punch from the bowl on his stand. She smiled at Viv saying, "I won't be long." She then walked off toward her friends.

Viv was handed a kebab with onions and chilli sauce. "Hmm, this is so tasty!"

"Not as tasty as you!" was Alex's all too corny reply.

"That's something you will never know!" Viv retorted, looking away from him. As she did, her gaze fell upon a roasted pig rotating on a spit. It made her feel uneasy. It reminded her of what Henry must be going through. *'It must be hell for him!'* she thought, as she reached for her now empty glass. Alex, the voice and *'letch'*, refilled her glass quickly and passed it to her with a big, perverse smile.

"Thanks," she said, not looking directly at him. Viv

drank deeply hoping the drink would take away her guilt, or at least some of it. She walked back to the bench to wait for Dandy's return. After a short while, a talkative man sat by her, so she made excuses, stood up and began to stroll around whilst she waited. The normal reaction she experienced from alcohol had not made her feel tipsy in the usual way, instead she had a feeling of extreme tiredness. However, she was determined to enjoy this barbeque.

Everyone seemed to be having a great time. Laughter and girlish screams surrounded her. She had even caught sight of BV in the distance to her right, warding off an overzealous girl who demanded his attention. This was a brunette, the blondie must have been elsewhere. She felt sorry for him as he looked so harassed. But, now was not the time to approach him. *'I don't know him well enough to try and rescue him,'* she sighed, *'plenty of time for that later, hopefully.'*

Just within sight, Viv saw a back view that resembled Dandy, with a man who was definitely *not* Daniel, and she was being steered toward the orchard. Viv decided to follow, but found it difficult as there were too many people in her way.

Viv walked faster through the crowd and came upon a naked couple, half-concealed in the shadow of bushes, with their arms and legs wrapped around each other. They were too engrossed to bother if she were there or not. Viv felt embarrassed and was about to turn and leave, when she noticed a few feet away, something familiar lying on the grass in a patch of light. It looked like Dandy's cardigan!

* * * * * * * * * * * * * * * * * * *

Chapter Fifteen

A Frightening Episode for Dandy and Viv

Cautiously, Viv moved closer and stopped in startled amazement. A strange man had Dandy propped against a tree and he was kissing her! Viv felt angry and determined to intervene, so she ran toward them. Dandy was putting up a feeble struggle. *'How dare this man take advantage of Daniel's wife, not to mention, my friend!'* Viv thought as she went to confront them.

"Leave her alone!" Viv shouted. The startled man jumped back and fled, cursing as he did so. Dandy's arm was completely out of her shirt which had been pulled down enough to expose both breasts.

"Viv, help me, I'm so drunk," she drawled. "I've only had two. I know I've only had two drinks. I don't understand it?"

Viv knew what she meant. Her head felt woozy, too, but nothing similar to the way she had ever experienced before. It must have been the punch. She remembered thinking it tasted too strong, instead of being evenly mixed with fruit juices. Dandy made no effort to dress herself, so Viv attempted to help her, although she felt very much like sitting down. Her eyes were losing their focus.

"You don't want Daniel to see you like this," Viv whispered, trying to get an arm back into the sleeve. "Dandy, do try to concentrate, please! What on earth happened here?"

As Viv pulled the material upwards, Dandy moaned. She placed her hand over Viv's, making it rest on her naked breast. The nipple hardened, and Viv felt a strange impulse to put her lips around it. New, odd sensations surged through her body, and she was confused. She recalled similar feelings when caressing her own breasts as the nipples stiffened. Viv could not help but stroke the exposed, tantalizing nipple as if it were her own.

Dandy pulled Viv's face closer. It felt so natural to kiss Dandy's soft neck whilst gradually moving down onto her firm breast. Viv let her lips caress the flesh, taking the nipple into her mouth. Dandy moaned louder, obviously enjoying this sensation. Suddenly, a noise in the background took Viv out of the sensual cloud enveloping her.

"Come on Dandy! Help me get you dressed, please!"

There was urgency in her voice which got through this time. Although it was difficult, she managed to get Dandy looking respectable again. Both were unsteady on their feet, but they had to get back to Daniel. They clung to each other walking everywhere, except in a straight line. Viv could not focus or walk properly; the drink had begun to have a real effect and she could hardly stand.

Through half-closed eyes, Viv saw Daniel walk and then run toward them. He caught the nearly unconscious Dandy as if she were a child. He called out to the nearest person to follow and help Viv into the house. Through her haze, Dandy felt relieved that someone would help Viv, but it was short-lived when she recognized the leering face of Alex picking Viv up!

* * * * * * * * * * * *

"That's it Dandy, drink all of the coffee. It's strong darling, but you need it." Daniel said, as he held the cup to her lips. He still did not understand why the two women came back from the orchard, or why they had become so intoxicated. Daniel felt only a little effect from the punch and had not taken another drink whilst talking to the friends he had bumped into, whilst in BV's house. He was also worried why Alex, the man he had entrusted Viv's care to, had not brought her into the house yet, unless, she had preferred to remain out in the fresh air.

When Dandy came around enough to talk, she asked for Viv and felt horrified to hear Viv was in the same drunk condition and put in the care of Alex. She told Daniel to go look for Viv immediately, but he felt too concerned for his wife, preferring to stay with her. Dandy was insistent and upset, so Daniel only agreed after she promised to remain in the room, until he returned for her.

Daniel hurried back out into the party, passing the many embracing couples. At the far side, by the summer house, he found Alex leaning against a post. He was observing a pretty young girl who just as keenly watched a good-looking young boy, performing handstands. He walked impressively on his hands in circles.

"Alex!" Daniel shouted. "Where is Viv? Where is the woman I left in your care?" Alex hunched his shoulder up and down, then turned back to watch the girl.

Daniel reached out and took him by the arm. "I told you to help her into the house! Where is she?" he demanded.

Alex pulled his arm free. "I couldn't do what you said," he groused unconcernedly. "Some guy took her off me." He began to walk away.

Daniel grabbed Alex by the arm and swung him around. The men faced each other briefly, and when Alex raised his hand in a fist, Daniel punched him hard on the jaw. The blow sent Alex flying over a stool.

"Pay attention!" Daniel shouted. "Describe the man who took her! Tell me which way they went!"

Alex angrily picked himself up and glared at Daniel. Rubbing his sore face, he shouted, "I don't know! It was some weirdo in a cloak and a mask. I couldn't do anything; he was bigger and taller than me. About your size and besides that, he hit me in the ribs. I'm fed up with being hit!"

"Which way did they go?" Daniel repeated.

"I didn't see!" he shouted, falling back on an up-turned stool all the while rubbing his injured jaw.

Daniel looked around. Many people had come in fancy dress and some were wearing masks. He wondered where to look for this cloaked man and if he would still be wearing the same costume.

"Where were you exactly when this happened? Where did the man go to?"

Alex considered carefully, it seemed as if he did not want to volunteer this information, as he guiltily declared it was away from the outside of the house. Daniel knew Alex was lying, and it became hard to control his temper. He reached again for Alex, who conveniently remembered the cloaked man went in the direction of the orchard.

Daniel left Alex and made his way as speedily as possible to the orchard. People were in his way, oblivious to how important it was that he get through and past them. Everything had gone wrong and he liked Viv. She had trusted him and Dandy, and now may be in serious trouble. It was darker in the orchard, but the moonlight coming through the leaves and branches of trees helped in his search.

He looked along the wall and under the bushes there, continuing to search the grounds, but he would need some help. Not only that, he desperately wanted to get back to Dandy to ensure she was okay. Along the way, he stepped over couples having sex and avoided many lurid invitations to join them. When he finally got back to the house, Dandy had begun to sober up, but seemed extremely agitated.

"Did you find her Daniel? Please tell me you found her? That she's alright?"

"Can't find her anywhere, we'll have to call the police!" he told her. "We'd better tell BV first, if we can find him. Some of his guests may have drugs on them, and we need to give him a chance to get them out of here."

* *

Baron von Eider had noticed that Viv was different. He liked her self-assuredness and proud demeanour. He was also pleased she had not chased him. Especially, when first meeting her, he knew that she wanted him, too; had seen it when looking into her eyes. He looked at her now, so innocent and at his mercy.

When he had come upon them by accident and seen Alex begin to sexually maul Viv in her semi-conscious state, he had gone to her rescue. He carried her through the orchard to the door in the wall, to his special place, the *'den.'* The 'Lyons Den' as he privately called it, used only for personal reasons. His initial intention had been to revive Viv and then to take advantage of the privacy in getting to know her without interruption. He gently placed her on two of the bean bags, which were liberally scattered around. He kissed her lightly on the lips, meaning to go no further, not yet anyway, but could not resist his feelings.

Slowly, and gently, he pulled the clothing from her body. As he caressed her, there was a noticeable change in her breathing. His hands worked expertly over her flesh. They slid over her taught belly, mound and finally rested between her thighs. As he moved his fingers, she breathed faster. He worked them deeper and faster until she almost panted.

He pulled himself away and placed a light blanket over her sleeping body. He was too excited and wanted to save himself for when she regained consciousness. After all, he wanted her to take an active part, as there was no pleasure, well not much in taking advantage of an unconscious, desirable woman. He removed his clothes and put his cloak back on, waiting and watching her closely.

* * * * * * * * * * * * * * * * * * * *

As awareness returned to Viv, she wondered why she was waking up in a dark room lit by red light. She was sprawled out on some large bean bags with a light blanket draped over her. Her attempt to sit up was prevented by a strong hand, which reached over and gently held her shoulder down.

"Take it easy, or you'll feel sick," the resonating deep voice whispered. "Lie back and relax, you're perfectly safe here."

Viv did as she was told, staring in the direction of the man with the sensual voice. She tried to make out his face, but it was mostly covered by shadows. He stood up and walked away from her. She was nervous, confused and still woozy. Only a soft, light material covered her bare skin. *I'm naked!'* she realized. *'He's undressed me! Has it happened? Have I been raped?'* Her thoughts raced around madly as she tried to make sense of what had gone on. *'It must be a dream,'* she concluded.

It was difficult to focus her eyes, but that really was a cloak she could see and it was being worn by the man. The candlelight was bright enough to make his bright blue eyes shine as he turned. His cloak parted and a magnificently muscled man slowly walked toward her. *'Don't wake up, don't wake up,'* she repeated to herself. He knelt down on one knee by her side and she could see his chest, dark with hair. He moved his thigh aside, knowingly. She looked at his engorged penis which stood way out from his taut body. A sudden crinkling noise pulled her attention to his hands. He was opening something, and a condom was pulled out.

She watched fascinated as he placed it on his erection. Slowly, so slowly, caressing it down, until it was finally jammed tightly against his body. Their eyes met. Excitement coursed through her. Every nerve tingled with anticipation. Her throat and lungs tightened and she could not swallow or breathe properly. He was now moving toward her, and his erect penis gently swayed as he removed his cloak.

The apparition came nearer. Viv thought she should pinch herself, but did not intend ruining this dream. She felt incredibly aroused, quite prepared to meet her fate. The sight of him was almost too much for a mere mortal. The muscular body had thick hair that continued down in a line over his abdomen, thickening out again above a magnificent shaft of erect flesh. He was a very threatening, imposing figure, but it was not fear that she felt right now.

As he slowly arrived at Viv's side, her body shuddered involuntarily. Slowly, he slid the blanket from her aroused body. His touch and slow kisses made her tremble. His lips fitted perfectly over hers and the pressure of aroused flesh on flesh was exquisite. Several times his hardness brushed her thighs and each time she craved for him to enter. He began to kiss his way down her body.

Viv gripped his muscled shoulder and the back of his head, desperately trying to bear the intense feelings, without screaming out loud. He kissed his way back up her body and used his fingers expertly on her, in the way he had already discovered she enjoyed. This time she yelled out as the pleasure began to exhaust her. He allowed his swaying penis to rest on her legs, tantalizingly.

He held his mouth close to hers and she raised her head to press her lips against his. The kiss was gentle at first, but became so passionate that her body shuddered with yet another orgasm. She continued to moan in pleasure as his hands cradled her face. He arched his back and slid forcefully and deeply into her.

* * * * * * * * * * * * * * * * * * * *

Chapter Sixteen

Dandy Discovers Conflicting Emotions

{NB: 'BV' is the Baron von Eider.}

Dandy still felt fragile, but on her way to recovery. She and Daniel had left messages for BV and awaited his response on their cell phones whilst doing a quick search of the house. They had not been finished long when the phone rang. Daniel quickly picked up to answer.

"Hello, who is this?" He hoped it was Viv phoning from somewhere. Dandy watched him expectantly.

"What's wrong Daniel?" asked the Baron, on hearing the alarm in his brother's voice.

The Baron soon heard of the confusion he had helped cause and told them not to panic. He said for them to come around the orchard to the den, where he and Viv were.

Daniel looked incredulous. Yes, the den, it was the only place they had not searched. They did not even remember to look there as it was such a private place. It was so out of bounds that Daniel had only been invited there once before, when it was first built with its concealed door in the downstairs cloakroom. There had also been a concealed entrance in the wall in the orchard, but Daniel did not know exactly where that would be. The Lyons' rushed to the cloakroom arriving at the door which was held open by BV. They were ushered inside.

Viv greeted them with a flushed smile. The Baron apologized for not telling them sooner about their whereabouts. With a broad grin, he stated, "Circumstances were not in my control."

Viv flushed deeper.

Daniel told BV he had confronted Alex, who said a masked man took Viv away. "I was still suspicious of Alex though, did he hurt Viv?" He looked at Viv with concern, but also great relief to have found her safe. "Did he hurt her?" he asked BV again.

"I will tell you more, just let me catch my breath," he said with a sly smile. "Let's get a hot drink inside us all first. You know how much I like my tea!"

"Catch your breath?" Daniel asked perplexed.

Dandy smiled. "At least you two managed to get together, but we could have done without the worry! What happened with Alex? Why didn't he bring you into the house, Viv?"

"Dandy sit down here beside me," Viv said, tapping the bean bag she was sitting on. There was ample room for both of them. "BV will have to explain more about that… I was rather, er, out of it! How are *you* feeling now?"

Something nagged at the back of Dandy's mind. She also felt worried about Viv getting too fond of BV, wondering why the feeling seemed so similar to jealousy. *'Couldn't be,'* she thought. *'It doesn't make sense.'* She only felt brotherly love for BV, so it was illogical to react in this way. *'Viv must be the cause,'* she realized, feeling confused again. She could remember becoming strangely aroused with Viv earlier in the orchard. *'Now why did that happen and could that be the reason for my so-called jealousy?'* She wondered.

BV put an arm around his brother and walked him into the small, but well-equipped kitchen to get some tea for everyone. They left Dandy and Viv hugging each other with relief.

"I'm so glad nothing bad happened to you, Viv," Dandy said, full of concern.

"We'll leave the girls to catch up some," BV said, adding casually, "they seem very close, have they been friends for long?"

"Yes, they are close, but have not known each other long." Daniel replied. "BV, did Viv tell you why they were both in the orchard?"

"No, she hasn't. What do you think they were up to?" BV grinned. "Shall we ask them? I'm quite interested to know why, too Daniel."

"No. Not now. I'll ask Dandy tomorrow, when she feels better and more like talking," Daniel said, as he picked up two cups of tea. He walked over and handed a cup to Dandy, who moved off the beanbag onto another one, so her husband could sit by her. BV brought a cup over to Viv and sat down with his arm around her. Daniel's eyes went up into his brow. Dandy laughed at his reaction. Looking at how cosy BV and Viv were, it made her feel pleased and wary at the same time, with the familiarity shown by BV to her friend.

Viv was content and liked being around these people. She looked from Daniel to BV, surprised to realize that she now only felt warmth toward Daniel. *'I'm over it, and BV doesn't feel like a copy at all,'* she happily thought, as a sigh escaped her lips.

"And why are you sighing like that?" BV asked.

"I'm just happy, is all," she replied with a smile.

After some general chit chat, Dandy announced they should be getting home. She asked if Viv was ready to go yet, as she cast a sideways glance at BV.

"I could use some sleep," Viv said, still feeling the after-effects of the earlier incidents. "After tonight, it's going to be very quiet at my place!"

"You can stay with us tonight, if you want? You can lay in tomorrow. We probably will!" Dandy assumed Daniel's approval. His worried expression was noticed by BV.

Viv answered that she appreciated the offer, but would rather go home tonight. There was so much she needed to think about. The Lyons said goodnight to BV, and went outside to wait for Viv to say her goodbyes.

"You're unusually quiet sweetheart," Daniel said, as they walked to their car. "Nothing wrong, is there?"

"No," Dandy said distractedly. "I'm just tired." She was picturing BV holding Viv close, kissing her. She wondered why Viv never mentioned what had obviously happened between her and BV. She could not ask, nor did she really want to know the answer.

Back in the house, the couple were saying goodbyes. "Are you called anything else, apart from BV?" Viv asked.

He replied with a huge smile. "Sure, but those names are unmentionable!"

After the intimacy they had shared, it seemed strange to ask his name. Telephone numbers and emails were exchanged. They looked at each other in silence, both lost in their own thoughts.

"I would like to see you again. Can you phone me soon to arrange?" BV asked.

Viv nodded. One last delicious, lingering kiss, then she was escorted to the waiting car.

On the drive back, Viv tried to apologize for the trouble that had been caused. Daniel stopped her. "If anyone's to blame, it's that Alex! It seems he went around spiking drinks!"

Now Viv understood, although she was still puzzled by the identity of the man in the orchard with Dandy. She felt uneasy about mentioning the incident and hoped Dandy would volunteer the information later. *'Could Dandy have been with Alex? Surely not BV? No, the man had been much smaller in stature.* Apart from that, she detected no chemistry other than friendship between brother and sister-in-law.

Viv was safely delivered home and Dandy stepped out to enable the car seat to go forward, for Viv to climb out of the two-door car. She called out goodnight to Daniel, as she stood close to Dandy. They had not known each other that long, but the incident brought them closer. Daniel wondered if it was normal for women to hug in such a friendly way this soon when saying goodnight to each other. He surmised it was due to his wife being relieved that Viv was safe. After Dandy settled back into the car and they had driven off, Daniel became quiet.

"Penny for your thoughts darling?" Dandy asked.

He dare not tell her as it would make him sound neurotic. Instead, he smiled at her and looked back at the road. "Oh, I was just thinking about it all and relieved you're both okay."

Dandy hoped her husband had not fallen for Viv. Everyone else seemed to have and she wondered if the spell was on her, too.

* * * * * * * * * * * * * * * * * * * *

BV could not stop thinking about Viv. He lay in his bed wondering how dangerous it would be to get involved with such a woman. All his life, he had been a free spirit, with no one to answer to, but himself. There were numerous casual relationships, but he had yet to find that *one* woman he wanted to settle down and share his life with. Viv was different and possessed a kind of magnetism. There was definitely something special about her, but it would mean changing his life completely, which he might not be able to do.

And what was all this about her and Dandy? Something had happened, he could sense it. Dandy had paid quite a bit of attention to Viv. Perhaps it was because she was over-protective of Daniel? He felt reasonably confused as he drifted off to sleep.

* * * * * * * * * * * * * * * * * * * *

Chapter Seventeen
Back at the Ranch

Henry found it impossible to relax although he was writing, which always took him out of himself. He had been trying to finish a short story to post to his website, but hated the way it turned out. The story was about an average guy who worked diligently each day. In the evenings, this man walked the streets and dispensed vigilante justice to the thugs and criminals. The media built him into quite a legend. The man met, and rescued a wonderful girl who was in a bad situation. This girl had stolen his heart and he wanted to spend his life with her.

The hero was just about to ask the girl to marry him when he was spurned. He lost her, although there was as yet, no reason why. Henry turned from his computer in disgust. He moved away from the desk and paced the floor. It was too similar to the turn his own life might be taking, apart from the superhero part. In fact, his life had been relatively ordinary and uneventful up to this point, although comfortable.

Henry thought back to his father and the wonderful times they had spent together. He promised his father to make something of himself and gain recognition in life. His father had comforted him with these words, "Just do your best and everything else will fall into place. You will find happiness." Henry always believed those words and came to live by them.

So why now, after all of these years of sacrifice and hard work, was he still unhappy? He realized now it was because that one special ingredient was missing in his life. Namely, the love of a woman he was just 'crazy' about. There were some special women in his life over the years, but none that matched Viv, or, the strong feelings he had for her. Why had it taken him so long to find a woman like her? And now after finding her, she might be lost to him.

Henry grew angry and tried to figure out why Viv did not feel for him, the same way he felt about her. After all, he was a good enough guy and they certainly did have a bond. But then again, maybe the old adage was true. Nice guys really do finish last and how could he compete with Daniel's looks, not to mention a baron who was single and looked similar? Why did he not wonder about that before? What was that about? A co-incidence? He had enough to worry about and moved his thoughts on.

Henry's mother had gone to bed. He could always tell, once the sound of her footsteps in the flat above stopped. That had happened a good few hours earlier. He loved his mother, enjoying her company and being able to see her each day. But, he was in need of a different sort of company now. He needed the companionship of someone to take his mind off Viv and the degree to which she might be enjoying herself tonight. Henry thought about how she must be laughing and enjoying being with the baron. She could be literally dancing the night away with him.

The very thought drove him up the wall, until he could no longer contain his anger. He just had to get out of the house, anything to take his mind off the situation.

He walked to the pub, hoping a few drinks would help him feel sleepy and help dilute his worries. Upon his arrival at the local pub, he found it packed as usual, for a weekend night. He entered squeezing his way through to the bar. After his first order of Booth's gin, he remained at the bar to drink it. As he sipped away at his drink, a screech of laughter hit him full in the right ear. His eyes followed the noise, to rest upon a peroxide blonde seated on a bar stool a few seats over from him. She basked in the attention of three male admirers, who each wanted to outdo the other in order to impress her.

"I could make you feel much better than that," she was saying, in a high-pitched, irritating, girlish voice.

Henry turned away and wondered why people had to act so ridiculously. An attractive woman appeared by his side, flashed him a big smile and began to rummage around in her handbag in an attempt to find her purse. She gave up, said she had mislaid her purse and asked if he would buy her a drink.

"I'm sorry," he replied quickly and a little embarrassed to be in this place to begin with. "I was just leaving." Henry put his glass down, as her well-manicured hand rested on his arm.

"Please don't go, I would like to talk with you," the young lady said hopefully. "I could do with the company." She then extended her hand gently into his, introducing herself as Harriet.

"I'm Henry," he said, politely disengaging his hand from hers. Her need for company seemed to match his, so he asked what she wanted to drink.

"A gin and tonic would be great," she replied.

Henry called to the bartender and ordered her drink and another Booth's, for himself.

"Thanks, I appreciate this!" She sipped her drink. "You don't look like a Henry," she stated, after a moment's consideration. "You look more like a Richard!"

"What's wrong with Henry?" he asked a little hurt. He liked his name.

Smiling, she replied, "A big old cart horse would be called Henry."

"That about sums me up, only I'm slightly more refined!" He laughed. "I feel like a cart horse most of the time!"

Harriet chatted on happily and Henry was content to listen, responding every now and then. He bought Harriet another drink when he bought himself a re-fill. Whenever his mind wandered back to Viv, he threw himself into the conversation. The bell went for last orders. Henry finished his drink and announced it was time he left.

"Oh, please don't go yet, Henry!" Harriet said intently. "I've only just met you and you're such a sincere and interesting man. Those qualities are not easy to find these days."

Henry looked at her imploring, pretty face. She used only the slightest amount of make-up to enhance her features. If Harriet had entered his life before Viv, he would have felt inclined to be more sociable toward her.

"I'm flattered that you're interested in me, Harriet, but I'm very involved with someone else right now," he said to her thinking, *'Even if she isn't with me.'*

Harriet drained her glass. "Would you please be kind enough to walk me to the door, Henry?" They pushed their way through the crowd, and out into the street.

"Thanks for the drinks, Henry, but, I wish we could have talked longer!" She kissed him on the cheek.

Henry smiled awkwardly. Harriet's hand still rested on his sleeve as she began to speak quietly, but earnestly.

"Before I go, I want to tell you something." She faltered. "I never believed in love at first sight, until now and here you are, about to walk away from me. I've only confessed because I'll never see you again!" Her sad eyes pleaded with him.

Henry stood there, shocked.

Harriet spoke again. "Even if you weren't involved, we wouldn't have stood a chance." Her voice became even quieter. "I have a secret and I wouldn't normally share it with just anyone, but for some reason I can tell you. I don't know what it is, but there's something so special about you Henry. I noticed it almost immediately."

"Thanks," he cut in, feeling embarrassed. "That's a very nice thing for you to say, even though I cannot understand how you feel you know all that. But, anyway, I am too wrapped up, or maybe messed up, with this current relationship. Everything's too involved for me to be of much company to you, even as a friend." Henry sensed Harriet wanted to tell him her secret so he added, "By the way, don't feel compelled to tell me anything that makes you feel uncomfortable to share about yourself. It's not necessary."

"No, I think it's important, Henry, because I feel we could've been very good friends. I need to tell you something very special," she said intently.

"Alright, go ahead then," he responded.

"Henry, I used to be a man!"

With this revelation, she turned and briskly walked away. Her high heels clicked on the pavement and she looked every bit a lady.

Henry was stunned as he stared at her disappearing slim figure, in total disbelief at her words. Then he felt a sudden urge of sympathy. He knew all about loneliness and how deeply it hurt. He called out to Harriet to wait and ran to catch up with her. She was almost as tall as he was, although strangely enough, he had not noticed that about her, at first.

When he reached her, she looked surprised to see him. Tears were streaming down her face and Henry felt his eyes begin to sting in empathy.

"Don't cry," he said softly. "Isn't there some way we could be, er, friends, just friends?"

Harriet cheered up immensely. "Of course, there is, Henry! I'd love that, and I'd love to be introduced to this lady friend of yours later too, if that's possible?"

"I hope it will be," he replied honestly, as the gnawing pain returned in his stomach. He wondered what Viv might be doing at this very moment. It still hurt him too much to think about it.

Harriet offered coffee and added that her house was only a short distance away. Whilst they walked, Harriet chatted as if she had known Henry all of her life. He stole glances at her and wondered if she had really told the truth. Her features were very feminine and she looked nothing like the people he had seen on television documentaries. Even with loads of make-up, their masculine features were normally visible and it usually showed in their stature and walk.

Harriet wore her hair straight and just onto her shoulders, with a side parting. It looked very natural, as did the reddish-brown colour. Henry looked at her hands. They were smallish and certainly better groomed than some of the female hands he had noticed before. It occurred to him that he may have misunderstood what she said. What could she have said instead? *'I used to have a man?'* It could have been that, but why on earth would that upset her so much? Then again it might. It all depended on the circumstances.

Harriet turned out to be quite a character and convinced him she was indeed a transgendered person. He had never heard so many outrageous tales or realized how much mental anguish these people had to go through. Henry was so intrigued, that he stayed longer than intended. Harriet was so easy to be with, and he told her of the events which led up to this evening. She did her best to make him laugh by poking fun at herself, anything to keep him from worrying about his troubles.

Harriet told him there had not been anyone for

her, since becoming a woman properly. She had always been a loner and previously had a boyfriend, for a few short months. "Before my operation," she told him, "at a party whilst I still had a penis, but as usual dressed as a woman, I found the women's toilets were occupied. My bladder was too full to hang about waiting, so I went into the men's bathroom after checking no-one was in there. I should have at least gone into a stall, but I had too many drinks and was not thinking properly. I quickly hitched up my skirt and took a whiz standing up, as I usually did up until having my op.

My boyfriend back then, walked in behind me and flipped out! At that time, I still hid my true sexuality from people and always dressed up as a woman, so he actually believed me to be one. He almost went into shock," she continued. "He ran out of there so quickly. I never saw him again and always wondered why he couldn't talk to me about it. We had dated for a while and became quite fond of each other."

"If you don't mind me asking," said a red-faced Henry. "How come he didn't know you were er, still a man?"

"You are wondering how he didn't notice my manhood," Harriet laughed. "Well, we did stuff, and he would never have known I was not a real woman. I never let him touch me below the waist, and he never saw me completely naked. That's one of the reasons I'm so straightforward now. I just don't want to ever mislead anyone, ever again." Harriet seemed relieved it was all out in the open.

She also hoped there was a chance to be with this man she had instantly fallen for. *'It's not his good looks in particular, it's the kindness that comes off him in waves,'* she thought. *'And besides, if this other woman was the right one for him, he would not be out on his own looking so unhappy.'*

Henry learned many surprising things from Harriet, and he wanted to share them with Viv. He wondered if she would be interested. *'Probably not,'* he thought sadly. *'She must be having the time of her life. Why would she care about me, or my feelings?'* For all intents and purposes, she had probably written him off, carrying on her liaison with the baron, whilst fantasizing over Daniel.

'What an idiot I am!' he thought. *'How could I have been such a fool?'* Henry now thought he should have been more aggressive and let Viv know he was willing to fight for her. Or, perhaps he should have been less polite and more possessive. *'Is that what she really wanted after all? Who knows with women? Why should I care?'* He thought miserably.

Well, if he did not care, then why did it hurt him so much to think of her with another man? *'And, if she were only enjoying a strange man's company at a casual party, it could lead to more than just that. What then?'* The thoughts came in waves now and were just killing him.

"Would you like anything to eat?" Harriet asked, which startled Henry back to the present.

"No thanks," he replied. "Just another cup of tea, if it's not too much trouble, then I'll be getting on home."

Harriet smiled, headed off to the kitchen and threw a backwards glance at him as she left. He sat wondering. *'No way was that attractive, feminine creature ever a man. She's also such lovely company and so easy to talk to.'* Henry decided he would like to become friends with her.

Perhaps it was the effect of the drinks that evening, even with the tea diluting it, but sitting there on Harriet's settee, he wondered how it would feel to make love to a transgendered woman. *'Would it feel different somehow? No, I mustn't think that way!"* Henry uttered to himself in a panic. *'Try to think of Viv,'* he told himself.

But, as difficult as it was not to think about Viv during the course of the day and evening, he now found it equally difficult to try and think of her. *'What could possibly happen next?'* He thought miserably.

* *

Chapter Eighteen
Henry and Viv Both Get a Shock

Viv woke up late in the afternoon, surprised at still feeling groggy from the night before. She also felt slightly sore in certain areas, but it was not all unpleasant. The telephone rang earlier, but she had been too sleepy to answer it. All at once, a thrill shot through her, as she remembered the previous night's events. '*It had been simply wonderful,*' she thought, gently stroking herself. Sex would never be the same again. Not even Lawrence could have made love to her like that. Well, at least he was so far removed from today that his memory had been toned down. Or, perhaps it was just as good, but this had just happened, not several years in the past.

Thank heavens she had been under the influence of drink, or her principles would have prevented her from becoming part of a wonderful fantasy. On second thought, she may have thrown her principles out the window, depending on the mood at the time. Oh, what a fantasy! Whichever way this relationship developed, or did not, she would always cherish this amazing memory. '*It will be my fantasy, to keep forever,*' she smiled to herself. '*Another one I can add to the past fantasies!*'

Viv had been awake around two hours when the police arrived and knocked on the front door of her home. This all seemed so unreal, and she had no idea why they had arrived. To be sure, she left the thick, strong chain on before partially opening the door to the two police detectives. They introduced themselves and showed their identifications to her satisfaction. She let them in.

Questions were asked about the barbeque, such as, had she seen any suspicious characters. She now thought everyone looked suspicious. Eventually, she heard that the man called Alex Labelle, had been found dead. Alex was murdered sometime during, or shortly after the party. The police discovered his body in the orchard, when it was reported by a party-goer who had gone back to find his missing keys. The murder spot seemed to be just past where Viv saw Dandy and the strange man together that night, by the first set of trees.

She was stunned, but when the detectives said the primary suspect in the case was Daniel, her stunned silence turned to complete shock. They were holding him on suspicion of murder at this very moment!

Viv sat down before she fell. Terrible thoughts raced through her brain. *'Poor Dandy! How was Daniel coping?'* Her head was still spinning, but she gathered her strength and provided the police with all of the information she could remember, that might have been relevant. Unfortunately, the events of the prior evening were still mostly a blur. She tried not to say anything which might make it worse for Daniel, or BV. The detectives left, asking her to call if she remembered anything else that might help in their investigation.

Viv had purposely left out the part about Dandy and the stranger, not because she thought it was unimportant, but more to preserve Dandy's dignity. After the police had gone, she wondered about the Lyons. She had known them only a short time, but even so, there was no way Daniel could be a murderer! There was nothing much of the early time at the barbeque Viv could remember, due to the effect of the drink.

She remembered Dandy saying how angry Daniel was with Alex for not bringing her into the house. She also recalled after being left in his care, Alex had grabbed her by the wrists and tried to kiss her. Her struggles had been totally ineffectual in her groggy state, and he was persistent. As she was about to lose consciousness, BV suddenly showed up from apparently nowhere and hit Alex in the ribs telling him to get out. Alex groaned, falling to the ground breathless, but still conscious, and the *'masked man,'* then rushed her from the scene.

Viv tried to recall if BV had been angry enough to hit Alex more than once, but it did not seem that way. Nothing made sense. Daniel could not have knocked Alex unconscious, or he would have admitted it. Her thoughts turned to Dandy.

Perhaps it would be best if Dandy stayed with her, until everything got sorted out. The poor woman must be a mess of emotions at this terrible time. They had both been put through so much, in just the past twenty-four hours, that it made perfect sense to look after her for a while. Viv thought it best to call right away and invite her over.

Viv reached for the telephone, but it rang before she could dial Dandy. It was Henry, who asked if she had heard about Daniel, which she confirmed. He continued, by saying the murder was all over the news. There had also been an update on the serial killer who killed gays. Several more deaths had occurred, in places not too far from where she was, but the police had no further developments with their investigations.

Although Henry seemed concerned about Daniel's plight, he had been worried that she might have become the victim. He obviously avoided asking her what happened regarding the baron, and she never volunteered any information on it either. Henry then started to confuse her when he spoke of a new friend he wanted her to meet. Someone who needed to 'belong.' She tried to listen, but it was impossible. Her thoughts returned to Daniel and how tormented he and Dandy must now be. She told Henry she was inviting Dandy over and hoped he understood she did not have much time for him, just at the moment. Henry was okay about it, saying he would call her later that day, just to check and see if she was all right.

* * * * * * * * * * * * * * * * * * * *

Chapter Nineteen
Daniel Starts to Lose Hope

Daniel was unable to take it seriously at first, but that last visit from his solicitor and long-time friend, Mr. Howard Lane, really worried him. Mr. Lane heard the news from Dandy when she paged him on his emergency line. He raced to the police lockup as fast as possible. Mr. Lane was a short, portly man, with a receding hairline. He wore tiny spectacles that made his face look much wider and rounder than it actually was.

He had been out playing tennis with a client of his that afternoon and arrived at the police station, still dressed in his white shorts, polo top and tennis shoes when he asked to see Daniel. After presenting his credentials, he was led down the corridor of examination rooms. A guard stood vigil in front of them. After showing his security pass, Mr. Lane was admitted. Daniel sat there, head down, elbows on the table, jaw leaning in the palm of his hands.

"My friend!" exclaimed Lane, as Daniel jumped up, and the two of them embraced. "Geez, it feels like somebody died in here," Lane said tactlessly.

"I feel like *I've* died Howard," said Daniel, as Lane sat down across from the prisoner, in the examination room.

The room consisted of a simple card table with a small stained metal ashtray on top of it. There were two small, uncomfortable chairs that faced one another. A bright, hanging light protruded from the ceiling in between them. The room was otherwise fairly dark, except for the light that protruded from the wall of mirrors on the side of the room. It also had the distinct, but faint smell of stale cigarette smoke.

Mr. Lane and Daniel had often sat down to discuss business, but obviously under different circumstances than today. Unfortunately, today it was this room that provided the backdrop for their meeting.

He explained to Daniel that the initial coroner's findings in the Alex Labelle murder read as; "The autopsy determined death occurred from a cranial embolism, due to a blow or blows to the head. The authorities believe these injuries ultimately caused the death of Alex Labelle."

"What does that mean, Howard?" Daniel asked.

"Well, it says 'ultimate' cause of death, because there were also marks on his face, bruising to his ribs and a bruise on his chin."

"Blows to the head?" Daniel repeated in disbelief. "I only hit him once, and that was on the jaw! That explains the bruise on the chin. Someone else must have hit him elsewhere and in the head, after I left him to look for Viv!"

Mr. Lane looked doubtful. "We'll have to prove that Daniel. You were the only one he openly disagreed with that night! It was you who was seen not only arguing with him but also punching him on the jaw.

By all witness accounts, you were extremely angry with him and looked like you really meant business."

"There were two kids nearby, when I hit him. They could back me up!" Daniel said hopefully, leaping up from his chair. He recalled BV saying he hit Alex in the ribs, but he was not going to mention that.

"Yes, they were there," Lane responded, "and they saw everything, or so they claim. They saw you argue with Alex and heard you ask about Viv. They saw you grab and hit him." He paused, to move his short legs and make himself more comfortable on the wooden chair.

Mr. Lane continued, "They ran off from that spot, claiming they were afraid for what might happen next. They obviously did not want to get involved, Daniel. The kids said you were violent and irrational. They could not recall exactly how many times you hit him or where, apart from on the jaw. Incidentally, Alex had a black eye too.

Daniel interrupted him, "I only hit him once and certainly not in the eye!"

Well, their statements leave that open unfortunately, so, that does not help our case. It actually could prove to be quite damaging to us. Their testimony is the last recorded recollection of events prior to Labelle's death. Those recollections prominently mention you!"

Daniel felt dejected as he sat back down on his chair. He placed his hands over his eyes and began to lose hope again, "This is bad, isn't it?"

Mr. Lane stood up. "I'm on it already Daniel!" Much of the evidence here is purely circumstantial and probably would not hold up in a court of law. After all, no one actually saw you *'murder'* Alex Labelle. I mean, you didn't murder anyone. On the other hand, I say most of the evidence probably will not hold up in court, but you can never predict how a jury will view things."

"They may believe you, but sometimes a jury can get vindictive and want to put someone away, just because they do not like them. After all, look at you. You're a young, successful, attractive man. Some folks out there might resent that and want to put you away just by virtue of jealousy. Gosh, I sometimes wished I were you, but not just now!"

Mr. Lane trailed off before catching himself. "But don't worry. I'm going to do the best possible job for you, my friend. Look on the bright side Daniel. At least they don't have the electric chair in this country." The solicitor's words did not console him.

"Besides, if you get any jail time, Daniel," Mr. Lane continued, "I'll ensure that it's only for a minimal duration. And, that you get sent away to a minimum security facility. They can be quite comfortable you know, almost a country club environment."

"Wonderful!" Daniel replied, "You make it sound so much better." He tried to smile, but could not conjure up one.

"Yeah, you get time off for good behaviour, special privileges for staying out of trouble, plenty of recreational activities and TV. The time passes by quickly. Gosh, you could be out in three, or four years," Mr. Lane said triumphantly, as though Daniel's incarceration was already a forgone conclusion.

Mr. Lane's words stung Daniel. He knew his friend actually wanted to lift his spirits, but the exact opposite occurred. Not his fault, but Lane never was one for tactfulness. Daniel became more depressed than he had ever been in his life. He could not fathom the prospect of not being with Dandy, or in giving up his freedom for years. Especially, for a crime he had not committed. It all seemed too outrageous and impossible. None of what was happening could be real. Yet, here was Howard Lane, speaking as though it was a distinct possibility he would do time in prison.

"By the way Daniel, have you got a message for Dandy that I can pass on for you?" Lane asked, lifting himself out of his chair.

Daniel looked up at his long-time friend. "Yeah, Howard, give Dandy my love. Tell her to make sure my brother knows about this and ask her to try and think of something to get me out of this mess! She's usually good at solving puzzles."

He tried to sound optimistic, but his despondency was hard to hide. The prospect of losing his freedom and being without the woman he loved, even for a brief period of time, was more than he could bear. Death would be more humane.

"Sure!" Mr. Lane said, as he banged on the door to summon the guard. "Sorry, got to run, but you hang in there pal, okay? Oh, sorry, didn't mean to use the word hang. I meant, stay tough Daniel."

He could see the morose look on Daniel's face and grew concerned. He had been Daniel's friend for a long time and knew him to be upbeat and full of spirit. That was not the man he was about to leave behind him right now.

As soon as Lane exited, Daniel began to wonder if he were set up. If someone with a motive saw him punch Labelle, they might have taken advantage of the situation. *But, who and why?* He hoped a motive would come to light. Someone, somewhere, must have seen something. '*There just has to be hope,*' he thought, as the guard came to take him back to his cell.

* * * * * * * * * * * * * * * * * * * *

Chapter Twenty

Humiliation Followed by an Eye-Opening Talk

Henry promised to let Harriet know if all was well, but instead of a phone call, he decided to call on her in person. She was very pleased to see him. When he left so abruptly only a few nights before, Harriet wondered if she would ever see or hear from him again.

So much happened that evening, with Henry leaving saying he was tired and a bit drunk, also that he had way too much to think about. That was understandable of course. Harriet had thrown a lot at him, in addition to everything else he already had to think about with Viv. Apparently, she had not overwhelmed him too much, considering he was back here now.

When he told Harriet about the murder of Alex Labelle and Viv's involvement, her mood changed and she became very thoughtful.

"Alex Labelle," repeated Harriet. "I just know I've heard that name before. But, where?" She continued to think about the name as she went off to the kitchen to make some coffee. Meanwhile, Henry walked about the lounge and noticed some interesting pictures on the wall. He was admiring them, especially one of a large tiger, when Harriet returned with two cups of coffee.

"How do you like it?" she asked.

"Oh, just a little cream and sugar, please," he responded, not remembering she had made him coffee the other night.

"No, silly! How do you like the picture? I noticed you were admiring my work," Harriet inquired, placing the tray of coffee, milk and sugar on the coffee table.

"Oh, yes, sorry! I love them all, particularly the cat in the jungle scene. It's so real and looks like it's going to jump right out of the picture and pounce on me!"

Harriet was pleased and wished she could pounce on him right now. "That's my favourite too! I did that one whilst on holiday in Africa."

"You're quite a brilliant artist," he said, whirling around to face her. "You could earn a living at it!"

"Actually, Henry, I do," she smiled. "I sell them at markets, and shops have bought some. I have my usual clientele for commissions and a couple of exhibitions coming up."

"That's marvellous! Have you any others I could look at?" he asked.

"Yes," Harriet replied sheepishly. "They're upstairs in my studio, if you dare come up to see them with me!"

"Why not?" he said, with a false air of confidence.

Harriet happily led Henry upstairs into a small studio. The walls were covered with works of art. The frames varied slightly, but everything was tastefully done. He was given a guided tour and explanation of the pictures. He examined each one with pure amazement. Never had he seen anything quite like this type of work before. She possessed such talent and so much to show for it. He marvelled at the discipline involved, whilst Harriet stood by and beamed with pride.

"You're so clever I could hug you!" he said, turning around to face her.

"Be my guest," she retorted, as she opened her arms to him.

Henry put his arms around Harriet and hugged her tight. She stayed that way and would not allow him to let her go. He found himself wondering how it would feel to have sex with her. She looked up longingly, her arms still wrapped around him.

"I do love you, Henry. I'm sorry, I can't help it!"

Her lips were close, so tempting. He did not resist as she placed her lips gently against his, nor when she took his hand and placed it over her breast. His hand lingered for a second or two, before being pulled back. Harriet was not to be put off. She slowly began to undo her buttons, removing her blouse to reveal a pretty pink bra. She wiggled out of her skirt and whispered, "I've got panties to match!"

Henry was not sure what to expect, and it surprised him to see how female she looked. Slim, slightly muscular, but still shapely. He felt a pang of guilt, as he thought of Viv. His curiosity began to get the better of him, and he did not like it at all. Harriet suspected as much.

"I know how you feel about Viv," she said, reading his thoughts. "All I ask is that you accept me meanwhile and let me give you pleasure, just until things click between you and Viv. Nothing will change, I'll put no holds on you!" She undid her bra and slid the straps slowly over her shoulders revealing her round breasts. Her bra fell to the floor.

Henry was too intrigued to stop her, but felt very apprehensive as she stepped out of her panties and walked toward him. She began to undress him, and he tried to think of a polite way to escape. When Harriet tugged his trousers down, he knew it was too late.

* * * * * * * * * * * * * * * * * * * *

Half an hour later, they walked back downstairs arm in arm. Harriet picked up the tray of coffee she had made earlier and went to make some fresh coffee. When she came back with more, she felt bad that Henry still looked upset.

"Shouldn't we be having a cigarette right about now?" Henry asked with mild sarcasm.

Harriet laughed and sat down beside him. "Shame we don't smoke!"

"Nothing to smoke about, and it certainly doesn't call for a cigar!" Henry mumbled quietly.

Tears stung Harriet's eyes, as she looked at the man she cared too much for.

"It doesn't matter, Henry, really it doesn't! Lots of men can't get erections for one reason or another. Particularly when they're under stress, it can be very difficult. Believe me, I'd know! I was a man myself once, remember!" Harriet realized they were not the best choice of words, but also knew she could not really convince him or herself! She then tried another approach. "It was all my fault anyway," she continued. "I shouldn't have started it!"

Henry looked at her sad face. It hurt to see how much she cared for him. He let her down because he could not even react to her femininity. Probably, because he could not stop thinking about Viv, or could it be the knowledge of Harriet's operation? More confusion, just what he did not need.

Harriet went to a desk drawer and brought out a photo album. "Let's go through this one," she said cheerfully.

They sat down next to each other on the settee and she set the album in his lap. She helped him turn the pages and he saw a normal-looking baby. It turned into a cute toddler. A couple of pages later and the teenage boy definitely had a feminine look.

"This photograph," Harriet said pointing to a very pretty boy, in shirt and jeans, "is me, at fourteen years of age."

It could not be denied. Even with her hair cut short and dressed up in football shirt and boots, Harriet's breasts were noticeably developing. They pushed her shirt away from her body in a way not seen on a boy. Henry felt slightly better, at least she had never looked manly, but he regretted such intimacy had occurred between them. What if she wanted him to try again?

Page after page of memory was turned. At one point, Harriet laughed as she pointed out the name 'Philip,' written under a photograph.

"My parents had grown alarmed at this stage and no more pictures were taken."

Henry wondered how he would have coped, if this gender problem had happened to him. It was a terrible thought. He winced, realizing what she had cut off! What a decision to make!

Harriet noticed the look on his face. "What's the matter?" she asked.

"I just thought, well, wondered, how you had the nerve to have the chop?" He flinched at his own words.

Harriet grinned broadly. "Do you want the lurid details?"

He thought seriously for a moment. "No. Not yet anyway. Just the idea of it makes me ache! Ouch!" He grimaced.

His comments amused Harriet. "If I hadn't told you, would you have known?"

Harriet waited patiently whilst Henry recalled the embarrassment of his performance, or rather, the lack of it. He tried to visualize what he saw of Harriet's *personal parts.*

His answer eventually came. "Probably not, so what made you tell me on our first meeting? You don't tell everyone you get friendly with, do you?" Although an innocent question, he could see her feelings were hurt.

"Of course, not," she replied. "It was just that I thought I'd never see you again. I wanted to give you something special to think about! About me!"

"Ah, ha!" said Henry. "Perhaps you were always a woman and you found a clever way of getting me interested!"

Harriet feigned annoyance. "Henry, how can you say that? You've seen my photos and *'Philip'* written underneath some of them!"

"You looked like a girl all the way through," he laughed. "Anyone can write a name under a photo!"

"Okay. You asked for it! Here are the lurid details!"

Henry tried to interrupt her, but it was too late. She began anyway. "Well, I already had the formation of breasts due to the abnormal production of estrogens in my system. The surgeons just went in and inserted some implants to increase the size and add a bit more shape and contour to them. That was the easy part. Shall I go on?"

Henry interrupted her. "No, no! I believe you! Anyway, it's getting late. I've got to be going!"

Harriet held up her hand and stopped him. "Henry, sit down! First, I had to get two psychiatric evaluations to recommend me as a candidate for transgender surgery. I saw two recognized doctors in the process. Secondly, I had to get a letter from an endocrinologist that outlined the history of my hormone therapy. In all, I had to undergo nine months of psychiatric and laboratory tests to determine that the operation was the right life choice for me. In the end, it was decided I was a good candidate. Because the surgery is irreversible, everyone wanted to ensure I didn't enter a situation I'd regret later."

"Sounds fascinating, see you tomorrow then," said

Henry, as he got up to leave once again, not wanting to hear any more.

"Stop, you can't go yet!" Harriet continued. "The operation is called Labiaplasty. First, a needle and suture thread was pushed through the head of my penis. Then, it was surgically removed at the root and pulled along the needle and thread. Next, the surgeon trimmed my penis down to size to form a clitoris. He cut open a cavity and used the remaining penis tissue to create a vagina. The skin from my penis was used to line the new vaginal cavity. If the surgeon didn't have enough material to work with, a skin graft may have been needed. The skin is usually taken from the groin, or butt."

Henry's eyes began to water, and he fidgeted uncomfortably. Knowing Harriet would continue with her grisly story, he resolved himself to hear all of the gory details. He sat back on the settee, hoping his initial nausea would subside.

Harriet continued, "Fortunately, no skin grafts were required as my penis was long enough to begin with, so enough skin was available to make a nice deep vagina, around five inches deep. That was important, since I still planned to have a healthy sex life some day. Finally, the surgeon removed my scrotum. Later, I went back and he finished the job by removing my remaining scrotal hair with a laser."

"Carry on Harriet," he said, feeling glad to have got through the worst of it.

"Well, I think you're ready for the more placid details of the surgery now, so here goes."

Henry nodded since the worst seemed to be over.

"To start properly at the beginning, I arrived at the centre and was taken to my room and settled in. A nurse came in and gave me a pre-med to relax. When she left, I held my penis for the last time, as if to say goodbye to it."

Henry winced, and without realizing it, placed his hand over his crotch to ensure everything was still intact.

Harriet went on, "I was prepped for surgery and wheeled to the operating theatre. The nurses lifted me onto the operating table and I was given a general anaesthetic. I couldn't remember anything, until I woke up in the recovery room. The operation itself lasted about four hours. I slept most of the remaining day and an IV stayed in my arm. Powerful pain medication and sleeping tablets were given, with ice packs applied over my groin, constantly."

"Ouch!" He said, "That sounds painful in itself!"

She continued. "There was a large suture tied over a roll of cotton in my pubic area, along with a urinary catheter and drains. At first I felt weak, but my strength recovered quickly. I left the hospital after the eighth day. Before leaving, my vaginal packing was removed, and I received instructions on how to keep my new vagina dilated. That's important, because in some cases the opening will contract and close up and then most of the surgery is for nothing. I was prescribed some strong painkillers and sent home to recuperate. And, here I am," Harriet said triumphantly. "Hey, would you like to see the video?"

"What? You have a video of the procedure?" Henry exclaimed, before lapsing into utter silence. He was amazed at what this poor woman had undergone, in order to become the person who sat beside him today. He had a renewed sense of admiration for her and to top that, she had a video of it!

"Yes, the medical staff videotaped the entire operation. I have it on a few cassettes. Would you like to watch them?" Harriet asked, with a broad smile on her face.

"Perhaps another time Harriet; there's been just so much to take in this evening." Henry tried to be tactful, but he really wanted any reason to excuse himself at the moment. He felt a bit queasy from Harriet's vivid descriptions of her ordeal. "Let's save it for another time, okay?"

Harriet again made him promise to keep in contact with her. Henry truthfully told her that he would and left dumbfounded. He still reeled from the revelations made to him this evening, but he knew he did not need to see the video...., ever.

* *

Chapter Twenty-One
It All Hits the Fan

Daniel was determined to get out of this mess. For one thing, he could never adapt to prison life. If convicted of murder, he might end up in a hard-core prison full of known murderers, rapists and thieves.

He waited three worrying days for his bail hearing and hoped it would go favourably. It had not. Mr. Lane pleaded his case vigorously enough, stressing that Daniel had no prior convictions or arrests. But the circumstantial evidence worked against him, and the prosecutor convinced the judge that Daniel was a flight risk, given his wealth and connections. Now, he knew his life would be turned inside out.

He was headed back to the real prison, until things could get sorted out. If that were even possible! Daniel pondered the obvious. If he were not able to belong to a gang it would leave him vulnerable to attack, especially, given his age and boyish good looks. He was bound to receive numerous threats. Whilst he could not take all of this seriously, it was well known that big trouble always happened in prisons. He hoped he could keep away from it, but it was bound to look for him everywhere. To survive, a different psychology would be necessary, but it would take a while to learn it. Meanwhile, he would have to cope, somehow....

"Oh, please, Dandy, do something to get me out of here!" he lamented under his breath, as the guard handcuffed his hands and feet to place him in the police wagon for the ride to prison. This was the lowest point he had ever experienced in his life.

* * * * * * * * * * * * * * * * * * * *

Dandy and Viv spent three days together. They waited patiently for word from Mr. Lane on the outcome of the bail hearing. It was an uneventful three days, except for the one time Dandy was allowed to see Daniel. She went to the prison, accompanied by Mr. Lane and sat down behind the glass partition to greet her husband. When she saw Daniel, horror struck her. He was ashen and unshaved, with the worry obvious in his eyes. She picked up the telephone on her side of the partition and spoke to him.

"Oh, Daniel, you look terrible. I'm so worried for you! How are you doing?"

"Don't worry, Dandy, I'm alright for now. Just do everything you can to get me out of here, please," he pleaded.

"Howard is working on it now, darling. We'll be together soon," Dandy responded, her voice cracking.

Suddenly, Daniel broke down in tears and was unable to continue. He called for the guard and was led out of the room. Before he left, he glanced over his shoulder at Dandy, but said nothing. His look conveyed it all, *'Get me out of here!'*

Dandy also burst into tears and Mr. Lane escorted her out of the room. He drove her to Viv's house, where she could continue to stay for emotional support and wait on the outcome of Daniel's court appearance.

It felt strange for Dandy not to have gone home, although she had needed to be with Viv for the first three days, but she could not face their house without Daniel being there. They did have other friends she could have stayed with, but Viv had been part of the circumstances and she was glad to spend time with her. After a short time of going over her thoughts, she shared them with Viv.

"I've played out this scenario in my head a thousand times. It's just so ridiculous that Daniel could be charged in this murder. Why can't the courts see it that way and let him come home?" Dandy lamented.

"I feel that way too, Dandy, but there's no way he's going to stay in prison, now try not to worry and be optimistic!" Viv responded, although she was in no way sure herself. She turned on the television to try and break the tension.

"The serial killer is still on the loose," the reporter announced. "He continues on his bloody rampage and it now appears he has struck close to home..." Before the reporter could finish, Viv turned the television off.

"No need to hear about those terrible things. We have enough to worry about," Viv said.

Normally Dandy might have replied that it was necessary to know about criminals on the loose, but with all that was going on, it seemed impossible their luck could worsen.

The days passed painstakingly slow, when finally

the day of the bond hearing arrived. The women had just finished their afternoon tea when the telephone rang. Dandy answered and it was Mr. Lane, their solicitor.

"Just what I expected," he sputtered frantically. "They're charging Daniel with manslaughter! We're looking at several years in prison here. He's a dead man, no, don't take me literally, I mean I'm going to get him out of this mess! Don't worry, okay? I'm on my way down to the prison now!" he shouted, half out of breath. The telephone went silent.

Viv saw the blank look on Dandy's face. She looked very upset as she set the telephone back in its cradle.

"Bad news?" Viv cautiously asked.

"It couldn't be worse, Viv. That was Howard. Daniel's being charged with manslaughter! I can't bear it!" Tears were flowing down her cheeks.

"Manslaughter? But what about the autopsy report? I thought it was inconclusive?" Viv asked, bewildered.

"The autopsy showed an embolism, a sort of blood clot on his brain. They believe it was due to these 'blows' to the head, but we know Daniel only hit him once," Dandy explained. "And that was on the jaw, not in the head!"

"Perhaps one blow anywhere in the head area, is enough to cause an embolism?"

"No, Viv. It doesn't ring true. There needs to be hard external pressure in the region of the embolism, unless it was a natural internal trauma which occurred with no-one else to blame. But, why did Mr. Lane say that Alex had a black eye? His death must have been due to someone and something else!"

Viv felt helpless, but her mind still went around in circles trying to think of something constructive. Dandy paced the room, sitting occasionally, but found that too much of a strain. She got up every few minutes pacing nervously. Eventually, she said they should find out what they could, but to be very careful and not to trust anyone. The police already questioned as many guests as they could trace, but came up with nothing other than the testimony of the young couple.

Dandy sipped the last dregs from her third cup of coffee and then told Viv, "Let's go! We need to search that orchard. My man is not going to rot away in jail!"

Viv wondered what they could possibly find in the orchard and asked, "Any idea of what we'd look for?"

"No idea really," Dandy responded. "We could look at any remaining rubbish. BV probably didn't have a chance to clear up properly. By the way, he may be back by now. Wonder where he went off to, in such a rush? We only spoke a few words about Daniel's predicament, but he sounded concerned. Maybe he's tracking down and talking to his guests. He might find out something, Viv!"

"It's possible, but don't raise your hopes too much," she replied, picking up her car keys. "We may as well go now, are you ready?" They got into Viv's Alpha Sud car which was smallish, but very good on acceleration.

The journey seemed a lot further in the daylight,

and most of it spent in silence and their own personal thoughts. Viv mentioned she thought it strange that BV had not yet been to see Daniel, although his reason that it was more constructive to help on the outside, made sense. Surprisingly, she also learned the brothers were not that close. The two lived quite separate lives, mainly due to Daniel's desire not to get involved in BV's various lucrative, but sometimes, dangerous business ventures. Viv wished she could learn more, but felt this was not the time to ask.

They pulled into the drive, parked and alighted from the Alpha. As expected, BV was not at home, but they hoped he would return home before they left. With some luck, he may have information that would help. The women walked in a decreasing circle around the orchard, whilst looking about carefully. They examined the empty packets of cigarettes for some undiscovered clue. Sometimes, names and telephone numbers were exchanged on them, so that could prove useful.

Dandy led the way to the place where the body was found, as described by Mr Lane. This area had been mostly cleared of garbage and a broken chalk drawing in the grass, depicted the exact area of the dead body. There were still bits of leftover food and empty plastic cups strewn on the grass, to the side of the outline of the body. They searched through it all, but the whole exercise began to feel futile.

Viv wondered if BV would be pleased to see her, when she heard a noise, and looked up to see his car pull into the drive, a short distance away from where they were standing. Viv and Dandy exchanged glances as BV alighted from the large, black, well polished, SAAB turbo. He looked harassed, but still delectable to Viv. Not that much different from Alain Delon, the actor, except in size and hair, she suddenly realized. Her heart skipped and she felt her cheeks redden as he approached. Viv returned his wave and walked nearer to the trees strolling into the slightly longer grass and gazed around. She needed to steady her nerves before talking to him. BV asked Dandy how she was coping, received a hug and was provided the latest information.

Viv's thoughts were all over the place. She commanded her eyes to scan the grass instead of being directed to where she really wanted to gaze. Suddenly, something shiny caught her attention. The sun reflected on what looked like a metal object. Viv approached the object and as she gently parted the grass, saw it was a hat pin. She picked it up wondering what Sherlock Holmes would have made of it. Probably nothing, but an idea had occurred to her.

Viv walked over and showed them both the pin. They stared thoughtfully at it. Dandy smiled and said it could not possibly be a clue, unless the murderer wore a hat!

Viv thought hard. "Well we do know something. Someone wore a hat in the murder area, and he or she, might have seen something suspicious."

"The police would have interviewed all of those they could trace from the party," BV said, "but I remember a girl named Annabel talking to Alex; she wore a hat. I didn't see them in this area, but it's possible they were, at some point during the course of the evening."

Dandy asked if many hats were worn that night, stating she had seen Annabel, who she had vaguely known at a previous BV party. No-one could remember any others. She smiled and said, "I think I'll just make sure that Annabel was interviewed."

She turned to BV and asked if he had a list of everyone's address. He answered that some guests were strangers, but he had given the police about thirty or so addresses and numbers, including Annabel's. He knew the remaining guests only vaguely, from bumping into them at the various clubs he frequented. The club members' names that he could remember were given to the police. BV showed the two women into his drawing room. Viv was glad she was not in the den again, that would have been far too embarrassing. Coffee was brought in by a friendly, but business-like maid. Everyone sat silently for a short while with their own thoughts.

Dandy spoke first. "This is a long shot, but I have a theory on what might have happened. I noticed Annabel was standing with people I already knew to be drug pushers from earlier parties. She looks as if she had been, or is, on the hard stuff. Now, let's say Alex was a peddler…. And, Annabel wanted some drugs from him in return for sex. He got the sex; she didn't get the dope. She got mad and hit him, not once, but a number of times making her hat shake about and that's when the pin could have fallen out of her hat!" She raised her eyebrows, as she waited for a response.

"Possible, but Dandy," interrupted Viv, "the pin could have fallen out any time!"

"Okay, but the rest of my theory still fits because Daniel only hit him once on the chin. The police said Alex had a black eye, some bruising over his ribs and a cranial embolism!"

BV leaned forward. "Even if you're right, proving it could be impossible."

"You could ask Annabel," Viv said enthusiastically. "Persuade her to tell the truth. It obviously could be proved the death was an accident!"

"No," he replied. "She's not likely to say a word if drugs are concerned."

They were all lost in thought. Viv tried to remember the idea forming in her mind as she found the pin, when the phone rang. BV answered and after a moment, announced to the women that Mr. Lane was on his way over.

"Good," said Dandy. "We can tell him what we think might have happened. Any news about Daniel?"

"I didn't get the chance to ask. He didn't want to say much on the telephone. You know how abrupt he is."

Viv's eyes opened wide. "The hat pin! Now I remember. I was reading not long ago about an improvable murder. That's to say, it was improvable until the murderer gave himself up!" All eyes were on her. She continued. "The police found the body, but there was no evidence of how death occurred. They only found out when the murderer told them that he had pushed a hat pin into the brain behind the ear, in the hairline!"

Dandy shuddered. BV was lost deep in thought

and then remarked, "Death could have been caused by an embolism due to the insertion of the needle!"

"That's what I was thinking," replied Viv.

"That could mean Annabel killed him deliberately!" cried Dandy. "But when and how did she get the hat pin into his skull? How did it fall in the grass? It should have still been in his head, right?"

"He could have felt a sting and knocked it out, but that doesn't explain the other bruises on Alex's head," remarked Viv.

"I think your original theory might still hold to a certain extent, Dandy," said BV. "If she had become angry with Alex withholding drugs, she might hit him, but surely would not want to kill him. No sense in that!" He was deep in thought.

Dandy told them, "Depending on how furious she felt, Annabel might have snuck up later, to stick him with the pin. If still enraged, she could have hit him over and over, even if he were on the ground. The hat pin could fall out of his skull during that time. If the murderer were Annabel, she could have panicked and rushed off, forgetting all about the murder weapon."

"We could ask the coroner for another autopsy," Viv suggested, "paying particular attention to the scalp. If the coroner found a red pin prick mark, he might be able to trace it down to the embolism? We can only hope!"

"That's better than nothing. Maybe Daniel will get bail then." Dandy tried to sound positive.

They talked on with BV listening most of the time,

until Mr. Lane pulled up in his BMW sports car and screeched to a halt in the driveway. He rushed to the door and hammered on it with his fist. Dandy opened it to greet him, but he rushed straight past her.

"Boy, I need a drink!" Lane exclaimed and headed to the bar to help himself. In between gulps, he explained he had just left Daniel. "The judge decided not to allow bail in this case, since Daniel had the means to leave the country and so was considered too much of a flight risk. Otherwise, he's holding up okay. Better than me at least," he gasped.

Dandy told him of their speculation and Mr. Lane just laughed. "What's next? An Ouija board?" He half joked, until he saw everyone's apparent disgust with him. "Okay, I think it's about as likely as me sprouting breasts and dancing at the Windmill Theatre, in Soho. But, I'll ask the coroner to investigate, okay?"

Everyone nodded. He took one last quaff of his drink and departed, in the same rush as he had entered.

Dandy said that she had to get back to the agency to tie up some loose ends. She and BV glanced at Viv.

"I'll be glad to take Viv home, Dandy," offered BV. "I'd like her to stay a bit longer anyway."

"Oh, I don't want to leave Dandy alone though," replied Viv.

Dandy held up her hand, "No, I'll be all right, Viv. Just lend me your car keys. I'll see you later then."

"All right, Dandy, see you later at the house," Viv answered. She kissed Dandy and handed her the keys. She then turned to face BV. Although she was in a serious mood when her eyes met his, she melted inside.

* * * * * * * * * * * * * * * * * * * *

Chapter Twenty-Two
The Baron's Stunning Revelations

As soon as they were alone, BV told Viv that now was not the time to dwell on personal matters. *'Why not?'* Viv thought. BV appeared quite serious. He had to tell her something important, and no one else was to know about it. He hoped she would continue to care about him, even after hearing what was about to be revealed.

"Viv, what I'm about to tell you can't go any further, understand?" He held her firmly by her arms, whilst looking deeply into her eyes.

Sensing the urgency in his face, she exclaimed. "Oh my God, you're not bisexual, are you?"

"No! Of course not," he replied mildly irritated. "It's just that sometimes, well, I deal in drugs."

A feeling of disgust gripped Viv deep in the gut. She looked at BV and fumed, "You bastard, letting me fall for you and not even telling me this before! I thought you were special!"

"Wait, Viv, let me explain. It's not what you think."

"Oh, and what am I supposed to feel, relief?"

"Viv, now listen to me, please," he implored.

"Just how deeply are you involved in drugs then?

Do you stand around on street corners selling to little school kids, and that kind of stuff?" she asked.

"No, and sarcasm doesn't suit you. It's nothing like that at all. It's on a much bigger scale actually and very complicated. I can't tell you everything, but suffice it to say, I got involved with the wrong people. That's the way this heroin deal came about. I didn't want to get involved, but there was no choice at the time."

"Well, go on, tell me," she retorted, still annoyed.

"Alex Labelle worked with the suppliers. He was there to keep an eye on things and make sure the deal went down okay. One thing led to another, and I was in too deep. You don't know the people I'm dealing with here. They don't let you out, not alive at least."

"Why didn't you go to the police?" she asked incredulously.

Exasperated, he explained, "You don't realize, Viv. These people have connections everywhere, even with the police at the top. It's that big."

"What's that got to do with everything happening now, BV?"

"I believe someone at the party, could have mistaken Daniel for me, when he saw Daniel hit Alex. It's possible they used that chance to frame me by finishing Alex off. The problem is that innocent Daniel got framed instead! It's killing me since he had nothing to do with this, and I can't believe I've got my own brother into trouble."

BV looked miserably at the floor, then stared

straight into Viv's astonished eyes.

She found it difficult to digest his words. "That may be the case. But, BV, you involved with drugs, that's terrible! This is so difficult to accept. How can we possibly have any future?"

BV knew his problems were now affecting his chance at a relationship with Viv. He was very sorry about that as he had already fallen in love with her. But the main thing now was to get Daniel off the hook; also, how to go about it without exposing his own illicit involvement. Now that his brother was in serious trouble, he had to do something.

Viv saw the dejected look in his face. "You'll have to think of something," she said. "It may well be your fault that Daniel's in this trouble!" She yearned to put her arms around him and make it all better, somehow.

BV looked helplessly at the carpet which divided them like an ocean. "Don't waste energy on your opinion of me, Viv. Just try and think of a way to help Daniel."

"What if you question this girl, Annabel? You know her, don't you?"

"That would be too obvious, Viv. She wouldn't tell me anything different than what she's already told the police. But there's a chance she might tell you exactly what happened. Girls share a lot of secrets, I know!"

"You mean even if it was murder with the hat pin?" she asked, not believing Annabel would confess to such an act.

"Well, if she acts suspiciously, you could ask her if she has all her hat pins. If she looks alarmed, you can surmise that she's involved in the murder," BV said.

"Well if that happened, do I then go to the police and hope they'll question her and break her down? Do you have any idea why she might've done this?" Viv eyed him suspiciously. "Come on, tell me if you suspect anything!"

"Well, Annabel had a boyfriend, but I didn't see him at the barbeque. Her boyfriend's brother was involved to a greater extent than Alex was," he continued. "I'd previously offered him insurance. That's help, if he ever got caught. The usual way is through a good solicitor. As it turned out, the police picked him up and he called me for this help. I never kept my part of the bargain because he talked too much, and I didn't trust him. Safer for everyone with him on the inside."

"What happened to him, BV?"

"He went to prison. I wouldn't get involved, so he stayed there. I was able to cover up and decided that it was better that he do his time, to teach him a lesson and distance him from my activities. It was a relief to get him out of the picture." BV mused, adding "He is a very unsavoury character, even for a low-life. His name is Robert Scully."

"Do you think he's trying to get back at you through Annabel?"

"Perhaps he is. It's just an idea."

"Do I wait for the results of the new autopsy, or do I go around as soon as possible?" asked Viv.

"Sooner the better, thanks, Viv." He gave a disarming smile. "I'm really sorry for involving you in this mess, but what else can we do?"

"Dandy might find out eventually, but I'll try and keep this to myself, at least for the present," said Viv. "I'd have loved to share this with her, but I'll have to deal with it on my own."

"I appreciate your help, Viv. Especially after everything I've just said. I'll make it up to you, somehow."

Viv stood up. "If you'll just give me Annabel's address then? I'd like to go home now."

Nothing personal would come between them with all this going on, but she yearned for him to hold her, to help forget all this bad business. If only he had not told her about his sordid history and this drug involvement. BV handed her a piece of paper with some details on it.

"Well, I'm ready now," Viv announced and stood up.

"Oh yes, I forgot you didn't come on your own and Dandy took your car." He picked up his keys motioning for her to follow. Before opening the door for her, he turned and put his hands on her shoulders. "I wanted a meeting far different than this. Didn't you, Viv?"

Viv felt heady, so many emotions swam around her head. "Yes, I did too." she murmured. We'll have to put it on the back burner for now.

Suddenly his lips were on hers. Softly, but firmly, he kissed her. When he released her, she fell back a little. He had not lost his touch. If he had asked her back inside, she willingly would have gone. She seemed to ask that question with her eyes as BV responded, "Perhaps now is not the best time, Viv. Come on, I'll take you home."

With that remark, BV opened the car door for her and then climbed into the driver seat.

The drive back did not take long. Viv's car was still not present which meant Dandy had not returned from the office as yet. BV did not attempt to come in and Viv did not invite him. After the events of the day, she was glad to hear his car pull away. Or, was she? Something inside told her this man was trouble, but she sensed he was still worth it. After all, a man who made love the way he did, could not be all that bad, could he?

Viv was busy with her scheme when Henry telephoned. Instinctively, she knew it was Henry. *'Good heavens! With all the ordeals over the past few days, I've forgotten to get back to Henry and he's left so many messages!'* She guiltily returned his cheery greeting. She told him as much as possible, but omitted BV's involvement, the drugs and everything else really. She agreed that it might be a good idea for Henry to come around at some point that day so they could compare notes and decide on a course of action to save Daniel. He readily agreed, and she was relieved he did not badger her about *'their'* relationship or where it was headed.

Henry had thought a lot about Viv over the past several days. Perhaps it was true that absence made the heart grow fonder, but his mind was such a ball of confusion right now. Thinking straight was difficult. Life had become such a mess. This murder was a terrible thing, and Daniel's involvement, or lack of it, was another matter. As terrible as it was to admit, though, Henry did find the current course of events a welcome distraction from his otherwise mundane life, especially, not having to face up to any unwelcome decision Viv might have made.

Up to this point, his life had been complacent and ordinary. Every day predictable. All things had a time and a place, and everything went according to routine. He grew used to schedules and usually kept to them. But now? Good grief, Henry did not know what to think. Every day, every moment, was another life-changing experience for him.

There was Harriet the transgenderist, Daniel the murderer, Dandy in an emotional mess and of course, Viv. The love of his life at the moment had possibly fallen in love with two other men. The only constant part of his existence was his feelings for Viv and the fact that he loved her very much. The worse part being that he had not even been able to see her alone to find out how she felt about him, since the barbeque.

Henry arrived at Viv's house later that day. When she opened the door, he was extremely pleased to see her, but grew worried by the lack of response. She looked up briefly, then glanced into the house and motioned him to come in. He dreaded the question but had to ask, "Are you going to say goodbye to me now, Viv?"

"Certainly not, Henry! But I can't really think about us right now. Let's not talk about that yet, okay? There's too much going on at the moment!"

"Oh yes, all this trouble with Daniel. It must be hurting you terribly, not to mention Dandy!" Henry said, looking concerned.

"Oh, you fathead!" she said and hugged him. "So much has changed. There are different reasons for different things, and I don't know which ones to tell you about." Henry was a bit stunned by her remarks, but her affection, was certainly welcome. It made him feel optimistic.

Viv still felt safe with Henry. She had known him before her life had changed so drastically. Before she became involved with a drug baron and a murder!

They sat down on the sofa and Henry placed his big arm around her shoulder. *'This is how it should be,'* she thought, *'little wifey, no worries. Big 'ol Henry to take care of things!'* She looked up into his kind face. She cared about him a great deal, but still needed BV and felt so worried about Daniel! *'Is it possible to love two men at once, each for his own different qualities?'* She wondered. At least, Daniel was out of the equation now.

Viv listened to Henry, as he explained all that had happened between him and Harriet. He omitted the events which took place in the art studio. After all, it was pointless to mention that right now, if ever. Nothing really happened and besides, it might hurt Viv. It certainly would damage any friendship that could ensue between her and Harriet. He anxiously looked forward to both of them meeting and sharing the friendship.

Viv was intrigued. "I should be jealous Henry, but I'm not exactly an example of *'proper'* behaviour myself." She laughed. "Harriet sounds wonderful. Why don't you invite her over and the two of you come around here tonight for drinks? Dandy and I could do with the company. We need to take our minds off everything that's going on right now."

Henry was not sure if it was a good idea to let them meet each other just yet. He knew they would get on, but wanted Viv all to himself. He went ahead and telephoned Harriet after asking Viv's permission to use her phone. Harriet picked up and said she would be very pleased to come around. She said there was no need to fetch her as she could head over right now, if that was okay.

Henry asked Viv if it was alright with her. She replied it was fine and they could all have a meal. No sooner had she told him so, when they heard a key at the front door and Dandy walked in.

"What a nightmare, will all of this ever end?" she asked in an exasperated manner throwing herself into an armchair. "I've brought your car back now Viv, but earlier when I used mine, had to leave it at the shops and get a cab back. The darn thing wouldn't start." Henry told her that after they had eaten, he'd take her to the car and get it started.

"Thank you so much! It's times like these that a woman needs a good man around. I need Daniel," she said sadly.

After a half hour or so, a car pulled up in the driveway. Henry peeked out the curtain and saw Harriet. She exited her car and approached the house. When Viv opened the door, she was greeted by a cheerful young woman, dressed in a burgundy, tight-fitting skirt with pearly grey blouse and high heels.

"Hi! You must be Viv, I've heard so many good things about you. I'm Harriet."

* *

Chapter Twenty-Three
Viv and Harriet Become Detectives

Viv looked at the smiling, feminine Harriet in quiet amazement, as she stepped into the house.

"Welcome to my home, Harriet. It's great to meet you too," she said, giving her a big smile. Harriet was then introduced to Dandy. Henry approached and planted a kiss on her cheek, ending it with a hug.

'Interesting,' thought Viv, *'but why the hug, as well as a kiss on the cheek?'* She felt a pang of jealousy which surprised her.

It was not long before they were all immersed in deep conversation. The atmosphere was easy and the talk revolved around Daniel's plight. Harriet was brought up to date on the latest news. Once again she reiterated that the name, 'Alex Labelle,' sounded familiar, although she could not place it.

Viv did not mention anything about BV's conversation or his involvement in drugs. However, she felt the need to confide in Harriet, who seemed to know, Alex Labelle, the murdered man. Perhaps her memory could be jogged.

The opportunity arose when Harriet offered to wash up the tea things with Viv. She felt pleased that Harriet was so likeable and fun, but not as much as it pleased Henry who could not stop smiling. Viv could not help but think Henry would be much better off loving Harriet, than her. It was almost impossible to believe Harriet had ever been a man. Her face was smooth, no sign of shaved-off hairs. Her hands were a normal woman's size and also hairless. Even her feet were in proportion, they certainly did not look big, Viv noticed, peeping at them over the tea cloth she was using to dry the dishes.

Harriet noticed and laughed aloud. I know what you're thinking Viv! You were wondering if I had feet like a man's!" She laughed again. "I am lucky in that way, my bone structure is small!"

"I'm sorry Harriet, I didn't mean to be so impolite, but I did wonder." She grinned sheepishly, having been caught out.

"No harm done," she replied. "You were bound to be curious and I'm happy to answer any questions you might have."

"Thanks Harriet, I probably will have some questions later, as I've never met a transgendered person before." Viv replied. "The question I'd like to ask now is can you try to remember anything about Alex Labelle?"

"I've been trying to, Viv, but I just can't! Wait, I remember now. I have a friend called Ruby, and we bumped into Alex and some of his friends at a party. Yes, that's right. He was such a loathsome character. There was some kind of informal exchange and he introduced me to a girl and her boyfriend. They tried to sell me some dope. The girl's name, Annabel, has just popped into my head."

Viv wanted to know more about this *'boyfriend'* of Annabel's. Perhaps he had been at the barbeque, too, possibly in costume and involved somehow. Unfortunately, Harriet could not remember his name, and her description of him could have been of anyone. Jeans, t-shirt, training shoes, average looks.

"Oh wait," she exclaimed. "Yeah, he said *'cool it'* a lot."

That really struck a note. Viv remembered hearing that comment at the barbeque. She first heard it when Alex poured the punch for her and Dandy. Then again, in the orchard when she half-carried Dandy out after something odd occurred. A strange feeling shot through her. Viv remembered Dandy's excitement when she helped her to dress. She forced her mind back to being a detective again.

"Do you know where these people hang out, Harriet? A particular pub, club? Something like that?" Viv asked.

Harriet became alarmed. "You don't plan to speak to them, do you? That could be very dangerous!"

"I know it could be, but what else can I do? I must help BV as well as Daniel!" She looked steadily at Harriet, and then decided to share the secret with her. "Promise to keep this quiet. I've given my word for silence, but I need to share this with someone before it drives me mad. It's about BV!"

"Oh, I do know a little about that situation with Henry hoping that you would not fall for the baron. He was so worried about how you'd feel after meeting him."

"It isn't about that Harriet, well not at this moment. I have yet to find out what is going to happen there." Viv did not feel annoyed that Henry had confided in Harriet and welcomed this woman's honesty.

"I think I understand. You haven't known the Baron for long enough yet to make a decision as to who you prefer to be with. Am I correct?" asked Harriet.

"You have that right, but I haven't had time to be concerned about relationships at all, now that all this trouble has gone down." Viv did not want Harriet to know about the intimacy shared or the depth of her feelings for BV. She could not share that. "I have a secret about BV's possible involvement in Daniel's arrest. It's not something I can share with Dandy, or Henry. BV asked me to keep it to myself, but I need to discuss it with someone I can trust, to help me work out how I can use the information to get Daniel out of prison. He wouldn't have been in that trouble if it wasn't for me going there with them!"

Harriet felt honoured that Viv could confide in her. "Thank you, Viv," she replied. "I will help in any way I can and also keep it a secret with you."

Viv pulled out a kitchen chair and sat down. Harriet did the same and then called out to Dandy and Henry in the front room, "We're bringing out coffee in a minute."

Henry came in to say that he was taking Dandy to pick up her car, and they could have their coffee when they got back. He kissed Viv on the lips before leaving, giving Harriet a quick wave. Viv felt pleased they were still that close, she needed it.

"Bye Dandy," Viv called out. "We should be finished with the dishes by the time you both get back."

Dandy called back, "Okay!" and the front door closed behind them.

Henry assumed that Viv and Harriet wanted time to get acquainted and feel out how much each of them was involved with Henry. He also thought it was the best opportunity for Viv to get to know Harriet. It would be great if the two could be friends. Neither Dandy, nor Henry realized that a plot was about to be hatched in the kitchen.

* * * * * * * * * * * * * * * * * * * *

Chapter Twenty-Four
Viv and Dandy Become Closer

That night, after all her visitors had gone, Viv lay in her bed wondering how much Harriet really meant to Henry. She could be a real comfort to him, easing the blow, if it did not work out the way Henry hoped and BV were the chosen partner. Anyway, who could help but like Harriet? She was kind enough to become involved in Daniel's trouble without even knowing him. Viv had to admit she still had feelings for Henry and would continue the relationship, if BV turned out not to be worthy company.

Viv had arranged a meeting with Harriet the following evening. Henry was disappointed he was still not able to see Viv alone. Plenty of time for that, she assured him. Viv had insisted it was important she see Harriet alone. Although she did not give him a reason, Henry did not push her to tell him. He supposed she would discuss everything with him later, when she was able to.

Viv felt restless and was unable to drop off to sleep for thinking about all her new friends. There was Daniel wasting away in prison, Harriet, sweet Harriet, Henry her loyal friend and Dandy, who had already become like a sister to her. When she thought of BV, her stomach lurched. It always did.

Viv often thought of the first time they made love. Even with being 'out of it', she remembered the emotions vividly and had already fallen for BV, although realising that lust had a great deal to do with it.

Suddenly, a warm, naked body climbed in bed and an arm went over hers.

"I hope you don't mind, Viv. I just don't want to be alone tonight."

"Dandy!" she exclaimed. "Are you okay?" Dandy's body trembled, so Viv moved closer to share her body warmth. "It's all right Dandy, I understand you feel lost without Daniel."

They snuggled up into a comfortable position with each other's arms wrapped around one other. Viv leaned forward and gave Dandy a kiss on the cheek. She turned so that it landed on her lips.

"I just feel so scared for Daniel," Dandy cried. "What will happen to him in prison? What can happen? He's so vulnerable in there, I can't bear it! When I spoke with him on the phone earlier today, he was crying and telling me that something terrible had happened, but he couldn't speak about it. He just kept sobbing! Viv! Daniel is the strongest character I know. If he can't cope, well, I'm afraid for him."

"Why didn't you tell me this before? What a terrible thing to keep to yourself!" Viv was horrified to think she had not noticed Dandy had been much quieter than normal, even with all the company earlier. She pulled Dandy's face around so she could put her cheek against hers. When she did, their lips touched.

Dandy gave Viv a quick, soft kiss on the lips and said, "Thank you for being with me at this terrible time."

Viv was about to reply when she felt the soft, full lips over hers again kissing with real feeling. It felt uncomfortable, but she did not want to move away in case it humiliated Dandy. Beside that, she wanted to try to show her love in this way if Dandy needed it. Their bodies pressed harder against each other. Viv felt a hand begin to fondle her full breasts, and fingertips flicking her hardening nipples.

"I'm sorry!" Dandy exclaimed. "I don't know what's got into me, except that I miss Daniel's loving so much."

"I think I understand, but I've never done this with a woman and don't know if I can." Viv could hardly believe this conversation was happening.

"Nor have I been with a woman before Viv, but I need this comfort if you are willing?" Dandy was also surprised that she was reacting this way to Viv, but it felt natural and comforting somehow.

They continued to cuddle and Viv began to relax. It was difficult to believe she could enjoy a woman's touch, but it felt good. Tingles went through her body from head to toes, as she imagined it was BV making love to her. Viv also imagined Daniel with this woman, his wife, enjoying her this same way. The two women began to passionately kiss and fondle each other with an excitement that had been pent up for much too long.

Dandy murmured, "I felt something about you that first day you came into the office. I never felt this way about a woman before." Her hand was now between Viv's legs. It touched and stroked gently. Dandy moved under the covers and kissed up the insides of Viv's thighs making her tremble. Both of their needs grew stronger and whilst they used fingers and lips on one another, all problems had left their minds. It was exquisite for both of them, but Viv missed the fleshy rod of a man and could not imagine becoming satisfied this way. The quickness of Dandy's fingers started to bring her to an orgasm. It was a strong, long one, and only once did she think of BV. As they lay side by side holding onto each other, Viv realized what she must do next. She got up from the bed and went to the dresser drawer. She chose a personal massager from her collection.

As Viv glanced at Dandy, she could see the pleasure in her eyes. Dandy lay back and waited, as Viv prepared to do what she surmised experienced lesbians must do, and worked with Dandy's body language to give her the time of her life. Afterwards they lay contented, turned onto their sides with Viv snuggling into the arch of Dandy's back, inhaling the fragrance of her long hair. They both lay intertwined, exhausted, totally relaxed and fell deeply asleep.

* *

Chapter Twenty-Five
Back to the Orchard

Late, the next afternoon Viv woke up to the sound of the telephone ringing. It was Dandy, calling from the agency. She had woken early in the morning, dressed quickly and left, not wanting to disturb Viv. She had just spoken with Mr. Lane who said the second autopsy had been completed. The coroner shaved Alex's head and found a line of broken capillaries that led from the embolism in his brain to a spot on the surface of the scalp. There was now a definite possibility of a hat-pin murder.

Dandy became very excited. "This means the girl did murder Alex. At least, it proves Daniel had nothing to do with the death." She calmed down and asked, "How on earth can we prove it was the girl?"

Viv had some ideas and if she was lucky tonight, it could all be over soon. She told Dandy it could be a late evening, so not to wait up for her. The telephone call was short as Dandy was tending to a client, but Dandy had told her thanks for the 'lovely' night.

* *

Chapter Twenty-Six
The Interrogation

Before long, Viv was in her car, on the way to meet Harriet in 'The Three Bells.' This was the pub where the 'Alex' people liked to frequent. Viv had already called BV and told him the news about the coroner's report as well as where Harriet and she planned to go tonight, just in case something went wrong. Only now, Viv began to worry about how it would all go down. She did not relish the thought of being amongst such deviant people. She went over the plan in her head many times hoping it would work without too much ad-libbing. At that moment, Harriet came around the corner and met Viv at the door. They stayed outside whilst Viv told her about the autopsy.

"Right," said Harriet, "here goes!" They walked in and ordered their drinks at the bar. Luck was on their side. Harriet recognized Annabel, but no one else with her seemed familiar.

They found seats near the girl and started to chat to each other about mundane events. Appearing to do so by accident, Harriet looked straight at Annabel and spoke to her. "I remember you, I talked to you at a party not too long ago. How are you, do you remember me?"

Annabel stared at Harriet, trying to place her.

Suddenly, she smiled and came over to the empty seat at their table.

"Hello," she beamed. "Yes, I remember you, great to see you again!"

'*She's hoping I want to buy some dope*,' thought Harriet.

Annabel now recognized Viv. "I saw you at the Baron's barbeque, didn't I?"

"That's possible, but I don't remember you, I'm afraid," said Viv honestly. The hat Annabel had worn before must have covered quite a bit of her face, or at least left it unrecognisable in a shadow.

"Oh, yes," Annabel continued. "I was there all right. Oh, and that horrible death. Did you know him? Alex Labelle?" Turning to Harriet she said, "You may remember him, he was at the party we were at, a real poseur!"

"Hmm, I vaguely recall an Alex," said Harriet, as she tried to look thoughtful.

"I've been questioned by the police because I'd been standing in the area of the murder!" Annabel said.

She looked almost pleased with herself. All went well so far, and they did not expect information to be volunteered so easily. They slyly looked at each other. It seemed impossible that a guilty person would act the way Annabel did.

"Well, actually, I heard a girl was the last to see him alive. Were you that girl?" Viv asked as naturally as possible.

"Seems so!" Annabel replied. "I didn't like him much, but not enough to want him dead. That's something else. He annoyed everyone, but for someone to hate him enough to kill him, that's just something else." She appeared genuine.

Viv and Harriet exchanged glances. Viv continued, "When the police questioned us, they thought you wanted dope in return for sex from Alex!" It was a shot in the dark, but it was part of the plan.

"How dare they!" she retorted. "I have a boyfriend and anyway I don't act like that!" She became upset.

"Is your boyfriend here?" asked Harriet, glancing around. "I didn't see anyone with you."

"No," Annabel replied quietly and sadly. She looked very young now. "He doesn't take me out much anymore. He may have found someone else."

Viv and Harriet both felt sorry for Annabel, but there was more work to do. They continued with their questioning, whilst Annabel's impatient friends called out for her to join them again.

"A hat-pin was found near the body," Viv ventured. "Were you wearing a hat with a hat-pin?"

"Yes, I was," she replied. Annabel did not know why a hat pin was so important, but she soon found out.

"The autopsy report today said that death was caused by a puncture from a hat pin," Viv said slowly.

Annabel's eyes grew huge with horror. She was sensible enough to keep her voice down. "They might suspect me of the murder! Do they think the hat pin is mine?"

Cautiously, Viv replied that she did not know, but they would probably find out soon.

Annabel began to tremble and muttered something about 'David.' They could not quite get the last name as she was so upset, but it sounded like 'Scully.' Harriet told Viv it was best to get the girl out of the pub to talk further, if possible. It also might sober her up a bit, make her think more clearly. Her friends were absorbed in their conversations again, so Annabel was asked if she minded talking outside the pub. Annabel agreed, but swayed, so Viv steadied her as they walked a short way to a bench. The questioning resumed when they sat on the seat.

"Murdered with a hat pin, maybe my hat pin, how horrible!" The girl was too intent on her thoughts to hear what Harriet and Viv were now saying to her.

Harriet started to believe the girl innocent, and repeated her question. "Do you think there is a possibility someone wanted it to look as if you murdered Alex, by dropping the hat pin there after the deed was done?" This remark had the desired effect.

"Could be!" Annabel's face puckered with effort as she thought hard. "He must have done it! David! He was messing around with my hat earlier!"

"David, is that your boyfriend?" asked Viv. "David Scully? Was he at the barbeque?"

"Yes," she replied. "I didn't know he was coming. He was wearing a wig and false beard. People like to dress weird for BV's parties."

Viv thought more along the lines that David did not want BV to know of his presence at the party.

"Oh, what shall I do?" wailed Annabel. "What a mess!"

Viv raised her eyebrows and gave Harriet a look to say, *'Quite good so far, but how do we prove who did what?'*

Annabel sobered up fast and began to cry. Harriet offered to have Annabel over to her house for the night if necessary, to help her get over this shock. Annabel agreed as she hoped they would help her sort out this bad situation.

Annabel travelled with Harriet, whilst Viv followed. It did not take long for them to arrive. Harriet's home looked cosy and welcoming. Viv thought the paintings were particularly good, just as Henry told her, but she said nothing, the girl was the priority. Harriet passed them a brandy each. She gave Annabel a double but mixed lemonade in with their single shot.

They were soon to find out that Annabel was only nineteen, Scully being her first lover. He had also got her hooked on cocaine! She talked freely now the brandy had loosened her tongue. Eventually, they learned more about what happened that fateful evening.

David had come up with the idea for Annabel to lure Alex into the orchard so he could then take over and talk him into trying to persuade BV, using blackmail to help get his brother out of jail. He intended using threats of going to the police about BV's drug involvement. Unless BV co-operated and came through with the 'insurance' as he had promised, using his own high-powered barrister to free Robert.

Harriet asked what happened next with Alex and what was said.

Annabel looked embarrassed. "Well, I never got to ask Alex anything, although I had started up a conversation with him. David was nearby and he motioned me away just as I was going to say what I had been told to. Maybe he thought I wouldn't do it properly. I went back to join the party."

"So, David could have thought he'd approach Alex himself," Harriet said, with obvious ideas going through her head.

Harriet and Viv looked at each other once again, both with raised eyebrows.

They realized that Scully might have changed his plan possibly deciding to murder Alex and set BV up for the crime, after seeing who he *'thought'* was BV, hitting Alex. They all went quiet considering this point, although Annabel did not seem capable of taking much of it in.

"Did Scully, er, David, stay in the orchard after you left?" asked Viv.

"Yes, I waited for him to come and find me, but he was gone for ages. I don't know if he actually spoke to Alex. We didn't see each other again until quite a while after. I suspected he'd found a girl to talk to. He usually did."

'Poor girl,' Viv thought. *'I'm sure she's quite innocent!'* She glanced at Harriet who appeared to be thinking the same thing. *'But, perhaps the girl was a good actress and just wanted to pin the blame on her boyfriend.'* That had to be a consideration.

"When was he messing around with your hat?" asked Harriet. "Before you went to speak with Alex?" Viv asked. Abigail's eyes looked from Viv to Harriet as she answered the questions fired at her. It looked as if she were watching a tennis match.

"It was when we were both by the pig roast, that he kept poking my hat with his finger and even threw it in the air! I was really annoyed, but he just laughed and did it several more times!"

"He could have taken the hat pin then," stated Viv.

Annabel looked puzzled. "There's no reason why he should have set me up. If the police arrested me, I could tell them everything like I've told you and he'd be in trouble!"

"Possibly not," said Harriet kindly. "If David was disguised, how could you prove he was there? No one else could verify your story."

'That's right,' thought Viv. BV had told her Annabel's boyfriend was not present. It looked bad for Annabel, who looked extremely miserable.

"Harriet," Viv said. "I think the murderer accidentally dropped the hat-pin after the dastardly deed. Someone may have disturbed him, and he was not able to search for it, or if he did, he never found it."

"After all," continued Viv, "he wouldn't want to leave any clues which might lead to Annabel, as that could lead to him eventually. But why would he kill Alex, when he needed him to make the blackmailing deal with BV to get his brother Robert out?"

"Yes," agreed Harriet. "But, it doesn't make sense for David to change his plan. Killing Alex and setting BV up would not get his brother out of jail."

"But he could have suddenly wanted revenge!" Viv replied. "The blackmail might not have worked as he would have implicated himself if he went to the police with drug information on BV, who would be sure to drag him into it as much as he could. If it was BV he was setting up, he couldn't have known Daniel would get involved instead!"

"I'm just wondering why David didn't think Daniel, the twin, might be the one, instead of BV, who punched Alex? With that being the case, he would not be able to set BV up," Harriet said.

"I know through Dandy, that Daniel did not mix with BV's friends, and he would have had no reason to talk to Alex, let alone get mad at him!" replied Viv. David could not have known that Daniel was angry with Alex over not bringing me into the house when he was told to. So, he surmised it could only have been due to 'business,' that BV ended up punching Alex, and so David or the murderer, made sure that was the last time Alex was seen alive."

"What shall I do?" Annabel asked in a pitiful voice.

"I suggest we take you home and you get some sleep. In the morning, go straight to the police," said Harriet. "It's best you say nothing about us, or they'll think you only went to them because we found out. That will not look good for you. By the way, where do you live, Annabel?"

"Just a few streets away from here," was her quiet response.

"I'll drive her back," suggested Viv. "It's on my

way!" Immediately, she realized her mistake. How would she know which street was being spoken about? BV had given her the address previously and she had nearly let the cat out of the bag. Viv glanced at Annabel, but luckily, she was too upset to notice.

Harriet would have offered to drive, but she hoped Viv might find out something else on their way back, as she had run out of questions and wanted to think about all the information. Annabel thanked each of them for all their trouble. Viv said she would phone Harriet later that night, after they both had a chance to think.

Out on the road, Annabel stayed lost in thought and Viv could not think of anything of importance to say, so they drove in silence until, 'The Three Bells,' was in sight, when Annabel spoke, gesturing toward the pub.

"If you don't mind Viv, I would rather join my friends," she said. "They might still be in there and will take me home."

Viv slowed down and stopped the car. "If you prefer it, then of course, but don't mention anything about our conversation; it may not be safe and you don't know who will find out. Don't forget to go to the police with your information, or they'll pay you a visit and it will be far worse for you." Viv hoped Annabel could appreciate the seriousness of this comment, but her response was only to nod in agreement.

"You know where Harriet lives and if you want further help, I'll give you my number. "

Annabel smiled wanly. "Thank you ever so much."

Viv reached into her pocket for a pen. All she had was a business card for the Dandy Lyons Dating Agency. She wrote her own number on the back of it.

"Here, Annabel, take this card and if you need to talk, just call me. Don't let anyone see this, for your sake. Now promise me?"

"Okay, Viv, thanks!" With that, Annabel gave her a hug, thanked her again and then disappeared into the pub.

Viv was not in the mood to drive home yet, so she drove to see Harriet instead. Back there, she told Harriet what occurred.

"She wanted her friends to take her home," Viv told her.

"Did you find out anything?" asked Harriet.

"No, nothing more, the poor thing had quite a shock. Harriet, we've got to hope the police can make this David Scully confess.

"Yes, I felt she was telling the truth too!"

They talked on and Viv had the distinct impression that Harriet did not like BV. Of course, no mention had been made about their session at the den. There was only mention of BV carrying her into the house after the altercation with Alex. Viv did not want it to get back to Henry, which it might, even by accident. Not that she could imagine an ounce of spite in Harriet, who she noticed, had quite an amount of admiration for Henry. She did not want to ask how involved Harriet was with him. Instead they discussed the dating agency. Viv suggested Harriet try it and laughingly said, it could be the start of a very hectic life.

Harriet thought for a minute then sadly said, "It's difficult to have relationships. It would only work on a totally honest level and that frightens most men, if not all of them."

Viv thought Harriet probably told Henry almost straight away about her gender change and he would have accepted it due to his kind nature. She then thought that if not for her being in the way, Henry and Harriet might get on very well indeed. *'She must know that and yet she doesn't dislike me.'* Viv felt an odd kind of guilt. After all, not only had she already fallen for another, but it was far easier for her to find a man to fall in love with.

No, that was not quite true, or she would not have gone to the dating agency in the first place. It was not that easy to come across men like Henry either! BV was incredible, but Henry was absolutely lovable and security personified.

Harriet waited for a response to what she had just asked.

"Oh, sorry!" Viv said. "I was miles away!"

"Who were you thinking of? Henry, BV, Daniel or all three?" Harriet asked with a smile.

Viv was very surprised by the mention of Daniel, then she remembered telling Harriet about her first meeting with him.

Viv replied with a question. "What happens when you love two men at once?"

"That sounds very greedy to me," Harriet laughed. "And lucky!"

"It's not really like that. Two are available, well only

one is really, because the other one is involved in drugs, but he's very special too."

"I wouldn't want anyone who's involved in drugs. Who knows what else he might be covering?" questioned Harriet.

"I don't know to what extent, but I find it difficult to believe that BV is as bad as some of them. Trouble is I'm already physically involved!" Viv did not mean to admit this and felt horrified.

There were a few seconds silence, before Harriet spoke. "Whatever you do, don't let Henry know that, especially not until you've made a decision. Even then, if you choose Henry, it is far kinder for him never to know what you just told me. I believe when this murder thing is cleared up, you'll realize that Henry is the one for you. I can tell you have a great respect for him, so the rest will happen. I know he's totally besotted by you, Viv!" These last words obviously hurt Harriet, but she was still kind enough to say them.

Viv felt sad for her again as she said, "I wish you were not so lonely, you don't deserve to be!"

"Don't you worry about me, Viv, I've found some lovely new friends and I'm much happier!"

Viv felt very warm towards Harriet, who had already won a place in her heart. She had every reason to be bitter about life, but was far from it.

"Well," said Harriet, "It's time you drove home. You did remember to give Dandy a spare key didn't you?"

"Oh, yes. Don't worry, she'll probably be in bed by the time I get back. Hope she hasn't taken all the covers. I mean…"

"That sounded as if she's in the same bed as you!" Harriet cut in.

Viv's face burned. Now that her secret was out, she decided to share the rest of it with Harriet, leaving out a few details here and there.

"Dandy needed a little extra comforting whilst Daniel's away." She tried to make it sound as natural as possible.

Harriet grinned. "Viv, you *are* far too greedy, but 'tiz nobody's bizness' 'cept yours! My lips are sealed!"

Viv smiled helplessly, what could she say?

They hugged each other on the doorstep and said they would be in contact the next day.

* *

Chapter Twenty-Seven
Harriet Takes on More than She Can Handle

Harriet's mind raced. There were too many things to sort through and so many revelations were made tonight, more than were necessary. Many new questions had come up too. Annabel certainly shed a great deal of light on what happened that fateful evening in the orchard, but could she be trusted? After all, her boyfriend, David Scully, might have murdered Alex Labelle. He had the opportunity to do so, but why? And how much could he have over BV, to be able to blackmail him? What connected the two men? How had someone as young and seemingly innocent as Annabel, ever become involved with someone as low as Scully in the first place?

Harriet deliberately kept her mind off the information gleaned regarding Viv's private life and knew that snap judgements were not to be made. Things happen, even to the most moral people. She ought to know. Just as she would never divulge what happened between her and Henry, she would keep quiet about Viv's indulgences and hoped that it would work out well for everyone.

Harriet was in the midst of thinking through various scenarios when she heard a knock at the front door. *'It must be Viv,'* Harriet thought. *'She must have forgotten to tell me something.'* But, when she turned on the porch light and looked outside, no one was there. It seemed as if children were messing about. Harriet went into the kitchen to make a cup of tea before turning in for bed, when she heard another knock on the door. Again, she opened it to find no-one there. She walked outside to the curb, looking up and down.

"Who's there," she shouted, "Damn pranksters!" and went back into the house.

Harriet had barely stepped back inside, when the sound of footsteps rushed up behind her. Suddenly, a terrific shove to her back sent her sprawling across the floor. The surprise, combined with the abrupt hit to the back, momentarily knocked the wind out of her. When she looked up, there was a tall, dirty-looking man standing inside the doorway. He glared at her, then closed the door behind him and stepped closer.

Harriet did not shout out, she was too shocked, but soon regained her composure as much as possible under the circumstances. Then, she grew angry at this humiliating treatment. It was not something that she accepted passively. When angry, she grew stronger. All of the years growing up teased about being an effeminate boy taught her to fight and take care of herself. She became well-schooled in self-defence and could hold her own against almost anyone.

"Who the hell are you?" she demanded picking herself off the floor to face the unkempt man.

"Shut your freakin' mouth bitch!" he growled, advancing toward her menacingly. "Who the hell do you think you are, putting lies into people's heads?" He spat, the drool foaming down his stubbled chin.

When he came closer, Harriet smelled the strong scent of whiskey on his breath. Suddenly, with a shock, she realized who it was standing before her. It was Scully!

"I was at the pub tonight. Saw you an' your friend talking to Annabel," he growled. "Overheard some of what you were sayin'. Thought I'd follow you here an' get the story for myself."

Harriet could only stare in disbelief. He was indeed an obnoxious, nasty man and a violent one at that. It made her even angrier.

"Get out!" she shouted. "Or I'll call the police! I'm warning you for the last time! I don't want you in here!"

"Why not?" he leered. "Exactly what do you think you're gonna do about it? I noticed you and your friend didn't mind speakin' to little Annabel earlier now did you? I'm going to enjoy takin' care of you three and makin' sure none of you speak to anyone, ever again."

"You better not harm Annabel, you, you dirty bastard!" She almost said *dirty murderer,* but thought better of it, for the moment at least.

Scully rushed at her and Harriet prepared for the swing of his fist. She ducked making his arm sail over her head, as she punched him hard in the solar plexus. It would have been somewhere else if he had been in a different position.

It was a well-placed punch and he momentarily

doubled up, only to come back at her again. His face twisted with surprise and rage. He lunged at her, but she sidestepped his advance. He grabbed her blouse, tearing it and gave her a hard, unexpected back-handed punch across her face.

Scully's blow sent Harriet crashing against the credenza. She saw stars as she fell to the floor. Household items scattered everywhere. A glass vase rolled up along her side, which she picked up to defend herself against his onslaught. When Scully reached down to grab her, she slammed the vase into his nose with all her strength. He staggered backwards and held his bleeding nose.

"What you doin' bitch? You tryin' to break my freakin' nose?" Skully gurgled through the blood that poured from his face and mouth.

Somewhat dazed, but aware of the opportunity to make her move, Harriet crawled to the fireplace and grabbed a poker. She raised it, holding tightly with both hands.

"I know you killed Alex," she shouted. "The police are looking for you right now. They know what you did," she lied, but hoped it would have the desired effect.

Scully smirked, with a lop-sided grin as though he did not believe her. That look was enough to trigger more anger in her, and with renewed strength, she rose to her feet.

Scully advanced on her. "You're a liar! I've got friends in the police. Nobody's lookin' for me right now, thanks to that fool, Lyons, they've got locked up. Couldn't 'ave been more perfect."

"So you did murder Labelle?" Harriet replied, astonished. Admittance to the crime she did not expect and this was very close.

"But, you'll never 'ave the chance to tell anyone. Enough of these games, freakin' bitch. Now you die," he snarled.

"Get out you scum! Get out of my house you dirty, filthy murdering scum! And, don't you *EVER* call me bitch!"

The demeaning look he gave, enraged Harriet further. She swung the poker around and clocked him hard along the side of his head. He turned to deflect the blow, but was only partially successful.

Pieces of his hair, skin and blood, sprayed against the living room wall. Scully staggered, momentarily losing his balance. He cried out in pain and fell to his knees. Harriet lost her balance, stumbled backwards, and hit her head on the hearth. Dazed, but realising the immense danger if she stayed down, managed to get to her feet.

Scully staggered to his, with one hand holding his bleeding, injured head. He held up his hand and grimacing from the pain said, "Hold on! Take it easy, you crazy bitch! "Cool it! You hear me? You hear what I'm sayin'? Are you listenin' to me? Cool it bitch!"

Harriet advanced toward him, poker in hand, rage in her eyes. She raised the poker over her right shoulder preparing to deliver the hardest blow yet, when a strange feeling came over her. The sight of this man in his weakened state, made her feel compassion.

Harriet hesitated in her assault on the bloody man and for an instant, dropped her guard and lowered the poker. When she did so, Scully staggered toward the door, hand still holding his head.

He stood unsteadily, as he slurred at Harriet, "You're crazy bitch! You 'aven't seen the last of me. I'll get you! You'll never know when or where, but I'll get you! Hear what I'm saying?"

When Harriet did not raise the poker, Scully took the opportunity to make his escape. He fumbled with the front door and then bolted out as quickly as his damaged body could manage to carry him. Obviously, he had not been prepared for her fury and was lucky to escape with his life, if not quite intact.

Harriet regained some composure and ran to the door, calling out after him, "If we ever meet up again you filthy bastard, you're a dead man! That I promise you! Do you hear me? You're a dead man, Scully. I promise you that! Mark my words Scully! Mark my words! I promise you'll be a dead man the next time we meet!"

With those words uttered, Harriet slammed the door shut, immediately falling down dazed. '*I should have killed him,*' she thought. '*What was I thinking? Maybe I should call the police?*' But, if she did, they might need to know more than she was able to tell of the events that led up to what had just happened. She was in a very difficult position. Her head hurt, maybe needed attention, but she felt too weak to do anything about it, except to lie there for a short while.

No, the police would not help matters, at least not just yet. She had to keep Viv's secret about BV's involvement which meant not relating information that would make sense of why this man tried to kill her. She could not risk letting Viv's secret out, or it would implicate BV. But, what if something terrible happened to Annabel? Scully was a very disturbed man and capable of anything, even murder. It seemed now, that he *was* the murderer.

Harriet glanced at her watch trying to think of what to do next. She was a bundle of nerves; it was difficult for her to think straight. Not only that, her head was swimming furiously. She wondered why she felt dizzy and remembered her fall onto the hearth. When she touched the part that ached, her hand came away with blood, and now it had begun to trickle down her face. She picked up the cell-phone and tried to find Viv's phone number, but could not focus well enough to see it. At least she had gone home safely and Dandy was there as well. Best to tell Viv what just happened, tomorrow.

Harriet regained her composure only for a moment, but the room began to whirl around even faster. Harriet panicked, as she attempted to grab the back of a chair to keep her balance. *I must have hurt my head more than I imagined.* Before she could finish her thoughts, everything went dark.

* * * * * * * * * * * * * * * * * * * *

Chapter Twenty-Eight
Another Murder Occurs

A few hours later, Harriet woke up on the living room floor. She controlled her feeling of nausea to sit up and then to slowly stand, clutching the chair for support. The recollection of the earlier fight came back as she noticed the blood spattered wall. With one hand on her throbbing head, she used the other hand to lean on furniture to aid her unsteady walk to the phone.

Harriet's first thoughts were to call Viv, although with the wounds Scully had suffered tonight, she knew he would not have felt like going on to break into Viv's house. Beside that, Dandy was there, so Scully would have two irate women to contend with. Harriet walked unsteadily to a side table and picked up her cell phone.

The decision to phone or not, was made for her, as her eyes could not focus enough to see any numbers. "Good grief, what a night!" she said aloud. Harriet still felt woozy but managed to stumble to her bed, where she collapsed on top of the covers and gradually drifted off to sleep.

When Harriet woke in the morning, she had a stinker of a headache, so took some strong painkillers and lay back down to allow them to work quicker. Harriet's first thoughts were for Annabel's safety and where Scully had gone after the attack on her. He might have needed hospital treatment. Harriet could not waste time waiting for the pills to work, so she picked up the telephone to call Viv.

Several tries to the home and cell phone were unsuccessful. Thinking Viv could have been in the shower, Harriet decided it best to drive over to her house as quickly as possible. It was painful taking her shower, soaping her body and hair over the bumps and bruises, which were starting to show deep mauve colours. Drying herself with the towel pumped the blood to her head, but the headache pain had started to lessen.

Harriet dressed as hurriedly as her aching head allowed and on combing her hair she yelped. The comb had gone over a sore lump on her scalp. Then she looked closely in the mirror to fix her make up. She was most surprised to see the beginnings of a black eye staring back! "Damn!" she said, and digging out some old make-up from a drawer, she eventually found some eye shadows that matched the purplish colouring. The mauve and green shadows would do for later, when the bruise began to come out. Very skilfully, she applied the make-up to the normal eye and touched up the injured eyelid and surrounding area.

'Well,' she sighed, *'at least they look similar now!'* Harriet did not like the heavy look, but it was the best she could do. She phoned Viv one last time with no luck and thought she might be found in her garden, if the showering had finished. Harriet's mission could be important, as there was the possibility that Viv may be next on Scully's attack list.

Viv had been luxuriating in the bath, so had not heard the telephone ring. When Harriet arrived, Viv was making breakfast. On seeing the battered Harriet at her door, Viv anxiously ushered her inside. She wanted to take Harriet to the hospital for a check up, but received a definite refusal.

"I feel completely fine now, no adverse effects at all, well apart from the bruising, so don't you worry!" Harriet was only concerned with revealing all of the previous night's disastrous events, which were hurriedly disclosed to her friend. A shocked Viv, then rattled off several questions.

"We must inform the police, surely there's a way? What if Scully attacks again? Could this attack and his implying he was involved with who he *thought* was BV being locked up, be enough to prove he's the murderer? What if he's already hurt Annabel? What if he's murdered her? Oh, Harriet, what are we going to do?"

Harriet thought hard. "We have to tell the police about our conversation with Annabel, but then she might not have had a chance to go to them first, which would make it look bad for her. We should try to contact and ask her if she's visited them, but perhaps that doesn't matter any more. Beside that Viv, I need to report this vicious attack and describe Scully to the police. He needs to be arrested and whilst in custody, they can tie him in with the killing."

"Anyway, you should let the police photographer take pictures of your wounds quickly, before they fade too much," said Viv. "We're in such a bad position here for meddling. What a mess!"

Harriet sighed. "We could wait to see what angle the police come up with. They're bound to contact you if anything happens to Annabel. You said you wrote your phone number on Dandy's business card and they are bound to find that. We're too involved, we just know too much and all we were trying to do as amateur detectives will come out if I report the visit and beating Scully gave me!"

"But," Viv interrupted, "Annabel might be too scared to tell them her story. Scully may have frightened her into silence, if he's not done something much worse already!" Harriet now looked alarmed. "You're right, we'd better tip off the police somehow. I can talk to them from the pay phone a few streets away and speak in a strange accent." There did not seem to be any other way.

Harriet left to find a telephone booth a good distance away and was soon speaking with a policeman about Annabel. In between trying to keep her acquired 'German' accent constant, she explained that Annabel had been very upset and had news about a murder which she planned to speak to them about that morning. Harriet spoke rapidly, not allowing the policeman any chance to interrupt her, knowing they would be more interested in who she was, rather than in taking the message down properly.

Harriet stated how important it was for them to call on Annabel if she did not turn up, to make sure everything was all right as her boyfriend was a known thug involved with drugs and a murder. She read Annabel's address out to them, but could not be sure if the policeman was taking it seriously enough to write it down.

After Harriet delivered all the info she could, the policeman insisted yet again, that she tell her name. Instead of complying, she interrupted him loudly, saying it would be the responsibility of the police if something bad happened to Annabel, adding the girl was linked to the death of Alex Labelle. Before the frantic policeman could ask her any more questions, Harriet hung up the phone. She then drove quickly back to Viv's house.

"So, she's not been in yet to see the police," they almost said in unison.

"We're guilty of putting Annabel in danger, Harriet!" Viv said.

"Seems so, but it was unavoidable. We just have to hope she'll be all right," said a thoughtful Harriet.

An hour had gone by when the telephone rang. Viv answered and heard Dandy's voice. The police had just been to see her and she appeared to be quite shaken up.

With her voice breaking, Dandy told Viv, "Poor little Annabel has been murdered. She was found this morning in her apartment. She was badly beaten and her neck snapped. How could such a terrible thing happen? The police wanted to know if I knew anything. They found my business card in her handbag with your telephone number on it. How could that have happened anyway? Why was Annabel carrying my business card around?"

Viv just sat there numb. "Annabel was murdered?" she mumbled.

Harriet returned the look of alarm, wondering

if her call to the police had helped them to find Annabel. But, surely enough time had not past between her visit to the phone booth and them finding out this new information?

Viv told Harriet, "Now, the police are asking Dandy if she knows anything and of course, she doesn't know anything!" Speaking back into the phone, Viv continued her conversation. "Okay, Dandy, now calm down. We can talk about everything when you get back from work."

Dandy was still upset, but said, "Oh, all right. Talk with you then. Everything is just so unbearable right now." She hung up the phone.

Viv and Harriet sat facing one another. They were both shaken by the news of Annabel's murder.

"We are guilty," Harriet said slowly, "but, perhaps he intended killing her anyway!"

"We have to tell the police everything now, Harriet, including your attack. Let's hope they believe what we have to say."

Viv phoned BV, and luckily he was home. "We need to go to the police BV. It's time to come clean with everything we know," she told him.

Surprisingly, he gave his permission, even down to his involvement in it. He knew all the details would have to be divulged now and he told Viv to get hold of Mr. Lane straightaway. Lane could arrange for them to go and see Detective Mayfield, who was in charge of the case.

"Okay, I'll do that BV. I'll meet you at the police station in about an hour then? I'm calling Mr. Lane now."

Luckily, Mr. Lane was available and rushed over to meet with Harriet and Viv within the hour. He listened impatiently to their story and interrupted them constantly, walking up and down the room, as they tried to explain all that had happened.

"Bunch of putzes!" he exclaimed. "Why is it that everywhere you people go, bodies start turning up? How could you possibly think that you could do a job that the entire police department was not capable of doing? What do you think this is, some kind of game where you get to dress up and play detective? This is serious business! You should never have got involved in any of this mess! Bodies everywhere!" He was even more agitated and tactless, than usual.

"Bunch of putzes!" Mr. Lane reiterated in disgust to no-one in particular. "Okay! Time for damage control, big time. Let's get down to the police station, pronto! I'll call the detective in charge of the case. Mayfield I think, like the singer. I have his phone number in my organizer. I met Mayfield down at the lock up. Now, damn it, where's that damn thing?" he mumbled, as he turned everything out of his coat pockets. "Here it is, hold on…." He looked up Detective Mayfield's number and dialled it.

"Hi, Mayfield, it's Lane. What? Yeah, yeah, the short, obnoxious bastard, right. You're a real comedian, Mayfield, but no time for that now! Listen, I'm bringing down some witnesses. Daniel Lyons is innocent! We need to talk. Okay, I'm on my way." He hung up the phone. "Let's go then," he said, motioning everyone to the cars. "Time to come clean folks and pay the piper. Bunch of putzes!" He muttered.

Harriet thought if she heard him say that one more time, she would pop him one right on the nose!

"I'd better just phone Dandy and tell her where we're going," said Viv. "She may want to be there too." After a very short phone conversation, it was obvious that Dandy was going to meet them at the police station.

"Putzes!" said Lane again. "Come on now, no more time wasting."

Viv and Harriet looked at each other, as if they were both thinking the same thoughts. They already knew they should not have become involved, and would probably be told the same thing again at the police station. Viv was sure of two things. An innocent woman had been murdered and Scully's whereabouts were unknown. Even worse, this dangerous, deranged man knew where to find them.

Scully was a desperate man. After the attack on Harriet, in her own home nonetheless, this man was capable of anything and probably would not stop until he was stopped. Viv turned these thoughts over in her head as they made their way to the station in the black Mercedes, to meet with Detective Mayfield.

* *

Chapter Twenty-Nine
The Wheels Turn To Set Daniel Free!

The ride to the police station was quick and uneventful. On the way, Viv did not feel up to explanations, so she asked Harriet to call Henry on her cell phone to tell him what happened, as she wanted him to be in on the picture. When Harriet got through to Henry, he sounded frantic.

"Where are you Harriet?" he said. "I've been trying to find you. I stopped by your apartment and found blood all over the path! Are you okay? What's happened? Where's Viv? Is everyone okay?"

"Calm down Henry, Viv's with me. Just meet us at the police station, that's where we are heading with Mr Lane. We can explain things to you there. We're all right. Speak soon then, bye for now."

In reality, Harriet needed a chance to collect her thoughts before explaining anything to Henry. She intended telling more, but Henry seemed too upset to take it in properly. It was difficult trying to explain anything of a serious nature over the telephone at the best of times. Harriet looked out of the cab window and wondered about all that happened over the past several days.

When the group arrived at the police station, BV,

Dandy and Henry were already outside. They had been in conversation and, to Henry's surprise he found that he liked the Baron. But, still he hoped Viv would not choose the titled man. Everyone rushed into the station and Mr. Lane walked briskly up to the desk sergeant.

"We need to see Detective Mayfield. Now! Now!" He repeated, breathing noisily and heavily from the fast walk up the steps to the station.

"Take a seat," the sergeant said, unimpressed. He glared at Lane, and motioned with his pen to the row of empty seats in the lobby, whilst he continued to fill out forms.

Mr. Lane slammed his hand hard on the desk. "Listen, pal!" he seethed. "We're talking about a murder here. I don't have time for your attitude! Understand?"

The desk sergeant jumped back in surprise, quickly turning angry. "Sit down!" he said in a sharp tone, motioning Mr. Lane away.

The sergeant picked up the telephone and called Detective Mayfield, who suddenly appeared from behind the door that led to the offices. He was anything but the stereotypical image of a police detective. He was a tall and distinguished looking man. His attire was out of the ordinary also. He wore a red and yellow tailored blazer, neatly pressed indigo shirt and straight black trousers. His clothes which fit his large frame perfectly, looked as though they had just been pressed that morning.

His alligator black shoes shone like mirrors. Around his neck he wore his detective's badge on a long, silver chain that complimented his rings and thick genuine Rolex watch. He wore his dark hair with greying sides onto his collar, combed back over his ears. There was a faint scent of cologne wafting from him which added to his manly appearance. An eyebrow went up, as he looked the group over who collected in the lobby, along with an irate looking, short, overweight red-faced man waiting for attention. He walked toward them and introduced himself.

"Hi, I'm Detective Mayfield," he said in a rich, baritone voice. "You must be the witnesses mentioned on the phone. Let's go to my office, please." He held the door open and motioned with his free hand for everyone to enter the squad room.

Mr. Lane rushed ahead saying, "About time we got some service here. Everyone on a coffee break or something?" He was his usual restless self.

Detective Mayfield led Viv and her friends through a large, open room that seemed to brim with chaos. Everyone was shouting to be heard and moving speedily about the closely assembled desks. People and stacks of paper seemed to be everywhere.

Viv could only pick up bits and pieces of conversations, but everyone seemed to have a sense of urgency about them. It made her feel uncomfortable. The room was brightly lit with several overhead lights. The smell of cigarettes, coffee and stale sweat, permeated every square inch of the crowded room.

"This way please," Detective Mayfield stated, indicating for the group to enter his office. He then closed the door behind them all. "Now, what can I do for you? It seemed rather urgent when we spoke on the telephone, Mr Lane. Are these all witnesses?" Mayfield was answered with a swift nod from Lane. The detective then glanced at the remainder of the group and asked them to sit down.

Mr. Lane was quick to speak. "Well you see, it's like this…" But, before he could get the full sentence out, Harriet started to interject.

"No, let me explain. The killer is Scully. He killed Annabel."

"No, Harriet," interrupted Viv. "I think we should start with Annabel."

Mr. Lane tried to talk over them. BV and Henry both tried to shush Viv and Harriet who continued to talk, whilst Dandy wailed, "Oh, please set my husband free!"

The scene was total chaos.

Detective Mayfield stood up, walked to the door, opened and slammed it shut. The room immediately went silent. He kept his back turned, then slowly faced the group, his left hand still on the doorknob. He spoke quietly, but with authority.

"Glad I have your attention at last," he said. "Now, who's going to speak first? And one at a time or this meeting is over. Do I make myself clear?"

He glanced at each one individually, looking straight into their eyes, to let them know he meant business.

"Yes," responded Mr. Lane. "One at a time, so I shall go first. I apologize for our behaviour, detective. I know you're a busy man. I'm Lane, the guy you spoke with on the telephone, yes, I know you know me, so let me explain first."

Detective Mayfield let go of the doorknob, went over and sat down behind his desk.

"Okay, I'm listening," he said.

Mr. Lane then explained everything he knew and meticulously described all of the events that led up to the meeting here. He asked Harriet and Viv to interject from time to time to clarify some points. Detective Mayfield listened intently, as did BV and Henry. When the story was finished, the detective looked pensively around the room and finally spoke.

"If everything you're telling me is true, then we have an innocent man locked up behind bars."

Dandy jumped with joy, clear out of her chair. "Does that mean you'll be letting him go? Can Daniel come home with me now? Please tell me he's going to be set free? Please, please tell me my husband is coming home with me now!"

She felt faint after uttering these words, and Henry quickly leaned over to steady her.

"Come on Dandy, sit down," he said. "Can I get some water around here somewhere Detective?"

"There's a water cooler just outside the door to your left," Detective Mayfield motioned. Henry hurried out the door to retrieve some for Dandy.

"What I was trying to explain Mrs. Lyons, is that our jails are full of innocent men and we just can't let your Daniel Lyons out. The fact remains he did have sufficient motive and provocation to commit the crime, let alone the opportunity. There were witnesses as well, who placed him at the scene of the crime and who did see a fight ensue."

"But that said, you've certainly made a strong case that this other man, Scully, might be involved in the crime. We're looking for him right now in connection with the Annabel Lewis murder."

Viv and Harriet looked at each other. They mumbled something.

Detective Mayfield coughed, and then said, "If I may go on? It turns out that Scully lived with Annabel as her live-in boyfriend. Now he's disappeared just when her dead body was found in the apartment they shared. That's pretty strong circumstantial stuff." He sipped some water from a glass on his desk and continued.

"The problem we have, though, is that Annabel was the only person who could testify unequivocally that Scully was at the party, albeit in disguise. You folks are telling me that Annabel said he was there, but since I can't get this information from her directly, then it's hearsay. I like you folks, sure, but how can I believe that everything you're telling me is true."

He looked at each one in the room, then asked, "Where is the factual evidence, the tangible stuff that I can take to the Prosecutor and say, 'Hey, here is indisputable evidence, let this guy go!' After all, you do have a strong motivation here to set Daniel Lyons free. Who's going to say you're not lying even though your intentions are good?"

Everyone looked at each other incredulously.

"So, we're still back to where we started," Dandy said dejectedly.

"No, not necessarily," Detective Mayfield continued. "With this new evidence, there's strong probable cause that points to another suspect. If your Mr. Lane here is so inclined, he can file the appropriate petitions to request an immediate bail hearing."

I think your Daniel Lyons can be set free on bail, at least until everything gets sorted out. In the meantime, we'll find this David Scully, who'll hopefully come clean with us. And, that should be the end of it."

"That's it," shouted Dandy, knocking the cup of water Henry still held. The water splashed his face and clothes.

"Thanks," he said, with a grin, as he dried himself off.

"I'm sorry, Henry, but I'm thrilled." She turned to Mr. Lane, "Howard, get busy and do the paper work! Get bail for Daniel!" She shouted at him. "Why are you just standing there?"

"I'm already on it!" he shouted back and raced out of the room. He was pleased his friend would soon be out of jail.

Detective Mayfield continued, "We'll find this David Scully, I can guarantee you that. We can charge him for his attack on you as well, Harriet. Are you up to speaking with one of my men to get a picture taken of the injuries and make your statement?"

"Of course," said Harriet. "By the way, do you suspect Scully of killing Alex?"

"Perhaps," said Detective Mayfield. "We can't jump to conclusions. There's a lot to sort out and make sense of, after the things we've heard from you all here today. Another thing is, we searched Annabel's room when we found her body. Well, after the landlady found her body this morning. We found her diary. It was written up to date and it included her conversations with you two," he said, pointing to both Harriet and Viv. We would have got around to seeing you both for statements, had you not arrived here.

Mayfield continued, "Annabel had written that Scully apparently attacked her after she got home, the same evening he attacked you Harriet. We have got no solid clues as yet to who killed her. We know she was severely beaten and then strangled, with enough force to completely snap her neck. It takes a strong man to do that."

Harriet and Viv winced at this news. Dandy was still delighted about her husband and about to be freed, and so was not focused on anything else.

"But Scully may have come back to her that night, after she had written those notes!" said Harriet. "Besides, he's a very large man. He certainly would have been capable of snapping poor Annabel's neck." She felt a pang of guilt as she said these words.

"Sure, anything's possible," replied Detective Mayfield. "But we don't know that yet. We can't prove anything until we have the opportunity to question this Scully character."

"It's a good thing she kept her diary up to date, so that substantiates many things," said Viv.

"Couldn't we see the diary? We may be able to help there," asked Harriet.

"No, but thanks all the same," said Detective Mayfield. "It's all evidence right now, so that would not be possible. Perhaps after we've gone as far as we can, we might reconsider, but it would not be appropriate right now." He smiled. "You've all played detective long enough, and look where it's gotten you. Thanks again, but I have all the help I need. Besides, right now I need to speak with Baron von Eider here. He called me earlier to tell me that he had some *interesting* things to tell me." Mayfield dismissed and accompanied the small crowd, who began walking out of his office.

BV looked at Viv and shrugged his shoulders. She hoped things would not be too hard for him after he explained everything to the detective about the drugs and his involvement. Viv held BV's hand and gave it a squeeze for good luck. He gave her a smile in return. Henry noticed and felt hurt by this gesture.

Mayfield told the group, "Thanks for your help, but don't get involved in any more of this!" Then he and BV walked back into his office for their private talk.

As the group of friends left the police station, Mr. Lane called Dandy's cell phone from the courthouse. He had filed the petition and would now have to wait to see what happened next. He warned them not to speak to the police again unless he was present. They promised. It was decided they go back to Viv's home for a cup of tea and for Dandy to pick up some of her belongings as she was in no mood to go back to the agency and work, being far too excited by the prospect of Daniel's release from prison.

Viv went in the car with Henry, and Harriet accompanied Dandy. Henry was happy to have the company of Viv and knew it was best only to make small talk. He enjoyed being alone with her again, if only for this journey back to her home.

They were soon at her house and after Dandy had packed a small suitcase, she asked why she had been left out of so much of what led up to these terrible events.

"We kept it from you for your own good," she was told by Viv. "You've had enough to cope with. Anyhow, you know it all now!"

After a short banter, Dandy picked up her coat and suitcase. Her face beamed with excitement as she thanked Viv for her hospitality, asking that they keep in close contact and let her know what was happening.

"Promise!" Viv and Harriet agreed, in unison.

When Dandy had gone, Viv asked Henry and Harriet if they would mind giving her some time to herself as there were things she had to attend to.

Henry looked curious and slightly put out, but Harriet replied, "Of course. We'll talk to you later Viv." Harriet had an idea where Viv was going, but was not going to mention it.

"I hoped to see you today Viv," Henry said. "Can I see you later?"

"Phone first though, Henry, to make sure I'm back. I'm not sure how long it'll take," she replied.

Henry was visibly upset, but accepted it. Both gave Viv a hug as they departed.

Henry whispered to her, "I'll see you later."

Once everyone was gone, Viv freshened up. She decided not to drive, but to get a taxi and pay a surprise visit to BV's home. That way she would have more time with him when he brought her back. She hoped his meeting with Detective Mayfield, would not take too long as she planned to wait for him until he got back. There was so much she needed to know and discuss with him.

* * * * * * * * * * * * * * * * * * * *

Chapter Thirty
BV Has a Chance to Win Viv Over

It took some time to get a taxi, but when Viv eventually pulled up in front of BV's estate, there were cars already parked in the driveway. She recognized BV's black Saab and parked alongside it was a classic old Humber Hawk. Viv exited the taxi at the top of the driveway and paid the driver. She then waited amongst the bushes trying to figure out what was going on.

Eventually, the front door opened and she watched BV and Detective Mayfield leave the house, to stand just outside the door. They exchanged a few words, then BV waved goodbye and went in closing the door behind him. Mayfield got back into his car and drove past without noticing her.

* *

Detective Wesley Mayfield drove to his favourite watering hole, the 'Lamb & Flag.' He really needed a drink after this evening's events. He ordered his usual, a double neat scotch and then he lit a cigar. It had been years since he had quit drinking, but lately, it seemed like the thing to do. It soothed his pain.

He sipped his drink and pondered the past few months. He had been so close, or so he thought, in his investigation of that damned serial killer, 'El Diablo.' That was until the killer decided to strike way too close to home. The killer had taunted Mayfield on and off for weeks, always leaving those tempting messages and small clues which should have culminated in a capture. Daring Mayfield, in fact, who remembered events vividly every day leading up to that fateful and dreadful night. His thoughts trailed off. It was so hard to come to grips with it all.

Mayfield reflected on his career. He had started with the police force over twenty-seven years ago. He was just a green rookie back then, fresh out of the military and looking for a career. Police work was interesting, and besides, it was a steady job and with a reasonable pay-cheque. He moved up the ranks quickly, in spite of the barriers he faced being the only black man on the force.

Soon, Mayfield realized that he truly liked this work. It suited him, and he particularly took a pride in his appearance. His uniforms were always tailored and neatly pressed. Shoes highly polished, gun cleaned and oiled. Yes, a sharp appearance was very important, and Mayfield took great pride in the way he looked.

After only eight years on the force, he made detective, which was almost unheard of at the time. Mayfield was proud of his work record and achievement. He met his wife, Angela, on the job. She worked as a receptionist, and they had casual conversations now and then.

Finally, he worked up the nerve to ask her out and one thing led to another. They were married after seeing each other for only six months. She was the love of his life, and they would have celebrated their twenty-first wedding anniversary this week. Unfortunately, they were never able to have children.

He called the publican for another drink. Life seemed so meaningless these days now that Angela was gone. He took out her worn photograph and placed it on the bar. He toasted her.

"Here's to you sweetheart."

He remembered that evening well. Several months ago, he was assigned to lead the task force trying to catch 'El Diablo.' Somehow the killer worked out Mayfield was in charge and not only phoned him, but also sent messages constantly.

Then one day, when he arrived home, his beloved wife did not greet him. He thought it odd, so pulled out his service revolver on entering the home. What he found in the living room grieved and horrified him.

Angela was gagged and bound to a chair. Her throat was slit and a note had been placed on her chest, written with her blood. It read; 'This one's for you Mayfield!' Even to a hardened cop like him, it was too much to bear. Grief overcame him and later all he could think of was killing the monster. He always tried not dwell on this memory, it was far too devastating, but he could not prevent the horror from surfacing as often as it did.

It had been all over the news, 'Serial killer strikes close to home.' 'El Diablo,' killed Mayfield's beloved wife to scorn him.' That certainly fell outside the typical prey…..gay men. Mayfield thought that as the killer had branched out to killing women that he might now have acquired a taste for it.

Mayfield choked back the tears; it still drove him insane when he thought of it all. Unfortunately, his superiors immediately took him off the case. They told him to take as much time as possible to recover, even to consider retirement. He had enough time on the force to leave it right now and collect a decent pension. But he could not leave, not now.

Mayfield had been reassigned to the general case files when Alex Labelle was murdered. He was pleased to be assigned to this new case, needing badly to take his mind off the past and back onto real police work. Reluctantly, his superiors had agreed. Now, here he was, in the middle of two murders and 'El Diablo' still on the loose.

'Oh well,' he thought, coming back to the present. 'At least we might be able to wrap up some of this mess soon. Just need to apprehend that low-life Scully.' He re-lit his cigar and ordered another scotch. "Happy anniversary darling," he choked back tears and sadly toasted the picture of his wife once again.

* *

Viv moved out from behind the bushes and walked the rest of the way to the front door. Without hesitation, she rang the ornate lion bell. BV answered quickly, thinking Mayfield had forgotten something and come back. BV recovered his composure and ushered Viv in. It may have been her imagination, but he looked slightly ruffled. His hair stuck up in one place, as though he had run his hand through it.

"Everything all right?" she asked.

"It wasn't too bad really," he answered, steering her into the lounge. "it could have been worse. I'm pleased to say the police are not too concerned at the moment about my part in the drugs. The murders are their priority. Bigger fish to fry I guess," he said, adding, "so far."

Viv was curious. It was not like the police to just overlook illegal drug activity just because they were preoccupied with another crime. "Is there something else you want to tell me, BV?" she inquired.

"It is lucky that Annabel kept a diary," he offered, still evading her question.

Viv persisted, "I saw Detective Mayfield leave your house, BV. What was all that about?"

BV once again avoided her question. "The police didn't really say anything about what was in it, the diary that is. I only know that it exists, and that it might help them catch the murderer. It looks as if it could only have been Scully. Who else would want to keep Annabel quiet?"

"BV, answer me, please! What's going on here?" Viv persisted.

"Mayfield thinks he is on to something, but he's being very cautious," he said, taking her hand. "There is some great news I can give." A smile lit up his face. "Daniel is being released on bail. Finally! Hard to believe he's been in there for almost three and a half weeks." Feeling pleased with himself he added, "Let's celebrate, Viv, and go where it's really comfortable."

"Do you mean the den?" she asked, looking at his inviting lips.

"Yes. It is about time we really relaxed, is it not?"

For an instant she wondered whether or not to persist with her line of questioning. But as she looked into BV's eager, blue eyes, there were none she could think to ask. She was still perplexed by Mayfield's involvement with BV and hoped to find out more before leaving his home. Her thoughts were disrupted by BV's hand sliding up her thigh.

Viv tensed up. "I must phone Harriet," she said. "If I'm going to stay the night, that is?"

"Yes, of course," BV said, with a smug look on his face as he retrieved her handbag from an armchair. Viv dug into the bag and found her phone. Harriet picked up on the second ring.

Although Harriet understood, she tried to talk Viv out of staying there for the night. She reminded Viv that Henry wanted to see her."

"I'll wait for him to call me but if you see him first, tell him whatever you think is best, Harriet. I don't want you to lie, but try not to hurt him."

"How do you feel about all this?" Harriet sounded concerned. "Have you decided on BV instead of Henry? He'll be broken-hearted and you could be making a very big mistake, Viv!"

"Don't worry Harriet, I have a feeling that BV is not as bad as he seems to be. I also have a feeling he's keeping a secret and I want to find out what it is."

"Yes, I know! That's because he's probably the murderer, Viv, for God's sake!'

"No, he's not, Harriet, I can tell," Viv replied, noticing that BV was out of the room, which gave her the chance to say, "There is something odd going on. BV hasn't been arrested even though he's come clean with Detective Mayfield, who has been around here today with him. I have the feeling that they know each other quite well."

"But, Viv, I am so worried about your safety!"

"Please don't be. BV knows I'm telling you right now that I'm here, and probably staying the night. I'll be quite safe, honestly, Harriet. Just trust my instincts on this."

"Okay, I don't seem to have any choice anyway. Take care, please, Viv!"

"Yes, I will. Promise! Now stop worrying about me and have a good evening. I expect Henry might pop by to see you."

"Okay. But you take care now!"

"Sure I will. I'll call you tomorrow when I get home."

"Okay, Viv, bye for now."

"Bye, Harriet, see you soon." Viv ended the call and returned her phone to the handbag, just as BV arrived back at her side.

* *

Henry had been calling Viv to ensure she was all right. When there was no answer at her home, he decided against calling her cell phone in case it annoyed her to be interrupted. But, he became worried and called Harriet. She told him Viv had spoken briefly to her about an hour earlier. Henry told her he had already left a message on Viv's answering phone, asking her to phone him when she got back in. Harriet invited him over, saying she would discuss the conversation between her and Viv when he got there. Henry agreed, and within a half an hour was at Harriet's front door. She opened it dressed in an apron, jeans and wearing long rubber gloves.

"Just been cleaning up the mess," she said. "You know, I had a bit of an incident last night."

"I know," said Henry, who glanced at the blood-spattered wall that Harriet was trying to scrub clean. It was still stained in places. "Don't you think you should leave that for the police? It could be evidence."

"It's okay, they were here this morning. They took a load of photos and said it was okay to clean up. By the way, you smell lovely," she said and kissed him lightly on the cheek.

"At least it's not being wasted," he smiled. "Where is she, Harriet? Well, to tell you the truth, I'm worried. I hope she's not in danger. They haven't picked Scully up as far as I know. He could be lurking about anywhere!"

Henry's words did not exactly comfort Harriet, and he felt terrible as soon as they left his lips. After all, if anyone knew about the danger of Scully running about free, it would be Harriet. She felt his wrath first-hand and Henry could see the uneasiness his words caused her.

"I'm sorry, Harriet, that was so clumsy of me. Forgive me. I'm sure the police will have that creep in custody any moment now. Oh, my gosh, your eye! Was that from last night? Damn that creep, I'll kill him!"

"It's okay, I'm going to be all right. Just a bruise. Don't worry about Scully. I don't. You can't live your life in fear."

She thought it best to tell him that Viv had gone to BV's house that afternoon. He would also have to know the rest. She felt relieved Viv had given her permission, so no lies would have to be told.

"I have something important to tell you. Sit down and I'll make us some coffee."

"Good idea," he said. "I could use a nice strong cuppa. Didn't get much sleep last night, and I'm starting to feel the effects of it." He made himself comfortable on the sofa.

Harriet went off to prepare the coffee. She returned quickly and handed him a cup, seating herself at his side.

"When Viv called me earlier, she wanted me to tell you where she was." Harriet felt it best to be blunt as was her style. "After we all left her house, she went over to BV's."

"Oh, no!" Henry exclaimed, as he spilled some coffee on himself. It was hot and must have caused quite a bit of discomfort, judging by his reaction. He picked at the cloth of his trousers to relieve the heat.

"Just what I needed," he said. "Please go on, let's hear the rest of this bad news, I guess."

Harriet passed him a box of Kleenex and continued. "Viv only intended to be there an hour or so, but felt there was something she needed to find out. She may also be spending the night."

He looked extremely unhappy and thoughtful. It hurt Harriet very much.

"I thought it was important that you knew, and beside, Viv told me to tell you where she was and not to worry." Perhaps she should not have revealed this unsavoury information so abruptly to him, but could think of no other way.

Henry moved uncomfortably on the sofa. "Now what do I? I can't see how I can make sure she's not in danger without looking like a jealous fool!"

"She shouldn't be in any danger at BV's, Henry. Maybe they're going over a few important facts right now." As soon as Harriet spoke these ill-chosen words, she regretted them.

"I'm worried about that too!" he exclaimed. "BV's my rival, and although he seemed like a decent guy, I don't like this. I haven't even had the chance to talk Viv out of considering a relationship with him yet. But that would have made me look silly I suppose, especially if she knew I wanted her so desperately."

He hung his head, rubbing his hands together. "Now they might be lovers, so it makes things even worse. Not only that, I'm sure she feels a lot of guilt over Annabel's death. That's got to be driving her crazy."

"Forget about it now," said Harriet. "It's not worth making yourself sick over it. You need to wait and see the outcome. There's nothing you can do until you speak to her." Suddenly, Harriet remembered the coffee he had spilled and only mopped with a Kleenex. There was a large stain on the trouser leg. "Hey, look at the mess you've made. Give me those trousers, I'll put them in the wash." She added; "I'm sure Viv will contact us again soon."

Henry unbuckled his pants and climbed out of them. His thoughts were far away as he absentmindedly handed them to Harriet for washing. Her quick, smiling glance up and down his body made him have second thoughts.

Harriet looked at him standing in her living room in his shirt and underwear. "You look, scrumptious, Henry. Now don't you go anywhere, okay?" She laughed as she went off to wash his trousers.

Henry sat back down on the sofa and thought about Viv. 'My girl and BV together, in a passionate embrace by now probably. The man is so damn good-looking, how could she resist him?' Too many upsetting scenarios raced through his mind as he sadly thought it was him who should be with her tonight, not BV!'

* * * * * * * * * * * * * * * * * * * *

Chapter Thirty-One
A Difficult Choice for Viv

Viv was relieved she had spoken to Harriet. Now she could relax knowing Henry would be told by Harriet where she was and in the best way possible, if there was such a way. Henry would have worried about her, if he could not speak to her, especially, with all these murders about. She hoped he would understand that she had to see BV. It felt horrible, hurting Henry like this, but at least he could count on Harriet for company. BV kissed her neck. The goose pimples felt delicious, and she anticipated an incredible evening. They talked for a short while about Annabel's murder.

Suddenly Viv remembered and told BV, "I forgot about Scully still being free and had meant to ask her if she wanted to stay with me. He could be planning to come back and finish Harriet off. I'd better call Henry to ask that he keeps an eye on her, although he's probably at her place. But, I do need to make sure." Viv's cell phone battery was running down, so BV passed his phone over for her to use. She dialled Harriet's number.

"Hi, Viv," Harriet said. "Yes, Henry's here. He's half-naked in my living room right now, she chuckled. I'll go get him for you. Hold on, I'll give him the phone. Henry, it's Viv," she said, handing him the telephone.

She giggled at giving him away.

"Hello, Viv," he said extremely pleased to hear her voice.

"Well, it looks like the two of you have certainly started to hit it off in a big way. Hope I'm not interrupting," Viv sounded indignant, although she had not made up her mind between the two men as yet.

"I don't understand," Henry said, as he glanced back at Harriet.

"Never mind," Viv said. "I phoned to ask you to keep in touch with Harriet, to make sure she doesn't get into trouble again. Just until Scully is caught, although I intend asking her if she wants to stay at my place for a while. I thought if you weren't actually around at her place you could call round or phone there. We don't know if he'll come back and try to finish the job."

"Sure, I'll keep an eye on things. Harriet will be all right. But, I'm worried about you Viv! How can you be sure you're safe with BV?"

"Henry, I can't talk now, we can meet up tomorrow probably. I'll call you." BV was nestling up to her, making it difficult to talk or hear Henry, who was trying to ask when she was coming back. Viv replied she didn't know at the moment as there were still many questions. She sent her love to them both and hung up.

Viv turned her attention back to BV, and they took up where they left off.

BV carried her onto the large, soft bed in the den. They undressed and lay down beside each other, holding hands. She turned her face toward his, and they kissed. She loved the manly smell of him and tried to inhale as much of it as she could. The kissing became so passionate they were both left breathless.

'BV's the best I've ever had, like Lawrence, but maybe better,' she thought happily. It was not just that he knew exactly how to turn on her passions. She loved the way he responded to her as well. It was so exciting, and the only 'down' part was his involvement in drugs.

"Why do you affect me this way?" she asked, breaking away from him for some air. "I feel so good with you." She put her head on his chest and held him tight.

"I guess it's chemistry baby. I feel exactly the same about you," he answered, in between quick kisses.

Viv wanted to say more about how she felt, but wished he would say it first. *'I know I'm in love with him, but he may not love me,'* she thought.

"Would you do oral on me babe? I'd love to feel your lips around it!"

"Just let me get into position and I'll kiss away," she said moving down his body.

"In a minute," he said, sitting up so he could reach her breasts.

"I just love these," he said. He could not resist and put his lips around her stiff nipples, sucking and nibbling, giving them plenty of attention.

Viv allowed herself only so much pleasure, before pushing him back to continue her work. She kissed his body slowly, all the way down to his erection.

She kissed him expertly, varying the pressure and positions, until he squirmed with pleasure. He gasped as trembles shot through his body. He was amazed she could keep her tongue flicking him whilst moving in a circular motion the whole time and loved the way she changed the tempo.

'*I can't believe I love doing this so much,*' she thought, enjoying his extreme reactions to her method. It took some practice not to gag when she took him deeply, but it was a practice she enjoyed learning immensely. BV manoeuvred his fingers inside her, giving them both double the pleasure. He was even more turned on by how ready she was for him.

She peeped at his face, he was in ecstasy, just like her and it was obvious he was about to explode. His love fluid tasted sweet, as it began to ooze across her tongue, but she couldn't stop, even though she needed him in her very badly. He knew this and quickly changed positions, entering her deeply. Sweat fell in droplets from his face onto hers, blending with her wetness. It lasted longer than she imagined, giving her time for multiple orgasms. Suddenly, she felt his explosion and was able to match it with hers. They both cried out with pleasure and release, as he collapsed on top of her, quivering. Only the sound of their harsh breathing could be heard, as they held on to each other.

"I guess I owe you one," he managed at last.

They cuddled up and fell into a deep satisfied sleep.

Before morning they made love several more times, and each one was a truly wonderful experience.

* *

When late morning arrived, the sun shone straight in on them. They awoke with their arms still wrapped around each other.

"Good morning, my sweet darling," he said huskily.

"Thank you," she replied, trying to open her eyes. *'Wow! That was the best time I've ever experienced,'* she thought contentedly, stretching her arm across him. It was so good waking up to this gorgeous man lying beside her.

"Viv, I realize more than ever, that I love you and need you. I want you more than anyone or anything I've ever wanted in my life. The problem is that I'm leaving soon. Will you come away with me?"

"Leaving? What are you talking about? Where are you going? Why so suddenly?" she asked, sitting up to face him.

"Abroad. Switzerland probably. Just for a year or so, then after that, who knows? I need a change of scenery. Need to get away." He propped himself up on his elbow and looked intently into her surprised eyes. "Will you come with me, darling?" he repeated.

Viv was worried. She wanted so much to be with him, but she did not want to leave her new friends, not yet anyway.

"I love you too, BV, so much it hurts and I would need to be with you, wherever you are. But everything has happened so fast, I need time to work out things. When were you thinking of going?"

"Within a few days," was his quick reply.

"Oh, no! That's far too soon! Can't you wait a bit longer? A few weeks?"

"No, I really can't. There are reasons why I must make my move so quickly. I can't for your sake tell you more just now. I can give you a phone number and the address of where I'll be, so you can join me, but no one else must know about it. It could mean my death! Do you understand, darling?"

"Not really, BV. You're scaring me, why such a rush? Why so secretive? Is it something to do with the diary and the drugs? Mayfield?" she asked desperately.

BV thought for a moment and then responded, "In a way, Viv, yes. It is also to do with Mayfield, but I'm not at liberty to say more. Anyway, it would be best if I got out of the way. Now that Daniel is safe, I can make sure that I'm safe as well."

"Can't you even tell Daniel that you're going?"

"I thought about that, but I just don't know. On the one hand, it's probably best that I don't, for his sake, but then again I might tell him. The police will expect me to wait until this murder thing is all over. They haven't said anything to me about not leaving the country yet. I wanted to stay a step ahead of them and get out whilst the going's good."

"But, they might have more questions to ask you."

"I hope not, or it might mean I'm in trouble."

Viv could tell by the look on his face, he was not entirely truthful and seemed to be holding something back. She did not want to be told more secrets than was necessary, but she asked just one more question.

"Are you going to see Daniel before you go, even if you don't tell him your intention to leave? He must want to see you."

"I'll try to see him tonight, or tomorrow. Maybe I'll tell him I'm leaving without going into any details about the reasons."

"I'll miss you dreadfully, BV! Can't you just wait a few more days so I can sort everything out clearly in my head?" Viv asked, hugging him as tightly as she could.

She needed to think about her feelings for Henry. She still needed him, but was it really possible to be in love with them both? 'Yes, I definitely love BV. I could spend the rest of my life with him,' she realized. 'But I could with Henry, too.'

She felt so strongly, for Henry, but why? His lovemaking was good, but in a totally different way. Not exciting, but deep and spiritual. Was that why she loved both of them, for their different qualities?

BV replied, "No. I'm afraid I can't delay. That's why I'm asking you to make up your mind. If you don't come with me now, you may never see or hear from me again! It would not even be my doing, and apart from that, I need your strength to help me through all this." He gave her a lingering kiss. "We love each other. It happened straight away Viv, didn't it? You can't deny that. You will come away with me, right? Yes?" BV's sexy blue eyes implored of her.

There were no words she could say. Viv felt so many emotions. She felt elated that he loved her so much, but was devastated in case she might lose him. Instinctively, she kissed him from deep within her soul. She had no idea what might or could happen next.

That evening after Viv had arrived back home, her

mind was in a terrible state. She still had so many feelings for Henry, but did not want to refuse BV's request. With everything that was going on, a decision had to be made. She could not believe all these problems were happening when she should be so happy. She wished there was more time to think it through properly to prevent making a huge mistake.

Henry would have to help her decide. It was late afternoon, so she phoned him on her way home. He answered and it was arranged they have dinner together. He arranged to be around for her within the hour. Viv did not go into any detail on the telephone, and Henry did not question her either. The previous evening could be discussed later, face to face, he hoped.

* * * * * * * * * * * * * * * * * * * *

Chapter Thirty-Two
Henry Lays It on the Line

Viv and Henry sat in a sidewalk restaurant that overlooked the river. The afternoon was quiet and peaceful unlike the previous week's chaos. The sun still shone brightly, and a gentle breeze blew off of the water. Viv decided she had no option but to have a heart-to-heart with Henry. Many things needed ironing out, if possible, on both sides.

"It's lovely here," said Viv, as a prelude to the bombshell she was about to drop. Henry nodded, staring at the menu in silence. When he spoke, it was in general terms about the quality of the food. For a few moments, the conversation continued in this casual vein. However, they both realized more serious matters needed to be discussed and the atmosphere was full of tension.

Henry reached over the table and gently grasped Viv's hand. Then he began.

"Viv, I've known you a very short time," he faltered. "I do know one thing. I love you, I love you very much. I realize now that I fell in love with you from the moment I laid eyes on you, from that very first meeting when I walked through your door, even though you thought me a rambling fool. That first time I saw you, listened to your voice, smelled your fragrance, saw your smile, heard you laugh, looked into your eyes, it was magical for me.

"Nothing or no one else mattered from that moment on. Time stood still for me, and I realized how much I needed you in my life. Desperately, in fact. Without you, my life was, is, meaningless. That's how I feel; it's how I've always felt, but I just never told you. Actually, I can't believe I'm telling you these things right now, but I must. Please hear me out, we have a problem," he said, looking worried.

"I know Henry, I know," she sad sadly.

"I love you, Viv. By the same token, you have a life to live and must do what's right for you. I'd like to think that I love you enough to want to see you happy, even if that happiness is not with me."

Henry became uncomfortable and glanced over the river.

"Henry," Viv began, but he held his hand up to silence her.

"Please, let me finish, Viv. Obviously, you're an extremely beautiful and lovely woman, who can have her choice of any man. I know that. I'd only hoped that over time you'd fall in love with me. That I'd be the only man in your life, even the most important person in your life. I realize now, that as much as I love you, you don't really love me back. Not yet anyway."

Henry's expression showed his pain and tears formed in his eyes when he looked at her. Viv was sorry she was the cause, and pulled back from his grasp to sit straight up in her seat.

"Henry, I'm having big problems with my emotions at the moment. I still need time to think. The trouble is all these thoughts are going around in circles in my head. Perhaps, you've become deeply involved too quickly? Maybe we just need to give things a little more time to see where they'll lead. I know there's love in my heart for you, please realize that. I'm sorting my feelings out and getting nowhere right now."

Henry continued. "I know, Viv, but that's not enough for me. I need to know what's going on. I'm in turmoil."

He began to hear a contradiction form in his head, but he persisted. He had just told Viv that he knew she did not love him as much as he loved her and she seemed in agreement with this. Henry now wondered if she had made a choice and did not know how to tell him.

"We meant so much to each other in Spain, Viv. Something clicked when we were there. I knew then, more than ever, you were the woman I wanted to spend the rest of my life with. I'd never have let my barriers down, if you weren't sending me the same types of signals. I could feel your vibes, saying you wanted and needed me. I couldn't have been that far off beam, could I?"

Viv thought carefully about his words. In a way, he was right. She had a wonderful time in Spain and loved being with him.

She looked at Henry. He made her feel warm and secure, but there was no excitement, nor danger about him. He was stability personified and very routine. Whilst those were all excellent qualities in a man, she needed excitement in her life. Why? She knew the answer of course. It was BV.

He epitomized it all, danger, excitement, life on the edge, passion, a real magnetic type of man. Almost a bit animalistic in a sense. The nearest Henry came to being exciting was in the stories he had written. They were dramatic and intriguing, but nothing like Henry's ordinary life. Actually, it was hard to believe he had it in him to be exciting. Not like BV, to whom it came so naturally.

"Viv?" Henry said. "You're far away even now. Are you thinking about BV?"

"No, no, of course I'm not," she lied, feeling guilty. "I'm considering what you've been saying." She continued. "I was wondering if I could ever have excitement with you, Henry. Oh, that sounds so nasty, I don't mean it that way. I'll admit, Spain was great, it was so spontaneous. I loved being with you. Apart from the fun, I liked that element of thrill. But, I don't like day-to-day things with too much routine."

"Oh, I see. 'Routine' is the problem," Henry said a little too loudly. "You see me as routine, and you don't like routine, so you can't imagine living a fun life with me!"

Viv hated when men turned like this. She was about to interject, when he held up his hand again to stop her.

"No, no, let me continue. Viv, there's nothing wrong with routine. Everyone has to settle down eventually. Sure, everyone wants a little excitement in their lives. That's why people take vacations, so they can get away and have a little excitement once and awhile. Excitement doesn't just have to be planned though, it can be spontaneous."

"I know that, Henry," she began to say, but he continued.

"Viv, it happens every now and then, like in Spain, but you can't live your life in a fantasy forever. There's everyday life, there's work, there are every day commitments, family, friends. It's all important and it all plays a part in what we are as people and what makes us feel fulfilled. But your feet have to touch the ground eventually. It's not just about living life on the edge constantly. That's not reality, Viv. It exists for the moment and it's exciting, but it's not reality."

Viv thought about this and realised BV was 'reality' to her and constant excitement. "Henry, right from the start you knew I'd only just joined the agency. I told you there were important issues for me to sort out. You knew I didn't want commitment with the first man I met."

He grimaced. "I know. You were honest with me. I can tell that you no longer have feelings for Daniel. Becoming Dandy's friend probably helped. Unless your feelings have turned to his twin? Even so, how can I stop loving you, just like that? Do you want me to try and back off?"

"I know you have pride Henry, and I hate doing this to you. I'm in a terrible position here. I feel as if I'm being such a horrid person and yet none of this is deliberate." She felt miserable. "I can't imagine why you still care about me, really I can't."

He stopped, as a sudden thought came to him. "I know, Viv. How about us getting a band together and doing a few gigs a week? That would give us a paying, sociable job and we'd have so much fun! That way we could at least have a fun future together in some way."

"I don't think so, Henry. I know you are a drummer and a sax-player, and I can dance professionally enough, but I haven't sung for a long time!"

"You're good enough, Viv. I've heard you sing when you thought I wasn't listening, you're very good actually!"

"Well, that's something for me to think about. I'd enjoy that, it would make life more interesting. We'd definitely have the kind of fun I long for."

"Oh, good. I guess what I mean is, well, can you see a future with me?" Henry asked.

Viv knew there could be a great future with him, but she would miss BV too much. Henry was a great guy, no doubting that. *It's driving me mad trying to make a decision,* she thought unhappily. Both of the men who loved her had excellent qualities, although one of them seemed to be in a great deal of trouble. She was never one to walk out on a friend in need, which made it more difficult to commit to one or the other.

Viv had been given no time to think about the consequences if she failed to make a commitment to either one of them.

"I've not discarded you, if that's what you mean Henry. I have to make decisions, sure, but none have been made as yet. But, I can tell you I'm being forced to make decisions when I'm not ready and it's killing me."

"Is this to do with BV? Did he ask you to make a decision last night?"

"Well, kind of, yes." She wondered whether to tell Henry any more, but he must have read her mind.

"No, please don't tell me too much. I couldn't handle it, Viv." He wanted to know that nothing happened with BV, but couldn't stand the pain if she had gone further with that relationship.

"I need to go away for a while to get my thoughts straight, Henry. Actually, I was thinking this morning I needed a break. Need to go off somewhere, within the next day or so really and escape with someone who might help me to decide." The words were out before she realized it was a mistake.

"With me?" Henry asked eagerly, and his eyes lit up with excitement." I knew it when I saw you this morning. I could sense it. We could go back to Spain for a while, recapture the magic we felt there. Wonderful news, Viv. I knew if I had the chance to speak with you alone, after all this chaos had settled down, you'd see things differently. You were just confused. I'm so happy, I could kiss you. Actually, I think I will." He jumped up from the table and gave her a big hug and a kiss.

Viv was most alarmed. What was she going to say now that he had jumped the gun? She would have to think of something to say which would not cause hurt. But, she could not think of anything.

"Henry," she started. He was smiling at her. "I'm sorry, but it's not with you. I need to spend more time with BV, I love him too!"

Henry slumped back in his chair, feeling deflated and foolish.

'Oh hell, I've done it now!' she thought.

"It's a wicked world, Viv. Seems people fall for the ones that fall for someone else. Must be some kind of masochism. What's wrong with me? Why can't you love only me? What must I do to win you?"

"Henry, you're not listening to me! Can't you see the state I'm in? I love you both so much! Equally, I think. What am I supposed to do? Run away from both of you?" This was such a mess, she almost wished she had not met either one of them.

Henry felt very uncomfortable. "If you can't love me more, then just lead me on for awhile. Pretend, mislead me, abuse me, anything is better than feeling this way. Can't you just sort of nurse me away slowly, so it doesn't hurt so much?" He looked so spiritually crumpled.

"Henry," she said in exasperation, but with sympathy in her heart. "I'm not getting through to you here. I don't want to do any of those things to you. I don't want to push you away from me, I love you too much! I just can't make a damn decision and BV is going away! I want you BOTH! If I were a Mormon, I could have two spouses. That would sort all this out for me! BV's asked me to go away with him, but I want to stay here as much as I need to go with him. If he were able to stay awhile, I would have the time to make the right decision. This way it's being forced on me and it's not fair Henry!"

"Oh, I see. That's how it is. Horrible. I'm trying to put myself in your position." Henry went silent for a short while. "Nope, I can't! But it still seems a dreadful predicament for you and I am not sure who I feel sorriest for, you or me! "

Viv continued. "Think of it this way. You didn't intend falling for me. I never intended falling for both you and BV. Especially, not needing BV when I feel this way about you, too. It doesn't make sense. I should be able to choose, but I can't. This hurts me so much, too, you know! I'm in the middle. I'm being squashed with all these emotions, they're too much for me!"

Henry looked at her sad face and realized what she was going through.

"Viv, I'm so sorry, this is terrible for us all, I think, especially you. Yes, I'm including BV. If he loves you anywhere near the way I love you, he must be going through hell, too. You did tell him you loved me as well, didn't you?" He asked hopefully.

"Of course, I did. He's prepared to go without me if he has to, but he's putting pressure on me as well."

"Okay, I see where you're coming from." He tried to smile, but it was not convincing.

Viv suddenly thought of a possible way out. "There's another option open to you, Henry, if you can't, or won't wait for me. Harriet's really fallen for you, or haven't you noticed?" It greatly hurt her to remind him of this.

"Yes, I do know that, but I also know she's accepted the fact that I'll never feel the same way about her. With you, it's different, Viv." He paused not wanting to ask this, but he had to. "I need to ask you a question here. Is it inevitable that you'll end up with BV? I can see why of course. He's a sexy man, and his trouble causes an extra need for you. I know how you care about people and this might give him more leverage. I understand that and I can't really blame you." He was trying hard to be considerate as he continued.

"But you should be worried about his involvement with unsavoury characters. I wanted to warn you before but was worried about how you'd take it. Now, I think it's too late. It appears that you've entered the point of no return in that relationship. Just be careful. You're playing with fire there. He has money but can't give you a stable life and home!" Henry hoped Viv could not see his pain, but would understand the potential danger for her.

Viv pondered Henry's words carefully. Of course, she had been led astray by BV's looks, his animal magnetism and now, his great need for her. That is what attracted her to him from the start and why she continued to long for him. She could not bear for him to suffer on his own. Her love was real enough to share his troubles and for her to be there for him. Viv tried to offer Henry some comfort.

"What if," she said. "Say, if it does happen with BV and me, could you be happy with Harriet? With me out of the way, could you give her a chance?"

"That can't be a serious question, Viv!"

"Yes, it is! For heaven's sake."

Henry thought for a while. "No, Viv. I'd always remember she used to be a man. There's no getting around that. She's a wonderful woman and in many ways, she's always been a woman, although at one point trapped in a man's body. But the fact that she lived her life as a man; that may be too much for me to overcome psychologically. I have a great deal of affection for Harriet, and it only holds that in a real relationship I'd want that affection to eventually turn into a physical one." Henry continued, "The problem is, I don't know if I'd ever be turned on enough to be sexually aroused. It sounds selfish and superficial, I know, but realistically that would be unfair to both of us." His face grew hot as he remembered the failed sex session in Harriet's art studio.

"I can't be the only person for you Henry," Viv persisted. "People always get over each other, eventually. You really can't believe all that rubbish about not being able to get over a broken heart. People do it all the time, and still manage to find another love."

Viv did not really believe all she was telling Henry. She still remembered her love for Lawrence all of those years ago. She often had flashbacks, leading to the pain his memory always caused her. But, here she was now, in love with two men! She had walked away from Lawrence in case some other woman tempted him, and away from the imagined worse pain of losing him. That was a terrible choice she had to make back then, but this choice in this moment, was an impossible one. Maybe Henry would be unable to get over her and what if she could also not get over him? She was brought back to reality by the sound of his sad voice.

"But, Viv, that's because they have to, or maybe they want to get over a relationship. I don't want to get over you! I can't lose you, and I don't want to get over a broken heart in the process. I'm the one who is best for you, can't you see that? If I couldn't make you happy, then you'd be better off with no one... I mean, until someone who could.....″ He broke off before finishing the sentence as his emotions began to overwhelm him.

Viv felt terrible. She watched his hurt and how he attempted to be so brave. Pretending to cope, when he could barely contain his emotions. It hurt her very deeply inside as she really did not want to lose him either. *'God, I love him so much, too, and it's not just because he loves me. He's so special,'* she thought, close to tears herself now.

"What do you want me to do, Viv?″ There were tears in his eyes, and his voice cracked. "I can't stop loving you and I will never stop loving you.″

She did not know what to say, but surprised herself with the words that came out of her mouth.

"I want you to pay the bill and come home with me, Henry. I want you to stay with me tonight!″

Henry sat in stunned silence. "Are you sure that's a good idea under the circumstances? But why? I don't get it. I mean, I think that's an excellent idea, but I don't get it! I feel a bit like a guinea pig!″ He grinned. "But okay!″ He called over to the waiter for the cheque.

"Why a guinea pig?″ asked Viv.

"They're used for experiments, right?″

"That's not a nice way to put it, Henry!″

"No, I suppose not. I'll try not to think of it that way.″

"You can back out if you want to!" she told him sternly.

Henry looked very thoughtful. "This may be the only way you'll ever get your thoughts in proper perspective. It'll help you straighten out how you truly feel and should be for the best, I hope! I must admit I'd have preferred it to have been more natural, but I'm not complaining."

"Yes, I know, I know," she replied. "Can we go now?"

* * * * * * * * * * * * * * * * * * * *

Chapter Thirty-Three
Getting To Know Harriet

Now that Daniel was home with Dandy, BV decided to talk to him. The telephone conversation was brief, some of it about Daniel's prison ordeals. After Daniel hung up, he went into the kitchen to Dandy who was preparing the evening meal. He told her what had been said and that BV was about to leave the country, soon.

"That's odd. Why the rush? Oh well, BV was always impetuous," Dandy said. "What is important is that the police know you're in the clear. Once they pick that Scully character up, everything will be fine."

"Perhaps he wanted to go away before he gets roped into explaining why most of his guests were involved in drugs," Daniel said. "I hope he doesn't get into trouble over that, but I know he's dealt with way too many unsavoury characters in his time to be completely safe. BV's always lived his life on the edge. I hope it's not all catching up with him right now. You live life on the edge, you can end up falling over a cliff!"

Dandy put the food into the oven to cook and accompanied Daniel into the living room. They sat on the sofa. She looked at his sad face and knew he was thinking about his lack of performance in bed the previous night.

"It's okay Daniel, my love, don't worry about what happened last night. You're just too stressed to cope with everything right now. You only got out of that dreadful place a few hours ago. You'll see, in time you'll relax and be your old self again."

"It's not only that Dandy. There's something I'm finding difficult to tell even you. Oh, well, I guess I need to talk about it. It's got to be now or never," he said pensively, looking down at the floor. "It's what I went through. The things I saw, that day you came to see me in prison."

"It's okay, Daniel, no need to talk about it now. Let's wait until you're feeling better," Dandy said thought-fully. "Besides, I know that you're still bothered about your brother and his phone call. Imagine, out of the blue, BV just calling and telling you that he's leaving the country. That you may never see or hear from him again. It's enough to send anyone into a tailspin."

"No, no. It's not just that Dandy. You see, well, if I don't talk about it now then I'll never get it out," he replied. "Well, those first few days in prison, I was placed in, with what is known as the general popula-tion. I temporarily shared a cell with a young man who'd been sentenced for forgery. He was a tall, very shy kid, probably only in his early twenties. I never got to know much about him actually, and cannot even remember his name." Daniel was determined to tell his wife about this terrible ordeal he went through.

He continued, "My second night there, the door of the cell opened and a bunch of guys came in. Not guards, these were inmates and they took this kid and beat him terribly. Then they stripped his clothes off and bent him over the bunk, whilst they took turns raping him. All the while, calling him disgusting, degrading names. It was just terrible and I was told to stay out of it, or worse would happen to me. I didn't know what to do, so I just sat there helplessly, like a snivelling coward! I still hear that poor kid's screams.

That kid looked at me from time to time, his eyes begging for help, but I did nothing! Nothing! I was too horrified. They beat him so bad that he lost consciousness. Actually, I thought they might have killed him. When they left, I was reminded in no uncertain terms that much worse would definitely happen to me unless I kept my mouth shut."

Dandy held his hand tightly. "Forget it, Daniel, there was nothing you could do. How terrible! What happened to that poor man? Did they…, I mean, did they kill him?"

"I don't know. He was in real bad shape. I called out to the guards, who had some medics come and take the poor kid away on a stretcher. The boy was limp and bleeding terribly. I never heard anything about him again. I spoke with one of the guards the next day about the incident. He told me, off the record, that for my own good, I had not seen anything. Also, to survive, I should find a man to be my partner. Someone I could willingly have sex with."

"What? How could they!"

"Evidently, in that way I'd be protected, preventing the same thing happening to me. He said the kid owed one of the older inmates a carton of cigarettes. That's how they barter in there. When he couldn't pay it back, this guy expected the kid to have sex with him. It's a common game the older, more experienced inmates and gang members use against first-timers and younger guys."

"But why can't the guards do anything about it?" asked Dandy.

"You'd be in worse trouble for 'snitching.' That isn't done at all. They make sure these cons are indebted to them. Once that's done, these guys are coerced mercilessly for sex to pay the debt back. Most of them go along with it because they figure it's better than getting gang raped, or worse, raped and beaten up by a bunch of inmates. The gangs are very powerful and run the prison. This one kid refused and tried to stand up to them, so the gang were there to teach him a lesson. They made him an example to the others."

"Oh, Daniel, how terrible! Darling, I'm so sorry! We should report this to the warden or someone. We need to put a stop to all this!"

"That would never work, Dandy. The guard I spoke to went on to tell me it was the way things were, and I should get used to it. I can't stop having nightmares about it all. Just as you got me out of there, these same guys were starting to send me threatening notes. They were constantly jeering at me, making crude remarks. If I stayed in there one more day, I'd have been just another victim of the system."

"I would have been dehumanized, and no one would have done anything to stop it. Just like me, when that kid was getting brutalized and needed help. If I had been there longer and knew what was going on, I would have picked them off one at a time. But this time, I could do nothing. No one would have lifted a finger for me either, when I had reprisals. It's just too terrible to think about, but for me not to have helped that poor kid, I don't know if I'll ever forgive myself for that."

Dandy held Daniel in her arms and cried with him. After a short while, the doorbell rang and she got up to answer the door.

"Oh, I'm so sorry, baby. I forgot to tell you, I invited Harriet over to meet you and show us some of her artwork. I'll have her come back some other time," she said, wiping her eyes and getting up to answer the door.

"No, don't worry," he replied. "I need the company to keep my mind off things. I'll be okay Dandy, I promise. Let's talk about it all later, okay?" He wiped his eyes with a tissue. "Just relax. I'll get the door."

When the door opened, Harriet was shocked to find a clone of BV standing there. It looked as if BV had shaved off his moustache and grown his hair longer. Overcoming her surprise, she introduced herself. Daniel liked her right away, thinking she looked more feminine than he had imagined. He was glad of this chance to show his appreciation for her help in setting him free, and intended to buy some of her paintings. That would be a good start at least.

Harriet was thrilled to show her work off. She was in the business to sell art and the Lyons would give her work a good home. Daniel helped bring her canvases into the house. During one of these brief trips back and forth to the car, he began an informal conversation.

"You know my brother BV," Daniel said casually. "He called to say he's leaving the country soon."

It surprised him to share this information readily with Harriet, but she had tried to help him and was a good friend to Dandy and he needed to talk. The thought of not seeing his brother again, at least not in the near future, bothered him very much.

Daniel continued, "I worry about BV Harriet. I know he hangs out with the wrong crowd of people, and I'm convinced that has something to do with his going away. He's been involved with the 'fringe' sort of people all of his life. It's just in his nature, but something has gone terribly wrong. The problem is he's unwilling to open up and tell me about it. That worries me."

"I'm sure there's good reason for it," replied Harriet, although she had her suspicions about BV, too. Especially, with his involvement in drugs. She did not want to bring up the topic, so it was best Daniel brought up the subject of BV's friends, and not her.

"BV seems a bit impulsive, but he must have an excellent reason to leave so abruptly, Daniel. He wouldn't just leave everyone and everything behind. Perhaps it has something to do with his business?"

"Yeah, he is impulsive," replied Daniel. "That's why it doesn't come as a complete surprise. It's just that, as his brother, I can sense when something's wrong. We've had those feelings for one another all our lives. Whenever one of us was in trouble, or there was something wrong with the other, we have always sensed it. It's uncanny, but true.'

In reality, Harriet was not surprised to hear that BV was about to leave the country, but she did not air her views. Some things were better left unsaid. After all, Daniel was his brother and it would be hard to explain why she did not like BV. Harriet also did not like the fact that Viv was so involved with him, but for her own sake it was better for Viv to be involved with BV, than with her Henry. Harriet secretly hoped to have Henry for herself. Even though he did not show it at the moment, she knew that eventually, if Henry was left to her alone, he would fall for her. She did not blame Viv for the way it was going down either. Harriet understood all about emotions, and she also knew Viv suffered from caring too much for both men.

Once Harriet's art possessions were in the house, the trio assembled in the living room. They cleared a large enough space on the coffee table where Harriet was able to display each painting and drawing. She brought some of her favourites to show them, including a portrait of Henry. It was set in the living room of her home. The painting was of him standing in his underwear, holding a coffee cup. It was a bit abstract, but a tremendous likeness, and Daniel found it hilarious.

"Sorry, that one's not for sale," Harriet explained. She wanted to keep it for her studio. It also reminded her of that first intimate encounter with Henry. Daniel could not help but notice the fine detail and meticulous structure given to the drawing, which was done in pen and ink.

"The detail in these drawings is absolutely remarkable," he exclaimed. "You're incredible Harriet. You have outstanding talent. Please show us everything that you've brought over, I can't wait to see it all!"

Harriet continued to show her work, explaining that a story was attached to every one. The old cliché that every picture tells a story certainly rang true when it came to Harriet's work. She had drawn a picture of a pacing lion, during one of her visits to a zoo in the States. It was at a time when she had gone through her own emotional turmoil over the sex change operation. Trying to come to terms with whether it was the right decision, or not.

Harriet had observed the 'lion' for ages managing to capture its majestic look, and the finishing touch was the beautiful frame. She called it 'True To Your Nature' because she realized that no matter how caged or domiciled the lion was kept, it was still a dangerous animal and a perfect killing machine. Only, it killed to survive and not out of mere aggression. In the zoo, it was out of its environment, just like she was, but it was also a tremendous family animal. It stayed true to its pride and protected them. Most of the time, anyway.

Harriet often felt melancholy knowing there was no one who cared enough to protect her. She could have used the reassurance and comfort of a family with all that continued to happen in her life. She was alone, but that was nothing new.

She had been lonely all of her life, even as a child. It was no oversight that her parents stopped photographing her when she turned fourteen. As she began to portray more and more feminine character-istics, her parents just could not handle it. Instead of being friendly and supportive, they felt humili-ated and rarely spoke to her. It hurt that her parents turned their backs when she needed them so des-perately. Especially, since she had to defend herself almost daily from the taunts and attacks of her peers. Parents were supposed to be there to protect, sup-port and help, but instead they turned away from her.

It was almost a blessing when she dropped out of school a few years later and made her own way in life. When she left home, there was little fanfare, or emotion. Her parents provided some money and waved goodbye, telling her to look after herself.

They would suffer no more humiliation and felt re-lieved she no longer lived with them. It became their last contact as they never replied to any of her let-ters. Harriet heard that her father had passed away a few years ago and that her mother followed shortly thereafter. She still thought about them, and her childhood, at least up to the point when they ostra-cized her.

Harriet's departure from home still left vivid mem-ories. She was just seventeen when she took up with a friend, named Mark. Of course, he had no idea that Harriet was falling for him or of her sexual feelings toward him. It disturbed her being unable to express any feelings towards him since she looked like a man too. They rented a flat together, as friends, but Mark occasionally brought women back to the flat which caused her to feel jealous.

One night, after Mark's break-up with a particular girl, they drank heavily and commiserated about past relationships. One thing led to another and soon they were kissing. Harriet performed oral sex on Mark, and they fell asleep in his bedroom. Even though the drink had affected both of them, Harriet, (Philip) became worried about how Mark would handle the knowledge of what just occurred, when the drink wore off and his brain turned on.

When they awoke the next day, Mark was indeed horrified at what had happened in their inebriated states. Harriet was accused of being gay and in trying to turn Mark into one. He angrily ordered Harriet out of his bed and she then spent days alone in her room crying. She had wanted him to make love to her, the same as he would have with a woman. No penetration had occurred on either person and she was not 'gay.' Already being feminine, Harriet knew she did not want gay men to treat her like another 'gay' man. Her need was to be loved as a woman, not as a man. Breasts, vagina appreciated, and the coupling in the proper orifice. She had no feeling for her back passage to be impaled in any way.

When Mark was able to speak with her again, she tried to explain that it was not a 'gay' thing and about her true feelings of being feminine. He ridiculed her and accused her of making excuses about fancying her own sex. But it was more than that. Harriet had started to fall in love and only then had she wanted the physical closeness with him.

It was true, however, that at no time during puberty, or after, had she any sexual feelings toward a woman. She could appreciate their beauty, and liked to hear the women speak about clothes or make-up. That always fascinated Harriet. But, she always preferred to be in men's company, until they started talking about women and football. These subjects held no interest for her at all.

Weeks passed, with the atmosphere growing far worse. It hurt Harriet dreadfully to only have polite conversations with Mark. It felt even worse, when he brought women back to the apartment again. Harriet would sit alone in the next room, trying to relate to the feelings of the woman. She knew Mark would never love her. When the heartache grew too much, she had to move away from him and go it alone. The hurt stayed, although she was able to escape in her drawings and paintings when feeling particularly down. And there were times when she could get extremely depressed. In fact, she felt quite suicidal, attempting it a few times, although unsuccessfully.

The first time was a clumsy attempt shortly after she left home. She tried to cut her wrists with a broken piece of glass and scraped it over them repeatedly. As it turned out, the sight of blood made her squeamish. She had to stop and ended up cleaning the superficial wounds and covering them with bandages.

The second time was not long after leaving the flat she shared with Mark. She overdosed on the sleeping tablets her doctor had prescribed for her insomnia. Another time was a couple of years before her transgender surgery. She had just spent another holiday alone and felt very scared about the decision to be made. There was no one to talk to about this life-changing operation, and she felt melancholy and totally unloved or needed.

The loneliness and indecision hurt so badly that she took an overdose of Valium. That never worked, and she ended up asleep for three days. The only other memory of what happened that evening was the terrific headache she woke up with. She felt completely useless, not even being able to get suicide done right.

Harriet experienced frequent episodes of depression over the years, even after her successful operation. She felt particularly down the night she first met Henry. Why was he there at that bar, at that precise moment? Neither of them ever frequented bars, but they just happened to meet there that night. They had now become such good friends, although Harriet would always yearn for a more intimate and long-lasting relationship.

It seemed fate sometimes entered the lives of people, to intervene and help them cope when they were unable to take any more. She had not been doing well emotionally for several months, when she entered the bar for a drink and hopefully, some good company. In reality, a successful suicide was on her mind that lonely night, although she never disclosed or even discussed those thoughts with Henry, the man who was brought into her life by fate.

Somehow, Henry reignited a spark and made Harriet feel alive again. Life was worth living after all, and he was a big part of it. It felt so exciting when she was in his company. Sure, there would be complications in their relationship. Mainly due to Harriet's sexuality and his involvement with Viv, but certainly those problems could be overcome or ignored.

Henry seemed a bit shy that one night, but who would not be if confronted with a similar situation? Love would conquer all in the end, and Harriet was totally in love with Henry. He was gentle and caring, with such honesty showing in his kind eyes. He was a good man, she could tell, and it would be impossible to imagine life without him. Harriet had searched for such a partner all her life and after the suffering she had been through, deserved this happiness.

Harriet also believed that in time, love would win out and they would find happiness together. Finally, she would have a family. Henry would be her family, along with all of the wonderful friends made in the past few weeks. It gave her comfort to think such warm thoughts.

"Harriet, can you hear me, you seem to be miles away," Daniel asked, as he interrupted her thoughts, bringing her back to the reality of their abode.

"Oh, I'm so sorry," she said. "What were you saying Daniel?"

"I've just got to have that one," he said pointing to the lion picture. "Just you name your price!"

"Sold!" she said, delighted. "The lion to Mr Lyons!" He immediately picked up the lion portrait and went to hang it on the wall behind the dining room table.

When he returned, job done, cheque written for the agreed amount and given to Harriet, she continued to show her pictures. In particular, one group that illustrated her extravagant use of colours.

"I love these, Harriet," Dandy said. "The colours are so vividly lovely!"

"I'm really glad you like them," Harriet beamed, adding, "Hey, perhaps I could do a portrait of you and Daniel? It will be a gift for both of you. I brought my brushes and paint things. Won't take me long to fetch them from my car!"

"We'd love that!" exclaimed Dandy. "Would it be finished this evening or require more sittings?"

"I'm quick," Harriet responded. "I may be able to finish it tonight, but if not, I can come back tomorrow if that's convenient?"

"Oh, I can't wait!" said Dandy excitedly. "We would hang it right here over the mantelpiece, er, where the lion is at present."

"Yes," replied Daniel. "Place of honour and we'll choose the next best place to put the lion."

Harriet went outside to retrieve the equipment from the trunk of her car, brushes, paints, inks, easel and canvas. As she assembled all of her supplies, a brown, paper parcel fell out of her bag with a thud. In light of everything that had happened, and with Scully loose, Harriet was nervous enough to want protection. After much thought, she had gone to a pawn shop earlier that day and purchased a handgun from 'beneath the counter.'

Harriet never owned a gun before. She did not believe in them or in violence, except as a last resort and even then, it disturbed her. She had been at the receiving end of way too much abuse and violence during her lifetime. As a consequence, she realized that tit-for-tat rarely accomplished anything. Except that it left the recipients feeling the need to seek retribution in kind. It was a vicious cycle where no one ended up the winner.

A friend had told Harriet using a gun was easy, *'just point and shoot.'* Her gun was a simple looking weapon, but actually quite beautiful in its form and function. It was bright silver and the pawn shop clerk had told her it was a Colt .357 magnum revolver, with a ventilated 8 inch barrel, whatever that meant. All she knew was that the shells were huge, which meant they should find and stop their target, no matter how inexperienced the marksman might be. As that friend once told her; *'You want something that gives you maximum fire power without having to worry about having a perfect aim.'*

Harriet admired the weapon momentarily and ran the fingers of her left hand over its smooth barrel. She placed it back into its brown wrapper and secured it under the wheel well in the trunk. *'God forgive me if I should ever have to use such a terrible thing, even in self defence,'* she thought. She quickly gathered her art supplies up and headed back for the house.

Harriet thought the Lyons were a wonderful, lovely couple. They were really meant for each other and it showed. She could also see why Viv had been so attracted to Daniel, with his disarming good looks. In reality, Daniel was completely devoted to Dandy and would never stray from her. It was obvious that he adored his wife.

'I wonder if Henry and I will end up like that,'

Harriet thought, as she carried her supplies in. '*Of course we will. Over time he'll love me completely just like I love him now. But then again, maybe I'm not meant to be loved. I might be one of those people who have friends, but not a partner. There are some people like that; they're just so different that no one can ever be happy with them. They end up in seclusion, loneliness or both and then die alone.*'

The heavy feeling of melancholy which hit Harriet soon dispersed as she entered the living room where the Lyons anxiously awaited her. She smiled at them.

"Okay, let's get started." Harriet smiled, and expertly covered up her feelings of despair and sadness. After all these years of training, she was good at that.

* * * * * * * * * * * * * * * * * * * *

Chapter Thirty-Four
The Shattering of a Rapturous Union

Without warning, Henry lifted Viv and carried her into the bed room. This surprised her, as she waited to see where it was going. Memories returned, uninvited, of the intense pleasure she shared with BV.

Henry placed Viv on the bed, kissed her deeply and buried his face between her breasts. He pressed himself against her with urgency. It was hard to believe he had this animal streak in him. Henry had seemed more conservative and laid back, but, now he was a wild man. Just as she thought Henry was about to lose all control, he stopped, stood back and placed Viv gently into a sitting position.

"I'll fix us some drinks first and bring them in," he said.

"Oh," she said re-buttoning her blouse. "Well, okay, Henry, you know where I keep everything." She was most intrigued by Henry's sudden change in character and liked it.

He walked into the next room and got busy with some bottles. Upon his return, they sipped their drinks, falling into occasional silence. When the glasses were finished, he leaned over and they kissed slowly, but the passion soon overcame them. The pressure of his open-mouthed kiss excited her, and they became enmeshed in the physical rapture of sensuality. Clothing was discarded, and no thoughts permeated her mind, except for the anticipation of what was to come. Her head reeled as Henry's hands moved all over her partially clothed body. Without waiting, or a change of position, he entered her, and she could barely breathe.

She clutched his strong muscular back, as pleasure overwhelmed them both to the point of ecstasy. Her whole body tingled and pulsated whilst he continued to kiss her. The thrill of it all amazed her and she was about to experience her first orgasm with Henry. Was this really Henry? She looked at him to make sure and yes, it was! They moved in rhythm, each movement raising the intensity. She heard him gasp several times. The sight of his manly strong chest and tight abdomen, as it contracted with the effort, was something she would never forget. This was every woman's fantasy, love and lust together. She experienced two rapturous orgasms, before feeling him quiver and change to quicken his rhythm.

Their kissing had ceased, due to the need for oxygen, and they both cried out loudly in relief and sheer pleasure. He fell forward onto her and his face rested beside hers. They panted, until a gentle calm came over them and then fell asleep wrapped tightly in each other's arms.

Viv was the first to wake, and she recalled that before arriving at her house, a nervous feeling had overcome her. It felt like the first time of really dating Henry. It also seemed as if she was just beginning to know him. Viv caressed Henry's hair with her fingertips. He awoke and smiled up at her.

"That was wonderful, Viv. Let's take a bath and then make dinner."

He guided her into the bathroom, his arm around her. She was still in a misty cloud of satiation as he held her and ran the bath. He also managed to pour in the great smelling Badedas bubble bath, one-handed.

"How are you feeling?" he asked, with a warm loving look in his eyes.

"Pretty good actually," she replied softly. "Mostly a bit surprised, that's all. But wonderful!"

Viv climbed into the fragrant smelling bath and lay back, letting the bubbles soothe her body. Henry soaped her body, massaging her all over. She wriggled when he touched her private parts. Viv felt him get into the bathtub, but was too relaxed to open her eyes. He soaped his body quickly. Through half-opened lids, she watched the man she loved, get out and dry himself.

"Are you ready to get out now?" he asked her.

"Yes, I am, Henry."

He lifted and placed Viv on the bathmat then dried and snuggled her in a towel. He carried her into the bedroom where the curtains were still drawn and the semi-darkness soothing. He gently placed her on the bed and lay down beside her. She could see the concern in his expression.

"Thanks Henry. I feel all right, honestly! Just surprised at the feelings you gave me."

She smiled to reassure him. They cuddled up and very slowly Henry removed her towel. Viv enjoyed the feeling of his flesh against hers and became excited again. She caressed him, and he tried to control himself, but his hardness told her differently. All the warmth from their previous lovemaking swarmed back, and it happened again. They both felt blissfully satiated. There was so much love as well as lust between them, which gave a more complete feeling to their relationship. Viv did not want this intensity to stop. She had now made her decision based on a total package, rather than be blinded by the excitement which accompanied BV and, which could also bring problems and insecurity for her.

Henry was her man, but she felt anxious wondering how she could cope with not seeing BV ever again. After a short while of hugging each other tightly, they got up and dressed.

"I'll make us something to eat," Viv said.

"Thanks, I'm famished," said Henry. "Could you use some help?"

"No, thanks, darling, I'll be okay," she embraced Henry and they kissed deeply.

Viv departed for the kitchen. It was good to have a few minutes to herself to think. She must decide how and when to tell BV, and it would have to be done soon. She knew there would be pain and not only for her. How to do it? What to say? Before she could answer her own question, the doorbell rang. She jumped, her composure gone temporarily. She called out to Henry to open the door.

"Got it," he replied.

Suddenly she heard a loud crash and the sound of raised voices.

"Guess you were just in the wrong place at the wrong time, pal!" she heard someone shout.

"Who the hell are you guys?" she heard Henry shout back, followed by more crashing sounds. Apparently, a fight had broken out, and Viv was terrified for herself as well as Henry. Viv picked up her cell phone and hit the speed dial for Harriet, whilst trying unsuccessfully to dial 999.

She was shaking too much and dropped the phone. Then she thought of running out the back to a neighbor for help, but a man stood there, with his back to the door as if he was keeping a lookout. She panicked, but then thought of Henry. She grabbed the first thing nearby, a vase, and peered into the room with the action. Henry was surrounded by three men. One large man, in particular, seemed more menacing than the other two. He held a wooden club and swung it about. The man to his right lunged and Henry smacked him hard in the mouth with his fist. The man reeled backwards, grimacing in pain before hitting the floor.

The next man whacked Henry across his back with a club causing him to momentarily stumble, arching his arms back in pain. He regained his balance and blocked the next blow with his forearm. There was a cracking sound as the club connected. With his other hand, Henry punched the man hard in the ribs which sent him into a heap across the floor. He turned to face the third man and was hit hard across the back of the head with a club. Henry dropped heavily to the floor.

He lay on the floor motionless, the large man waving the wooden club stood astride him. A big sneer spread across his face.

'*Oh my God, Henry's dead!*' Viv thought. A sick feeling grabbed the pit of her stomach and her knees began to buckle.

As she watched in horror, the large man stepped over Henry's body to reach his two unconscious companions. He gave both a kick to wake them up. Slowly they staggered to their feet and stood. Both went over and gave Henry's inert body a kick in the kidney area. Viv's heart raced, hoping to see Henry move. She screamed for them to stop, but had no idea of what to do. Suddenly, the large man turned and looked at her. She wanted to hide, but it was too late.

"You!" he screamed. Then, in a slow, menacing voice, he said, "It took me a while to find you! I got your description from a friend of Annabel's, but you're prettier than they said."

His words sickened her.

"What do you want?" Viv asked. Her nerves were such a mess, she could barely utter the question. She knew this was Scully.

"The police are trying to get me for Annabel's murder! That would not be happening if it wasn't for you and your freakin' bitch of a friend. The one I smacked!" he boasted. "Don't worry though, she's going to get much worse than that, believe me." With an evil grin, Scully motioned to his two accomplices to move ahead.

He took out his cell phone, and called his other companion standing vigil by the back door.

"Get back in here!" Scully shouted.

He then walked toward Viv, leering at her. She started to back out of the room. The sound of someone coming in the back door startled her. There was nowhere to run.

All at once, Scully's three accomplices were all over her, whilst Scully stood in front, all the while waving his wooden club. Two of the men clutched her by the shoulders, whilst the third one ripped the front of her blouse. Soon, it was ripped completely off. Her attempts at kicking and punching were useless, and her arms were held firmly by her side. Scully approached and pulled down her bra, exposing her large breasts. He began to grab and maul them. The men laughed hysterically as the room began to spin out of control for Viv. She felt dizzy and wanted to vomit.

Scully, moved in closer. She could smell the alcohol on his breath. "I wanted to hurt you for your part in this," he leered, "but I've other plans now."

He tore at her skirt, revealing her thighs, as she continued to try and fight him off. Soon her skirt was a tattered mess which he flung across the room. His attention was distracted momentarily by the sound of Henry, who groaned on the floor.

"Thank, God, he's still alive," she whispered.

"Go get him," Scully said, "finish the job!" He motioned towards his three friends to attack Henry again.

The three accomplices advanced toward Henry. This caused just enough of a distraction, for Viv to pull away and run behind the sofa. She glanced at Henry, who was still motionless on the floor. *"My poor Henry, I've got to think of something."*

Viv was terrified as she watched the three advance toward him. This was truly a horrific scene unfolding before her eyes. Henry surprised her by suddenly staggering to his feet. A thread of hope rushed through her.

Henry regained his balance and prepared to fight, using his good arm. The shorter man was the first to swing at him. Henry responded by moving sideways and giving a well aimed karate kick to the groin. The man buckled as Henry followed with a terrific chop to the throat. The man fell to the ground clutching his throat and gurgling. He soon became motionless. It must have been a lethal blow.

The other two jumped on Henry, who put up as brave a battle as possible, landing some good kicks against the overwhelming odds. Viv knew he was fighting for both his life and hers. If only she could reach the door, it would be possible to run for help. But Scully was too close and blocked her escape.

Scully threw himself over the sofa and pulled her down with him. She struggled hard, but her strength was no match for him. By his movements, Viv knew he was opening his trousers. She bit his lip when he tried to kiss her. She saw his arm rise to hit her, but he reeled over before delivering the blow.

Somehow Henry had escaped the battle with his two antagonists, who were clutching various parts of their bodies in pain, giving him time to hammer his fist against Scully's jaw. Viv closed her eyes in relief and felt Henry helping her to her feet. But, it was short-lived as Scully recovered pulling out a knife. He opened it with a quick flick of his wrist to expose a gleaming steel blade.

"I'm going to cut you to bits," Scully sneered at Henry.

The two accomplices came upon him from both sides. Henry threw his elbow at the nearest one with such a force that it shattered the man's nose on impact. Bone fragments flew into his brain. The man staggered several feet across the floor, holding his bleeding face. Then he fell and did not move again.

The other man picked up an iron poker from the fireplace as Scully advanced with the outstretched knife. Henry reached for the first thing he could to defend himself, but it was just a pillow from the sofa. Suddenly, using the pillow, Henry shoved the man with the poker, into Scully and the men fell over each other. Henry turned to defend himself against Scully, who was rising from the floor angrier than ever, and as he did so, the other man hit him hard with the poker. Henry fell to the floor unconscious.

"Enough of these games," Scully sneered. He turned to face Viv. "Now, you die little girl!" he sneered as he and his partner advanced towards her. They were just about on top of her, when a voice disturbed them from the doorway.

"Have you forgotten my promise?" barrelled a voice. The two men turned and were startled to see Harriet standing in the open front door. She slammed the door closed and glared at them. In the excitement, Harriet had forgotten to use her trained higher-pitched woman's voice and had resorted back to the deeper voice of a man.

Scully laughed and then his partner began to laugh.

"Hey, look! Our victims are coming right to us. Don't worry victim, I'm just going to take care of some business here, then it's your turn. You're going to like what I've got planned for you. But first, I'm going to enjoy doing you, baby!" Scully said, as he raised his knife toward Viv.

"I said…. Do you remember my promise?" boomed Harriet, emphatically and even deeper this time.

Scully turned quickly and screamed at her, "What's that, bitch? What did you promise me?"

She looked down quickly at the poor, injured Henry. He glanced up at her with glazed eyes.

"Harriet?" he mumbled. She motioned him to stay down, as anger coursed through her veins.

"It's all right, Henry, stay still." Looking at Scully she said, "I made you a promise the last time we met, scumbag! Don't you remember?"

"No, enlighten me you crazy bitch!" he snarled.

"I promised you that the next time we met, I'd kill you!"

From behind her back she produced the Colt revolver and pointed it straight at Scully.

Scully's eyes bulged from his head with surprise, then rage. Finally, it overcame him and he lunged at Harriet, but it was too late. There were two clicks followed by two loud cracks as the gun fired and the bullets hit him square in the chest. Scully was knocked clear off his feet by the impact and the knife flew out of his hand.

He landed on his back several feet away, blood spattering everywhere. Scully let out a brief moan and then lay motionless. His accomplice tried to run into the kitchen, heading for the back door to safety, but two more clicks, two more loud cracks, and he fell dead in his tracks. Scully and his accomplices were dead.

Viv rushed to Harriet, hugged her quickly, then crying hysterically went to Henry. He moved and muttered, "Harriet saved us," then passed out. Harriet called the ambulance and police. She helped Viv dress and explained how she saw Viv's number come up without a message, so knew something was wrong. Within fifteen minutes, there was a knock on the door. It was the emergency personnel, accompanied by Detective Mayfield.

"My God! What happened here? Looks like a slaughterhouse!" exclaimed the startled detective as he entered the house. "Okay, okay! You two ladies ride along with Henry in the ambulance. We need to make sure you're all right; you can answer questions later. Looks like it's going to be a long night." Mayfield called for additional backup to help secure the crime scene.

On the way to the hospital, seated on either side of Henry, Viv and Harriet could only stare at each other in total in silence. Henry suddenly spoke. "Viv?"

"Yes, Henry?" she answered quickly.

Henry muttered very groggily, "I love you, Viv. I'm so happy now that you love me too. Let's get married, soon, okay?"

"Yes, Henry!" How could she say anything else, when he had almost given his life for her? Viv looked at Harriet's sad face and started to say sorry, but Harriet stopped her.

"I know, Viv," she said. "You love each other very much." Harriet felt pleased to have saved both of their lives even if it meant losing Henry to her friend, but it still hurt her deeply. "Everything's going to be fine," she said to Viv, with a reassuring smile. "Just fine."

* * * * * * * * * * * * * * * * * * * *

Chapter Thirty-Five
'El Diablo.'

Detective Mayfield looked at the bodies scattered about Viv's house. It had all begun as a routine murder investigation in the death of a small-time criminal. Now he was faced with five additional bodies. These four hoodlums, as well as Annabel Lewis. It all looked relatively straightforward. Scully was involved in most of it, and the scene here looked like a clear case of self-defence.

Of course, there would be the issue with Harriet and the unregistered handgun. The prosecutor might see that as premeditated and bring charges. On the other hand, there were extenuating circumstances involved. It appeared Scully had attacked her previously and was also about to do so again. It would be easy enough to get some corroboration from Viv and Henry to that effect.

Mayfield was reminded of the other huge case he was still involved in, if only emotionally. He thought back to just a few months ago, when life was quiet and simple. There was nothing much happening, a loving wife to go home to, and the prospect of retirement. He distinguished himself throughout his career and could leave the force in good standing with high regard. Then he received that call from his squad leader. An international task force had been formed to track down and apprehend this serial killer known as, 'El Diablo.'

Bodies were showing up all over Europe, and it appeared the killer had begun to strike close to this small town, just outside London. The task force asked his squad leader to recommend a top man to participate in the investigation. Mayfield's name was proposed immediately. He accepted the assignment without hesitation. Finally, back to some real police work. Little had he known at the time, that it would lead to the horrific murder of his beloved wife.

His first goal after joining the task force was to develop a profile on the killer. The package provided him gave some of the details. As it turned out, El Diablo was sought in connection with eight murders, and suspected in dozens of others. Apparently, he was a master of disguise as well.

To date, each of the victims had been seen with a man fitting slightly different descriptions. He must have set himself into their lives to gain their complete confidence. There never appeared to be a sign of a struggle, he just befriended and killed them, always in their own homes.

In each case, the victims were drugged. El Diablo probably mixed it into a drink and then once his victim slipped into unconsciousness, he bound them. The first two victims were asphyxiated with a plastic bag. But lately, he killed in increasingly violent ways, and each of the last six victims were cut up with savage brutality. He always left some evidence behind specifically targeted at the police. He loved to taunt them. Each time, the killer had scrawled the word

'Pig,' somewhere on a wall, mirror, floor, or on lampshades, in the victim's own blood.

To date, El Diablo targeted only gay men, with the exception of his wife. Usually, younger men, single, successful and relatively attractive. Which made Mayfield suspect that the killer also fit at least part of that physical description. In the last murder, El Diablo severed the victim's head and placed it on the mantelpiece with a note inside the mouth. Only the word 'Pig' was written on the note. The most recent killing occurred only a few hundred miles away, and Mayfield knew he had to prepare himself for this maniac.

Somehow, the killer managed to stay a step ahead of the police, and he always seemed to know their next move. The media even speculated that the killer might be connected to the police, perhaps a cop. He seemed to possess too much inside information.

Mayfield discounted that theory. He suspected the killer was some type of technology whiz who had managed to tap into the police computers. Technology ruled everyone's lives these days, not like when Mayfield joined the force all those years ago. Back then, a good detective relied heavily on intuition, his contacts, a note pad and a sharp pencil. Now computers ran everything and so did those clever enough to hack into them for illicit purposes.

That was one of the reasons it did not surprise Mayfield when he began to receive personal messages from someone purporting to be the killer. The first phone call came late one evening just two weeks into the case. Mayfield was finishing up some reports and following up on witness statements. It had been another long day, and he wanted to wrap up before going home for the evening. Around midnight the telephone rang.

"Detective Mayfield here."

"Hi Mayfield. I'm a big fan of your work," said a deep and sophisticated voice on the other end.

"Who's this?"

Mayfield had immediately motioned to his staff to start the trace on the call.

"Well, my real name isn't significant to you. Not yet. After all, I change it to suit my mood. But for purposes of our communication, I believe everyone is referring to me as 'El Diablo.' That's funny. Me, the 'Devil!' Don't know how the papers picked up on that one. At least it's better than what they used to call me. You know, the killer of gay men."

"All right, Diablo. It's good to speak with you. Now, just tell me when you want to come in to talk. Or, better yet, just let me know where you are, and I'll be glad to pick you up personally, so we can have a private chat. I think we've a lot to talk about."

"I don't think that would be a good idea detective. You might want to throw me in jail, trap me, or even worse."

"Why would I want to do that, Diablo? You haven't been charged with anything as yet."

"Because, detective, all those murders you are investigating right now. Well, I committed them. I killed those men and you know it."

"Which men are you referring to? I haven't said anything about a murder," Mayfield looked out the internal window of his office to see if a trace had been completed as yet. His staff just shrugged their shoulders. It appeared that they were having difficulty getting the trace.

The caller laughed. "You amaze me detective. So sincere. What are you doing right now, trying to trace this call? Forget it, you'll never be able to do that. You'll never catch me, you know. I'll just continue to kill."

"Why do you kill, Diablo? Why gay men?" Mayfield asked.

"Oh, but it's not just gay men, Detective Mayfield. That's just the tip of the iceberg. You people will never begin to grasp the magnitude of my work. How many have you found by the way?"

"I'm not at liberty to discuss any details of the case with you, Diablo. I can only say that the number is significant."

El Diablo laughed again. "Significant. Yes, I guess a few dozen is a significant number when you're talking about body counts. But relatively speaking, it's just a small number. How many have you found? Probably not many. I only offer those clues to keep you people occupied. It gives the newspapers something to write about, too. I do enjoy my simple pleasures and my notoriety."

Detective Mayfield stood up and motioned, even more agitated than before to his crew, who continued to try and trace the call. 'Still no luck', was their response.

"Okay, Diablo. When are you going to stop all of this nonsense? Turn yourself in, why are you doing this?"

"Because, detective, because I can. I'm going now, but just one more thing before we finish."

"No, don't go yet Diablo. We're just getting started," said the frantic Mayfield.

"Sorry, detective, I've got to leave. I just wanted to say I've a surprise in store for you. Actually, it's already done. Talk to you later then. Oh, incidentally, I've branched out. I'm not only killing gay men any more. But that will be evident to you very soon. Bye… for now."

With that, El Diablo hung up on him.

"Did we get a trace on the call?" he yelled out to his staff.

"Sorry, Sir, this guy's slick. He must've been using some type of scrambler to jam our systems. We didn't even get one number, it's incredible!"

"I knew it," said the detective. "This guy's using technology against us. Great, just what we needed. A computer nerd, gay-killing, serial killer."

Detective Mayfield finished up his work for the night and went home. His wife had called earlier and told him that she was making his favourite dinner that evening. He really looked forward to it. Of course, nothing prepared him for what he discovered later that night. Apparently, El Diablo's 'surprise' was his slaughtered wife.

Sure, he was now off the case, 'officially,' but it had become personal. It would not be over until El

Diablo was apprehended, dead or alive. If Mayfield got his hands on him first, that choice would be an easy one to make.

* *

Mayfield's eyes refocused on the carnage in front of him. He'd get this sorted out and then pursue his own personal vendetta.

The forensic team arrived.

"Okay guys," he told them. "Let's get on with it then. Looks like a long evening for all of us. I'm going back to the station now. Keep in contact with me and see if you can't get me a full report within twenty-four hours. We'll need to meet first thing in the morning and see if we can wrap this all up."

Mayfield departed the scene leaving it in the hands of his capable team of experts. He felt extremely burdened. 'Killing, violence, what makes people want to do this?' Each time he investigated a murder scene, his wounds opened up and left him raw. He was determined to catch 'El Diablo,' against the rules or not.

He would not let this man go to trial. Too many things went wrong when the litigators got hold of a case. Evidence would get tampered with, or disappear. The defence would cry 'not guilty,' by reason of insanity. All of a sudden, in spite of top police work, the offender would get off on a technicality. No, El Diablo would never see the inside of a courtroom, if Mayfield had his way. And he would make sure that he did.

* *

Chapter Thirty-Six
Viv Gets to Know More about BV

As it turned out, BV had been working with the police as an undercover operative for over six years. It was the only way he could assuage his conscience. In the university he had befriended a young man named Paul, who grew dependent on drugs. BV tried so hard to help him get clean. Whenever Paul went 'cold turkey,' he became so ill and panic-stricken, begging BV to get him the drugs. Each time, BV succumbed to the pleas having to meet with dealers and pick up packages for Paul.

BV grew very angry with these illicit men, who cared little about the pain and addictions they caused. He would have set them all up for the police, if it had not been for his best friend's involvement. He supported Paul and helped him stay off drugs for as long as possible. However, when the sweats and trembles started, it grew harder each time to watch him suffer.

On one occasion, when Paul went through cold turkey, he collapsed and trembled violently. It frightened BV to watch his friend's body deteriorate. Paul would get pins and needles in his limbs, and his vision turned black at the periphery. It was at these times, BV relented and went to get the drugs to save his friend from his terrible suffering. It served to continue the addiction, but the pleas from his friend for help could not be ignored.

One particular day, Paul was going through these withdrawals, trying his hardest to come through his addiction. This time he begged BV not to give him any drugs. BV complied, but cried as he held his dear friend, wrapped in blankets, sweat pouring from his head. It must have been too much for Paul's heart this particular time, and he died whilst BV held him. That was the start of BV's guilt and his overwhelming hatred for drug dealers.

BV told the police about his complete involvement and his wish to work for them. He wanted as many of these immoral people to pay for their deeds as possible. There would always be drug pushers, but he wanted to prevent additional people from falling victim to them.

BV helped the police with problems in the University, and then, for six years 'officially' trained and became one of their undercover 'narks.' It was a very dangerous job, but extremely rewarding, too. To date, he possessed an envious record, but his luck had now run out. Scully had found out about BV's involvement, through an informant who worked in the police department. Consequently he tried to blackmail BV, who refused to pay him. In retaliation, Scully leaked his name to the mob, telling them that BV was a squealer who worked with the cops.

It seemed the trouble was serious enough that BV needed to run for his life. Detective Mayfield had asked him to come into the police department, to meet up and discuss the Scully case and his options.

BV was there now, at the station, talking to the detective and almost finished with the business of it all.

Meanwhile, Viv had left Henry recuperating in the hospital, so she could meet Detective Mayfield who wanted to get a statement from her. Henry told Viv to go on afterward and see BV, to tell him of their decision to marry.

The desk sergeant called Mayfield to let him know of her arrival.

"Viv has arrived to give me her statement. We should finish this business first, BV," said Detective Mayfield. "There are a few people I need you to speak with. The officers from the Witness Protection Program."

"It's okay, Wesley," BV replied to Mayfield. Why not have Viv come on in? Best to let her know what's going on with the Labelle case. I can explain the *'other'* important things to her in more detail later."

"That's okay with me, BV." Detective Mayfield phoned the desk sergeant to bring Viv into his office.

She was surprised to see BV there, but assumed it had something to do with the murder investigation. They hugged, kissed quickly and then sat down to listen to Detective Mayfield.

"You wanted to know why Annabel's diary was so important to us, well now I can let you know," Detective Mayfield said. He handed the diary to Viv, opened at the day before BV's barbeque. It read, *'must remember to wear the large hat with the hat pin as David asked. He seems adamant. Cannot imagine why, but it won't hurt to wear it!'*

"You see," said Mayfield, "as it turns out, this David, who you know as Scully, was a very bad character. He was heavily into drug trafficking among other things, and Alex Labelle was his contact to BV here."

Viv looked up at Mayfield. "Oh, so you knew about BV's involvement in that? The drugs?"

She felt surprised, then worried about the outcome. Perhaps that was why BV was here today. He was to be charged with trafficking and would be sent off to prison for a long time!

"Of course, Viv. We know the Baron very well."

Before he could continue, BV interrupted, "Viv, there's a lot I need to tell you, but please hear Detective Mayfield out first. I'll tell you what I can later."

"Okay, BV, but I'm so confused," she replied.

"Well," Detective Mayfield continued. "BV arranged to receive a shipment of narcotics from Labelle, who was a minor distributor. He obtained all of his drugs from this guy Scully. As it turns out, Labelle had plans of his own. He had no idea that BV was working with us."

"What!" exclaimed Viv as she shot up from her seat. "What do you mean working with you?" she asked, looking directly at BV.

BV looked dishevelled. "It's a long story, Viv, and I'd prefer to tell you in private. I've been working undercover with the police department for a long time now. We were trying to identify everyone in the drug pipeline from small fry to the big fish. It took a long time, but it worked. There's a lot to tell. Please be patient, I'll explain later."

Viv sat back down, in total confusion.

Mayfield continued, "It turns out, that Labelle was supposed to receive the drugs from Scully just a few nights before the barbeque. BV had done business with them many times in the past. Now the plan was to get the drugs and deliver them to BV, who would have the money deposited directly into an offshore bank account."

"This plan had been used several times before. It was a system that seemed to be working fine. Incidentally, by working with several other law enforcement agencies, we were able to use the bank account numbers to make several high-profile arrests. But, back to Labelle."

Viv sat in awed silence.

"Anyway," said Mayfield, "this time, Labelle decided to be a wise guy and keep the drugs. He intended to sell them and make big money for himself. It's hard to believe Labelle was so stupid not to realize who the guys were that he was ripping off. These people don't play games, and they don't take getting ripped off lightly. They wanted payback."

"We've since pieced together bits from what happened next from Scully's brother, Robert. He's in prison and was also Scully's confidant. He's opening up now and singing like a canary, to try and get his sentence reduced. He's provided us with some key details in the process. Incidentally, did you know that it was BV here, who helped put him behind bars to begin with?"

Viv sat in silence, amazed as the story unfolded before her. Mayfield continued.

"Since it was Scully who had delivered the shipment, his orders were to get the drugs back from Labelle, plus the money for them and then to get rid of Labelle. Scully planned to sneak into the barbeque by wearing a costume, escorted by Annabel. She was already an invited guest, and then when the time was right, he was to kill Labelle." Mayfield continued. "At the barbeque, Scully approached Labelle and asked for the drugs and the money. When Labelle couldn't, or wouldn't produce anything, Scully killed him. The hat pin was used by him to finish off the job. Incidentally, we found the drugs hidden in Labelle's apartment this morning."

"But why did he kill Annabel, Detective?" Viv asked. "What part could she possibly have played in anything?"

Mayfield replied, "Well, Scully just sort of stumbled onto the idea of killing Labelle with the hat pin. He wanted to try and shift the blame to Annabel. Luckily, she wrote quite a bit about that in her diary there. Apparently, Scully confided many of the details of Labelle's murder to her the night she was killed. Just after you and your friend Harriet last saw her that evening, Viv."

"Does that mean that Scully didn't kill her? I mean she had time to write all that in her diary. Didn't she?"

"We can't rule him out," replied Mayfield. "He could have gone away and thought about what he'd confided to Annabel. Later, with drink in him, he could have regretted it and decided to murder her." Mayfield smiled. "Yes, maybe it happened like that."

Viv felt huge guilt. Had she insisted that Annabel stay with her that evening, perhaps she would still be alive. Although, more likely, Scully would have hunted her down and killed both of them. Viv shivered at the thought, then resumed listening to Detective Mayfield.

"So, Scully left her alone for a few hours. Then, perhaps thinking better of it, went back and finished her off, so she couldn't talk to the police. He may not have known that Annabel kept track of everything in her diary, just in case anything ever happened to her. Now, it's proving invaluable to us."

"So it seems that Scully killed both Labelle and Annabel," Viv said. "That man is a monster!"

"Yes, that's a safe assumption, but of course we have to prove that now. His greed would have been his undoing." Detective Mayfield continued. "He could have become braver after killing Labelle, and decided to move on to bigger things. Somehow, he got hold of information about BV's involvement with us. We obviously have an inside informant in the department, and we're now dealing with that situation."

"It turns out it was someone in records, a woman who used to date Scully. Anyway, Scully started to make plans. Since he didn't have the drugs, he decided to get the money from BV and give it to his bosses in order to buy their favour in the syndicate. He felt that $1 million would make him a big man in the organization, so he decided to blackmail BV. He called BV that evening and told him that it was going to cost him $1 million to keep quiet."

"Keep quiet, or he would tell his bosses about BV and his involvement with the police?" asked Viv.

Mayfield continued. "Exactly. BV came to us immediately. We'd already decided to pick up Scully for questioning when all of you suddenly got involved! Next thing we knew, Annabel was dead."

Viv's face turned ashen.

"We were looking for Scully when he met with his final justice at your house, Viv. Now we just have to tie everything up with the evidence, so that Daniel Lyons can be completely exonerated."

"Thank goodness," Viv sighed.

"During my investigations, Viv," Mayfield said in a deeper voice, "I found out that you were in the…" he coughed, "den, around the time of Alex Labelle's death. Are you sure you did not hear, or see anything suspicious that might help us in our investigation? Just to help us tie up all of the loose ends here?"

Viv was horrified. "You can't suspect me, I didn't have a motive to kill anyone, I don't take drugs, it was the first time I'd even met BV!" she blushed, realising what she was admitting to, and it was no crime. "Do I need my solicitor?"

"No, no you don't! Just hold on, Viv, I'm not accusing you of anything," said Mayfield. "I'm a detective, and it's my job to ask questions. With all that's happened, it would be easy to forget some small piece of information that might be important here. I think I've all that I need though. Please keep in touch in case we have any further questions, okay?"

Viv felt that Detective Mayfield may have hoped

she knew something which could help him, but now felt reassured by his words and demeanour.

"Right. Sorry detective. I'm still such a bundle of nerves over all that's happened. It still seems so unbelievable. Incredible, really."

"I know," replied Mayfield. "I don't have any further questions right now. Why don't you let BV take you home and get some rest?"

* * * * * * * * * * * * * * * * * * * *

Chapter Thirty-Seven
Heartbreaking Experience for Viv and BV

BV drove Viv back to his home, leaving her car parked by the police station. The conversation on the way was light and uneventful. Each of them thinking how best to break the news to the other about what the future held. When they entered the house, BV asked Viv to sit down in the main room whilst he fixed a couple of drinks. *'I've been drinking quite a bit recently, considering I don't drink,'* Viv thought.

BV returned and began to speak. He appeared nervous, which she had not noticed at any other time.

"Viv, I love you. I've never known such emotion and passion as I've felt with you, and that's why it's so important that I tell you everything. I'll try to fill in the gaps Mayfield never covered with you." His tender words caused her eyes to sting. She felt the same way in many respects, which made it even more difficult to have to tell him goodbye.

First BV explained about his friend, Paul and his painful death. Also mentioning that being the reason he started the work against drug pushers. BV continued, "I got messed up with some very evil people; one thing led to another. There was no way out for me once I became involved. I didn't know what to do, so I had to continue my work with the police. I went deep undercover; that's why I couldn't tell you before. There were too many things to sort out, and some very bad people went down as a result."

"It would have been fine, but then Scully showed up. He wanted to blackmail me, as you know. Somehow, he found out that I was working with the cops. I didn't know how at the time, but he knew things that could harm me. When I wouldn't pay him, he squealed on me. Now there are some very dangerous people out to kill me."

"I have to run and hide, and that's not easy for me, Viv. I've never run from anything in my life, and now it all has to change. That's why I asked you to leave with me in such a hurry. I have no real life without you, but by the same token, I have to go. I know you don't deserve to be on the run as well, but we need each other! There's no winning for either of us here." He choked back real tears and his voice betrayed his pain.

Viv's head began to swim. She had learned so much with BV being an undercover informant and not involved in a bad way with drugs! That put a different spin on things now. *How could I have believed he was bad?'* she thought, feeling guilty for misjudging him. *I want to go anywhere BV goes,' she realized. 'I don't even care if I'm on the run, too!'* She was wracked with anguish for having committed herself to Henry and knowing that she could not let him down now. She could never hurt dear, brave Henry.

He loved her far too much, so it seemed she might have to hurt BV and herself, instead.

"I just don't… I can't now..! Oh, BV," she collapsed sobbing, into his loving, strong arms.

Now that Viv knew BV was not the bad person she thought him to be, all her love for him resurfaced. His kiss reminded her of their closeness and lovemaking. How passionate and intense that had been. It had definitely been love at first sight. She realized that it was possible to be in love with two men at once. She felt so happy to be with BV, but grief stricken because of the circumstances she now found herself in.

Their mutual need for one another created a huge bond. Now that Viv knew his secret and could see deep into his character, her barriers collapsed. She constantly thought of Henry's love too, and the guilt was consuming her. It would be impossible to hurt BV now, and beside that, her love for Henry had grown also, so how could she hurt him? He almost lost his life saving her, although Harriet was the ultimate saviour.

They now sat closely together on the sofa, whilst BV explained that as a 'protected witness,' he might never have normal freedom again. If she joined him, it would be a very different world being on the constant run and look-out.

"I love you too much to put you through all that, Viv. But, I'll never stop thinking and yearning for you to be mine alone."

These words were too much for Viv, and she again broke down in tears. She sobbed on his shoulder for what seemed like hours. The entire time he held her close to him and frequently planted kisses on her forehead, cheek, wherever, whatever he could reach in that position.

When her tears ceased, Viv tidied her smudged make-up using the mirror from her bag. Her eyes were red and a little swollen, but to BV she still looked wonderful. He took her hand gently and led her to the bedroom.

Viv wanted to tell him she was marrying Henry, but could not bear to say the words. They lay down on the bed and hugged as tightly as possible. They kissed fervently, almost in a frenzy just to emphasize their feelings and because they knew it might be their last time together.

BV looked so handsome and Viv wondered how she would cope, never seeing this wonderful face again. They continued to kiss and before they knew it, their lovemaking began. The intensity was high from the very start because of their mutual need for each other. They both had longed for this physical closeness. Also, there was the sorrow of the inevitable parting, and this being the last time to ever share such feelings, or their love.

There were no words to describe the heights they achieved. They were like drowning people, desperately getting their last few gulps of oxygen. The last time they would ever physically bond. In between their passion, both of their hearts were breaking. The emotional pain and the physical pleasure made a strange combination.

As good as they felt in each others arms, they

hurt so badly. They tried to make the sex last as long as possible, until the inevitable orgasms came. Afterward, they lay close, huddled together, side by side, with her head resting on his chest, her tears trickling onto him.

They stayed together on the bed in silence and made no move to dry their tears. They just held each other tightly, as if to indent this memory forever in their minds. It would be all they would ever have to remember each other.

Viv found it hard to breathe, and the pain in her chest was heavy and very real. It was the pain of loss, and to Viv it seemed as if she grieved for a dying partner. In a way, it was grief for a love that should have been. They fell asleep in each other's arms.

When they awoke, Viv started to cry all over again. BV hugged her tightly, as he said, "Just remember that I love you more than anything. I will never love another woman and will keep your memory sacred." He tried hard to fight his emotions. "If I ever find a way to contact you that won't put you in any danger, I shall. You can be sure of that, my darling. It's my promise to you!"

His blue eyes brimmed with tears now as he added, "I'll find a way once I have a totally new identity. Although I won't change my appearance, for I'd truly lose myself then. Once I find seclusion in a busy place, I'll send for you. Then we'll be safe and together, never to be separated!"

Viv, through heaving sobs, wondered if he were saying all this to make them both feel better. As if they stood some kind of chance to be together again to make the parting more bearable. But she was grateful for this thread of hope. She needed to cling to it, so that she could bear the torment that went on inside of her. Her ribs and insides ached.

The telephone rang. As BV undid himself from her, he tried to smile, but his eyes were still full of pain.

"Hello?" BV asked into the telephone. "Oh, yes, I'm ready. Okay then, thank you."

Viv knew before he got back to her, that it was his call to go. Someone was about to pick him up. She felt a deep surge of panic churning her stomach.

"Darling, I'll have to get you a cab now and we must say goodbye. Just for now. True love will find a way, you'll see!"

Viv stood up and they embraced as if they would never let each other go. Her tears rolled freely, wetting both of them. His eyes brimmed with tears he desperately tried to hold back.

As they held each other, BV made the call for her taxi. Never had she remembered such pain, both emotional and physical.

She stared into his eyes and said, "I'll never forget you, BV, or our love! No matter who I end up with, I'll come to you when you call for me!" Her words were quiet, but BV heard them all and pressed her closer to him.

"Let's go out into the grounds and walk to the drive. We still have a few moments before the cab comes," he said, gently leading her by the hand.

Viv looked once more around her, as if to keep this atmosphere in her memory. They had time to hug each other again, and then the cab pulled into the drive. They looked into each other's eyes and tried to impart themselves deeply and spiritually, into one other. To keep each other's essence forever deep inside.

The cab driver pulled up in front of them and waited. They hugged tightly and kissed, whilst their tears mingled. BV managed to pull away and straighten his posture, then gave Viv a sad, but broad, forced smile. She returned it the best she could, but tears still flowed down her cheeks. He took her hand and led her to the opened cab door, helping her into the back seat. The cabbie had the decency to look the other way and was now ready to drive off.

Viv was unable to let go of BV's hand, so he gently unclasped it from his as she tried to hold on. He kissed her hand before he released it and then kissed her firmly on the lips to seal his promise of them being together again. She was unable to speak at all through grief.

BV then said to the driver, "You can go now, thanks." He turned once more to Viv and said, "Bye for now, darling, it won't be long! I promise!"

She nodded, unable to answer, and the tears flowed copiously now. The door closed and it felt like the closing of a prison cell door to Viv. She watched BV, through the haze of her tears, as he backed away from the car. The tears rolled down his cheeks unchecked now. The driver revved the engine, and drove her away.

Viv turned around to look out the back window at the true love of her life. He waved and she waved back, sobbing loudly now, hardly able to breathe, until he was out of sight. She slumped back in the padded seat, feeling so much pain that death would have been a welcome release for her.

* *

Chapter Thirty-Eight

Can Viv Go Through With the Marriage?

The week passed and Viv visited Henry each day in the hospital. She hated returning to her home every night where the terrible incident occurred, but she had to get over that. Henry never questioned how she finished with BV which she greatly appreciated. In between, she talked to Harriet who wanted to discuss plans for the wedding, but Viv never let on about the turmoil she was going through for obvious reasons.

Dandy was told the whole story, and she shared the pain in the best way possible. They had managed to spend a couple of nights together as Daniel had kindly agreed that Viv needed support. The time spent with Dandy was a mixture of talking, under-standing and comforting, with Dandy wondering how it would feel if she lost Daniel. How she would feel just like Viv did now, if she could never see her husband's handsome face ever again. The same face and body type that Viv was desperately missing. She more than anyone, knew how Viv was feeling. The girls were physical, but not in a sexual, needy way. They were sharing the emotional pain through be-ing physically close. Viv needed the closeness in the way Dandy had, when Daniel was imprisoned and the gesture was willingly returned.

Viv tried to look happy on the day she collected Henry from the hospital. His arm was still in a plaster cast, he had stitches in his head, but the rest of his wounds were not so visible. They discussed the marriage as they had also done when Harriet visited at the hospital and Viv did her best to appear excited about it. Occasionally, Harriet would look sideways at her, knowing there was sadness, but it was not spoken about. Henry hoped with time, the memory that was obviously upsetting Viv, would fade. He was also pleased that they did not see a great deal of Dandy and Daniel, as the memory would take a lot longer to fade with her being reminded of her lost love. But, they would of course be at the wedding and he hoped it would not spoil Viv's happiness on that day.

Henry's mother was surprised and thrilled to hear about the forthcoming marriage, although she had sensibly not been informed of the previous violent incidents. She wanted to meet Viv, so after a few weeks of recuperation, Henry arranged for them to have dinner at a fancy restaurant.

Viv was not nervous at all. She was still worried about BV and attempting to hide her distress. They would never make love again and her stomach churned each time she thought about how it could have been for them both. If not for Henry, she would have followed BV anywhere. Viv hoped this feeling would disappear with time, as she wanted to have love only for her husband. It might be good to share some of these thoughts with Harriet at some point, to get a woman's perspective who was not enamoured by the Lyons' good looks.

Viv's taxi pulled up outside 'Manny's Lobster House,' and she was greeted by a smiling Henry who introduced his mother, Martha. After a few pleasantries, they all entered the restaurant. The entire time they walked, Martha looked Viv up and down. Once seated, Henry's mother started the conversation.

"So. You two met through a lonely heart's club?"

"Mum!" Henry interjected, as Viv choked on her glass of water. He quickly answered the question for her. "We met through a dating agency. It's the way busy professionals meet these days."

"Oh. Well in my day, they called them lonely heart's clubs. Most of us didn't use them though. I met Henry's father at a dance. His name was Henry too, that's why we named Henry here after him. Anyway, what a dancer! Gosh, he swept me off my feet! He was so tall and handsome, just like Henry here," she smiled in his direction and he glanced down in embarrassment.

Viv chuckled to herself. It was obvious that Martha was very old-fashioned in her beliefs, but still it was sort of cute the way she doted on him, as a mother should on her child.

"Anyway, what do you do for a living, Viv? I hear you work in an office. Are you doing secretarial work or something like that?" continued Martha.

"No, actually, I'm a manager with a large consulting firm downtown," Viv said.

"Yes, Viv's a professional woman, Mum," said Henry, his face reddened due to his mother's comment.

Viv was thinking, *'Martha probably still believes that women could never advance professionally and their place is in the home, raising children!'*

"Oh, I see." Martha replied. "So, do you have any children, Viv?" she asked.

Now it was Viv's turn to blush, and her face began to burn, "No, I don't, Martha. I…"

"Have you ever been married before?" Martha interrupted.

Viv tried to think how best to answer this question. She had told Henry briefly about Gavin, but it was not something that seemed appropriate to discuss with Martha. At least, not on a first meeting. After a moment of contemplation, she responded.

"Henry and I still need to talk about children. Although, I would love us to have children, when we're ready."

"Oh, that's wonderful!" gushed his mother. "Grandchildren, finally! You know I don't have any grandchildren and was starting to worry about that. Began to think I'd never see the day! It would be wonderful to hold my own grandchild. Thank goodness! How many children do you plan to have then?"

"Mum, take it easy will you? We're not married yet!" Henry gently scolded her. "Viv and I still need to discuss children, but I'm glad she thinks the way she does." He looked at Viv with a twinkle in his eyes.

"All right, all right. But don't take too long. You're not getting any younger Henry, well actually, neither one of you is for that matter. Gosh, you're what now, Henry? Forty something?" Martha asked.

"I'm thirty-eight Mum, and Viv is thirty-five. We've plenty of time, now let's get off this subject, can we? Anyway, it's starting to feel like an interview. Let's talk about something else for now. For awhile, okay?" Henry did not like this line of questioning and sensed that Viv felt the same.

"All right, but it never hurts to plan your future and your children certainly are your future Henry," Martha said. "So when is the wedding? What church and so forth? There are lots of plans to make."

"Mum," Henry said. "Viv and I want to have a Humanist wedding."

"What on earth is that Henry?" Martha blurted out, as Viv chuckled involuntarily.

"Well, it's a bit different than a typical wedding in a few ways. I'll try to explain it to you, Mum. We'll have a legal wedding with a couple of people present to witness our signatures in the registry book. After that, the couple and the witnesses go to an appointed place for the Humanist wedding. It could take place anywhere, such as a chapel, or a hired hall or theatre and even on board a ship. Some people hold the ceremonies in buildings, parks, forests or, well, anywhere they wish. Even their own home, with all their friends and family there."

Viv interjected, "We hoped that you might want to help organize the wedding, Martha, to make some of the arrangements and add the finishing touches to the Humanist service."

"I just don't know, Viv. I'm an old-fashioned girl and this ceremony seems a bit strange to me," replied Martha.

Henry continued. "It's actually quite fashionable and a true expression of a couple's love for each other, Mum. The night before the wedding, there's a party of loved ones and close friends. Poems, songs or speeches are delivered at the time of the wedding ceremony. Whilst this is happening, music, live or recorded, is played. The organizer, a specially trained woman, faces the couple, us, who are facing toward our friends and family. A much better way to be married."

"A better way than is done in the church," added Viv, who was not the slightest bit religious, not in the man-made sense of the meaning of it. Viv continued, "This professional has learned what she should say, from written copies of words the couple have made up for each other. They can still be given blessings through the Lord, if they believe in a God. Blessings can also be given for everyone in the room. The organizer goes through a script and then declares, "You are now husband and wife.""

"It's all legal then?" questioned Martha, whose eyebrows were almost touching her nose with the effort of trying to understand this unseemly ceremony.

"Soon it will be made possible for Humanist ceremonies to give out marriage certificates, but at the moment, a couple need to marry in a registry office first to make it legal," replied Henry. "So we would already have been legally married on paper earlier. They're going through the process of legislation to make Humanist weddings legal, with the registry signing at the same time, the way it should be and the way it is done already in Scotland. The couple have individual speeches, or can read something aloud to all, about how they feel toward each other. Then the guests are asked if anyone wants to say anything about their newly married friends. The whole ceremony is arranged around exactly what the couple wants and is a much friendlier event."

"Food and drink is already at the wedding venue and there are decorations put up, too. The couple even choose what kind of clothes they want their guests to wear which could be particular colours, or, fancy-dress, smart or just plain casual. Even the organizer wears the preferred colours. The whole occasion is one to be cherished and full of fun, with no piety or seriousness, just extreme joy and good wishes for the happy couple. Everyone takes videos and photos. No need for a professional photographer, so everything and anything is recorded. It's a wonderful time and a joyous memorable occasion for all."

"It sounds so lovely, Henry. I'll really look forward to this wedding and do my best to help with the organizing, Viv," said Martha, leaning over to kiss Viv on the cheek.

Turning to Henry she said, "As long as you're happy, sweetheart, that's all that matters. Your father would be happy for you, son."

She got up from the table and gave them both a hug. "How did you hear of this new style wedding, Henry?" she asked sitting down again.

"Viv told me about it and I agreed that it sounded a lovely way to go about a marriage."

Martha's eyebrows went up in the air, as she looked from one to the other, but she made no comment.

They got on with their meals, talking between mouthfuls. Martha talked the most, but Viv did not mind at all. She liked Henry's mother, although it made her sad that her own parents were not present. They had never even been interested enough to attend her first wedding. She wondered if they were still alive, if they would want to come to this wedding. Something she would never know now. *'Maybe they would be there in spirit?'* she thought, *'and maybe they both love me now, from that world.'*

When they finished at the restaurant, Henry drove them back to his home where they had coffee. Martha did not stay long and soon excused herself. She gave them both a hug and went upstairs to her flat. Henry offered to drive Viv to Harriet's house, where she was staying for the next few days. Viv still found it difficult to go back home, to the place where such terrible events had occurred just a few weeks ago.

"If you don't mind, Henry, could I stay here tonight?" she asked.

"Oh, of course," Henry replied. He wrapped Viv up in his arms and kissed her passionately. "I'd love to have you here. I keep telling you to move in, even before our marriage and then we can both move into the new marital home I've been getting ready for us, together."

"I love you too, Henry, very much," she replied, "but, it will be so good to be married and *then* live together. She really did love Henry, but it was still difficult to get BV out of her mind. "Do you mind if I take a quick shower? I have some fresh clothes in my bag, if I could just borrow a towel."

"Of course," said Henry tenderly, as he accompanied Viv into the bathroom. "How are you feeling?"

"Okay," she replied in a soft voice. "Mostly tired, that's all."

"Are you as excited about the wedding as I am, or are you missing BV too much?" Henry asked, which was unusually blunt for him. Viv was taken aback, but she had told him earlier about their goodbyes, without going into too much detail. She had also mentioned that BV had to go on the run due to his involvement as an undercover drug operative.

Still, Henry's question startled her and it was right out of the blue. Viv regained her composure and stated, "I just feel so sorry for BV. I hope he can get on with his life."

"If he cares about your happiness, he'll be pleased for you. He will still realise it would have been a terrible mistake for you to be on the run with him.   I don't believe any man who cared for a woman would want her to go through that ordeal."

"But, he's going to miss Daniel and have to start all over, to build a totally new life on his own!"

Henry knew Viv would still be concerned for him, at least until most of his memory had faded. He hoped that would not take too long.

"I know he's been involved with some horrible stuff, but he's gone through hell and now he's completely alone," Viv said.

"I know. I didn't have the feeling that he was a nasty person, but he's still involved with something you shouldn't get mixed up in."

Viv smiled at Henry and managed to hide her heartbreak from him. "I'll stop worrying about BV soon enough. But, I have chosen the right man."

Henry seemed pleased that the temptation of BV had been removed. Especially, when she told him of their sad goodbyes, but not of their despair and the promise to be together again. Henry never asked if they had sex as he did not want to know the answer. It was Viv's business and now she was his. That was all that mattered to him. He would make her so happy that she would forget all about BV.

In the shower, Viv's mind went back to BV. They had showered together a couple of times and it had been delightful. His caresses were so soft and he touched every part of her, even her soul. She would never forget him. He was the special fantasy man that every woman wanted, perhaps, even more so than Lawrence. Yes, she realized that feelings of nostalgia for Lawrence had been replaced by the deeper feelings she had for BV.

She wanted to think that BV would find a woman that he could find happiness with, so long as she could remain a sacred memory. But just the thought of him making love to another woman hurt her badly. The real part of her life was to be with Henry. Viv knew it would be good and she was as happy as possible under the circumstances, even though her heart was breaking.

* * * * * * * * * * * * * * * * * * * *

The wedding was arranged for four weeks time.

There were many congratulations and offers of help. Henry's Mum did her part, writing out the invitations and making lists. Viv had given her the addresses of friends in Cornwall and had sneaked Lawrence's in, too. After all, he was still her friend, and she wanted him to see her settled down. Harriet got on famously with Henry's mother, who shared much gossip and laughter with her, but not anything too personal.

Viv was amazed at the way Harriet could get on with anyone. Also, how she managed to share the duties with Henry's Mum in organizing the food for the reception. Harriet's main job was to hire the best band around for them. In between going about the arrangements, Viv mentioned BV. The conversation worried Harriet a great deal.

"Are you sure you should be getting married under these circumstances?" Harriet asked, although she hoped that nothing would go wrong. "Don't you think you should wait until BV is out of your system?"

"Oh, I don't know if that would ever happen." Viv replied. "Although I have accepted there could be no stability with BV, as we would never have a home to call our own. He can't even return to this country for the wedding. That is, I don't think he could, even if he wanted to."

"Viv, have you considered that BV might be hiding somewhere in this country and can't leave just yet. I mean, from what you've told me of his love, imagine how difficult it would be for him to board a plane and put all those miles in between you both?"

Viv looked as if she could faint. "Harriet, I don't

know what to do? I need to know how he is! I have his new cell phone number, but don't dare to contact." She had his new temporary address as well, but could not divulge this information.

"You must resist, Viv. Just be careful not to let anyone see his number. I presume you have it in code? You can call sometime in the future, just to see how he's doing. I expect it will help him feel better. Well, Viv, I can't say he's a bad man anymore, to make you feel better about Henry. But, I agree with what Henry said to you. There will be no life for you on the run, and what if he were caught by the baddies?"

Viv visibly flinched. "Don't say that, Harriet. I couldn't bear if he were to be killed!"

She could see the pain in Harriet's eyes and knew she was hurting too, although it was not totally on her behalf. Viv almost wished Henry could suddenly fall in love with the more deserving Harriet.

Harriet put her arms around Viv and hugged her. "I'm so sorry. Believe me, I feel the pain you're going through. But, I know memories fade and you're so much safer with Henry. You will learn to love him as much as he loves you, Viv."

She had been so happy for Viv and Henry in spite of her strong feelings for him. But as a woman, she understood the dilemma that Viv faced. She would not wish that on anyone, let alone her friend. But she was herself broken-hearted. She had lost her Henry. She was determined to conceal this incredible emotional pain from both Viv and Henry. Although, she resisted the urge to fling her arms around him whenever they were together. Instead of the real thing, she made do with day-dreaming about him day and night. She at least had him to herself then. It would have to do.

* * * * * * * * * * * * * * * * * * * *

Chapter Thirty-Nine
Pre-Wedding Party, Viv's Still Undecided

The four weeks passed by quickly and suddenly it was the night before the wedding. Harriet organized the pre-wedding party with the help of Martha, who so obviously doted on her son and wanted his happiness. She would be a delightful mother-in-law. In attendance were the Lyons, Harriet and Martha, a few friends from Viv's work and Henry's business associates. Detective Mayfield was unable to attend.

Apparently, there had been another 'El Diablo' killing, and this one happened quite nearby. While he was not officially on the case, he said there were some loose ends that needed to be sorted out. He apologized and wished the couple happiness and the best of luck, saying he would pop in, if possible.

The band played various genres of music, so everyone enjoyed it; especially the rock 'n' roll. Henry most of all, when he took a turn on the drums for some of the songs and received a great ovation. Viv was extremely proud of him, and even sang a few songs herself. *'It would be great fun to have our own band,'* she thought happily. She did not let thoughts of BV mar the day, although she still harboured regrets for the loss of him. She wished he could have been invited, especially, if he was still in the country. But, that would have proven difficult for everyone, and she might even have run off with him. So she could only hope BV was safe. BV would always be her fantasy and hopefully, she his.

There were a few times during the evening, when Viv noticed Harriet looking melancholy. Of course, Viv was not entirely without her sad moments, too. Daniel looked wonderful as usual. However, she no longer had any physical feelings toward him and was able to think of him as a friend. Still, it was difficult to look at him without thinking about her lost love with BV. In fact, looking at Daniel caused her pain now.

At one point, Dandy took her aside and asked if they could *get together* whenever possible. Apart from not wanting to be unfaithful to Henry, Viv did not feel like renewing her previous physical relationship with Dandy. It was difficult to explain without hurting her, so it was left that if it was spontaneous, it might happen, but Viv needed a friend more. This seemed to be understood, although Dandy unwillingly accepted the decision.

"I love your company, Dandy, and love you so much as a friend, but that will have to do for me. I am trying to be loyal, Henry deserves that."

"Well, Viv, you know it's different between us," Dandy replied sadly, "so if you ever change your mind, just let me know" She pursed her lips at Viv seductively and continued, "I love you in a different way than I do Daniel and still need your love in return." Their hug in public looked innocent enough. It was as if Dandy was only congratulating her.

Daniel whisked his wife off for a dance and Henry extricated himself from guests to come over and dance with Viv. As she danced, her eyes wandered often to the door. Although Lawrence had been invited, he did not reply as to whether he would be there, or not.

The party was nearly over and Henry was arranging their many gifts into the back of his car. Viv stood just inside the hotel door when a waiter handed her a note. At first glance, she thought it was a message from Lawrence.

She opened it, recognizing BV's writing, then quickly slipped it into her pocket. When Henry returned, she excused herself to use the restroom and rushed off to read this precious note.

Her hands shook as she tried to keep the paper still, so it could be read. Her eyes filled with tears which made it even more difficult to make out the words:

My Dearest Viv,

I found out that you are going to marry Henry. I hate that, but I understand and am glad he will be looking after you, until I can send or come to get you. You have stayed on my mind constantly, and it's just a matter of time before we are together, a year or two, at the most.

Should you change your mind and want to join me sooner, you have my number. Just call me. In fact, call me anyway. I need to hear your voice. If you don't call, I wish you a safe and happy time, until I find you again.

Until then,

All my Love and Thoughts,

Yours only, BV

XXX

Viv felt devastated and needed to call him this very minute, but it would be torture for them both. She wanted to postpone marrying Henry and would have liked more time, but that had been impossible. The thought of leaving her new friends as well as Henry at a time like this would be so inconsiderate and cruel. But, her whole being yearned to contact BV.

It occurred to her again, that BV may still be in the country. Harriet suggested he might still be around and how else had it been possible to receive this note? Where was the waiter who gave her the note? She could not see him anywhere. Viv composed herself, splashed some cold water on her face and walked back to join Henry.

Guests were saying goodbye to each other. Some were waiting by Henry's side for her to come back. Viv walked toward them and received many hugs and good wishes. She even received a hug and a kiss from Daniel which had a very strange effect on her. It almost felt as though she was with BV, but she reminded herself this was dear Daniel, who had gone through so much trouble for his involvement with both her and his brother. Viv gave him back the most affectionate hug, as if to say sorry and thanks for everything.

She smiled and tried desperately to hide her breaking heart. Harriet was the last one to leave and gave Henry a longer hug than she gave Viv. But Viv was beyond caring about that. She had a dilemma to deal with. When all the guests had finally left, she and Henry got into the car. Martha was already sitting in the back seat, looking tired.

They were soon on their way and, as planned, Henry would drop Viv off at her home. Harriet and Dandy were picking her up in the morning to meet Henry and guests at the registry office, then on to the Humanist Wedding and reception.

At the door Henry beamed at her. "I can hardly believe we're getting married tomorrow, Viv! I couldn't possibly be happier."

She beamed a smile just for him. "It's going to be a wonderful day, Henry, and the beginning of a great life for us." How she wished this would be true, for both of them.

Henry hugged her as if he might never see her again and then he climbed back into his car. She waved to both him and his mother. Viv walked into her house and flung herself straight down on the bed in exhaustion. Alone at last, she let the pain out and sobbed. Sobbed until her ribs ached, all the while clutching her cell phone and wanting to make that call.

* *

There was no sleep for Viv, and in the morning when Harriet and Dandy appeared, she was still getting ready.

"You don't look as happy as you should be," Dandy said adding, "I wish it could be under different circumstances."

"I expect its nerves, don't all brides have nerves?" Viv asked.

They all knew why Viv was not happy. Harriet was thinking that to get married whilst your heart is breaking, must be a dreadful thing to do. She and Viv had Henry in common, and both of their hearts were breaking. But if she was marrying Henry, it would have been the happiest day of her whole life. Life could be so ironic at times. She sighed and continued to help Viv get ready, occasionally making her laugh, whilst Dandy rushed around bringing snacks and drinks.

Harriet drove them, since Daniel and Henry were meeting up with them all at the Registry Office. Not long after the ceremony, Harriet would drive the married couple to the dock to board a ship for Barbados. Harriet and Dandy chatted happily all the way, although Harriet carefully watched the road at the same time as joining in with the conversation.

Viv quietly sat in the back seat, wearing a stylish designer cerise suit. She wore an ice blue sheer blouse underneath the jacket. Her shoes were a metallic cerise, high heeled, with an ankle strap. She looked wonderful, but felt dreadful. There was a practised smile on her face and she was able to hide her sadness, by knowing that Henry would soon be hers. Contradictory emotions were now very familiar.

The traffic was light and soon they were at the office, greeted by Martha and many friends. They all went into the registry office where Henry was waiting accompanied by Daniel and Howard Lane, the family solicitor.

Most of the invited people were there and the whole event took an hour. Viv was hardly aware of the ceremony, but smiled at the appropriate times. When told they could now kiss, she tried to show as much warmth as possible. She must have pulled it off well, as Henry still seemed extremely happy. But at the words; *"You are now man and wife,"* Viv involuntarily cringed. Her real love was on the run somewhere. It felt strange for her to be marrying her best friend, as that was how she felt about Henry most of the time.

The four witnesses signed the book, followed by the newly married couple, who were handed their marriage certificate. Then everyone rushed on to the venue for the Humanist wedding at the pre-arranged hotel which had been decorated the day before by Harriet and Martha.

This ceremony was far more intimate. Viv and Henry read their speeches to each other, declaring their love. He seemed a little surprised that her speech was not as *'declaring'* in its love for him. But she said how wonderful he was, and professed her tremendous luck in finding such a good friend and loving partner.

Various friends, including Martha, made their speeches about how well suited they were for each other. Viv managed to look happy, but she ached inside, wondering if she should phone BV. She had kept her word to Henry and had not humiliated or upset him by cancelling their wedding. Viv hung onto the thought that if BV truly loved her, he would ensure they ended up together some time, sooner or later, when he was settled and had a place for her to stay. She knew that moving regularly would be all right with her, just as long as they were together.

The party, after this lovely Humanist ceremony, was a very happy event for all in attendance. Viv felt pleased that everyone enjoyed themselves and appreciated the chance to speak with old friends. There was also the opportunity to catch up with gossip on Gavin. He had been seen around with numerous women, but none had lasted long. However, he was still very bitter towards her. Viv did not care and thought it served him right not to be able to settle down with anyone.

The band was the same one they had for their pre-wedding party. Harriet had found one of the best around. For a short time, Viv enjoyed herself, too, when she danced with Henry. The music took away some of her pain. When Henry went up to play drums again, she got up and sang her favourite country songs. It had gone down so well and Henry was very proud of her.

Soon it was time for goodbyes, and they changed into casual clothes, brought along in their suitcases. Harriet drove the newly married couple to the dock and saw them onto the ship.

Viv thanked her for all she had done. "We'll see you soon, Harriet," she said, hugging her tightly.

"And many, many thanks from me, too!" said Henry, giving Harriet a warm embrace and kiss on the cheek.

"It was a real pleasure!" replied Harriet as she tried to smile through her tears. "Just enjoy yourselves, I love you both so much!"

"So what are you going to do whilst we're away, Harriet?" Viv asked.

"Well, believe it or not, I've already gone to see

Dandy and registered my profile with the agency. Guess what? They have the portrait I painted of them in a prominent part of their offices!"

"We'll have to make a point of seeing that when we get back. I'm so pleased you're with their agency Harriet," Viv said excitedly. "That's wonderful news, good luck with it!"

"Yes, I met with both Dandy and Daniel for a couple of hours the other day. They were both so good and reassuring. They showed me the profiles of eligible men, and I already have a date lined up for later this evening. I'm looking forward to it," said Harriet.

Viv and Henry boarded their boat. As it pulled away, they could see Harriet grow smaller and smaller, in the distance. They did not see her tears falling heavily, nor were they aware of just how much her heart was breaking. Long after Harriet's form disappeared, the newly married couple remained on the deck leaning against the rail, arms around each other.

"No thoughts about BV? Well, not many I hope?" asked Henry.

"Hardly any," Viv answered. She accepted her state and planned to be happy with Henry for as long as they were together and would force out all memories of BV, whenever possible.

"I can't wait to see our new house," Viv said happily.

"I'm pleased to say it's completely ready," Henry beamed. He had bought it after he first met Viv and refurbished it. But, he would not let her see it until they were ready to move in, after their marriage.

"What if it had not worked out between us?" she asked.

"It would not have been a home without you, Viv. But Mum has got over Dad's death and she's quite independent now. No need for me to be there any more. I have a life, too; you helped me realize that. But, if I had to move in without you, it would have been necessary to change the colours. Everything was decorated with you in mind. If you were not there, the colours would have haunted me. Thank goodness everything worked out, though, the way it has."

Viv was glad to have Martha as a mother-in-law and Henry was pleased they both liked each other, or it could have been a bad situation indeed.

* *

Whilst on honeymoon, the couple had an idyllic cruise around the Islands. Their private moments were very intimate and the lovemaking intense. Except for the times Viv thought about BV. They travelled around to see all the sights possible and tasted every meal that was new to them. Sometimes, it felt like the time they spent in Spain, when their relationship was new. Viv was also surprised that she was falling deeper in love with Henry, and most of the time, felt very happy and content with the outcome.

Occasionally, they discussed their friends back home, wondering how they were all doing. They were looking forward to hearing how Harriet had got on with her date and hoped she would find someone compatible. The days raced by, but they made sure to collect suitable gifts for their loved ones back home. Amongst the souvenirs and presents, there was a special one for Harriet. It was a newly designed easel, in a pastel lilac colour, with many holders for the different brushes and shelves for her paints. On their return home, they stood on the deck enjoying the sound of the sea. Their conversation often drifted to Harriet.

"Harriet will really be pleased with the easel!" smiled Henry, as they leaned together against the stern of the boat, listening to the swishing of the waves.

"I hope she'll like it." Viv frowned.

"What's the matter? You look worried, Viv."

"Oh, it's just that I was wondering if Harriet will ever find someone to love, apart from you, I mean!"

"I thought she was over me. Do you really think she cares that much about me still?"

"She certainly does, Henry! I saw the sadness in her eyes. We can only hope that time will help her to get over it."

"Yes, time will take care of everything," replied Henry.

They both remained silent and dwelled on their individual thoughts as they gazed at the beauty of the ocean.

* * * * * * * * * * * * * * * * * * * *

Chapter Forty
The Lyons Arrange a Date for Harriet

Harriet busied herself all day to prepare for her date. The Lyons had spent considerable time with her and gone through the videos and screenings for the best possible match, or matches. It took plenty of convincing, since Harriet's image of the ideal man was Henry. For that reason, it would be difficult for another man to measure up.

After viewing the videos, Harriet finally came across a young man named Eric. Like her, he was in his early 30s. He described himself as: '…having a nice build and an accountant by trade, at one of the large banks. Also, very open minded and willing to try new things.'

"Well, I certainly fall into that category," Harriet laughed.

Daniel had called Eric and spoke to him briefly to establish the introduction. He then handed the telephone to Harriet. They seemed to get on well and arranged a dinner date and movie. Eric would pick Harriet up at her apartment. It was agreed to meet Saturday night, the same day Viv and Henry married and after they left for their honeymoon.

Harriet hoped the night out would help take her

thoughts off Henry. Whilst she looked forward to meeting Eric, her happiness was dampened with sadness. It had been almost unbearable to see them both leave on the boat earlier.

Harriet bathed and dressed in a tight-fitting gown, with a loose neck, almost a cowl. She also wore her most cherished possession, a silver necklace with a small, diamond pendant that her mother used to wear. Eight o'clock came quickly, and soon Harriet heard the doorbell ring. She answered, slightly apprehensive.

A tall, young man greeted her with a bouquet of flowers and introduced himself.

"Hi, I'm Eric." He flashed a smile which extended through to his bright, blue eyes. Harriet was immediately impressed with his clean good looks and manners.

"Nice to meet you, Eric. Let me grab my shawl and we can go."

She picked it up and the two departed for dinner. Eric drove a black, convertible Benz and played soft music on the drive into town to the restaurant.

"The Lyons told me a lot of good things about you, Harriet. I watched your video, but gosh, you're even prettier in person. The video doesn't even begin to do you justice!" He beamed at her.

"Am I? It doesn't?" She responded, surprised. "Thanks, Eric, that's very nice of you to say, although I must admit you're a very attractive man. I'm quite impressed," Harriet returned.

The two engaged in talk about family, touched

vaguely on growing up, and spoke about interests and hobbies. She did not give out too much information. As it turned out, Eric also loved to paint and he offered to paint Harriet's portrait.

"I'd love it if you would pose for me," he told her.

"That will be a first for me. I prefer to be on the other end of the canvas! But, sure, any time I suppose," said Harriet.

"Good, how about tomorrow night? I have some of my drawing materials in the car," replied Eric. "I carry them around with me so that whenever the mood hits me, or when I see something interesting, I can just stop and capture everything in my drawings. I'd love to show you some of them."

Harriet grew quite excited about seeing his artwork, but not sure about *posing* for him this soon. She decided to see him the next night, if all went well with them. Another time, when she got to know him better, she would feel better about Eric painting her portrait. Harriet felt thrilled that he was also an artist. It was not often she met people with a mutual interest in art. Well, there was Henry, but, she refused to think of him at the moment.

They had a pleasant dinner at the restaurant and then instead of the movies, they decided to go to his place. He lived in a small, but neat apartment, reasonably near and Harriet was surprised at its austere nature. For an artist, the colour schemes seemed a little bland and it was very sparsely furnished. Eric took her shawl and placed it carefully on the back of a hook, on one of the doors, making sure not to make a tent-like dent in the material.

Eric invited Harriet to sit down and then poured two soft drinks. Harriet sat down on the settee, which was the only piece of furniture in the living room. Newspapers and fast food containers were strewn about. *'Typical of a bachelor,'* Harriet thought, *'but a tidy mess.'*

"I see you believe in keeping things simple," Harriet remarked, looking about the room. It seemed odd that he owned a Benz and kept such a low quality home to live in.

"Oh, this place is just temporary, until I can afford another house. You'll understand when I say I'm recently divorced. Once my work starts to take off, which should be relatively soon, as I have a buyer in mind, I'll decide where I want to settle down. Besides, I'm rarely home with work and everything, so it serves the purpose. Simple, but functional," he said.

Harriet smiled and sipped her orange juice.

They only had a brief conversation as Harriet could not wait to see Eric's work. He showed her into his 'studio' where he kept all of his work and supplies. There was an easel in the centre of the room, with drop cloths and paints littering the floor.

Harriet laughed. "It's certainly an organized mess, and much like my studio back home. I can find whatever's needed. I guess you must too!"

"Yes," he laughed back. "I usually can find things!"

He moved some papers and revealed a stack of drawings. Harriet moved closer and inspected them one by one. They were very good. Excellent, in fact.

Different to her style, but good. There were plenty of flourishes to the landscape, with well-blended colouring.

Upon closer inspection, she saw that his brush work needed some improvement. He had not quite learned the required skill with all the angles, but she would not mention that minor point to him. He looked too pleased with himself, and she could not be sure how he might take constructive criticism.

Eric sat down on a rickety old stool, further back, and asked with a smile on his face, "You like them?" he asked.

"Very much so," she replied. "I can see another style over there; can I look at those too?"

"Of course, go on over. I expect you're used to moving about, around and over canvases!" He laughed, "But if you fall, please, not on my work!"

Harriet laughed with him. This stack of work was more portraiture, and very unusual. Whilst she liked detail, there was a disturbing bent to some of them.

Most paintings portrayed women in different stages of violence. Broken limbs, throats slashed, looks of shock or in the midst of open-mouthed screams. Some portrayed the same woman, partially clothed, but with varying hair colours. The figure was the same, so Harriet assumed he had used the same model for these peculiar paintings.

The model sat, lay and leaned, in various positions, but of particular interest was one in which she was seated in a chair, partially clothed, hands bound behind her back. The woman gazed blankly out of a window with a melancholy look on her face which he captured wonderfully. Harriet looked over at him.

"These are exceptionally good! Unusual, but good. Are you selling them? Or is it more of a hobby for you?"

"I've sold some," he said, "mostly to friends. I've never put on an exhibition, though I've thought about it!"

"You simply must, Eric! These are too good just to leave in a pile here! You could put a high reserve price on the ones you don't want to part with!"

She came over and stood by him. Eric stood too, and put his arm around her. "Let's go back into the lounge," he said.

After they were seated again, Harriet continued to discuss how he could get recognition. He stopped her with a kiss.

"I'd like to talk about you, Harriet. In fact you're so appealing that I'd like you to stay tonight, unless you feel uncomfortable with that?"

Harriet felt a twist of discomfort. "Well, actually I think it's a bit soon for that, Eric, although I like you very much." She added, "Don't think me rude, but would you mind taking me back now, I'm feeling tired. I woke up really early this morning."

He maintained his mild demeanour and agreed. "Only if you promise to let me see your artwork and take you out again!"

Harriet was pleased that he took it this way. Maybe she could get to like him enough to date him on a regular basis. On the drive back to her house, Harriet explained why she could not invite him in. It would take up too much time and not only was she wanting sleep, she had to be up early. It was partially the truth, but sounded like a good reason and a proper way to finish this first date. Eric was okay with that, and they arranged a date for the following evening.

As she lay in her bed, Harriet felt half-pleased with the way it all went. But, Eric was no 'Henry,' and she also knew instinctively that he would never be, either. She drifted off to sleep, her visions mixed between Eric and Henry.

* *

Harriet managed to get through the day, excited about another date with Eric. She really wanted to show her work to him, too. She only had one cry over Henry so far, but hoped that he and Viv were enjoying their honeymoon. After catching up with a bit of housework, she bathed and groomed herself. It was soon time for Eric's arrival, and he was right on time too.

He brought several rolled up drawings from the boot of his car into Harriet's apartment. He then unbundled his drawings and flattened them down on the floor of her living room. Harriet was amazed as the drawings were all done in pencil and charcoal. The detail amazed her.

These drawings once again portrayed various women in different tortured states. Whilst macabre, they exhibited extraordinary detail. It was uncanny, but they seemed almost like photographs.

"You never showed me these ones! They're wonderful too, Eric. You have a very keen eye for detail." They chatted about the work for a while and then Harriet asked, "Can I show you some of my work? Most of it's upstairs in the studio." He had already seen and admired her pictures on the wall.

"Oh yes, I can't wait to see more!" replied Eric, and he followed Harriet up the stairs to her studio. He marvelled at her work. "Harriet, all of these are beautiful. Such a wonderful use of colour. I usually stick to the basics, but you've certainly taken it to a new level!

Harriet felt overjoyed that she was with a man who was not only attractive physically, but he was an artist, too. He also knew enough to give her a proper evaluation and appreciated and loved art as much as she did. Not only that, he was available and not attached to anyone. It seemed too good to be true.

"Would you like to do my portrait now, Eric?" she asked him. "If there's anything you can use from my studio, help yourself!"

"Yes, I'd love to!" He replied. "I shouldn't need to go back to the car and get anything extra." He rushed about the studio, gathering handfuls of equipment and tucking her easel under his arm. He set everything up and asked where she wanted to sit and get comfortable.

Harriet went to the sofa and sat down. "How's this?" she asked him.

"Just fine, Harriet, now just you relax." As he spoke these words, Harriet pulled her blouse off of one shoulder to test his reaction. Eric was obviously quite turned on by her. She felt quite daring now and hitched up her skirt a little. Eric admired her shapely thigh.

Harriet could see that he appreciated her as a real woman! Of course, she was one really, but legally it was not accepted, so this new reassurance pleased her greatly. Besides, she had become fond of this charming, young man who appreciated her talents and womanly charms.

"Relax now, Harriet," he repeated with a twinkle in his eye. "We're in for an interesting evening."

* * * * * * * * * * * * * * * * * * * *

Chapter Forty-One
Harriet's New Date
is Not All He Seems

Eric felt at ease in Harriet's home and enjoyed her company. Conversation with her was not difficult, and they seemed to share so many mutual interests. In particular, their love of art.

"I'm going to try something a little different. I'll use oil on this canvas," Eric said as he took out some brushes and various tins and tubes of paint. After a few minutes of different arrangements, he put the brushes down. "How about a couple of drinks? Real ones?" he asked.

Harriet began to rise, when Eric stopped her. "No, I'll get them. Where do you keep them and what would you like?"

"In the kitchen, Eric, right through that doorway and to your left. I fancy some Bacardi with Coke, thanks."

He smiled, saying he fancied the same as he headed off to the kitchen. It seemed to take awhile, but eventually he returned and handed Harriet her drink with ice in it. They sat, sipped and chatted easily.

Eric began, "I haven't been in a steady relationship for quite some time. I saw the same woman for a year, but then it ended rather abruptly. You probably saw her portrait at my home. It was in one of the piles of drawings on the floor. I've been over that relationship for some time and what luck to meet someone as lovely as you, now."

Harriet slowly sipped her drink. It tasted more bitter than she remembered, but she felt relaxed and content. Eric had gotten through to her, and when he kissed her, she responded. Harriet was not ready when Eric began to work his hands up her skirt and she put her hand over his.

"Not so fast, baby, there's plenty of time!" Harriet sweetly said. "Let's get on with the portrait."

"Hmmm, yes, you're right. Sorry, I was getting carried away!"

"You and me both!" Harriet laughed. Eric put down his partly finished drink on the coffee table and went back to work. "You just find a position that you like, and I'll start!"

Harriet tried to focus on Eric's directives, but she suddenly felt a little woozy. *'Strange?'* she thought, *'that drink shouldn't be affecting me this way. I don't drink regularly, but just one drink? Gosh, what's wrong with me?'*

Eric continued to speak as he walked toward her. His voice and gestures almost appeared to be happening in slow motion. "Harriet, we need just a little more flesh here. Let me help pull this back a bit."

He began to push her bra strap and sleeve further down her arm, then began to stroke her neck and bare shoulder. "I could do better justice to your portrait if you removed a little more clothing, Harriet."

He caressed the blouse off her and gently undid her bra. Harriet felt far too relaxed to stop him, but she hoped he would be a professional and not make a quick move on her. Soon, her blouse was on the floor and Eric's hands began to stroke her skin and breasts.

Harriet felt aroused, although a little alarmed. She let him continue. He began to nibble her neck and then moved to her nipples. His lips felt so good. 'So this is how it felt to have a man touch you, as though you're a true woman,' she thought.

Gradually, Eric eased Harriet back and she felt her skirt and panties slide down her legs. It felt nice. Beside, she felt too overcome by the woozy feeling in her head to make any attempt to stop him.

When she was totally naked, Harriet managed to sit herself up and asked him, "Are you going to carry on with my portrait?"

Eric's expression changed, but he said, "Of course. You're ready now."

He went back to his easel and started to work again. Harriet felt self-conscious and was not sure where to put her arms. They seemed to be in the way, no matter where she arranged them. When she looked at her drink, it was finished and she felt so tired. Thoughts of Henry and Viv on their honeymoon bed went through her head. It still hurt her.

Eric spoke again, but Harriet could not understand what he said. His words seemed garbled and almost unintelligible. He came over and began to kiss her, slowly and tenderly. Her lips responded. She pretended it was Henry, but when thoughts of disloyalty to Viv came in, her thoughts returned to Eric. She looked at him and hoped it could be possible to be in a relationship. Eric seemed a nice catch for a boyfriend and they might be a good match. Harriet responded by kissing him back. He seemed to gather courage and slid his hands over her thighs to the inner sides. His fingers started to pry higher.

Harriet suddenly panicked. What if Eric could tell that down there she was a bit different from other women? She had been assured that it all looked like a real woman's genitalia by her surgeon as well as by Henry. Maybe Eric would think the same way, too, but as she tried to relax her thighs, they tensed and came together instead. Instinctively, her muscles would not relax enough to let them open to his touch.

Eric became increasingly urgent in his actions and started to get rougher. He forced Harriet backwards and pushed her legs with force. He had somehow already removed his trousers and was very erect. Harriet was afraid that the *first time* for her, may prove painful and she did not want to be torn.

"Slowly, please," she heard her voice say. Eric became gentler with her.

Harriet forced herself to relax. How else could she ever have a relationship? It had gone this far too quickly, but he really seemed keen on her. His body was on hers now and he eased himself into her. Harriet gasped.

She could feel him, so her nerves inside must be in proper working order. It felt good. The tingles ran through her body. Yes, she would enjoy this. It felt tight, but it did not hurt her too much. The arousal was heightened by the look of pleasure on his face and by the sight of his hips as he pumped into her. They moved positions a few times, and although she was a bit too woozy to properly feel it, she felt pleased to be recognised as a woman.

Soon, Eric's body began to move differently, his back arched and she knew he had reached a climax. She took advantage of this situation and moaned more, as if climaxing in time with him. She had no idea what that might feel like, but there was no sudden tingling pleasure, which she had read about. Soon, he lay limp on top of her. His arms were around her and she felt pleased that he still wanted to hold her.

"Lead me to your bedroom and let's sleep the sleep of the satisfied," Eric said, in a mock Shakespearean voice.

Harriet led him to her bedroom and they lay under the covers. Harriet was awake, but her head still felt peculiar. She was not sure if a woman was supposed to let the man go to sleep, or if she was supposed to tell him how good he had been. She decided to speak quietly to him.

"Eric, are you awake? I have something important that I want to tell you," she began.

"Huh, oh, of course, sorry, I must have dozed off," he responded leaning over to kiss her.

"That was wonderful. I really enjoyed it!" She attempted to kiss him, but swayed and missed his face.

"Can we go to sleep now?" he asked. "We can talk in the morning."

Harriet was unsure how to proceed and whether this was the time to tell him the truth. Perhaps best to just go to sleep, her head said as much. But, no, she had to fight the urge to sleep and tell Eric everything. It may be too difficult to tell him at a later date. Then she remembered the first night with Henry. She had just come out with it and been honest. That seemed to work, so she decided to be just as open with Eric. Lay everything on the line and see if he was still interested in her. If so, perhaps he really could become her boyfriend.

"I used to be a man!" Harriet blurted out.

Eric laughed hysterically. "That's a good one, Harriet. Is that the reason you woke me up? Come on now, darling, quit joking and go back to sleep." He rolled over to put his left arm around her shoulder, but instead she sat up and avoided his affection for the moment.

Harriet got out of bed and retrieved her photo albums, to show to the now *wide-awake* Eric. It was the photographic proof and her alcohol soaked brain made her feel an urgent need to be honest with Eric, at this very time, instead of waiting until he knew her better. She told him about the early rejection by her own family, how she ran away from home, her roommate, the sex change surgery, everything. Eric sat and listened. Gradually, his look changed from gentle bemusement to downright anger. At that point, Harriet regretted telling him anything. Her alarm bells rang and she knew he was not kind and understanding like Henry.

"You're telling me you used to be a man? So you've turned me gay!" Eric fumed. "You've affected me with the gay virus and now I'm gay?"

"No, no! It's nothing like that," Harriet retorted, trying to defuse the situation. But, Eric refused to listen, completely losing control.

"What's your sick game lady? I mean whatever the hell you are you, you freak!" he shouted.

Harriet rose up from the bed and tried to place her hand on Eric's shoulder in an attempt to console him. That was a big mistake because when she did so, he flung around quickly and hit her hard, right on the jaw. The punch caught her off guard, knocking her back across the bed. The combination of the liquor and the sudden shock to her brain, made her begin to black out.

Eric jumped across the bed and grabbed her by the neck. He screamed and shook her roughly. Harriet could not make out anything he said. His gentleness earlier in the night had disappeared and now he was just a ball of rage. The room began to spin. She tried to crawl away from him when he released her, but he prevented freedom and landed another hard punch to her head.

Harriet landed on the floor, and cried out, "Please Eric, listen to me!" Her pleas fell on deaf ears.

He was on top of her now, both hands wrapped firmly around her neck. It was impossible for her to breathe and in a matter of seconds, there was only blackness.

* * * * * * * * * * * * * * * * * *

When Harriet awoke, she found herself downstairs laying on the carpet in her front room. Her jaw ached, and she still felt dizzy. She tried hard to focus her blurry eyes and could just make out her easel and the canvas in the middle of the lounge.

Eric was nowhere in sight. *'Why do I hurt so much?'* Harriet wondered. Her head bounced off of her chest, as she began to slip in and out of consciousness. Finally, she awoke enough to be able to focus her sight. *'My God!'* *There's red paint everywhere and the canvas seems to be a portrait, done in the same gruesome red paint!'*

As Harriet focused through her pain, she looked down at herself, and absolute shock gripped her. Her entire body was covered in blood! Sitting up caused her intense pain. Her flesh had been sliced all over. Harriet's eyes lost focus with the sickening realisation and she vomited over herself.

She recovered enough to notice a bloody kitchen knife near her bloodstained feet. Her eyes followed the trail of blood, from the pool below her, all the way to the canvas. She saw a paintbrush lying near it and realized what had happened. The portrait had been daubed or painted in her blood!

As Harriet slipped deeper into shock, she noticed her mother's silver necklace in the corner of the room, where it had been torn from her neck and thrown. Then she heard a noise in the next room and realized in horror, that Eric had not left the house.

She picked up the bloody knife and staggered to her feet just as he entered the room. He too, was covered in blood and had a strange, pale look about him. He walked towards her and she painfully raised the knife.

At first, Harriet felt at peace with the tranquil feeling which overcame her, from blood loss. But, this was soon followed by one of absolute rage. She held the knife underhand, so he would not find it easy to take it from her. Harriet stood on shaky legs and lunged at Eric. He screamed and ran at her.

* * * * * * * * * * * * * * * * * * * *

Chapter Forty-Two
Trauma for Detective Mayfield

The honeymoon was over. Henry walked Viv down the garden path toward the home he had refurbished especially for her. At the door, he lifted her over the threshold. As soon as he put her back on her feet again, she ran happily from room to room, exploring.

"I love the colours, the furniture, the carpets and Harriet's pictures!" she said, almost in one breath.

Henry pointed to one in particular. It was a pastel pink with blue letters that declared, "HOME SWEET HOME." The painting was a portrait of their very own cottage!

"I love it! And I love this home!" she exclaimed as she threw herself into Henry's arms and hugged him.

It took a few days sorting out their possessions into the new home. When the place was a tidy as possible, they decided to invite some friends over for a house-warming party. Viv had telephoned Harriet numerous times since their return; the telephone just rang and went into answering mode. She had left messages, but still heard nothing from Harriet.

Viv checked with Dandy, who had not heard from Harriet either, not since her date. Although Harriet had left a short message on their office answer phone, saying she had enjoyed Eric's company and was meeting him again. Viv asked for Eric's phone number to check if she was with him and Dandy provided it to her. It had been a few days since then, and they were all worried enough to interrupt, even if Harriet was with company.

"Henry," Viv began. "Something's wrong. I don't know what, but I can sense it. Harriet would have been in contact by now! She knew which day we were coming home and she would have welcomed us back!"

Viv phoned several more times, also trying the number Dandy had given them for Eric. No one picked up. Henry confided that all could not be well and decided to phone Detective Mayfield, asking for a policeman to stop by Harriet's house, just to make sure she was okay. Henry would have gone himself, but there was so much to do before their guests turned up.

"Hi, Detective Mayfield? It's Henry. Viv and I are back from our honeymoon. Oh, yes, it was great. The weather was beautiful, thanks, yes we had a wonderful time. Listen Detective, I'm sorry to bother you with this. We haven't heard from Harriet since the time we left on our honeymoon, or since we've been back. Would you mind having someone check on her just to make sure she's all right?"

"Of course, Henry, I'll go by there myself," was the answer. "Actually, I'm not too far from her home right now. I apologize for not making the party or the wedding. El Diablo is far too close and I have to catch him."

"You're kidding, detective. But, I thought you were off the case."

"Yes, that's true. I took that retirement from the department and contracted myself out to the police. But, there's not only a reward for the capture of this maniac, but I have a personal score to settle. So, I had continued to pursue El Diablo, anyway. I was doing just that when all of a sudden the Chief called and asked for my help. So, I'm officially back on the case now. That retirement will have to wait."

"A personal score? I see, detective. I didn't realize that, but best of luck with everything. You don't think Harriet's mixed up with this dreadful killer, do you? We heard there was another murder the night of the party."

"Now don't go jumping to any conclusions, Henry. I'm still following up on some leads at the moment. That night of your party the police discovered the remains of a young woman. It was El Diablo's work."

"Really?"

"Well, yes. I can't go into the details with you. It's all confidential at this point and the police can't have a public panic on their hands you know."

"Sure, but we're still worried about Harriet."

"Henry, I'm on my way to Harriet's and I'll call you from there. I'm sure there's an explanation for all this."

* *

Detective Mayfield made his way quickly to Harriet's. What he had not disclosed to Henry was the fact that the young woman they discovered the night of the party had been decapitated. There was another strange twist though. This time El Diablo had also removed her hands and feet. All these body parts were present at the crime scene, but the body was missing. Another note was discovered, and it was directed at Detective Mayfield, mocking him again. For this reason, the police chief asked if he could become involved on an official level. They now needed his personal assistance in apprehending the madman. Mayfield was extremely happy to oblige.

He pulled into Harriet's drive and went to the front door. When there was no answer, he jimmied the door open and pulled out his service revolver. Very cautiously he entered. There was a putrid odour in the air and he placed a handkerchief over his nose. As he turned into the living room, he saw blood everywhere.

"Good God!" he blurted out aloud.

As he moved in closer, he saw a chair in the middle of the room. Bound to the chair was a bloody blanket, which appeared to have something wrapped up inside. All his years of police training taught Mayfield never to tamper with the crime scene. It was always necessary to wait until forensics arrived and secured the scene before touching anything. But, this was personal, and his feelings took over.

Mayfield took out his knife and undid the cords which bound the blanket, and the bloodied bundle dropped down at his feet. As he untied it, he discovered the bloody torso of a woman.

The genitalia had also been horribly mutilated and

the breasts removed. There was a portrait opposite the chair. It looked like a portrait of Harriet, some of it painted in blood. Hanging from the picture was a woman's necklace and locket. Mayfield opened the locket and inside were pictures of a young boy and a woman. It was inscribed, 'To darling Philip.'

"Damn it!" screamed Mayfield. "The bastard's killed Harriet!" He pounded his fist into the wall then regained his composure long enough to call the police chief.

"Chief, it's Mayfield. El Diablo's struck again. Better send the team right away. I'm at the Harriet Dewar residence."

Even for a hardened detective, the scene overwhelmed him. Mayfield thought of his wife and broke down in tears.

* * * * * * * * * * * * * * * * * * * *

It was early afternoon and the guests began to arrive for Henry and Viv's party. Dandy and Daniel, Mr. Lane, Martha, and later, a few other work associates arrived along with some casual friends. After awhile, the conversation started to centre on Harriet. No one had heard from her for several days. The party had been underway for an hour or so.

Unexpectedly, the sound of a car, pulling up fast in the driveway, caused Viv to look out the window. It was Detective Mayfield, who hurriedly got out of his old Humber Hawk. He was accompanied by two men in dark suits, and all of them looked serious. They approached the house and Viv opened the door to greet them.

"Sorry, Viv," Detective Mayfield said. "May we come in?"

"Of course, detective, but what's wrong? Is Harriet all right?" Viv asked.

Detective Mayfield and his partners entered and greeted everyone in the room.

"Viv, Henry, I'd like to speak with you in private?"

"No need," Viv replied, "we're all close friends of Harriet. Just tell us where she is detective. Is she all right?"

By now, everyone had stopped their conversations and activities to listen in complete silence to Detective Mayfield. He looked around the room and then very solemnly looked Viv in the eyes. He grasped her arms gently in his hands.

"Viv, I'm very sorry to have to tell you this, but Harriet's dead."

Dandy attempted to say something, but no words formed. She looked to Daniel for help, who sat down by her side and bit his lip tightly.

The words could not have hit Viv any harder. She had a feeling something was wrong for days, but could never have anticipated anything so terrible. Henry just stared straight ahead as if he could not believe these words.

"Harriet's dead!" Daniel exclaimed as he stared at the carpet. "But how? Who? Oh, God, how could this happen?"

There was silence, whilst the words sank in. Then Viv began to sob loudly, and Dandy started up too.

Henry's hand shook as he took his glass and gulped the contents down in one swallow. Tears welled in his eyes. He somehow felt responsible.

"Poor Harriet," he said eventually in a shaky voice. "What happened? Was it anything to do with Labelle?"

Detective Mayfield continued, "No, but she was murdered, Henry. We're looking for the guy right now. We have reason to believe it was El Diablo. He's been committing similar crimes all over the world. A global serial killer, if you can believe that. He has a pattern, or so we thought. Normally, he's attacked gay men, and umm, we found out about Harriet's, umm, previous gender."

He coughed, his nervous cough, before he continued. "But we found some drawings at Harriet's home that seemed to match those of some female victims of unsolved murders. Apparently, this guy has broadened his horizons. The problem is that he's a master of disguise and has a very uncanny way of covering his tracks. But I guarantee you, I'll find him. Police departments around the world are looking for this son of a bitch right now!"

Through sobs, Viv asked, "But how? Did she suffer?"

"It's hard to say Viv," the detective continued. "He cut and beat her up pretty bad, but she was drugged. We found some vials of what we believe to be GHB, meaning the 'date rape drug.' We're testing it right now. It's a powerful muscle relaxant that he apparently mixed into her drink, so I don't think she was too aware of what was happening at the time."

"Poor Harriet," Viv sobbed uncontrollably. Henry walked over to console her. He sat down and held her tightly, but the crying did not subside. It made it harder for him to cope with this terrible news.

"I'm so very sorry," said the detective. "It's never easy on any of us when these terrible things happen. Umm, I don't mean to be insensitive, but after our autopsy, we typically release the remains to one of the victim's family. It doesn't appear that Harriet had any family, though."

"We're her family!" Viv shouted through her sobs. "We'll claim her and take care of the entire burial arrangements, detective."

"Thank you, Viv, I appreciate that. You won't be able to look at the body though, I'm afraid she's too mutilated. I'll have someone call and work out the details with you later. Again, I'm very sorry, I really liked her. This whole business is terrible for all of us."

Suddenly, Dandy shrieked. "It wasn't that man we found for her at the agency was it? Please tell me it wasn't him, detective?" Her eyes implored the detective to say it was not, but instead he nodded.

"I'm afraid he could be the killer. I'm going to need all your files on this guy."

"Of course, Detective," Daniel offered. "Anything we can do to help. I'll call the agency now and tell them you're on your way and to co-operate fully."

"Thanks, Daniel, I appreciate that."

"Detective?" asked Daniel, "Has he always used dating agencies?"

"That's the way he typically finds his victims.

Normally, through the same-sex dating agencies, but this time he decided to choose a lady. We're dealing with a very deranged and twisted individual here. That's one of the things that makes him so dangerous, but I'll find him. The bastard murdered my wife, you know, butchered my woman." His voice started to crack, but he continued. "It's gotten way too personal. So I'm going to find the son of a bitch and personally send him to hell where he belongs. Mark my words." His voice wavered as he glanced at the other officers, who pretended not to hear those incriminating words.

Daniel held onto his sobbing wife tightly and felt like crying himself. 'It's our fault,' he thought. 'We're to blame!'

"Wait," said Viv. She went up to the detective and gave him a kiss. "Thank you, detective and we're so sorry about your wife." Tears welled in Mayfield's eyes. He nodded his head and left with the other detectives.

Viv and Dandy held each other and cried, but comfort would not come. Henry, who had tried desperately to control himself all of this time, left the room and allowed his grief to break.

* * * * * * * * * * * * * * * * * * * *

Chapter Forty-Three
The Day of Harriet's Funeral

The drive to the morgue was a quiet one. Viv and Henry barely spoke to one another. They simply stared straight ahead at the road. Occasionally, he looked down at the directions provided him by the morgue assistant.

"Just a bit further, darling," Henry said. "We should be there soon." He glanced briefly at Viv.

"I hope so, Henry," she replied whilst continuing to stare blankly at the road. "I hope we're going to be all right with this. I'm a bit nervous, you know. I've never had to claim a… claim a… you know ..."

"I know," said Henry. "Let's keep our chins up, though. Remember we're her only family. She would have felt comfort to have family with her now. She would have wanted us to do this for her. It's more just a matter of claiming the remains, I mean body, gosh, you know. Oh, there's the building."

Henry parked the car in the gravel lot in front of an old greyish, two-storey building. It was situated by itself, just off the motorway. Unless someone deliberately looked for it, no one would even know of its existence. The windows had been blacked out for the most part, and the only clue to the building's identity were the words, 'Greater London Morgue,' etched in small gold letters on the front door.

"Good God, what a dreary place!" Henry stated, as he exited the vehicle and came around to hold the car door open for Viv.

"It sure is," said Viv, her arm wrapped tightly around Henry's. She took a moment to gain her composure. "Okay. Let's go in."

They entered the building and rang a bell which had a loud, tinny sound to it. Within a few moments, a short, chubby man dressed in a white lab coat, greeted them. A badge on his pocket was inscribed with the words, 'Morgue Assistant.'

"Hi, can I help you?" he asked.

"Yes, we're the family of Harriet Dewer. We received a call this morning to come and claim her, uh, remains," Henry said as calmly as possible, although it was difficult to finish his sentence.

"Oh, yes, I called you earlier this morning. My name's Tony, I work here," the assistant replied. "Just follow me, please."

With that, he led them down a short, brightly lit corridor and then to a bank of elevators toward the back of the building. He pressed the button, and they took the elevator down to the basement where the vaults were located. Tony escorted them to a vault towards the end of the bank and grabbed the metal handle to open it.

"Wait," said Henry. He turned to Viv and grabbed her by both shoulders.

"You don't have to do this, sweetheart. Why not wait for me in the car? I can take care of things here."

"No, she was my friend, too, Henry. I need to do this," Viv said adamantly.

"All right, sweetheart." Henry nodded his head and the vault was opened.

Tony pulled out a long, shrouded, metal gurney containing a black, zippered body bag. The bag was about six feet long and made of a rubberized material. It appeared to be shrunken. On top of the bag was a small box containing Harriet's personal effects.

"Poor Harriet," said Henry resolutely. He picked up Harriet's silver necklace and locket then held it out to Viv.

She took it from Henry and held it in her hand, but could not look back at the gurney.

"We should bury this with her," Viv said. "It meant a lot to her. I'll make sure it goes with her. Henry, do you think we ought to have the bag opened, to say goodbye to her?

"No Viv, she's not here now, but has moved on and away from her body."

"Okay then," replied Tony. "I just need to have you sign some forms upstairs in the office. Then, you'll need to contact your funeral director to pick up Miss Dewar's remains."

Henry hugged Viv tightly to his chest and took one final look at the gurney. Tony took them back upstairs to sign the required forms. They were allowed to telephone the funeral home and made the necessary arrangements.

Once again in the car, Henry looked blankly ahead at the road the entire trip back home. Viv clutched Harriet's necklace and ran the silver chain through her fingers repeatedly.

"She's at peace now, Viv," Henry finally said.

"But do we really know that, Henry? The way she died was far too devastating and her spirit might be in torment now!" Again Viv's tears flowed and there was nothing further to say.

* *

The morning of the funeral arrived, and it was a crisp autumn day. Viv, Henry, Dandy, Daniel and Detective Mayfield were present to say their last goodbyes to Harriet. The casket was an ice blue colour with gold inlaid handles. Flowers were everywhere and draped the closed casket. The funeral director had arranged everything quite beautifully. The priest hired for the occasion supplied the sermon.

"Friends and loved ones. Welcome on this very solemn day, to pay your final respects to our dear friend, Harriet Dewer. Her parents could not be here today, as they have already gone on to prepare a special place for her in Heaven."

"Harriet was loved by all of you good people, and I'm sure that her spirit is in peace knowing the love you had for her in life. We mourn her; we miss her exuberant spirit, so full of life, and her willingness to help her friends. She was a dear soul who died much too soon. However, her life was not in vain as she touched everyone in this room. Her spirit will continue to live through each of you. God's blessings to you, dear Harriet. Godspeed on your journey, beloved friend and peace be with you. Amen."

At the conclusion of the sermon, the organist played and everyone took one final pass by the casket. Each of them placed notes, gifts and cards inside a small, brass box located on top of the coffin as they went by. Everyone said goodbye to Harriet and told her they loved her.

Viv placed the necklace and locket inside the small box. "I love you, Harriet," she cried.

Finally, the casket was loaded into the hearse for the ride to the cemetery. Henry, Daniel and Detective Mayfield with one of his associates, acted as pallbearers.

Viv and Dandy could not hold back their tears as they followed the hearse to the cemetery. Dandy told Viv that they had closed the agency and were now considering another kind of business. The Lyons could never forgive themselves for their part in Harriet's demise.

Dandy and Daniel wore very serious expressions. Henry took it particularly hard, and Viv could hardly believe that her new friend and confidante, Harriet, was gone. Their eyes showed pain, and both felt guilty for different, but similar reasons.

The hearse parked just inside the cemetery gates, and the coffin was carried to the open grave. Whilst it was being lowered, the priest prayed. The small, brass box of personal effects and notes was tightly sealed and lowered on top of the casket. The priest then picked up a handful of earth and dropped it on the coffin. He invited the rest of the group to do the same, and then he recited, 'The Lord is my Shepherd'. When the service was completed, the priest left.

There had not been anyone else at Harriet's funeral. Her relatives, at least the few remaining ones,

shunned her. Even upon death, they were not prepared to make their peace with her.

Henry carried the easel, Harriet's present. Daniel
helped him to lower it into the grave, on top of her
coffin. Henry found it difficult to breathe, let alone
control his emotional pain and his tears. He finally
spoke in a wavering and emotional voice, reading a
poem he had written especially for Harriet.

"This is felt by all of us here, and we say goodbye to
one of the best and truest friends ever, "Harriet Dewer."

Henry drew a breath and then started.

"We say a prayer for a loving soul,

Who had more heartache than we could behold.

Confusion, despair, torment and pain,

All of this suffering, all in vain.

An unhappy accident started at birth.

The troubles had, were met with mirth.

Truly a woman, though born a man.

Forgive them for mistreating you,

They could not understand.

You did not murder, thieve or hate.

What did you do to deserve this fate?

We think of the others whose lives are the same.

Forgive our misunderstandings;

In not being humane!"

Henry paused several times when the words became too much for him. Somehow, he managed to

get through the poem, although everyone was in tears long before the ending. Harriet's closest and only friends were dabbing their eyes with tissues.

Each one looked toward her grave, sending out their last thoughts. Then slowly they each walked away. Dandy was too upset to come back to Viv and Henry's place as planned, so Daniel took her home. Only Detective Mayfield accompanied them back. They were all quiet on the drive, but Mayfield's mind was working overtime. It was still busy untangling the complexities of the case.

The forensics team found blood that must have belonged to the assailant. From the amount of it, he would have needed medical treatment very quickly. Mayfield had contacted all hospitals and doctors in a fifty-mile radius. No one had been treated for serious injuries on that fateful night, and Mayfield was perplexed. He continued to think about the inconsistencies of the case on the drive to Viv's.

On arriving, he only stayed a short while with the couple. Viv constantly broke down and had to take tranquillisers before going off to bed. Henry was not much company, and the atmosphere was heavy with sorrow. Mayfield's thoughts kept returning to visions of his slaughtered wife.

After offering his condolences once again, he left and went back to his office to study the murder reports. Something just did not fit in with the evidence on this case. He went through different scenarios in his mind and reached one conclusion. The remains of the victim prior to Harriet had to be exhumed. The one he was called out to, at the time of Viv and Henry's wedding.

The problem was this new line of investigation would also mean exhuming Harriet's body. He needed to have something to take to the Court to get that done. Dismembered body parts turning up everywhere. The body that belonged to these appendages had to be somewhere. '*What about the body found dismembered in Harriet's house? Was it really hers? Some of the lab evidence suggested it was almost completely drained of blood, prior to its discovery.*

Of course the nature of the wounds would contribute to a significant blood loss, and blood was everywhere in the home. But would a body lose all of its blood in just five days? In addition, the body was in a far more advanced state of rigour mortis than it should have been. Was that possible? How could that be?

Could the victims be one and the same? If so, then where was Harriet's body, and why the elaborate cover up?' It did not make sense. But then again, it was El Diablo he was dealing with. Nothing this madman did made any sense. '*Perhaps it was another twist, or quirk of this sick bastard. What was he up to now? Anything to torment me, that's what.*' Mayfield picked up the telephone to call the police chief. He was going to need some help on this one.

* * * * * * * * * * * * * * * * * * *

Chapter Forty-Four
Mayfield Digs Deeper

It took some doing, but Mayfield finally convinced the chief to go along with his plans. After a call to the Prosecutor, the exhumations were scheduled. The remains of both bodies were to be examined by a renowned, board-certified forensic pathologist from the New York State Police Medico Legal Investigation Unit.

Due to the nature of the murders, Mayfield wanted the help of one of the best forensics experts in the world, Dr. Michael Baker. The two were also friends, having collaborated on several cases over the years. After a few calls, Mayfield had convinced the superintendent at Scotland Yard to fly in Dr. Baker and his team to assist with the case. The results would be fed into London's super criminal computer model, the HOLMES 2. If a correlation existed that would help Mayfield and other senior investigators apprehend the killer, the HOLMES 2 would find them. The superintendent agreed without hesitation.

"Hi, Wesley. Yes, I have the remains from both exhumations. We've already begun our initial exams and tests."

"What can we honestly expect to find, Michael?"

"Well, you've put forth an interesting hypothesis,

Wesley. That we have one and the same victim and not two individual homicides. To prove that, we'll conduct DNA analysis on various tissue and blood samples. We'll match the results up and see if everything belongs to the same person. We'll also conduct our typical 5-part autopsy on the full set of remains. I'll conduct an external exam, a couple of tests on the chest and abdomen, the neck, skull and brain. We can compare vertebrae from the severed head and see if it's a match with the torso."

"But, Michael. We need conclusive proof that only one victim's involved here. Will your results prove that conclusively? We want to discount any possibility that the second alleged victim was not the one discovered in the Harriet Dewar home. If that's the case, we still have a missing person. Possibly a kidnapping or even another murder."

"Yes, I can give you that, Wesley. But, there's more. If the torso does not belong to Harriet Dewar, it'll be necessary to identify the victim and the precise cause of death aside from the obvious factors."

"If it's not Harriet Dewar, Michael, then it's vitally important for us to determine the exact time the murder occurred. I've collected an extensive amount of information on the El Diablo case. Profiles on different suspects. An exact time of death would help tremendously in matching up their alibis against this victim's time of death."

"Well, everything tells a story, Wesley. We can give a very reasonable estimate of the time of death from some relatively simple clues. In all likelihood, there will be eggs present in the tissue. Eventually, whenever a body, or body part in this instance, is exposed to the elements for any period of time, insects find it. We can get an estimate of the time the eggs were laid in different tissues and match up how advanced they are in the gestation cycle. Insects play an amazing role in body decay."

"That's all very informative, Michael, but how does that help in this particular case?"

"All right. A couple of things happen to a decaying body. Once the body stops getting nourishment, its own enzymes begin to eat it, causing tissues to liquefy. That's the putrefaction part, which is why you were probably hit with a stench when you entered the house. But let's get back to this insect business. Once maggots get to work on rotting flesh, they can take care of it pretty quickly. You know, I once…"

"Sorry to interrupt, Michael, but time is money so to speak. We're working with a very short timeframe to catch this killer."

"Oh, yes, sorry. Anyway, my point is that by matching the eggs and the maggots, we can come up with an amazingly close approximation to the time of death. If the results match between the body parts and the torso, we can determine if the murder or murders occurred at the same time."

"That's great, Michael. Can you do it quickly?"

"Yes, of course. I'll have the full set of results for you in a couple of days, and the initial DNA screen in a few hours. Then I can compare results against the medical and dental records you provided me. That will tell us if it's Harriet Dewar here. But, one thing still bothers me about this case, Wesley."

"I know, a lot of things bother me about this case, Michael. What's the problem?"

"Well. Whoever did these things. He or she made it very easy for you to find the body and the appendages, even the head. It didn't take much work to find them. Everything was right out in the open. Whoever did these terrible things, must have known that it would be a no-brainer for us to get a match. But, why? Why make everything so obvious?"

"Because, Michael. That's the way this killer operates. He's mocking us."

"Oh, I see. Daring you to catch him sort of? Okay, I'll talk to you soon then, Wesley."

"Okay pal, I've work to do and will wait for your call. Make it quick. Thanks again, Michael."

* * * * * * * * * * * * * * * * * * *

Chapter Forty-Five
Viv Needs to Come Clean

Henry and Viv sat in the living room, trying as best they could, to remain calm in the face of everything that happened.

"Henry, I know that now is a terrible time for us all, but Harriet's death has me thinking about many things."

"Yes, Viv. I've been thinking, too. I can't stop thinking about the bastard that killed poor Harriet. If only I could get my hands on him, I'd...,"

"No, Henry. Don't speak of things like that. The police and Detective Mayfield are on it. Let's leave it to the experts. They'll get him. I saw that look in Detective Mayfield's eyes and I don't like seeing it in yours. It's scary."

"I know, Viv, but at least we have one another. Mayfield is alone."

"Actually, that's what I've been thinking about, Henry. You know that I love you and that I'd never do anything to intentionally hurt you."

"Yes, I know that, darling. There's no need to tell me that."

"Henry, there's more and I've just got to get this out now, or I'll burst. I realize that you're a big part of my life. But, this marriage was a mistake."

"What? Viv, you don't know what you're saying. We're both upset about what's happened. I'll make you a cup of tea."

"Wait, Henry. I've been tormented with this since before the wedding. I'll always need you as my dearest friend and will always want you in my life. I do love you, but without being in love with you. I hoped it might be possible for me to fall in love if we gave it a chance."

"Why are you saying this, Viv, after all we've been through?"

"That's just it, Henry. What we went through made it impossible to say no to you. That doesn't mean I don't love you, but I can't give all of myself when I can't stop this feeling for BV. And, it's nothing like that silly little crush I had on Daniel. As you know, absolutely nothing happened with him."

"I don't want to talk about it, or even know any more for that matter, but it looks as if I have to ask. Were you and BV lovers then?"

Viv felt guilty as she still remembered what took place between her and Dandy. *'Was that wrong?'* she wondered. The question Henry had just asked filtered through to her.

"Yes, Henry, it did happen between BV and me. I'm so sorry, but it was out of our control. We became very involved, but I still couldn't stop loving you."

Henry felt even more miserable. He could barely believe it possible this was happening and just after the loss of their dear friend.

He asked, "Are you telling me this about BV just

to get it off your conscience, or because you intend doing something about it?"

"Both of those reasons, Henry. I may be telling you all this and end up losing your love. I'd deserve that and maybe it'll be all for nothing."

"You're confusing me, Viv."

"I'm trying to explain, Henry, but this is one of the hardest things I've done. You, above all people should not have this happen to you. I'm so sorry. I don't know what the outcome will be. But, I need to phone BV to see if he's all right and I didn't want to do it behind your back."

"But, he had to change all his details, so how do you know his new number?"

"At our reception, after the Humanist wedding, BV got a note to me. He hoped I'd call him, but, I didn't, Henry."

"Why do you want to contact him now?" asked Henry, as he tried to understand and accept whatever he was about to be told.

"I just need to. You may not want to speak to me again and BV may be gone now. But, I couldn't do this without you knowing."

"Well, I appreciate you telling me first, but in a way I wish you hadn't. I mean, if he isn't there, I didn't need to know. But, what if he is? What if it upsets you, Viv?"

Viv was upset already, just having to hurt Henry in this way. Also, what if BV asked her to join him again? She was scared of what might happen either way, but could not keep her feelings to herself any longer. It was driving her crazy and all on top of the sorrow of Harriet's death.

"Henry, I've no idea what's going to happen. I'll have to see, but I want to phone now. I may be asking too much of you, but please be supportive afterwards. I'll need you to be."

"This hurts, Viv. I thought you loved me enough, but you know I'll try to understand, whatever happens."

They both knew what might happen and did not want to talk about the possible consequences. Henry put his arms around her and she snuggled in toward him. How she wished not to be in this situation. Viv enjoyed this warm moment, and then stood to go upstairs and make her phone call in private.

"I'd better get it over with, Henry, and make that call now." She wondered if he'd ever feel secure with her again.

"Yes, I agree. If you need to do this, better do it now; get it over with. I'll just have a drink. Would you like one, Viv?"

She thought for a moment then said, "Yes, please, a Malibu and Coke. I'll take it upstairs with me." She felt nervous about what was going to happen.

"Viv, you know how I feel about you and we are newly married. Please keep that in mind."

"I know, Henry. I hate myself for what's happened to me. We all have to be true to ourselves though, darling. I know you'd hate for me to spend a lifetime regretting my decision." Viv began to break down.

Henry felt like crying too, but it hurt him more to see Viv upset. Before he could speak, she continued.

"Please remember I truly love you, darling, and I always will, but I'm in love with BV. It's so hard to describe it any other way."

"Whatever you feel and however strong, you're telling me you love BV more?"

"Yes, I guess I am. My love for you is very strong, but it would be complete if I wasn't in love with BV."

"He's out of the country and can't come back, Viv. Why don't you just let it go?"

"No, he hasn't gone yet. I didn't know whether to tell you before. He's contacted me by text, since I didn't phone him as he asked."

"Oh, great!"

"I never replied, but I've been thinking about it for days now. It's been pure torment for me because of my love for you, darling. And, also because of how I feel for him!"

"I can't believe this. Why? Why?"

"I don't know, Henry. It's difficult for you to understand because you've had so few relationships. Perhaps you just wanted me so desperately, that it was impossible to see the obvious. That I wasn't in love with you enough."

"But, you said yes, to marrying me!"

"I did, Henry, but look what we'd just been through! How could I turn you down at a time like that? It looked like you might die and I felt to blame in a way."

"Okay, I see. Perhaps my timing was bad, but I thought I'd nearly lost you. You could have been killed and I needed to ask you then. I need you, Viv, but I won't beg. Not even now that we're married. I just need to know what you want to do. Where do we go from here?"

"I'll always want you to be a part of my life, darling. But, it's BV that I belong with. I need to contact him, even though it breaks your heart for me to do so. I must keep trying until he eventually answers. Then we'll decide what's to be done."

Suddenly, the telephone rang and they both jumped. Viv picked up, since Henry was pouring their drinks.

"Hi, Viv? It's Mayfield. We've got another new twist. A big one. The body discovered in Harriet's home didn't belong to her. She may still be alive."

* *

Chapter Forty-Six
The 'El Diablo' Case Takes a New Twist

"Viv, I need to ask you and Henry some questions. The body and appendages found at the two murder scenes match. It's one and the same person. We don't know who it is just yet, but Dr. Michael is working on it with the police. One thing's for sure. It's not Harriet."

"Oh, my God, detective, but then where is she?" asked Viv.

"That's a good question. I need to know if either you or Henry can remember anything that Harriet might have said about her past. For instance, I'm trying to ascertain if she hated men."

Viv pondered this comment for a moment. Harriet not like men? No, she certainly loved Henry enough.

"There's no way she hated men. She's had a crush on Henry though they are, er.. were just the best of friends, detective. Okay, well speak later. Bye."

As Viv hung up the telephone, Henry walked back into the room. He was still very upset.

"Who was that, Viv?"

"Detective Mayfield. The lab results came back and it wasn't Harriet. She may still be alive!"

"What? Good grief! This whole day's been one big shock. What does he want us to do?"

"He wanted to know if Harriet mentioned anything about hating men."

"She can't be a suspect in this mess! That's impossible. She was with us at the party when that other body turned up. That clears her, but then where is she? Oh, I can't think, Viv. We're still not through talking about us and our future."

"I know, Henry, but we have to face up to facts. I need to call BV sooner or later. You know that."

"All right. I've had some time to think. I'm still against it, but let's get that out in the open at least. And, what I'm about to say is against my better instincts. Why don't you call him and arrange for us all to meet here? As soon as possible. I love you enough to want to see you happy. But, I need to see BV once more. I must see the look in his face when he's with you. That will tell me if he loves you, too. Only then, could I possibly bear to see you go off with him."

Viv went upstairs to telephone the number from BV's text. Her initial apprehension turned to great comfort when he answered. After finding out that he was holding up well and still in the country, she explained the scene between her and Henry. BV was surprised to find out that Henry had agreed to meet with them both. BV thought that a good idea, and it was agreed that all of them meet at Viv and Henry's house the next evening. It was then she would make her final decision as to who would have her love.

* *

Detective Mayfield's mind worked in high gear. It was essential to know if Harriet had an alibi at the time the murders took place. If Henry could be her alibi for at least one of the murders, that would be extremely helpful. As impossible as it seemed, Harriet might be the serial killer. Perhaps she hated gays due to her tormented past. She could view gays as being happy to stay men, coping with loving other men and without losing their gender status.

She may have killed the victim the police discovered at her house. As it turned out, the body was a transgendered male to female, placed there to look like her. It would have been a perfect alibi. She would then never be suspected of being the serial killer or having her fingerprints taken. She may have changed her appearance and looked totally different now. Then why plant the other appendages so obviously? They were meant to be found.

More likely, Harriet was kidnapped. Whilst it did not fit the El Diablo profile, he seemed to be changing his methods a great deal lately. If he wanted to kill her, then why go through all the work of planting a body at the scene? No, he took her for some reason, which would be found out when the killer was ready to let it be known.

Mayfield checked all of the records on Eric at the Lyons dating agency. They only met him once and said Eric appeared to be charming. As it turned out, the information provided on the application was all fabricated. The company he worked at, his address and references. No one Mayfield checked with, recognized the name or picture. He must have disguised himself again. Or, was it possible that El Diablo had an accomplice? Multiple serial killers? The mere thought of that was overwhelming.

If Eric was involved and planted a body to look like Harriet, there must be a reason for this turn of events. Perhaps he knew her. No ransom demands were made and Harriet had no living relatives. The motive must be other than money. Mayfield remembered working on a kidnapping years ago with some parallels to this one. In that case, the victim was locked up, tortured for weeks, then left to rot.

Perhaps Eric had designs on torturing her. Along with multiple blood types found at Harriet's house, the lab also turned up evidence of semen on the bed sheets. Eric might have engaged in sex with Harriet and then went mad when he realized her gender. He obviously hated gays and might have been victimized at some point, either as a child or even in a prison. Something happened to fill this man known as 'Eric,' with such rage.

If he did have Harriet imprisoned right now, it would be ugly for her. Death would not come quickly. It could drag on for weeks or months, and only due to his having sex with someone he still considered to be a man. There had to be another clue. What about the drawings? It seemed Harriet had phoned Dandy to give her an update. She had described Eric's home and his drawings.

Some pictures were found at the murder scene, but where were the rest? Eric was a talented artist. He painted Harriet's likeness on a canvas left in her home. It was partially done, but the work was very good in spite of its macabre nature.

Maybe it was best to start from the very beginning. It occurred to Mayfield that after the murder at BV's barbeque, the serial killer began to strike locally. Now why was that? Probably a good idea to stop by BV's house and have another look around. BV asked him to keep an eye on his place anyway. Mayfield was just about to leave when his telephone rang.

It was Michael at the crime lab, and they had a break in the case. A fingerprint lifted from evidence found at the first crime scene matched that of a known felon. It belonged to a small time art forger and drug peddler.

"Doesn't really match the profile of El Diablo," Mayfield said. "But, if Eric and El Diablo are one and the same, it's worth following up. Do you have a last known address?"

"Yeah. The police are on their way to the place now. 135 Chelsea Court, Apartment 9."

Mayfield climbed into his Saab and floored the accelerator. He arrived just as the police pulled up. They all entered the building and knocked on the door. When there was no answer, they burst in and were greeted by a stench. They discovered a decapitated male body on the bed. The head was found in the refrigerator with a note in its mouth.

"Looks like another El Diablo killing, Mayfield," the investigator on the scene commented, handing him the note.

It read: 'Congratulations, Mayfield. I see you discovered 'Eric.' Now that you have come this far, you are starting to unravel the puzzle. But remember. I am still a step ahead of you every time. Get it detective? I am always a 'head' of you. I do so enjoy my simple torments. By the way, Harriet's still alive, barely. And one last thing, you will never catch me.'

Mayfield handed the note back to the lead investigator. "Any identification on the body?"

"Yeah, actually there's something here," responded the lead investigator as he removed some ID from the victim's clothing. "Well, would you look at that. This is that guy Eric we've been looking for. There goes our El Diablo theory, Mayfield, he wasn't Eric after all."

"I know," responded Mayfield. "He's still out there. And, so is Harriet, but where and for how long?"

* * * * * * * * * * * * * * * * * * * *

Chapter Forty-Seven
Kidnapped

Harriet awoke in chains in a dank, musty-smelling basement. Her body ached and burned terribly from previous wounds and the administration of new beatings. Her hands and feet were chained. All she remembered was having a fight with Eric. She had a knife in her hand about to attack him as he ran toward her. But then someone struck her on the back of the head. Now she was lying on this hard floor.

As she regained consciousness, her focus became clearer. She saw the outline of a large man standing out of the way, in the corner of the room. He wore a mask and he noticed when she looked at him. There was a prod of some sort in his hand which became clearer as he approached her. He raised the prod and then zapped her with several thousand volts of electricity. The pain seared through her body as she let out a terrible, blood curdling scream.

"No, please don't! No more! Why are you doing this? Stop! I'll give you money, if that's what you want?" Harriet shouted, as she wriggled in agony. Her wounds gained earlier were still stinging and painful, without this extra torture.

The masked man spoke to her. His voice sounded strange through the mask. She thought it recognizable, but could not place it.

He told her, "I won't stop, that would ruin my fun. I don't want your money, but you're going to pay for what you've done."

"What have I ever done to you?" Harriet pleaded, still unable to recognize her kidnapper.

"That will all be made clear, Harriet," he replied slowly.

"How do you know my name? What do you want with me? Do you know me?"

"Everything will be made clear. As far as what I want, that's simple. Only to destroy your spirit and then to watch you die!"

Harriet screamed as the prod again seared her naked flesh.

* * * * * * * * * * * * * * * * * * * *

Chapter Forty-Eight
Detective Mayfield Confronts
'El Diablo'

Mayfield left the murder scene both disgusted that El Diablo was still loose and upset over Harriet's disappearance. He considered different scenarios and decided to take a closer look inside BV's house. He only had his suspicions to go on at this point, but his hunches had served him well in the past. The murders started in earnest that night of the barbeque and it was strange for El Diablo to stay in one area for so long. Maybe BV knew the killer, or at least had some tie to him without realising it. It was a crazy thought, given that he and BV were such good friends. But, in all his years on the force he had learned never to take any clue or intuition, for granted.

With that thought in mind, Mayfield obtained a search warrant and arranged for the police locksmith to meet him at BV's house. On the drive over, he tried to sort out all that occurred during the past several days. Instead of answers, he only came up with more questions. First, he hoped to find something of use amongst BV's papers. There were a few loose ends to tie up with the Alex Labelle murder, anyway.

The detective pulled up into the drive of BV's estate and walked through the orchard, around to the entrance of the den. The locksmith was already there and waiting. The official police seal was half stuck on the building and blowing around in the wind. Mayfield was let into the house.

He pulled out his service revolver and cautiously entered the den. He ignited a cigarette lighter to see his way and found a light switch. He flicked it on and walked into the main room of the den. It was a mess, and a wave of apprehension hit him in the chest. His instincts told him something was very wrong here.

As he walked past the bar, there were several papers scattered on the floor. They appeared to be drawings. He bent down to pick one up. It was a drawing of a woman in a state of contortion and the pain in her face was sickeningly real. A wave of horror hit him. It was a picture of Harriet!

"Good God!" he said aloud. "How did it get here, in BV's den?"

He looked up at the wall and found the safe open. Upon closer examination, he discovered several more pictures torn up, along with other papers. In a metal bin, he found a charred file folder with the name 'Eric' still visible on the cover. He examined the contents and learned that a man had been paid to assume the role of Eric. He appeared to be a junkie who depended on BV for money and drugs. He was the individual who met with the Lyons and appeared on the dating video. It appeared that BV's connections had provided all the necessary false identification.

Fortunately, for Mayfield, BV must have been in a rush and not checked that everything had burned properly. Also inside the bin, there was a slightly charred diary. In it, BV described how he hired a building in the country to commit some of the murders. There was also a list of gay men, along with their addresses and telephone numbers. More surprising, and careless, was the list of his *'past'* and *'potential victims.'* Apparently, Eric or BV, had either photographed or painted some of the victims prior to their deaths. BV may have blackmailed Eric to assist in some of these murders, or 'Eric' may have just been paid to help. Obviously, 'Eric' had become surplus to requirements.

In a distressed state, Mayfield phoned the police chief to tell him of these discoveries. "Chief, it's Mayfield. You'd better get out here to BV's place. Turns out he's possibly the killer. Everything's here in his diary and papers. We just need verification of his writing. If it is, then yeah, BV is El Diablo."

Mayfield continued to sort through the papers in the safe and discovered some letters to Viv. From the contents, BV had obviously fixated on her with his love, but for some reason never sent the letters. Mayfield had known him for many years, yet never saw him in a serious relationship, let alone want to marry anyone. BV had even been over for dinner at his home, with his wife. Mayfield was overcome with anger and humiliation at being taken for such a ride.

Now, he had to accept that his long-time friend and undercover man was possibly the same person who savagely murdered his beloved wife. BV, the serial killer, El Diablo. Mayfield forced his mind back into professional mode. In a strange way, it made sense. He had been BV's friend for years and unwittingly discussed his work with him, even shared the murder details. His own brother, Daniel, said he did not know much of BV's activities and rarely saw him.

A real enigma. Suddenly, Mayfield stopped dead in his tracks. He came across a recent entry in the diary, which read; 'Everyone's going to pay. Harriet, Henry and Viv!' Mayfield dropped everything literally, rushed out, locking the door behind him and tried to reach Viv and Henry on his cell phone. It was early evening, and they should be home. He held his breath as he waited for someone to pick up. There was no answer. His heart beat like a hammer trying to burst through his chest. He ran to his car and jumped in without even belting up. He closed the door whilst the car was in motion and sped to their house.

"Oh, God please," he called out, "don't let me be too late!"

* *

Chapter Forty-Nine
Henry Meets His Rival

It was early evening, and as arranged, BV pulled up outside Viv and Henry's house. This occurred just as a phone in their cottage started to ring. It was ignored, as BV's knock on the door took precedence. He only had to wait a few minutes. Viv was upstairs, still upset, though she had taken Valium earlier to calm her nerves. Henry left her side to go down and answer the door. When Henry opened it, the two men faced each other. There was a nervous, strained atmosphere between them. Although they managed to shake hands, it lacked any warmth.

Viv came downstairs, her face still tear-stained. For the sake of not hurting Henry, she did not run into BV's arms although she longed too. Instead, she said hello and asked that they all go into the lounge. Drinks were offered and accepted.

When all were seated, Henry asked how BV was getting on with the witness protection scheme. BV explained that all was in place now, and he had been keeping out of everyone's way.

"But, now I've got tickets to get out of the country tonight," he told them. "I want to know if Viv will come with me." BV looked beseechingly at her.

"Why should she want to go with you, BV?" Henry

asked quickly. "You know she's married to me! Can't you be a sport about losing out?" He had not meant to put it so bluntly, but his temper was rising with the cheek of this man.

BV glanced at Viv, sitting in an armchair curled up like a child, with her legs underneath her. She was sobbing, not able to speak or take part in this discussion. Both of the men wanted to comfort her, but they had serious business to sort out first.

"Henry," said BV, trying to maintain his temper. "You realize that Viv only agreed to marry you, because she thought I was on the wrong side of the law?"

"Of course, I know that had something to do with her decision, but she loved me first, and I can offer her a comfortable life," replied Henry, trying to speak in a calm voice. "You'll be dragging her around with you and could never provide a stable home."

Although BV was the larger man, Henry was not going to give Viv up so easily. He knew his past training would come in very handy, and he was not afraid of BV in the slightest degree. He wished his injured arm had been completely healed, but that did not worry him either.

"She loves me more," said BV. "She'll grow to regret her decision if she stays with you."

"If you loved Viv, you wouldn't have sent her the note, BV, nor asked her to phone you. Her welfare should have been the main concern, not yours!"

Both men tried to stay calm, but their voices began to rise. Viv stopped crying and found she was still unable to choose between them. There was no doubting Henry was a terrific man. She stared at BV and felt a different love than the one she had for Henry. *'How on earth could there be two kinds like this?'* she wondered miserably.

"It's about time Viv was brought into this," said Henry. He looked lovingly at her, waiting for her to say something.

"Please, Viv, join in darling. What do you want to ask BV?"

"I don't know," she replied, looking from BV's expectant face, back to Henry's.

Henry took over again. "I think she needs to know how long you'd have to be on the move, BV?"

"Well, that depends on how long these *'big'* guys are looking for revenge. It could be two years, or less."

"How would Viv's safety be guaranteed? They might grab her, to make you give yourself up to them!"

Viv grew alarmed. She had never thought of that. Just then the phone rang again, but it was ignored once more.

Henry continued. "Do you really want to risk that, BV? If you truly loved Viv, you'd say goodbye and never contact her again."

Viv burst into tears. She knew Henry spoke the truth and it hurt. She looked from one to the other, realizing that she loved Henry more. However, she still could not bring herself to say goodbye to BV again. That pain was still raw in her mind and suffering like that was more than enough.

Suddenly BV stood up and faced Viv. "I love you and need you more than anything in the world. Please come with me. I'll keep you safe. I've got enough money for us to live in a world of our own. We could go somewhere in the middle of so many people that we'd just disappear amongst them."

Viv looked at Henry. Her friends were here and Harriet might still be alive. How could she leave at a time like this? Even if she wanted to.

"BV, you know I love you. The moments we spent together were precious." She looked at Henry and saw the pain in his eyes, but continued, "I'll never forget you, but I can't leave Henry. You and I said our goodbyes to each other, BV, and I'm married now. It's too late!"

The phone rang insistently and Henry almost picked it up when BV spoke again.

"But, you love me more, Viv! We have such a bond. You know that. How can I leave without you?" BV started to sound desperate. "I don't mean to insult Henry, but he isn't the one for you. I am!"

"You're wrong there, pal," Henry said, now visibly angry. "You're mixed up with the wrong sort and they're after you! You'll never be free of them."

Viv was most alarmed when they confronted each other. BV swung first and Henry ducked, using his forearm to take the blow. Soon there were fists and feet flying with blows connecting on each of them.

"Stop! Please, stop this!" shouted Viv. She picked up the phone to call Mayfield.

* *

Chapter Fifty
The CONCLUSION!

No sooner had Viv picked up the telephone, when she heard a car screech to a halt outside the house. She rushed to the window hoping it was Daniel and Dandy. They were due to pop in some time soon. Instead, it was Detective Mayfield jumping out of his car. She ran to open the door for him, shouting out.

"They're fighting! Stop them, please! Stop them!"

Detective Mayfield ordered Viv out of the room. She stayed put, so he shoved her out and closed the lounge door. Her two favourite men were fighting, but she obeyed Mayfield and stayed on the other side of the door.

Meanwhile, Mayfield pulled out his revolver and was horrified to see BV stab Henry with a large knife. Blood spurted from the front of Henry's jumper as he fell to the floor gasping for breath.

Mayfield aimed his gun at BV and shouted through the door for Viv to get an ambulance. She ran upstairs to make the phone call.

"You make a move and I'll shoot you!" Mayfield said, through clenched teeth. "In fact, MOVE, as I want to shoot you!"

BV stood still, not far from his victim laying on

the floor. He knew the game was up and stared insolently at Mayfield.

"It was you who killed my wife! You! My so-called friend and I protected you! You bastard!" Mayfield could hardly contain his anger.

Knives had been thrown at him before and he was taking no chances at losing this killer. Instead of telling BV to put the knife down, which he knew he should have done, he shot BV in the kneecap.

BV screamed out and fell, writhing in pain. He grasped his knee, and his face contorted in agony.

"What's happened?" yelled Viv, still on the telephone getting help. "Who's been shot?"

"Just stay there!" Mayfield shouted back to her.

"Where's Harriet?" he demanded, aiming at BV's other kneecap. "By God, I'm going to shoot you again, if you don't answer me now!"

"She's alive," BV managed between gasps of pain.

"Where is she? Tell me now!" Mayfield repeated, about to lose his control.

"No food, just water. She's not well though," he giggled. "Probably swimming around in her own defecation and urine about now." His laugh further infuriated Mayfield.

Viv was back on the other side of the door. "The ambulance is on the way. I told them someone was shot! Who's been shot? Let me in!" she screamed, trying to push the door open.

Mayfield leaned against the door to keep her out, whilst Viv continued to call out to him. But, he still had questions to ask BV.

"Talk!" he shouted. "Where's Harriet?"

"I don't have to answer anything, Mayfield," BV managed, clutching his knee, in obvious pain.

"Talk, you son of a bitch! Where is she?" he shouted, kicking BV in the wounded kneecap.

The pain was excruciating and showed on his face, but so did his anger. "I could kill you!" BV replied, as he narrowed his eyes with hate.

Mayfield shouted again. "The next time I won't kick, I'll shoot! Talk! What about my wife, you bastard? Why kill her? What did she ever do to you?"

"Oh, guess I shouldn't have done that."

"Too right! I'm going to kill you for that. I've no need for a life without my woman!"

"Then Harriet will die!" he growled. "How about a deal? Her life for mine?" BV knew how near he was to getting killed on the spot.

"Okay, deal!" Mayfield said. "I've no option here. Tell me and I'll just have you arrested. But tell me now! My patience has run out!"

BV told him the address and Mayfield phoned it straight through to the police chief. He then waited for confirmation that Harriet was, hopefully, still alive.

Meanwhile, the detective tried to find out more whilst waiting to see if BV had given the correct address. "Did you really expect to get away with this, BV?"

"I would have, if I hadn't waited for Viv! How did you get on to me anyway?"

"The stuff you burned, the papers, diary in the bin.

Well, they didn't burn! You shouldn't have rushed off without checking. You slipped up bad and I got all the info I need!"

"My mind was on convincing Viv to come with me! Trust a woman to be my undoing!"

"Why did you start all this? Why the killings?" Mayfield hoped to grow calmer, but his intention was still to stop this murderer from going to trial, only to languish in jail. The pain in BV's knee began to subside. He smugly answered Mayfield's questions.

"It started in prison. Remember when I had to get arrested to prove I was one of the drug barons? Well, I was abused very brutally in there and often. You didn't give me the protection you promised!" BV looked as if he expected an apology.

"Go on," said Mayfield, lowering his gun.

"I've been determined ever since to get both the police and gay men back for my humiliation." He grimaced as the pain got to him. "That's why I couldn't leave, even though my cover was blown, until I knew Daniel was out of prison. I'd just about finished getting my own back on those gays, when I fell for Viv and……."

Mayfield interrupted him. "Why kill women? Why my woman?" He started getting angry again.

"Games, just games. Wanted you to think Harriet was dead or make her look like the famous *El Diablo*.' He laughed and remarked that Eric had served his purpose and had to be eliminated.

Mayfield was amazed that BV showed no sign

of regret for any of the suffering he had caused. Enunciating each word Mayfield asked, "What kind of man are you?"

BV seemed in a world of his own now. "I expected her to go with me, Mayfield, but Henry stopped all that. I'd hoped he would have gone off with Harriet. I was counting on those two, but they let me down. That's why I wanted to kill them." He groaned with renewed pain as he tried to move. "Where's the ambulance?" he cried out.

Mayfield glanced at Henry, who was breathing shallowly. "Why mention killing Viv in your notes? I thought you loved her?"

"I couldn't share her with anyone else. If she didn't come with me, she would have died, as well as Henry."

There was a strange look on BV's face. It was not just twisted with pain; it also showed a type of madness in his eyes. He looked as if he would kill Mayfield too, if he were able to stand up.

Mayfield looked again at Henry, still unconscious, blood pooling around him. He shouted out to Viv. "Is the ambulance on the way?"

"Yes," she shouted back. "Let me in, please!"

Mayfield ignored her plea. In the background he could hear the wail of the approaching ambulance.

"And my wife? You bastard! Why did you butcher my wife? Answer me," he screamed.

Mayfield's cell phone rang and he got the answer he was waiting for. "Harriet's still alive, but just barely!"

He then turned back to BV, "You're going to suffer for this! I tried my best to help you, but couldn't get you out of prison any sooner than I did. And to think you held it against me all this time! My wife did not have to die!"

Mayfield kicked BV in his shattered knee. As he did so, Viv pushed the door open and saw this incident. She then saw Henry sprawled on the floor in a pool of blood. On her way to Henry, she noticed Mayfield's gun aimed at BV and saw his bleeding, injured knee.

"Oh, no!" she cried out to Mayfield, absolutely horrified. "It was you all the time! You are El Diablo!"

"You wouldn't dare shoot me now, *'El Diablo,'* in front of a witness!" smirked BV, feeling safe, now that Viv was in the room.

"I always told you I'd kill you *'Diablo!'* You're not going to trial!" Mayfield said, shaking with rage.

Viv could not understand what was being said here. Then she saw the knife wound bleeding from the unconscious Henry.

"Oh, my God! Henry's dead!" she wailed.

As she cradled Henry's head, sobbing, Mayfield aimed his gun at BV and shot him in the chest at point blank range. Viv watched horrified as BV collapsed on the floor, clutching his chest and breathing his last breath.

Viv could not believe it. The two men she loved so dearly, now dead?

She became overwhelmed with grief and lapsed into unconsciousness.

* * * * * * * * * * * * * * * * * * *

Chapter Fifty-One
The Final Consequences

Henry had been treated for a punctured lung from the stab wound and after his brief hospital stay was able to go home. He still hurt, but much of that was in his mind. Viv had gone through hell and he had no idea just how badly her mind had been affected, but Henry had been told she was totally unstable now. No-one told him details and he wanted to visit her as soon as he was allowed by her doctor. It was hard to believe, but, BV, alias, *'El Diablo,'* was dead. The police chief gave Mayfield some problems about his not bringing BV in, or calling the police out in time to prevent the *'showdown.'*

Mayfield wrote in his report that he shot BV in the kneecap after BV had stabbed Henry, when he would not put the knife down. The next part of the report explained how BV had, on one leg, still attempted to knife the detective. He had to shoot him in self-defence and of course Henry would back that up, if needed, although he had, in reality, been unconscious.

Detective Mayfield knew that Viv's mind had been affected badly. By the time she recovered in the hospital, if she ever did, she would be in no condition to dispute anything that happened. Viv had been totally confused about who was who, anyway. He felt extremely sorry for her and for the outcome, but *'El Diablo'* would never be a threat again. Mayfield was also pleased the paramedics kept Henry alive and that he was now on the mend. Mayfield had already visited Harriet in hospital, after giving her a few days to recover from the worst of her injuries. He had taken notes and a statement, and then given Harriet the news about her friends.

Henry was told it would take at least two weeks for Harriet to recuperate from her ordeal, physically at least. The Lyons had visited her together and Dandy had also visited alone. She was visibly upset on learning some of what had happened to Harriet. The suffering from knife slashes, starvation, dehydration and severe burns from the electric prod. Additionally, the heavy chains had badly chaffed her wrists and ankles. Since *'El Diablo'* had not allowed Harriet to use the bathroom at any time, she had gone through that additional humiliation also. Luckily, Harriet was not still suffering as much emotionally and had her strong mind to thank for that. Harriet was more worried about both Viv and Henry.

The doctor gave Henry updates on Viv, who was not doing so well in hospital. Both Henry and Dandy listened with extreme sadness.

When Viv had regained consciousness in the Psychiatric Hospital for the first time, she had immediately screamed the place down and had to be kept heavily sedated until she was calm enough to be assessed. Viv had suffered a complete mental breakdown.

* *

Harriet was sitting up in bed, looking tired and bruised. She smiled broadly, when she saw her visitor.

"Hi, Harriet," Henry said, as he entered her hospital room. "How's the brave patient, feeling better than last time I hope?"

"Fine, thanks, Henry, just a bit sore, here and there."

He gave her a kiss on the cheek and noticed how pale she still was. Harriet asked about Viv as she had already found out that Viv was in a different hospital and had learned of her tragic collapse.

Harriet fired questions at Henry. "Where's Viv now? How's she doing? Is she off the tranquillizers yet?"

On a previous visit, Henry had told her a few details regarding Viv's condition, although he had not been allowed to see her. He also explained what happened that day they met with BV, when Viv almost left him. Harriet also had explained her ordeal in detail and apologized for not being there for him.

"Viv will be fine. They seem to know what they're doing with her, but she has only been crying so far," he said, trying desperately to maintain his composure and not worry Harriet further. Harriet sensed something was wrong but did not persist. They talked until Harriet became tired and she was already dropping off to sleep as he left her room.

Henry visited Harriet regularly and in between had managed to visit Viv. On occasions he had accompanied Dandy, who desperately worried about the condition of her friend. She also felt upset at Daniel's grief over losing his brother and on finding out his true identity. Viv, in her tranquillised state, had not been very talkative, but the little she said worried Henry.

He continued to visit both women every day, occasionally with Dandy. Daniel was holding fort in the agency answering enquiries from prospective buyers. He found it difficult to come to terms with the knowledge of what his brother had become and of BV's violent death.

When it was time for Harriet to be released, Henry came and picked her up. On the drive to her house, Henry asked if she would like to move into his cottage as a guest. Harriet was stunned.

"But Henry, you're married and Viv needs you!"

"No," he responded sadly. "She doesn't. Every day she's asked me who I am and tells me both the men she loved were murdered. I tell her I'm her husband, Henry, and very much alive. Each time she's replied, 'No! Henry and BV were killed. I'm waiting for Lawrence now, he's coming for me.'"

"Oh, my! Henry, is it really that bad? Lawrence? She hardly ever spoke of him, although I did know he remained in her memory. Is there any hope of a recovery?"

"The doctors don't offer much hope. Harriet, I've heard this so many times a day, for weeks. I can't take any more. I can't help her in the place her mind has gone. That's why I want you to move in with me. Mainly, for moral support and because it makes me feel as if Viv is still with us. We can only hope she gets better soon."

"Oh, yes, Henry. Of course, I understand. Yes, I'd love to move in and take care of things. Thanks for asking, but I'm flabbergasted."

After a few days and once Harriet was settled into the guest room, they went to visit Viv. Both of them were extremely upset to see no improvement. She welcomed Harriet's hug, but did not recognize her. Although, she became upset when Harriet cried, there was no recognition for Henry.

"Go to your husband, let him comfort you," she said to Harriet, motioning toward Henry.

The same scene played itself out every time Harriet and Henry visited. Although it proved painful for them both, they continued to visit Viv on a regular basis. She no longer wore any make-up and tied her hair back in a ponytail. She never recognized them as her former best friend and husband, but instead greeted them as new visitors each time.

As the days and weeks passed, it became apparent that Viv was pregnant. Eventually, she gave birth to a baby boy. Viv ignored the baby and never acknowledged its existence. Since Viv and Henry had not officially divorced, he was considered the legal father. After the birth, he and Harriet took the baby home to raise. They called him Daniel, after the man Viv once had a crush on and who had now become a very good friend and godparent, along with Dandy, to his little namesake.

Harriet and Henry loved the child and as it grew strong and healthy, so did the love between both of the friends. They married as soon as his divorce came through from Viv. Dandy and Daniel were still

their best friends, but Dandy was the one who continued to visit Viv the most. She had wept buckets
over Viv's mental condition and knew she was lost
forever to all of them. But Dandy would always be
there for Viv, and a new special friendship developed between them. Daniel visited with her sometimes, but he could not bear to see such a different
person in Viv's place.

As for the child, no one could ever be sure whose
it was, Henry's or BV's. They did not want to know
and Henry did not want a test performed. The child
was theirs and a part of Viv, who they both still loved
very much. They preferred to keep the memory of
how she used to be and eventually stopped visiting
her altogether.

Later, they would decide what to tell little Daniel,
should the question arise, but Harriet was his 'Mum,'
and she loved the boy as if he were her own. She had
been given the precious gift of a child, who possessed
within him, the blood of the two people she loved so
dearly. Not for one minute did she ever believe the
child could be BV's.

Daniel had Henry's hair colour and the brightest
blue eyes. His affectations were all Henry. A personality that was so similar to Viv's, was also discern-
able. Daniel possessed a mixture of charisma and
vivacity and shone with his outwardness and curiosity. He was loved and cherished, in the same way
the memory of Viv would always be. It tied them all
together with a very special bond.

Harriet was especially grateful for the chance to be
a real woman and mother, things she had thought

impossible. She would always be grateful to Viv and would always love and take care of these two very special men.

Meanwhile, Viv's mental decline continued. She constantly muttered that Mayfield was the real killer, 'El Diablo'. That he killed Henry and BV, the two men she loved. At other times her story changed to Lawrence being the survivor, in Henry or BV's place, and that he was getting well in hospital and then coming for her.

"Why will no one believe me?" she screamed sometimes.

On the occasions her memory showed her what she thought was the truth, (as she saw it that tragic night) Viv became hysterical. The nurses would hurry in and give her another injection, momentarily making the pain and horrific memories disappear. Whenever the distorted realization hit her, the scene played itself out again with Lawrence as the survivor, placing her in this other realm. One she could cope with.

That was the way it continued for Viv. Eventually, she forgot most of her past life and then refused to look after herself. The nurses helped her dress and bathe, and she spent her good days wandering around the facility.

When she came across other patients, the refrain was the same.

"I had two true loves," she would say. "Both were shot and killed by a detective called, 'El Diablo', but Lawrence is coming to take me home."

The other patients shared similar stories with her. Each time Viv told her story, she was under the impression that it was for the first time. Little did she realize that she had repeated it every day for the last twenty years.

Eventually, she no longer felt guilt or pain in being made to choose between two men. Sometimes she felt relieved that the choice had been taken from her.

More recently, she would sit in the garden and wait. On these occasions, Viv brushed her beautiful, long black hair, usually still dressed in pyjamas and a housecoat. She often smiled and felt happy now, as she spoke aloud……..

"Lawrence is coming for me today. We're going to spend the day on his boat," she would repeat, to no one usually, but the wind.

~THE END~

———————————————

~Epilogue~

If some of the characters and events in this story seemed almost real, there was good reason. Most were drawn from my actual life and experiences, but the story was fictionalised to a certain degree. The Baron was a friend, not really a serial killer, and his name is an anagram. Henry, Daniel and Dandy were all real acquaintances and friends.

Harriet was an actual childhood buddy who underwent a transgender operation later in life. Alex Labelle was a real-life rapist, I encountered in West Kensington, London, UK, in the early 80's.

Viv was loosely based upon me, the author. The events portrayed in this story have been elaborated on to a great degree. Although, the cars, houses, places and personalities were mostly real.

This book has been an ongoing experience that has consumed my time, on and off over the past several years, due to my many house moves and divorces taking precedence. This story was started in 1983, then added to and revised as the years went by. The first draft was completed in 1997. This current edition was completed in April, 2005 for an e-book. A final edit finished in June, 2009 initially, for a paperback.

I give thanks to the writers from Fanstory, a writers site joined, who gave encouragement and helped with the early 2005 edits. Special thanks to our friend Jeff Bigger, a fellow musician here in Chicago with our 'Mama DeVille Band,' who has great faith in the book becoming very popular. A mention to my awesome friend, Debbie who with her hubby Rob, own 'Campione's Taste of Chicago' just outside Nashville, in Gallatin, Tennessee, where we were living for five years.

Great appreciation and thanks to my fifth, final and AMAZING in every way, (not kidding) husband, Victor, known to me as Rocky due to his power lifting and mental strength. Rocky literally saved me at a time when I had dropped to my lowest. Yes, at age 54 in the UK, I had finally given in and given up. Not long gone through a divorce with third husband, a successful businessman and Wiccan witch, and now going through my 4th divorce from an ex-SAS, self confessed assassin with the British Army, PB, (recovering alcoholic) who was also a bestselling author of a book on this very subject. Normally, he was most charming, but on our separation, he became unstable and drank heavily again. So, at this time I was barricaded in my own home over Christmas, due to PB's constant contact and threats to me, whilst drunk.

I was also in ill health with a few untreated conditions and at this time, had no friends or family to care about me. I only had my teeny Pomeranian, Ching. I decided that when she passed away, I would join her. I would lock myself up in the home, (or rather not unlock myself as the situation had already gone into

50% of that stage). My plan, after the inevitable demise of Ching, my 13-year-old Pomeranian, would be for me to sleep, go on the computer to write in my websites, drink water but not to bother with any food and grieve over my lost, loving companion. I had constant love from that tiny 6" ball of fur, over many more years than any human had given me. I was of sick of picking myself off the ground, only to be kicked in the gut again and again. In effect, the time had come to stop fighting life and stay down this time.

Then if a miracle can be called one, Rocky got in touch with me over the Internet and the ocean. We soon became friends and commiserated over each other's lives. His life was good, but unhappy and he lived in America. I never imagined we could end up together, as there was too much at stake for him, and I was too secure in my own home in England.

Rocky came over to rescue me, initially, against my wishes. Very literally, in more ways than one, he saved my life. My completed, published autobiography will attest to this. It is due to Rocky, that I completed this novel for him to publish. I thank my husband for so much more than the work he put into this book with me. Without him, this book would not exist, and very likely, neither would I.

I hope you enjoyed reading the book, as much as I loved writing it.

Donni De-Ville

Official Website; www.donnideville.com

About the Author

Donni-Jay De-Ville learned to read and write from the age of four years old, and has loved writing ever since. Many articles and short stories have been published, with an almost completed autobiography of her amazingly full life.

Living in America, as a wife to a Chicagoan, and a mother of two tiny Poms.

Currently, a prestigious 'Top Contributor', for Yahoo Answers.

Number Two ranked author of novels, in February and March 2005, in the Internet online writing website, Fanstory.com

Long time member of Authors Den. Recipient of numerous reviewer awards on Writing.com

Initially, trained as a nurse, became a model for a short while, then professional solo dancer and singer/guitarist with bands, also a songwriter, signed to record label in London, UK. Appeared in television and commercials.

Donni-Jay is also a self taught, portrait pen & ink artist.

First real achievement was in winning the Schools Art Competition, in her final year of school, with a pencil drawing of John Lennon (of the Beatles).

Birth Place: Millionaires Row, (now called Billionaires Row) Finchley, London, England.

Seva, Donni-Jay and Monkee.

Donni De-Ville

www.ingramcontent.com/pod-product-compliance
Lightning Source LLC
Chambersburg PA
CBHW021952120726

47898CB00001BA/81